PENGUIN BOOKS

THE PENGUIN BOOK OF
LESBIAN SHORT STORIES

Margaret Reynolds is the editor of *Erotica: An Anthology of Women's Writing* and of Elizabeth Barrett Browning's *Aurora Leigh*.

THE PENGUIN BOOK OF LESBIAN SHORT STORIES

Edited by Margaret Reynolds

PENGUIN BOOKS

PENGUIN BOOKS

Published by the Penguin Group

Penguin Books USA Inc., 375 Hudson Street, New York, New York 10014, U.S.A.
Penguin Books Ltd, 27 Wrights Lane, London W8 5TZ, England
Penguin Books Australia Ltd, Ringwood, Victoria, Australia
Penguin Books Canada Ltd, 10 Alcorn Avenue, Toronto, Ontario, Canada M4V 3B2
Penguin Books (N.Z.) Ltd, 182–190 Wairau Road, Auckland 10, New Zealand

Penguin Books Ltd, Registered Offices: Harmondsworth, Middlesex, England

First published in Great Britain by Penguin Books Ltd., 1993
First published in the United States of America by Viking Penguin,
a division of Penguin Books USA Inc. 1994
Published in Penguin Books 1994

1 3 5 7 9 10 8 6 4 2

PUBLISHER'S NOTE

These selections are works of fiction. Names, characters, places, and incidents either are the
product of the authors' imagination or are used fictitiously, and any resemblance to actual
persons, living or dead, events, or locales is entirely coincidental.

Pages vii–ix constitute an extension of this copyright page.

THE LIBRARY OF CONGRESS HAS CATALOGUED THE HARDCOVER AS FOLLOWS:
The Penguin book of lesbian short stories/edited by Margaret Reynolds.
p. cm.
ISBN 0-670-85425-5 (hc.)
ISBN 0 14 02.4018 7
1. Short stories—Women authors. 2. Lesbians' writings. 3. Lesbians—Fiction.
4. Women—Fiction. I. Reynolds, Margaret.
PN6120.92.W46 1994
820′.8′09287—dc20   93–34061

Printed in the United States of America
Set in Postscript Garamond No. 3

CONTENTS

CONTENTS

ACKNOWLEDGEMENTS

Thanks are due to the copyright holders of the following stories for permission to reproduce them in this volume:

Kathy Acker: to the author and the William Morris Agency (UK) Ltd for 'The Language of the Body' (1993)

Dorothy Allison: to Firebrand Books, Ithaca, New York, for 'A Lesbian Appetite' from *Trash, Stories by Dorothy Allison*, copyright © 1988 by Dorothy Allison

Margaret Atwood: to Bloomsbury Publishing Ltd for 'Cold-blooded' from *Good Bones* (Bloomsbury, 1992)

Ann Bannon: to the Naiad Press for an extract from *I am a Woman*, copyright 1959, 1983, 1986

Djuna Barnes: to the Authors League Fund as executors of the Estate of Djuna Barnes, 234 W 44th Street, New York, for an extract from *Ladies Almanack* (1928)

Alison Bechdel: to Firebrand Books, Ithaca, New York, for 'Serial Monogamy' from *Dykes to Watch Out For: The Sequel*, copyright © 1992 by Alison Bechdel

Nicole Brossard: to Coach House Press for 'These Our Mothers'

from *These Our Mothers* © 1983, Éditions de l'Hexagone and
Coach House Press; translation © 1983 Barbara Godard

Rebecca Brown: to the author for 'Bread' from *The Evolution of
Darkness and Other Stories*, copyright © Rebecca Brown, 1984

Pat Califia: to Alyson Publications, Inc. for 'The Vampire' from
Macho Sluts (Alyson Publications, 1988)

Colette: to Martin Secker and Warburg Ltd and Farrar, Straus &
Giroux, Inc., for 'Sleepless Nights', translated by Herma Briffault, from *Collected Stories* by Colette, edited by Robert Phelps,
© 1958 by Martin Secker and Warburg Ltd. Translation
copyright © 1934 by J. Ferenczi et Fils, © 1957, 1966, 1983
by Farrar, Straus & Giroux, Inc.

H.D.: to Peter Owen Ltd for 'The Wise Sappho' from *Notes on
Thought and Vision and the Wise Sappho* (Peter Owen, 1988)

Isak Dinesen: to Random House, Inc., for 'The Blank Page'
from *Last Tales*, copyright © 1957 by Random House, Inc.

Emma Donoghue: to the author and the Caroline Davidson
and Robert Ducas Literary Agency for 'Words for Things'
(1993)

Frances Gapper: to Sheba Feminist Press for 'The Secret of
Sorrerby Rise' from *Wild Hearts: Contemporary Lesbian Melo-
drama*, edited by The Wild Hearts Group (Sheba Feminist
Press, 1991)

Jewelle Gomez: to the author for 'Don't Explain' from *Lesbian
Love Stories*, edited by Irene Zahava (Crossing Press, Freedom,
CA, 1989)

Anna Livia: to the author for '5½ Charlotte Mews' from *Incidents
Involving Warmth* (Only Women Press, 1986)

Sara Maitland: to Michael Joseph for 'Lullaby for My Dyke and
her Cat' from *A Book of Spells*, copyright Sara Maitland, 1987

Merril Mushroom: to the author for 'How to Engage in Courting
Rituals 1950s Butch-style in the Bar' (*Common Lives/Lesbian
Lives*, No. 4, 1982)

Joan Nestle: to Firebrand Books, Ithaca, New York, for 'Esther's
Story' from *A Restricted Country*, copyright © 1987 by Joan
Nestle

Anaïs Nin: to Peter Owen Ltd for an extract from *Cities of the Interior* (Quartet Books, 1979)

Beth Nugent: to Jonathan Cape and Alfred A. Knopf, Inc., for 'City of Boys' from *City of Boys* (Jonathan Cape, 1992), copyright © Beth Nugent, 1992

Jayne Anne Phillips: to the author for 'Swimming' from *Sweethearts*. To Faber & Faber and Delacorte/Seymour Lawrence, a division of Bantam Doubleday Dell Publishing Group, Inc., for 'Blind Girls' and 'Accidents' from *Black Tickets*, copyright © 1979 by Jayne Anne Phillips, published in Faber & Faber, 1993

Jane Rule: to the author and Naiad Press, Inc., for 'His nor Hers' from *Inland Passage* by Jane Rule, Tallahassee, Fl. (The Naiad Press, 1985)

Gertrude Stein: to Virago Press and the Gertrude Stein Estate for 'Miss Furr and Miss Skeene' from *Geography and Plays* (Four Seas, Boston, 1922)

Dorothy Strachey: to the Estate of Mme Dorothy Bussy and the Hogarth Press for an extract from *Olivia* (The Hogarth Press, 1949)

Renée Vivien: to the Gay Presses of New York for 'Prince Charming', translated by Karla Jay and Yvonne M. Klein, copyright © Gay Presses of New York, 1983

Jeanette Winterson: to the author and Great Moments Ltd for 'The Poetics of Sex' (1993)

Monique Wittig: to Peter Owen Ltd and Georges Borchardt, Inc., for an extract from *Les Guerillères*, translated by David Le Vay, copyright © 1969 Les Éditions de Minuit; English translation copyright © 1971 by Peter Owen

While every effort has been made to contact copyright holders, this has not always been possible, and the publishers will be glad to make good any omissions in future editions.

For the new Sappho,
all woman
and twice the man

INTRODUCTION

In 1925 Virginia Woolf was thinking about Vita Sackville-West.

These Sapphists *love* women; friendship is never untinged with amorosity . . . I like her & being with her, & the splendour – she shines in the grocers shop in Sevenoaks with a candle lit radiance, stalking on legs like beech trees, pink glowing, grape clustered, pearl hung.

Vita was seductive. She was glamorous. Virginia liked all that. But there was more.

There is her maturity and full breastedness: her being so much in full sail on the high tides, where I am coasting down backwaters; her capacity I mean to take the floor in any company, to represent her country, to visit Chatsworth, to control silver, servants, chow dogs . . . her being in short (what I have never been) a real woman.[1]

In 1925 Virginia Woolf could look at another woman, name

---

1. 21 December 1925, *The Diary of Virginia Woolf*, ed. Anne Olivier Bell (Penguin, 1982), Vol. III, 51–2.

her as a lesbian, acknowledge her sexual magnetism and admire her independence and power. And in 1928, inspired by this vision, Virginia Woolf could add to a discreet tradition in literature now claimed as lesbian, distilling all her attraction and admiration in *Orlando* and presenting it as a love gift to Vita.

None of this could have happened before the twentieth century. Not the knowing, not the naming, not the pleasure, and above all, not the writing. Lesbian history is strange. It is made up of many unknowable private facts and a few public inventions. Lesbian literary history is stranger still. It has one early and powerful exponent in Sappho. Then, because positive concepts of lesbianism mostly disappear, anything that can be construed as 'lesbian writing' disappears too.

Women have always loved women; but the private story of past lesbian experience is hidden. We cannot know the contrived touch, the shared bed, the tender experiment. Nor can we know the personal bravery, the challenging of taboos, the life lived according to the lights of desire. Fragments of a more public lesbian history remain. Sometimes we hear of a romantic friendship, sometimes we hear of a woman dressing and working as a man, sometimes we hear of a witch burned or an actress vilified. And each one of these may testify to the persistence of lesbian choice.

Officially and legally, of course, lesbianism was always discouraged, sometimes forbidden, but generally ignored. Lesbian history and gay history are not parallel here. The practice of homosexuality between men was considered dangerous and disruptive; so it was outlawed. But lesbianism is about women, and all ideas to do with women include an ideology of difference which is generally an ideology of presumed inferiority. So that if women do not really matter, then lesbians and their ways do not matter much either. Relations between women are not going to be considered important if woman's 'natural' allegiance is supposed to be given to men, and if the social structures which maintain order and hierarchy only give a woman status dependent upon her relationship to a man, father or husband.

Given a set of cultural assumptions and social conditions along these lines, even explicitly sexual experience between women does not constitute much of a threat. Girls who go to bed together can be ignored or tolerated as adolescents going through a 'passing phase' or desperate freaks who have failed to find anything better.

This confident phallocratic view of the universe reached its apogee in the early nineteenth century. In 1811 Miss Marianne Woods and Miss Jane Pirie took Dame Helen Cumming Gordon to court on the grounds that she had destroyed their reputations. Dame Helen's granddaughter had attended their school in Edinburgh and reported that Miss Woods had been wont to climb into Miss Pirie's bed and lie on top of her. Miss Pirie had been heard to say, 'You're in the wrong place' and 'Do it, darling', and Miss Woods would leave saying, 'I think I have put you in a fair way to sleep now.' It sounds pretty much like sex to me. But in 1819 the House of Lords found for Miss Pirie and Miss Woods, first of all on the grounds that two decent middle-class women did not do such things ('No such case was ever known in Scotland, or in Britain ... I do believe that the crime here alleged has no existence'), and secondly on the grounds that they couldn't do anything anyway without the presence of a penis ('Copulation without penetration of the female is ... much like charging a rape as committed ... in the course of small talk').[2]

Thus, as far as British law was concerned, lesbians became invisible women and they stayed that way throughout the nineteenth century. Section 11 (the Labouchère Amendment) of the 1885 Criminal Law Amendment Act made homosexual acts in public or in private illegal from that date until its repeal in 1967.[3] It specifically refers to 'any male person' and women were not included, with or without the intervention of Queen Victoria's

2. See Lillian Faderman, *Surpassing the Love of Men: Romantic Friendship and Love Between Women from the Renaissance to the Present* (William Morrow and Co. Inc., 1981), 147–54.
3. See Jeffrey Weeks, *Coming Out: Homosexual Politics in Britain from the Nineteenth Century to the Present*, revised edn (Quartet Books, 1990), 14.

legendary ignorance. From a legal point of view lesbian relations still do not exist. In Britain, even today, a woman cannot be divorced on the grounds of adultery if her lover is another woman.

If the law said that lesbians did not exist, from 1869 science said that they did. In that year Carl von Westphal published a study of a girl who dressed as a boy and was attracted to women. He perceived that she exhibited tendencies which were inappropriate to her 'natural' female character: that is, she was active where she should have been passive, independent where she should have been submissive, outspoken where she should have been silent. And so on. Westphal identified her condition as biologically based and abnormal, and he named her as a 'congenital invert'. Westphal's work was continued along similar lines by Richard von Krafft-Ebing in his *Psychopathia Sexualis* (1882) and by Havelock Ellis in *Studies in the Psychology of Sex: Sexual Inversion* (1897). The tenor of these influential texts can be judged from the fact that Krafft-Ebing's key case was that of one Alice Mitchell who had cut her lover's throat, and whom Krafft-Ebing described as a 'typical invert'.

So here at last was a named lesbian identity. But it's a poisonous gift to have a name when you are also identified as mad, miserable and murderous. The pernicious legacy of these theories cannot be overestimated. The Victorian lover of women did not know what to call herself but she could get on with her life as an odd individual. The twentieth-century lesbian – if she chose so to name herself – had to deal with concepts of moral sickness which persisted well into the 1960s. And that's just among lesbians themselves. The popular imagination is of course all too willing to accommodate the paradox of legal invisibility with homophobic accusations of perversion and moral corruption.

1819 and 1869. Key dates for a queer history resulting in the key concepts of invisibility and abnormality, which remained in place for a hundred years. Then two things happened. The first was the sexual revolution. That was not much good, because the sex suddenly being talked about was mainly heterosexual. But the second thing that happened was feminism. And the effects of feminism, for lesbians, were truly revolutionary. A group calling itself Radicalesbians distributed a leaflet at a conference in New York in the summer of 1970. It began:

What is a lesbian? A lesbian is the rage of all women condensed to the point of explosion. She is the woman who, often beginning at an extremely early age, acts in accordance with her inner compulsion to be a more complete and freer human being than her society – perhaps then, but certainly later – cares to allow her ... She may not be fully conscious of the political implications of what for her began as personal necessity, but on some level she has not been able to accept the limitations and oppression laid on her by the most basic role of her society – the female role.[4]

It's not very well written. But it was very important. Feminism meant that women began to analyse the ideological processes which had made them unfree. To be a feminist did not make you lesbian, but lesbian women were very often feminists. And throughout the centuries lesbians – self-reliant and brave resisters – had been feminists long before either term existed. Lesbian practice was the forerunner of feminist theory.

From the middle ages to the nineteenth century lesbian practice, of itself, did not cause the authorities much anxiety. Men were in charge and women could be controlled in other ways. What did worry the powers of the day a great deal were the cases where a woman usurped the rights and privileges of a man. She might have dressed as a man, earned a better living by presenting herself as a man, she might have acquired extra social status as a man, she might have married and – worst crime of all – she might have used a dildo. This was real transgression.

Records show that these were the women who were tried and condemned. And this is where the history of lesbian existence is so closely intertwined with the history of women's politics. It is

4. 'The Woman Identified Woman' by Radicalesbians (1970), in Sarah Lucia-Hoagland and Julia Penelope, eds., *For Lesbians Only: A Separatist Anthology* (Onlywomen Press, 1988), 17.

no accident that the Woods and Pirie versus Gordon case should follow on the proto-feminist agitation that was part of the Romantic movement. Mary Wollstonecraft's *Vindication of the Rights of Woman* (1797) argued for female independence and sisterly unity. And where were women most likely to be entirely independent of men? The 1819 decision in the House of Lords effectively stopped lesbian solidarity before it began, simply by saying that it could not exist.

At the end of the nineteenth century, at the time when Westphal, Krafft-Ebing and Ellis were writing, there was a much larger and more powerful movement demanding education for women along with employment and property rights, suffrage and social independence. Again, a lesbian choice would have represented the most radical version of these requirements. The pontifications of the sexologists helped to frighten even the boldest of the 'New Women', setting women against one another and securing, for a while longer, the controlling ideal of the feminine woman. It is worth pointing out that, before feminism, the women that we know about who managed to live successful lesbian lives were the women who were free of family manipulation, who had careers and, above all, who had money. This is true whether one thinks of the Ladies of Llangollen, the aunt and niece couple who wrote as 'Michael Field', or of the remarkable Paris group of the 1920s and 1930s – a group which included Natalie Barney, Renée Vivien and Djuna Barnes, all of whom were heirs to substantial fortunes, and very sure of their own right to a place in the world.

Vita Sackville-West was no feminist. She wasn't much of a lesbian advocate either, for she had, after all, given up on her 'great adventure' with Violet Trefusis and opted instead for the safety of marriage and the externals of English good form. But when Virginia Woolf first met Vita she represented all the seductive power, all the self-confidence, all the glamour and all the overt sexual promise that a dyke, out and proud, can offer to another woman. And in the late twentieth century more women are able to make those promises and more women are free to take them up.

A pattern of long silence followed by oppressive labelling does not make for continuity in literary history. There are two distinct elements to the character of lesbianism in literature. The one that has the longest pedigree, born out of the years when 'real' lesbians were silent, but certainly still alive and well today, is salacious representation. The juicy tradition of the lesbian in literature appears in serious works such as Ariosto's *Orlando Furioso*, where Fiordispina is convinced of the unique character of her plight. It figures in erotic histories like Delarivier Manley's *New Atalantis* or John Cleland's *Fanny Hill*. It plays a large part in Diderot's *The Nun* and Baudelaire's *Fleurs du Mal* and Pierre Louys's *Songs of Bilitis*. It takes up whole tranches of writing in the works of less elevated pornographers. Then in literature, as now in blue films and girlie magazines, portraits of lesbians are used to reinforce notions of heterosexuality as normal, desirable and inevitable. Lesbian sex is always deviant and unsatisfactory, useful only as titillating foreplay before the hero comes along to finish the job. Lesbians figure in that literary history only as a freakish sideshow.

'Authentic' lesbian writing is hard to trace before the end of the nineteenth century and the giving of names. For the most part the best-known examples of lesbian writing from the nineteenth century are texts written either by celibates or by intellectual women who used relationships between women as political exemplars. Important lesbian texts from celibate writers include Christina Rossetti's 'Goblin Market' and Emily Dickinson's love lyrics and the letters which she wrote to Sue Gilbert. Prose texts might include Charlotte Brontë's *Villette*, with its curious cross-dressing episode, or George Eliot's *Romola*, where the wronged wife and mistress go off into the sunset together. It is possible, with the sophistication of modern theoretical perspectives, to find many more examples of 'lesbian writing' in the Victorian period. But without contemporary definitions and with a precise (if absurd) contemporary denial of lesbianism, there is something specious in that attempt. Their very proper romantic friendship can all too easily become our saucy affair.

That is why I have collected only one nineteenth-century text in this anthology. The first story here is Sarah Orne Jewett's 'Martha's Lady', published in 1897. Jewett herself was probably not a nineteenth-century innocent – she lived in a 'Boston marriage' with Annie Fields for forty years – but her story is typical of that delicate strand of romantic attachment which at one and the same time made lesbian love possible and invisible. There is no trace of embarrassment or confusion in Martha's old-fashioned chivralric love, nor in Helena's final acknowledgement of that devotion. This is the unabashed display of a love that has no name to speak.

The stories which follow in this collection reflect the lesbian history of the twentieth century which I have outlined above. To some extent Renée Vivien's 'Prince Charming' stays within the invisibility formula by removing events to an exotic Hungarian setting – romantic love between women is made possible in a distant place. The fairy-tale formula is underlined by the opening which is that of a fabulist narrative: 'I promised you, my curious little girl, to tell you the true story . . .' The same fairy-tale method is used by Isak Dinesen in 'The Blank Page': 'You want a tale, sweet lady and gentleman?' Dinesen's tale has been the subject of a highly influential feminist analysis by Susan Gubar.[5] She plays there with the 'blank page' of women's history, but does not see that the real unwritten history is that belonging to lesbians. The princess whose sheet remains white was a virgin on her wedding night, but the many women who stand in contemplation before it, the 'worldly wise, dutiful, long-suffering queens, wives and mothers – and their noble playmates, bridesmaids and maids-of-honour' know very well why there is no blood to be seen on her bridal linen.

Of the earlier stories collected here many show the influence of the sexologist theories which made lesbians into abnormal outcasts. Katherine Mansfield's curious early fragment 'Leves

5. Susan Gubar, 'The Blank Page and the Issue of Female Creativity', *Critical Inquiry*, Vol. 8, no. 2 (1981), 243–63.

Amores' suggests just such an ambivalence: 'nothing beautiful could ever happen in that room, and for her I felt contempt, a little tolerance, a very little pity'. Mansfield, herself bisexual in experience, was certainly knowing enough to be familiar with the gloomy diagnoses of Ellis and his like.

Their best-known literary victim, however, was Radclyffe Hall. Her Miss Ogilvy, a forerunner of Stephen Gordon, is a misfit in life and dies alone, thwarted from her true masculine destiny. As her own note on 'Miss Ogilvy Finds Herself' makes clear, Hall was experimenting in this story with the difficulties of writing about the life of the 'invert' which were later to occupy her in *The Well of Loneliness*. Virginia Woolf's famous feminist polemic *A Room of One's Own* has a very important relationship with Hall's novel. The case has been made by Jane Marcus, but the facts, briefly, are these. *A Room of One's Own* started life as a lecture given to the students at Girton College, Cambridge, in October 1928. Virginia was accompanied by Vita Sackville-West, her own one-time lover; the students were all girls; many of them were feminists; and all of them would have known that at this very time Hall's novel, with its explicitly lesbian subject-matter, was on trial, having been accused of obscenity. The trial was in Woolf's mind and it appears in her lecture:

. . . I turned the page and read . . . I am sorry to break off so abruptly. Are there no men present? Do you promise me that behind that red curtain over there the figure of Sir Chartres Biron is not concealed? We are all women you assure me? Then I may tell you that the very next words I read were these – 'Chloe liked Olivia . . .' Do not start. Do not blush. Let us admit in the privacy of our own society that these things sometimes happen. Sometimes women do like women.

The style is deliciously flirtatious. Add to that the fact that Sir Chartres Biron was the presiding magistrate in the *Well* case, and the lesbian context of Woolf's lecture is clear. It was clearer still in her original typescript where this passage reads:

'Chloe liked Olivia. They shared a . . .' The words covered the bottom of the page; the pages had stuck. While fumbling to open them there flashed into my mind the inevitable policeman ... the order to attend the Court, the dreary waiting; the Magistrate coming in with a little bow ... for the Prosecution, for the Defence – the verdict; this book is obscene + flames sing, perhaps on Tower Hill, as they compound that mass of paper. Here the paper came apart. Heaven be praised! It was only a laboratory. Chloe–Olivia. They were engaged in mincing liver . . .'[6]

It's not explicit. But it's there. Just for a moment, we are invited to imagine *what* Chloe and Olivia might share. And if you need any more sexy suggestion, just remember that in legend Chloe dressed as a man, and in literature Olivia falls in love with a girl dressed as a man.

Even when their work was not labelled obscene, many of the writings collected here reveal that some authors suffered from a very natural anxiety as a result of the prevalent view of lesbian sexuality as abnormal and deficient. In *Olivia* the heroine tries to turn her fantasies about her schoolmistress into a fantasy about a man. And in Anaïs Nin's *Cities of the Interior* her lovers, Djuna and Lillian, hold back from one another ('She wants something of me that only a man can give her . . .'), and try, hopelessly, to work out the context of their passion in relation to the dictates of heterosexuality. Bannon's novels, published in the United States in the 1950s, are also full of characters trying to reconcile their perceived gay identity with popularly held notions of moral sickness and (for women) sexual inadequacy. That particular despairing tone really disappears from lesbian writing – not a moment too soon – after the 1960s.

By contrast, the Paris group of the 1920s and 1930s managed to produce a remarkable body of self-confident writing of great quality. For these women their sense of difference gave them permissions rather than prohibitions. Renée Vivien, Djuna Barnes, H.D. and, especially, Gertrude Stein, were all Americans

6. Jane Marcus, 'Sapphistory: The Woolf and the Well', in Karla Jay and Joanne Glasgow, eds., *Lesbian Texts and Contexts: Radical Revisions* (New York University Press, 1990), 173.

living in self-chosen exile from their country, from the restrictive conventions of heterosexual life, and from the contemporary downgrading of feminine capacity. They saw themselves as different, and specifically went out to look for models which could contain their own self-conception of collective harmony among strong women; the tribe of Amazons and the disciples of Sappho were their favoured historic patterns. Shari Benstock's *Women of the Left Bank* tells the story of their enterprise.[7]

In many ways the Paris group resembles in little the flowering of lesbian writing which follows on the feminist revolution that came so much later. This is hardly surprising. In practical terms, these women possessed the independence, solidarity and self-consciousness which marks both periods. The effects in literary terms are therefore similar.

The self-analysis typical of the group is demonstrated in Stein's wry and witty account of the life of a gay couple in 'Miss Furr and Miss Skeene'. Djuna Barnes's *Ladies Almanack* is conventionally described as a 'satire' upon the group surrounding the hostess Natalie Barney. But satire implies criticism, and there is certainly none of that here. There is self-deprecating amusement; there is play with teasing in-jokes; sending up of values held dear . . . but there isn't any criticism. Far from it. Barney's character here, Dame Musset, is canonized because of her sexual skills and her zeal (her name is Evangeline, after all) in dedicating herself to the needs of women. Her speciality is

the Pursuance, the Relief and the Distraction, of such Girls as in their Hinder Parts, and their Fore Parts, and in whatsoever Parts did suffer them most, lament Cruelly, be it Itch of Palm, or Quarters most horribly burning . . . [for] . . . no thing so solaces it as other Parts as inflamed, or with the Consolation every Woman has at her Finger Tips, or at the very Hang of her Tongue . . .

This may be a joke but it's none the less admiring and the

7. Shari Benstock, *Women of the Left Bank, Paris 1900–1940* (University of Texas Press, 1986).

bravado of both the subject and the writing is intoxicating.

The piece by H.D., 'The Wise Sappho', also demonstrates the self-consciousness of Sapphic modernism. It is a meditation which blends history, fiction and theory to examine a past and continuing tradition for women, for lesbians and for writing. In all three of these pieces there is a playfulness which overlaps from the particularities of the writers' personal status and situation into a parallel literary experiment with language (Barnes's mock Renaissance rhetoric), with grammar (Stein's repetitions), with genre (H.D.'s amalgam of theory and imagination) and with all the conventions of literary form.

While the freedoms of the Paris group were in large part due to their private circumstances, it is certain that the larger freedoms accorded to women after the First World War also helped their situation. This is made clear in Radclyffe Hall's 'Miss Ogilvy Finds Herself' where Miss Ogilvy finds her vocation in an ambulance brigade in France. But Miss Ogilvy loses those 'masculine' occupations after the war and has to go back to gardening and nursing her whinging sisters. With the Second World War the same thing happened; women were again encouraged to participate in an active working life during, only to be forced back into domestic roles after.[8] The propaganda of gender stereotyping which brought this about was highly influential and we still feel its effects today. Hence cake-baking and the New Look for mummy; hence an expanse of desk and a clean jaw for daddy; hence Doris Day and Rock Hudson ... Only gays could play a straight so very convincingly.

And play at butch and femme is exactly what many lesbians did in the 1950s. Ann Bannon's novels reflect this phenomenon, and their roots in the common experience of their time were what made her work so important to her readers. Her stories are full of married women dressed in nylon underwear and high heels

8. See Allan Bérubé, 'Marching to a Different Drummer: Lesbian and Gay GIs in World War II', in Martin Bauml Duberman, Martha Vicinus and George Chauncey, eds., *Hidden from History: Reclaiming the Gay and Lesbian Past* (New American Library, 1989), 391–2.

and yearning for another woman to help her slip into something more comfortable. When she does succumb and admit (tearfully) that she really is a Lesbian – it always has a capital L in Bannon, see Beebo Brinker's definitions in the extract from *I am A Woman* – an Ann Bannon heroine has then to decide whether she is a femme or a butch. This is the dominant question of 1950s lesbian style. But contrary to straight opinion, this is not an inevitable element in the character of lesbianism. Rather it is the reflection of a particular sexual ideology in a particular place and time.[9]

Ann Bannon's Beebo Brinker is a classic fictional butch and she still retains her cult status. Joan Nestle lived in that lost world before feminism and her tender fictionalized memories in 'Esther's Story' are embarrassed but proud of the bravery of both butch and femme, seeing in that style an ironic and politicized resistance to heterosexual norms. Jewelle Gomez in 'Don't Explain' taps into that 1950s confidence in the macho bulldagger, but Merril Mushroom writes from the grown-up 1980s and makes a funny pastiche of decisions which, for the women who really did waver between the lumberjack shirt or the Fire-and-Ice lipstick, were deadly serious.

The huge changes in attitude which marked lesbian experience and public perceptions in the late 1960s and 1970s meant that many writers were excited by the experiment of their own newly free lives and wrote that experiment into their work. Like the Paris group writings, the work of Monique Wittig and Nicole Brossard blends fiction and theory in a heady cocktail. Unlike the Paris group, these later writers were working within a feminist politics which values individual experience, not as a precious oddity, but as something which can represent the larger trials of women everywhere. It's not a generalization that I would endorse, but it is very typical of lesbian-feminist writing in the 1970s.

9. See Lillian Faderman, *Odd Girls and Twilight Lovers: A History of Lesbian Life in Twentieth Century America* (Columbia University Press, 1991), 167–74.

Experience became the common term, and suddenly there was a market of reading dykes out there desperate for stories about their sisters, about themselves. The coming-out story came into its own.

Of course it has its place. Young people in our culture are not encouraged to identify themselves as gay. So for many women and men the process of acknowledging their sexuality is very closely associated with the process of arriving at a sense of one's own individuality. This creates its own narrative, but it is a narrative which always covers the same ground, and it is a narrative which becomes an exchange of calling cards within a gay community. The first stirrings of misplaced desire, the first recognition of one's own oddity, the first lover, the first discovery by one's parents, the first brave affirmation to friends/employer/husband/vicar/hairdresser – any one of these constitutes enough subject-matter for a coming-out story. There are masses of them. They are mostly not very good. But they are there and they serve a purpose. So praise be for the presses which produce them.

Sara Maitland's 'Lullaby for My Dyke and Her Cat' is not a coming-out story because the narrator signally fails to come out. This is a clever parody of the sisterly ramblings so familiar from the early days of feminism and still all too much with us. This narrator is one of the 'I'm not a feminist but . . .' school, showing some influence from that closely related group, the 'I like women too but . . .' faction.

It should be said that the effects of feminism on writing quality were not always bad. Quite the contrary. In the 1980s especially, a kind of reciprocal curiosity and sympathy meant that lesbian-feminists and straight-feminists began to look at each other with renewed respect. One of the most significant theoretical texts in this exchange was Adrienne Rich's famous essay 'Compulsory Heterosexuality and Lesbian Existence'. It's a polemic which is well known to all thoughtful lesbians, but it also has wide currency at least within academic feminist circles. Rich argued that lesbian union was directly related to the political affiliation of all women, whether or not they called themselves lesbian:

I mean the term *lesbian continuum* to include a range – through each woman's life and throughout history – of woman-identified experience; not simply the fact that a woman has had or consciously desired genital sexual experience with another woman. If we expand it to embrace many more forms of primary intensity between and among women, including the sharing of a rich inner life, the bonding against male tyranny, the giving and receiving of practical and political support ... we begin to grasp breadths of female history and psychology which have lain out of reach as a consequence of limited, mostly clinical, definitions of 'lesbianism'.[10]

Many out-lesbians think that this is wet. That it makes a rainbow bridge between us and the straight women who are colluding with the Enemy. Maybe. But it explains why feminist writers use lesbian situations in their fictions quite legitimately and fruitfully for political purposes. There are examples in the works of Angela Carter and Margaret Atwood where this is the case. In Part III, 3, of Carter's *Nights at the Circus* (not included here) the women in the prison band together in love and determination in order to overthrow an authority which is oppressive. Their freedom at the conclusion of the episode, their singing for joy, is a symbol of the general freedom from cultural and social tyranny that Carter herself so passionately believed in and fought for. Margaret Atwood's story 'Cold-blooded' has hardly any sex in it. It is about politics and alienation. But it is also about the independent existence of an all-female world which is very much the 'woman-identified' story that Adrienne Rich calls the 'lesbian continuum'.

The principles set out in another, perhaps less-well-known, Adrienne Rich essay stand behind Jane Rule's story collected here, 'His Nor Hers'. In 'On Lies, Secrets and Silence' Rich roundly condemned those women who acquiesce in the oppression of lesbians by keeping the pretence, however large or small,

10. Adrienne Rich, 'Compulsory Heterosexuality and Lesbian Existence', *Signs: Journal of Women in Culture and Society*, Vol. 5, no. 4 (1980), 631–60.

of heterosexuality.[11] The married lesbian, who thereby gains social status and respectability while she betrays and tortures the woman whom she claims to love, is especially condemned. Jane Rule's story takes these strictures to heart and her married lesbian ends by losing all.

If all this sounds serious and portentous in its hard-line regulation, the self-awareness of lesbian writing also has its jollier side. Lesbians are very good at laughing at themselves. The irony in Maitland's story is lightly sketched in and very funny. Merril Mushroom, Dorothy Allison and Frances Gapper are all playing, very seriously but amusingly, with butch and femme, the myth of the greedy dyke, and the desire for a recoverable lesbian history of noble cross-dressers and romantic friends. Above all, there is nothing quite like the work of Alison Bechdel to unite right-on and right-off dykes everywhere. The whole success of Bechdel's cartoons depends upon the way that women in America and Britain recognize her cast of characters and are thus called upon to examine their own prejudices and laugh at their own posturing. Ask any lesbian, and she will tell you that the scene at the k.d. lang concert pictured in Bechdel's 'Serial Monogamy' really has happened to her. And to her ex. And to Hilary, and Sarah, and to Beth . . .

The use of pictures and of 'real-life' characters links Alison Bechdel's work with the *Ladies Almanack* of Djuna Barnes. The same teasing – and the same happy sense of belonging – is in both texts. Significantly, they both make new lesbian time. The *Almanack* revises the character of the seasons according to the exploits of Dame Musset. Alison Bechdel's *Dykes to Watch Out For* series began as and still is a cartoon calendar which has regulated the lives of many lesbian households since its first appearance in 1990.

This kind of self-referencing is not unusual within a lesbian writing tradition. Just as Bechdel refers to Barnes, so Woolf

11. Adrienne Rich, *On Lies, Secrets and Silence: Selected Prose 1966–1978* (Norton, 1979).

referred to Hall in *A Room of One's Own*. Emma Donoghue refers to a heroine from an earlier age in offering a new angle on the life of Mary Wollstonecraft, and Anna Livia makes a connection between the personal tragedy of Charlotte Mew (1869–1928; poet, misfit, lesbian, suicide) and the sinewy and triumphant heroine of her '5½ Charlotte Mews'. More familiarly, the writers in this collection look further back in history for their models; to the Amazons (Wittig) and to Sappho (H.D. and Winterson). Lesbians reclaim their own.

These are the positive images which lesbians remake. These writings also take on the negatives of the lesbian vampire, which were popular at the end of the nineteenth century and remain a staple constituent in a certain kind of Hollywood film. Of course the association of the lesbian and vampire is part of the cultural policing which separates women, making them fear each other and trust only in the safe protection of men and heterosex. But, nothing loth, many lesbian writers take back these images, either by laughing at them (Allison on food and the body), or by re-examining their emotional impact (Acker and her dream vision of *The Daughters of Horror*), or by undoing the conventional oppositions of vampire/victim (Califia and her *two* vampires both equally powerful and each in pursuit of the other).

Another negative image that is recuperated by lesbian writing is that of the witch. This image, unlike the vampire, is (unfortunately) based in fact and the best example of a lesbian 'witch' story is Sara Maitland's 'The Burning Times' (not included here). But other stories take up the idea, especially when a younger woman is being initiated into strange mysteries by an older and more knowledgeable lover as in Mansfield's and Nugent's stories. The schoolgirl story, born out of some women's experience, but entering the collective imagination with the film *Mädchen in Uniform* (1931) is a familiar one.[12] The stories which represent that strand here are the extract from *Olivia*, Colette's 'Nuits Blanches' and Rebecca Brown's 'Bread'.

12. See Martha Vicinus, 'Distance and Desire: English Boarding School Friendships', in *Signs: Journal of Women in Culture and Society*, Vol. 9, no. 4, (1984), 600–622.

These are examples of common themes in lesbian writing which are drawn from lesbian history, both 'real' and imposed. But there are other shared characteristics which make sense within a theoretical context. In the beginning of feminist literary theory the women it addressed were presumed heterosexual. Adrienne Rich and Bonnie Zimmerman changed that and lesbian theory is now a growth area of study in Britain and America.[13] One of the feminist academics chastised by Rich in 'Compulsory Heterosexuality' was Nancy Chodorow, the author of *The Reproduction of Mothering* (1978). Chodorow argued that, because child care in our culture is specific to gender, i.e. women do it, then 'the mother remains a primary internal object for the girl, so that heterosexual relationships are on the model of a non-exclusive, second relationship for her, whereas for the boy they recreate an exclusive primary relationship'. Rich takes this psychoanalysis a stage further:

If women are the earliest sources of emotional caring and physical nurture for both female and male children, it would seem logical, from a feminist perspective at least, to pose the following questions: whether the search for love and tenderness in both sexes does not originally lead toward women; why in fact women would ever redirect that search . . .[14]

Why indeed? Nicole Brossard's 'These Our Mothers' recuperates the mother–daughter relation by setting up a group of speaker, her mother, her daughter and her lover. They are

13. Bonnie Zimmerman, 'What Has Never Been: An Overview of Lesbian Feminist Literary Criticism', *Feminist Studies*, Vol. 7, no. 3, (1981), 451–75. See also: Estelle B. Freedman et al., eds., *The Lesbian Issue: Essays from Signs* (The University of Chicago Press, 1985); Bonnie Zimmerman, *The Safe Sea of Women, Lesbian Fiction 1969–1989* (Beacon Press, 1990); Mark Lilly, ed., *Lesbian and Gay Writing* (Macmillan, 1990); Judith Roof, *The Lure of Knowledge: Lesbian Sexuality and Theory* (Columbia University Press, 1991); Elaine Hobby and Chris White, eds., *What Lesbians Do in Books* (The Women's Press, 1991); and Betsy Warland, ed., *Inversions: Writings by Dykes, Queers and Lesbians* (Open Letters, 1992).

14. Nancy Chodorow, *The Reproduction of Mothering* (University of California Press, 1978), 198–9, and Adrienne Rich, 'Compulsory Heterosexuality', ibid., 637.

mothers (or potential mothers) and 'the bodies of mothers entwined' becomes a 'beautiful expression'. Beth Nugent's seeking narrator in 'City of Boys' wants her lover to be her mother, but has fallen into the old trap of believing that this desire is proof of arrested sexual development. Jeanette Winterson's characters, on the other hand, have no such worries. Baby, lover, mother all come together. Nothing is prescribed. All is possible.

Related to this mother–daughter dyad, though separate from it, are the kind of psychoanalytic theories which argue that women's experience of continuing change in their bodies (at puberty, at the menopause, with menstruation and childbirth) means that they are less likely to conceive of themselves as whole, separate, autonomous individuals according to the old humanist (and masculinist) models. Instead, their sense of identity as fluid and shifting means that they can more readily recognize and share in the experiences of another individual. If this is true for women in general, how much more so for lesbians. Sexual sameness is the very source of attraction here, and 'thine and mine' (as in Colette's story) are interchangeable. The mirror image, 'which is you, and which me?', occurs many times in the stories collected here; in Jewett, in Nin, in Brossard, Califia and Acker. Of course there is narcissism here, but when has the free expression of desire not included some element of self-love?

Many of the stories in this collection are experimental. This is no coincidence. The literary map of Modernism, for so long a *Boy's Own* Treasure Island, is currently being redrawn by the radical criticism of writers such as Bonnie Kime Scott and Shari Benstock.[15] They propose that the true instigators of Modernist literary experiment were the women who, by virtue of their position as multiple exiles (as women, as lesbians, as foreigners,

---

15. Bonnie Kime Scott, ed., *The Gender of Modernism: A Critical Anthology* (Indiana University Press, 1990); Shari Benstock, 'Expatriate Sapphic Modernism: Entering Literary History', in Karla Jay and Joanne Glasgow, eds., *Lesbian Texts and Contexts: Radical Revisions* (New York University Press, 1990), 183–203. See also Mary Lynn Broe and Angela Ingram, eds., *Women's Writing in Exile* (University of North Carolina Press, 1989).

as those whose natural inheritance did not include a literary tradition) had most to gain from the breaking up of conventional literary forms. Stein, H.D., Barnes, Mansfield and Woolf were all part of that bold literary experiment. And their challenge to traditional form has been continued by other writers who appear in this collection, most notably by Wittig, Brossard, Acker and Winterson.

There are other reasons for this. Queers have to think about words. First of all they think about words for themselves, as Margaret considers the names of 'Tommie' and 'tribad' in Emma Donoghue's 'Words for Things'. Then lesbian writers have often resorted to word-play to make codes for things that cannot be named. This started out as a social necessity; Stein's *Tender Buttons* is a pretty rude title – but only if you know what 'button' means. Her erotic poem (?) 'Lifting Belly' is one long riddle to the uninitiated, and 'Miss Furr and Miss Skeene' must have been incomprehensible while 'gay' was still a shibboleth confined to its own community. Add to this existing secret language the tendency to play with pastiche and parody, and lesbian writing becomes a mass of conundrums or a private linguistic system depending upon your own orientation. In this collection alone the proper reading of Woolf, Colette, Stein, Barnes, Dinesen, Mushroom, Bechdel and Winterson relies entirely upon the competence of the reader.

So what is lesbian writing? It is writing which exhibits, within the confines of the text itself, something which makes it distinctively about, or for, or out of lesbian experience. That element may lie in the plot, in the subject, in the theory, in the code or the genre, but it has to be there in the writing. The writer herself may never have kissed another woman. Even if she has, she may not call herself a lesbian. Many of the writers in this collection are lesbian; some of them are heterosexual; some of them would call themselves bisexual; some would choose to call themselves by none of these names. Who knows? Who cares?

There is a danger in modern lesbian criticism which has only recently been noticed. That is the assumption that anyone who writes on lesbian subjects must be herself lesbian.[16] Assumptions in any direction are always a bad thing. For they iron out difference, forbid diversity, deny individuality. If there is one thing that I hope this collection makes clear, it is the variety of writing that is now on offer on just this one fruitful subject.

Variety. Yes, and quality. There are three new stories in this collection, specially commissioned – those by Emma Donoghue, Kathy Acker and Jeanette Winterson. Each is quite different from the other, yet each acknowledges a particular facet of lesbian history and makes it new. Each writer cares about language and knows how to use form. Each writer also knows the power of writing. How it can change ideas, how it can challenge the world, how it can let in more light.

'Why do you sleep with girls?' asks the small-minded questioner named Ignorance. Winterson's large answer has the force of poetry and the conviction of truth. Virginia Woolf was right. 'These Sapphists *love* women . . .'

Margaret Reynolds

1993

---

16. See Reina Lewis, 'The Death of the Author and the Resurrection of the Dyke', in Sally Munt, ed., *New Lesbian Criticism: Literary and Cultural Readings* (Harvester, 1992), 17–32.

SARAH ORNE JEWETT
MARTHA'S LADY

(1897)

I

One day, many years ago, the old Judge Pyne house wore an unwonted look of gayety and youthfulness. The high-fenced green garden was bright with June flowers. Under the elms in the large shady front yard you might see some chairs placed near together, as they often used to be when the family were all at home and life was going on gayly with eager talk and pleasure-making; when the elder judge, the grandfather, used to quote that great author, Dr Johnson, and say to his girls, 'Be brisk, be splendid, and be public.'

One of the chairs had a crimson silk shawl thrown carelessly over its straight back, and a passer-by, who looked in through the latticed gate between the tall gate-posts with their white urns, might think that this piece of shining East Indian color was a huge red lily that had suddenly bloomed against the syringa bush. There were certain windows thrown wide open that were usually shut, and their curtains were blowing free in the light wind of a summer afternoon; it looked as if a large household had returned to the old house to fill the prim best rooms and find them full of cheer.

It was evident to every one in town that Miss Harriet Pyne, to use the village phrase, had company. She was the last of her family, and was by no means old; but being the last, and wonted to live with people much older than herself, she had formed all the habits of a serious elderly person. Ladies of her age, something past thirty, often wore discreet caps in those days, especially if they were married, but being single, Miss Harriet clung to youth in this respect, making the one concession of keeping her waving chestnut hair as smooth and stiffly arranged as possible. She had been the dutiful companion of her father and mother in their latest years, all her elder brothers and sisters having married and gone, or died and gone, out of the old house. Now that she was left alone it seemed quite the best thing frankly to accept the fact of age, and to turn more resolutely than ever to the companionship of duty and serious books. She was more serious and given to routine than her elders themselves, as sometimes happened when the daughters of New England gentlefolks were brought up wholly in the society of their elders. At thirty-five she had more reluctance than her mother to face an unforeseen occasion, certainly more than her grandmother, who had preserved some cheerful inheritance of gayety and worldliness from colonial times.

There was something about the look of the crimson silk shawl in the front yard to make one suspect that the sober customs of the best house in a quiet New England village were all being set at defiance, and once when the mistress of the house came to stand in her own doorway, she wore the pleased but somewhat apprehensive look of a guest. In these days New England life held the necessity of much dignity and discretion of behavior; there was the truest hospitality and good cheer in all occasional festivities, but it was sometimes a self-conscious hospitality, followed by an inexorable return to asceticism both of diet and of behavior. Miss Harriet Pyne belonged to the very dullest days of New England, those which perhaps held the most priggishness for the learned professions, the most limited interpretation of the word 'evangelical', and the pettiest indifference to large things.

The outbreak of a desire for larger religious freedom caused at first a most determined reaction toward formalism, especially in small and quiet villages like Ashford, intently busy with their own concerns. It was high time for a little leaven to begin its work, in this moment when the great impulses of the war for liberty had died away and those of the coming war for patriotism and a new freedom had hardly yet begun.

The dull interior, the changed life of the old house, whose former activities seemed to have fallen sound asleep, really typified these larger conditions, and a little leaven had made its easily recognized appearance in the shape of a light-hearted girl. She was Miss Harriet's young Boston cousin, Helena Vernon, who, half-amused and half-impatient at the unnecessary sober-mindedness of her hostess and of Ashford in general, had set herself to the difficult task of gayety. Cousin Harriet looked on at a succession of ingenious and, on the whole, innocent attempts at pleasure, as she might have looked on at the frolics of a kitten who easily substitutes a ball of yarn for the uncertainties of a bird or a wind-blown leaf, and who may at any moment ravel the fringe of a sacred curtain-tassel in preference to either.

Helena, with her mischievous appealing eyes, with her enchanting old songs and her guitar, seemed the more delightful and even reasonable because she was so kind to everybody, and because she was a beauty. She had the gift of most charming manners. There was all the unconscious lovely ease and grace that had come with the good breeding of her city home, where many pleasant people came and went; she had no fear, one had almost said no respect, of the individual, and she did not need to think of herself. Cousin Harriet turned cold with apprehension when she saw the minister coming in at the front gate, and wondered in agony if Martha were properly attired to go to the door, and would by any chance hear the knocker; it was Helena who, delighted to have anything happen, ran to the door to welcome the Reverend Mr Crofton as if he were a congenial friend of her own age. She could behave with more or less propriety during the stately first visit, and even contrive to lighten it with modest mirth, and to extort the confession that the guest had a tenor voice, though sadly out of practice; but when the minister departed a little flattered, and hoping that he had not expressed himself too strongly for a pastor upon the poems of Emerson, and feeling the unusual stir of gallantry in his proper heart, it was Helena who caught the honored hat of the late Judge Pyne from its last resting-place in the hall, and holding it securely in both hands, mimicked the minister's self-conscious entrance. She copied his pompous and anxious expression in the dim parlor in such delicious fashion that Miss Harriet, who could not always extinguish a ready spark of the original sin of humor, laughed aloud.

'My dear!' she exclaimed severely the next moment, 'I am ashamed of your being so disrespectful!' and then laughed again, and took the affecting old hat and carried it back to its place.

'I would not have had any one else see you for the world,' she said sorrowfully as she returned, feeling quite self-possessed again, to the parlor doorway; but Helena still sat in the minister's chair, with her small feet placed as his stiff boots had been, and a copy of his solemn expression before they came to speaking of Emerson and of the guitar. 'I wish I had asked him if he would be so kind as to climb the cherry-tree,' said Helena, unbending a little at the discovery that her cousin would consent to laugh no more. 'There are all those ripe cherries on the top branches. I can climb as high as he, but I can't reach far enough from the last branch that will bear me. The minister is so long and thin' —

'I don't know what Mr Crofton would have thought of you; he is a very serious young man,' said cousin Harriet, still ashamed of her laughter. 'Martha will get the cherries for you, or one of the men. I should not like to have Mr Crofton think you were frivolous, a young lady of your opportunities' — but Helena had escaped through the hall and out at the garden door at the mention of Martha's name. Miss Harriet Pyne sighed anxiously, and then smiled, in spite of her deep convictions, as she shut the blinds and tried to make the house look solemn again.

The front door might be shut, but the garden door at the other end of the broad hall was wide open upon the large sunshiny garden, where the last of the red and white peonies and the golden lilies, and the first of the tall blue larkspurs lent their colors in generous fashion. The straight box borders were all in fresh and shining green of their new leaves, and there was a fragrance of the old garden's inmost life and soul blowing from the honeysuckle blossoms on a long trellis. It was now late in the afternoon, and the sun was low behind great apple-trees at the garden's end, which threw their shadows over the short turf of the bleaching-green. The cherry-trees stood at one side in full sunshine, and Miss Harriet, who presently came to the garden steps to watch like a hen at the water's edge, saw her cousin's pretty figure in its white dress of India muslin hurrying across the grass. She was accompanied by the tall, ungainly shape of Martha the new maid, who, dull and indifferent to every one else, showed a surprising willingness and allegiance to the young guest.

'Martha ought to be in the dining-room, already, slow as she is; it wants but half an hour of tea-time,' said Miss Harriet, as she turned and went into the shaded house. It was Martha's duty to wait at table, and there had been many trying scenes and defeated efforts toward her education. Martha was certainly very clumsy, and she seemed the clumsier because she had replaced her aunt, a most skillful person, who had but lately married a thriving farm and its prosperous owner. It must be confessed that Miss Harriet was a most bewildering instructor, and that her pupil's brain was easily confused and prone to blunders. The coming of Helena had been somewhat dreaded by reason of this incompetent service, but the guest took no notice of frowns or futile gestures at the first tea-table, except to establish friendly relations with Martha on her own account by a reassuring smile. They were about the same age, and next morning, before cousin Harriet came down, Helena showed by a word and a quick touch the right way to do something that had gone wrong and been impossible to understand the night before. A moment later the anxious mistress came in without suspicion, but Martha's eyes were as affectionate as a dog's, and there was a new look of hopefulness on her face; this dreaded guest was a friend after all, and not a foe come from proud Boston to confound her ignorance and patient efforts.

The two young creatures, mistress and maid, were hurrying across the bleaching-green.

'I can't reach the ripest cherries,' explained Helena politely, 'and I think that Miss Pyne ought to send some to the minister. He has just made us a call. Why Martha, you haven't been crying again!'

'Yes'm,' said Martha sadly. 'Miss Pyne always loves to send something to the minister,' she acknowledged with interest, as if she did not wish to be asked to explain these latest tears.

'We'll arrange some of the best cherries in a pretty dish. I'll show you how, and you shall carry them over to the parsonage after tea,' said Helena cheerfully, and Martha accepted the embassy with pleasure. Life was beginning to hold moments of something like delight in the last few days.

'You'll spoil your pretty dress, Miss Helena,' Martha gave shy warning, and Miss Helena stood back and held up her skirts with unusual care while the country girl, in her heavy blue checked gingham, began to climb the cherry-tree like a boy.

Down came the scarlet fruit like bright rain into the green grass.

'Break some nice twigs with the cherries and leaves together; oh, you're a duck, Martha!' and Martha, flushed with delight, and looking far more like a thin and solemn blue heron, came rustling down to earth again, and gathered the spoils into her clean apron.

That night at tea, during her handmaiden's temporary absence, Miss Harriet announced, as if by way of apology, that she thought Martha was beginning to understand something about her work. 'Her aunt was a treasure, she never had to be told anything twice; but Martha has been as clumsy as a calf,' said the precise mistress of the house. 'I have been afraid sometimes that

I never could teach her anything. I was quite ashamed to have you come just now, and find me so unprepared to entertain a visitor.'

'Oh, Martha will learn fast enough because she cares so much,' said the visitor eagerly. 'I think she is a dear good girl. I do hope that she will never go away. I think she does things better every day, cousin Harriet,' added Helena pleadingly, with all her kind young heart. The china-closet door was open a little way, and Martha heard every word. From that moment, she not only knew what love was like, but she knew love's dear ambitions. To have come from a stony hill-farm and a bare small wooden house, was like a cave-dweller's coming to make a permanent home in an art museum, such had seemed the elaborateness and elegance of Miss Pyne's fashion of life; and Martha's simple brain was slow enough in its processes and recognitions. But with this sympathetic ally and defender, this exquisite Miss Helena who believed in her, all difficulties appeared to vanish.

Later that evening, no longer homesick or hopeless, Martha returned from her polite errand to the minister, and stood with a sort of triumph before the two ladies, who were sitting in the front doorway, as if they were waiting for visitors, Helena still in her white muslin and red ribbons, and Miss Harriet in a thin black silk. Being happily self-forgetful in the greatness of the moment, Martha's manners were perfect, and she looked for once almost pretty and quite as young as she was.

'The minister came to the door himself, and returned his thanks. He said that cherries were always his favorite fruit, and he was much obliged to both Miss Pyne and Miss Vernon. He kept me waiting a few minutes, while he got this book ready to send to you, Miss Helena.'

'What are you saying, Martha? I have sent him nothing!' exclaimed Miss Pyne, much astonished. 'What does she mean, Helena?'

'Only a few cherries,' explained Helena. 'I thought Mr Crofton would like them after his afternoon of parish calls. Martha and I arranged them before tea, and I sent them with our compliments.'

'Oh, I am very glad you did,' said Miss Harriet, wondering, but much relieved. 'I was afraid' –

'No, it was none of my mischief,' answered Helena daringly. 'I did not think that Martha would be ready to go so soon. I should have shown you how pretty they looked among their green leaves. We put them in one of your best white dishes with the openwork edge. Martha shall show you tomorrow; mamma always likes to have them so.' Helena's fingers were busy with the hard knot of a parcel.

'See this, cousin Harriet!' she announced proudly, as Martha disappeared round the corner of the house, beaming with the pleasures of adventure and success. 'Look! the minister has sent me a book: Sermons on *what?* Sermons – it is so dark that I can't quite see.'

'It must be his *Sermons on the Seriousness of Life*; they are the only ones he has printed, I believe,' said Miss Harriet, with much pleasure. 'They are considered very fine discourses. He pays you a great compliment, my dear. I feared that he noticed your girlish levity.'

'I behaved beautifully while he stayed,' insisted Helena. 'Ministers are only men,' but she blushed with pleasure. It was certainly something to receive a book from its author, and such a tribute made her of more value to the whole reverent household. The minister was not only a man, but a bachelor, and Helena was at the age that best loves conquest; it was at any rate comfortable to be reinstated in cousin Harriet's good graces.

'Do ask the kind gentleman to tea! He needs a little cheering up,' begged the siren in India muslin, as she laid the shiny black volume of sermons on the stone doorstep with an air of approval, but as if they had quite finished their mission.

'Perhaps I shall, if Martha improves as much as she has within the last day or two,' Miss Harriet promised hopefully. 'It is something I always dread a little when I am all alone, but I think Mr Crofton likes to come. He converses so elegantly.'

II

These were the days of long visits, before affectionate friends thought it quite worth while to take a hundred miles' journey merely to dine or to pass a night in one another's houses. Helena lingered through the pleasant weeks of early summer, and departed unwillingly at last to join her family at the White Hills, where they had gone, like other households of high social station, to pass the month of August out of town. The happy-hearted young guest left many lamenting friends behind her, and promised each that she would come back again next year. She left the minister a rejected lover, as well as the preceptor of the academy, but with their pride unwounded, and it may have been with wider outlooks upon the world and a less narrow sympathy both for their own work in life and for their neighbors' work and hindrances. Even Miss Harriet Pyne herself had lost some of the unnecessary provincialism and prejudice which had begun to harden a naturally good and open mind and affectionate heart. She was conscious of feeling younger and more free, and not so lonely. Nobody had ever been so gay, so fascinating, or so kind as Helena, so full of social resource, so simple and undemanding in her friendliness. The light of her young life cast no shadow on either young or old companions, her pretty clothes never seemed to make other girls look dull or out of fashion. When she went away up the street in Miss Harriet's carriage to take the slow train toward Boston and the gayeties of the new Profile House, where her mother waited impatiently with a group of Southern friends, it seemed as if there would never be any more picnics or parties in Ashford, and as if society had nothing left to do but to grow old and get ready for winter.

Martha came into Miss Helena's bedroom that last morning, and it was easy to see that she had been crying; she looked just as she did in that first sad week of homesickness and despair. All for love's sake she had been learning to do many things, and to do them exactly right; her eyes had grown quick to see the smallest chance for personal service. Nobody could be more humble and devoted; she looked years older than Helena, and wore already a touching air of caretaking.

'You spoil me, you dear Martha!' said Helena from the bed. 'I don't know what they will say at home, I am so spoiled.'

Martha went on opening the blinds to let in the brightness of the summer morning, but she did not speak.

'You are getting on splendidly, aren't you?' continued the little mistress. 'You have tried so hard that you make me ashamed of myself. At first you crammed all the flowers together, and now you make them look beautiful. Last night cousin Harriet was so pleased when the table was charming, and I told her that you did everything yourself, every bit. Won't you keep the flowers fresh and pretty in the house until I come back? It's so much pleasanter for Miss Pyne, and you'll feed my little sparrows, won't you? They're growing so tame.'

'Oh, yes, Miss Helena!' and Martha looked almost angry for a moment, then she burst into tears and covered her face with her apron. 'I couldn't understand a single thing when I first came. I never had been anywhere to see anything, and Miss Pyne frightened me when she talked. It was you made me think I could ever learn. I wanted to keep the place, 'count of mother and the little boys; we're dreadful hard pushed. Hepsy has been good in the kitchen; she said she ought to have patience with me, for she was awkward herself when she first came.'

Helena laughed; she looked so pretty under the tasseled white curtains.

'I dare say Hepsy tells the truth,' she said. 'I wish you had told me about your mother. When I come again, some day we'll drive up country, as you call it, to see her. Martha! I wish you would think of me sometimes after I go away. Won't you promise?' and the bright young face suddenly grew grave. 'I have hard times myself; I don't always learn things that I ought to learn, I don't always put things straight. I wish you wouldn't forget me ever, and would just believe in me. I think it does help more than anything.'

'I won't forget,' said Martha slowly. 'I shall think of you every day.' She spoke almost with indifference, as if she had been asked to dust a room, but she turned aside quickly and pulled the little mat under the hot water jug quite out of its former straightness: then she hastened away down the long white entry, weeping as she went.

III

To lose out of sight the friend whom one has loved and lived to please is to lose joy out of life. But if love is true, there comes presently a higher joy of pleasing the ideal, that is to say, the perfect friend. The same old happiness is lifted to a higher level. As for Martha, the girl who stayed behind in Ashford, nobody's life could seem duller to those who could not understand; she was slow of step, and her eyes were almost always downcast as if intent upon incessant toil; but they startled you when she looked up, with their shining light. She was capable of the happiness of holding fast to a great sentiment, the ineffable satisfaction of trying to please one whom she truly loved. She never thought of trying to make other people pleased with herself; all she lived for was to do the best she could for others, and to conform to an ideal, which grew at last to be like a saint's vision, a heavenly figure painted upon the sky.

On Sunday afternoons in summer, Martha sat by the window of her chamber, a low-storeyed little room, which looked into the side yard and the great branches of an elm-tree. She never sat in the old wooden rocking-chair except on Sundays like this; it belonged to the day of rest and to happy meditation. She wore her plain black dress and a clean white apron, and held in her lap a little wooden box, with a brass ring on top for a handle. She was past sixty years of age and looked even older, but there was the same look on her face that it had sometimes worn in girlhood. She was the same Martha; her hands were old-looking and work-worn, but her face still shone. It seemed like yesterday that Helena Vernon had gone away, and it was more than forty years.

War and peace had brought their changes and great anxieties, the face of the earth was furrowed by floods and fire, the faces of mistress and maid were furrowed by smiles and tears, and in the sky the stars shone on as if nothing had happened. The village of Ashford added a few pages to its unexciting history, the minister preached, the people listened; now and then a funeral crept along the street, and now and then the bright face of a little child rose above the horizon of a family pew. Miss Harriet Pyne lived on in the large white house, which gained more and more distinction because it suffered no changes, save successive repaintings and a new railing about its stately roof. Miss Harriet herself had moved far beyond the uncertainties of an anxious youth. She had long ago made all her decisions, and settled all necessary questions; her scheme of life was as faultless as the miniature landscape of a Japanese garden, and as easily kept in order. The only important change she would ever be capable of making was the final change to another and a better world; and for that nature itself would gently provide, and her own innocent life.

Hardly any great social event had ruffled the easy current of life since Helena Vernon's marriage. To this Miss Pyne had gone, stately in appearance and carrying gifts of some old family silver which bore the Vernon crest, but not without some protest in her heart against the uncertainties of married life. Helena was so equal to a happy independence and even to the assistance of other lives grown strangely dependent upon her quick sympathies and instinctive decisions, that it was hard to let her sink her personality in the affairs of another. Yet a brilliant English match was not without its attractions to an old-fashioned gentlewoman like Miss Pyne, and Helena herself was amazingly happy; one day there had come a letter to Ashford, in which her very heart seemed to beat with love and self-forgetfulness, to tell cousin Harriet of such new happiness and high hope. 'Tell Martha all that I say about my dear Jack,' wrote the eager girl; 'please show my letter to Martha, and tell her that I shall come home next summer and bring the handsomest and best man in the world to Ashford. I have told him all about the dear house and the dear garden; there never was such a lad to reach for cherries with his six-foot-two.' Miss Pyne, wondering a little, gave the letter to Martha, who took it deliberately and as if she wondered too, and went away to read it slowly by herself. Martha cried over it, and felt a strange sense of loss and pain; it hurt her heart a little to read about the cherry-picking. Her idol seemed to be less her own since she had become the idol of a stranger. She never had taken such a letter in her hands before, but love at last prevailed, since Miss Helena was happy, and she kissed the last page where her name was written, feeling over-bold, and laid the envelope on Miss Pyne's secretary without a word.

The most generous love cannot but long for reassurance, and Martha had the joy of being remembered. She was not forgotten when the day of the wedding drew near, but she never knew that Miss Helena had asked if cousin Harriet would not bring Martha to town; she should like to have Martha there to see her married. 'She would help about the flowers,' wrote the happy girl; 'I know she will like to come, and I'll ask mamma to plan to have some one take her all about Boston and make her have a pleasant time after the hurry of the great day is over.'

Cousin Harriet thought it was very kind and exactly like Helena, but Martha would be out of her element; it was most imprudent and girlish to have thought of such a thing. Helena's mother would be far from wishing for any unnecessary guest just then, in the busiest part of her household, and it was best not to speak of the invitation. Some day Martha should go to Boston if she did well, but not now. Helena did not forget to ask if Martha had come, and was astonished by the indifference of the answer. It was the first thing which reminded her that she was not a fairy princess having everything her own way in that last day before the wedding. She knew that Martha would have loved to be near, for she could not help understanding in that moment of her own happiness the love that was hidden in another heart. Next day this happy young princess, the bride, cut a piece of a great cake and put it into a pretty box that had held one of her wedding presents. With eager voices calling her, and all her friends about her, and her mother's face growing more and more wistful at the thought of parting, she still lingered and ran to take one or two trifles from her dressing-table, a little mirror and some tiny scissors that Martha would remember, and one of the pretty handkerchiefs marked with her maiden name. These she put in the box too; it was half a girlish freak and fancy, but she could not help trying to share her happiness, and Martha's life was so plain and dull. She whispered a message, and put the little package into cousin Harriet's hand for Martha as she said good-by. She was very fond of cousin Harriet. She smiled with a gleam of her old fun; Martha's puzzled look and tall awkward figure seemed to stand suddenly before her eyes, as she promised to come again to Ashford. Impatient voices called to Helena, her lover was at the door, and she hurried away, leaving her old home and her girlhood gladly. If she had only known it, as she kissed cousin Harriet good-by, they were never going to see each other again until they were old women. The first step that she took out of her father's house that day, married, and full of hope and joy, was a step that led her away from the green elms of Boston Common and away from her own country and those she loved best, to a brilliant, much-varied foreign life, and to nearly all the sorrows and nearly all the joys that the heart of one woman could hold or know.

On Sunday afternoons Martha used to sit by the window in Ashford and hold the wooden box which a favorite young brother, who afterward died at sea, had made for her, and she used to take out of it the pretty little box with a gilded cover that had held the piece of wedding-cake, and the small scissors, and the blurred bit of a mirror in its silver case; as for the handkerchief with the narrow lace edge, once in two or three years she sprinkled it as if it were a flower, and spread it out in the sun on the old bleaching-green, and sat near by in the shrubbery to watch lest some bold robin or cherry-bird should seize it and fly away.

IV

Miss Harriet Pyne was often congratulated upon the good fortune of having such a helper and friend as Martha. As time went on this tall, gaunt woman, always thin, always slow, gained a dignity of behavior and simple affectionateness of look which suited the charm and dignity of the ancient house. She was unconsciously beautiful like a saint, like the picturesqueness of a lonely tree which lives to shelter unnumbered lives and to stand quietly in its place. There was such rustic homeliness and constancy belonging to her, such beautiful powers of apprehension, such reticence, such gentleness for those who were troubled or sick; all these gifts and graces Martha hid in her heart. She never joined the church because she thought she was not good enough, but life was such a passion and happiness of service that it was impossible not to be devout, and she was always in her humble place on Sundays, in the back pew next the door. She had been educated by a remembrance; Helena's young eyes forever looked at her reassuringly from a gay girlish face. Helena's sweet patience in teaching her own awkwardness could never be forgotten.

'I owe everything to Miss Helena,' said Martha, half aloud, as she sat alone by the window; she had said it to herself a thousand times. When she looked in the little keepsake mirror she always hoped to see some faint reflection of Helena Vernon, but there was only her own brown old New England face to look back at her wonderingly.

Miss Pyne went less and less often to pay visits to her friends in Boston; there were very few friends left to come to Ashford and make long visits in the summer, and life grew more and more monotonous. Now and then there came news from across the sea and messages of remembrance, letters that were closely written on thin sheets of paper, and that spoke of lords and ladies, of great journeys, of the death of little children and the proud successes of boys at school, of the wedding of Helena

Dysart's only daughter; but even that had happened years ago.
These things seemed far away and vague, as if they belonged to
a story and not to life itself; the true links with the past were
quite different. There was the unvarying flock of ground-
sparrows that Helena had begun to feed; every morning Martha
scattered crumbs for them from the side doorsteps while Miss
Pyne watched from the dining-room window, and they were
counted and cherished year by year.

Miss Pyne herself had many fixed habits, but little ideality or
imagination, and so at last it was Martha who took thought for
her mistress, and gave freedom to her own good taste. After a
while, without any one's observing the change, the everyday
ways of doing things in the house came to be the stately ways
that had once belonged only to the entertainment of guests.
Happily both mistress and maid seized all possible chances for
hospitality, yet Miss Harriet nearly always sat alone at her
exquisitely served table with its fresh flowers, and the beautiful
old china which Martha handled so lovingly that there was no
good excuse for keeping it hidden on closet shelves. Every year
when the old cherry-trees were in fruit, Martha carried the
round white old English dish with a fretwork edge, full of
pointed green leaves and scarlet cherries, to the minister, and his
wife never quite understood why every year he blushed and
looked so conscious of the pleasure, and thanked Martha as if he
had received a very particular attention. There was no pretty
suggestion toward the pursuit of the fine art of housekeeping in
Martha's limited acquaintance with newspapers that she did not
adopt; there was no refined old custom of the Pyne housekeeping
that she consented to let go. And every day, as she had promised,
she thought of Miss Helena, – oh, many times in every day:
whether this thing would please her, or that be likely to fall in
with her fancy or ideas of fitness. As far as was possible the rare
news that reached Ashford through an occasional letter or the
talk of guests was made part of Martha's own life, the history of
her own heart. A worn old geography often stood open at the
map of Europe on the light-stand in her room, and a little old-

fashioned gilt button, set with a bit of glass like a ruby, that had broken and fallen from the trimming of one of Helena's dresses, was used to mark the city of her dwelling-place. In the changes of a diplomatic life Martha followed her lady all about the map. Sometimes the button was at Paris, and sometimes at Madrid; once, to her great anxiety, it remained long at St Petersburg. For such a slow scholar Martha was not unlearned at last, since everything about life in these foreign towns was of interest to her faithful heart. She satisfied her own mind as she threw crumbs to the tame sparrows; it was all part of the same thing and for the same affectionate reasons.

V

One Sunday afternoon in early summer Miss Harriet Pyne came hurrying along the entry that led to Martha's room and called two or three times before its inhabitant could reach the door. Miss Harriet looked unusually cheerful and excited, and she held something in her hand. 'Where are you, Martha?' she called again. 'Come quick, I have something to tell you!'

'Here I am, Miss Pyne,' said Martha, who had only stopped to put her precious box in the drawer, and to shut the geography.

'Who do you think is coming this very night at half-past six? We must have everything as nice as we can; I must see Hannah at once. Do you remember my cousin Helena who has lived abroad so long? Miss Helena Vernon — the Honorable Mrs Dysart, she is now.'

'Yes, I remember her,' answered Martha, turning a little pale.

'I knew that she was in this country, and I had written to ask her to come for a long visit,' continued Miss Harriet, who did not often explain things, even to Martha, though she was always conscientious about the kind messages that were sent back by grateful guests. 'She telegraphs that she means to anticipate her visit by a few days and come to me at once. The heat is beginning in town, I suppose. I daresay, having been a foreigner so long, she does not mind traveling on Sunday. Do you think Hannah will be prepared? We must have tea a little later.'

'Yes, Miss Harriet,' said Martha. She wondered that she could speak as usual, there was such a ringing in her ears. 'I shall have time to pick some fresh strawberries; Miss Helena is so fond of our strawberries.'

'Why, I had forgotten,' said Miss Pyne, a little puzzled by something quite unusual in Martha's face. 'We must expect to find Mrs Dysart a good deal changed, Martha; it is a great many years since she was here; I have not seen her since her wedding, and she has had a great deal of trouble, poor girl. You had better open the parlor chamber, and make it ready before you go down.'

'It is all ready,' said Martha. 'I can carry some of those little sweet-brier roses upstairs before she comes.'

'Yes, you are always thoughtful,' said Miss Pyne, with unwonted feeling.

Martha did not answer. She glanced at the telegram wistfully. She had never really suspected before that Miss Pyne knew nothing of the love that had been in her heart all these years; it was half a pain and half a golden joy to keep such a secret; she could hardly bear this moment of surprise.

Presently the news gave wings to her willing feet. When Hannah, the cook, who never had known Miss Helena, went to the parlor an hour later on some errand to her old mistress, she discovered that this stranger guest must be a very important person. She had never seen the tea-table look exactly as it did that night, and in the parlor itself there were fresh blossoming boughs in the old East India jars, and lilies in the paneled hall, and flowers everywhere, as if there were some high festivity.

Miss Pyne sat by the window watching, in her best dress, looking stately and calm; she seldom went out now, and it was almost time for the carriage. Martha was just coming in from the garden with the strawberries, and with more flowers in her apron. It was a bright cool evening in June, the golden robins sang in the elms, and the sun was going down behind the apple-trees at the foot of the garden. The beautiful old house stood wide open to the long-expected guest.

'I think that I shall go down to the gate,' said Miss Pyne, looking at Martha for approval, and Martha nodded and they went together slowly down the broad front walk.

There was a sound of horses and wheels on the roadside turf: Martha could not see at first; she stood back inside the gate behind the white lilac-bushes as the carriage came. Miss Pyne was there; she was holding out both arms and taking a tired, bent little figure in black to her heart. 'Oh, my Miss Helena is an old woman like me!' and Martha gave a pitiful sob; she had never dreamed it would be like this; this was the one thing she could not bear.

'Where are you, Martha?' called Miss Pyne. 'Martha will bring these in; you have not forgotten my good Martha, Helena?' Then Mrs Dysart looked up and smiled just as she used to smile in the old days. The young eyes were there still in the changed face, and Miss Helena had come.

That night Martha waited in her lady's room just as she used, humble and silent, and went through with the old unforgotten loving services. The long years seemed like days. At last she lingered a moment trying to think of something else that might be done, then she was going silently away, but Helena called her back. She suddenly knew the whole story and could hardly speak.

'Oh, my dear Martha!' she cried, 'won't you kiss me good-night? Oh, Martha, have you remembered like this, all these long years!'

RENÉE VIVIEN
PRINCE CHARMING

(1904)

*Translated by Karla Jay and
Yvonne M. Klein*

told by Gesa Karoly

I promised you, my curious little girl, to tell you the true story of Sarolta Andrassy. You knew her, didn't you? You remember her black hair with blue and red highlights, and her eyes like a lover's begging and melancholy.

Sarolta Andrassy lived in the country with her old mother. For neighbors she had the Szecheny family, who had just left Budapest forever. Really, they were a bizarre family! It was easy to mistake Bela Szecheny for a little girl, and his sister, Terka, for a little boy. Curiously enough, Bela possessed all the feminine virtues and Terka, all the masculine faults. Bela's hair was a copper blond; Terka's was a livelier, rather reddish blond. The brother and sister strangely resembled each other – and that's very rare among members of the same family, no matter what they say.

Bela's mother was not yet resigned to cutting off the beautiful blond curls of the little boy or to exchanging his graceful muslin or velvet skirts for vulgar pants. She coddled him like a little girl. As for Terka, she kept shooting up, like a wild weed . . .

She lived outdoors, climbing on the trees, marauding, robbing the kitchen gardens. She was unbearable and at war with the world. She was a child who was neither tender nor communicative. Bela, on the other hand, was gentleness itself. He showed his adoration for his mother by making much of her and by caressing her. Terka loved no one, and no one loved her.

Sarolta came one day to visit the Szecheny family. Her loving eyes in her thin, pale face seemed to be begging. Bela greatly pleased her, and they played together a great deal. Looking wild, Terka prowled around them. When Sarolta spoke to her, she fled.

She could have been pretty, this incomprehensible Terka . . . But she was too tall for her age, too thin, too awkward, too ungainly, whereas Bela was so dainty and so sweet! . . .

Several months later, the Szecheny family left Hungary. Bela had an excessively delicate chest, being in general rather frail. On the advice of the doctor, his mother took him to Nice, along with his recalcitrant little sister. Sarolta cried bitterly over losing her playmate.

In her dreams, Sarolta always evoked the too frail and too pretty little boy whom she remembered constantly. And she would say to herself, smiling at the blond fantasy: 'If I must get married when I'm older, I would like to marry Bela.'

Several years passed – oh, how slowly for the impatient Sarolta! Bela must have reached the age of twenty, and Terka, seventeen. They were still on the Riviera. And Sarolta grieved through the joyless, long years, which were lit up only by the illusion of a dream.

One violet evening, she was dreaming by her window when her mother came to tell her that Bela had returned . . .

Sarolta's heart sang as if it would break. And, the next day, Bela came to see her.

He was the same, and even more charming than before. Sarolta was happy that he had kept this feminine and gentle manner which had so pleased her. He was still the fragile child . . . But now this child possessed an inexpressible grace. Sarolta searched in vain for the cause of this transformation which made him so alluring. His voice was musical and faraway like the echo of the mountains. She admired everything about him, even his stone-gray English suit. And she even admired his mauve necktie.

Bela contemplated the young woman with different eyes, with eyes strangely beautiful, with eyes that did not resemble the eyes of other men . . .

'How thin he is!' observed Sarolta's mother after he had left. 'Poor thing, he must still be in delicate health.'

Sarolta did not answer. She closed her eyes in order to again see Bela under her closed eyelids . . . How handsome, handsome, handsome he was! . . .

He returned the next day, and every day after that. He was the Prince Charming who is seen only in the childish pages of fairy tales. She could not look him in the face without feeling ardently and languishingly faint . . . Her face changed according to the expression of the face she loved. Her heart beat according to the rhythm of that other heart. Her unconscious and childish tenderness had become love.

Bela would turn pale as soon as she appeared diaphanous in her white summer dress. Sometimes he looked at her without speaking, like someone communing with himself in front of a faultless Statue. Sometimes he took her hand . . . His palm was so burning and dry that she thought she was touching the hand of an invalid. Indeed, at those times a little fever would show in Bela's cheeks.

One day she asked him for some news of the undisciplined Terka.

'She is still in Nice,' he answered indifferently. And then they spoke of something else. Sarolta understood that Bela did not love his sister at all. This was not surprising, what is more – a girl who was so taciturn and wild!

What should come next, came next. A few months later Bela asked to marry her. He had just turned twenty-one. Sarolta's mother had no objections to the union.

Their betrothal was unreal, as delicate as the white roses that Bela brought each day. Their vows were more fervent than poems: their very souls trembled on their lips. The nuptial dream came to be in the deepest silence.

'Why,' Sarolta would ask her fiancé, 'are you worthier of being loved than other young men? Why do you have gentle ways that they do not? Where did you learn the divine words that they never say?'

The wedding ceremony took place in absolute privacy. The candles brightened the red highlights in Bela's blond hair. The incense curled towards him, and the thunder of the organs exalted and glorified him. For the first time since the beginning of the world, the Groom was as beautiful as the Bride.

They left for those blue shores where the desire of lovers runs out of patience. They were seen, a Divine Couple, with the eyelashes of one stroking the eyelids of the other. They were seen, lovingly and chastely intertwined, with her black hair spread over his blond hair . . .

Oh, my curious little girl! Here the story becomes a little difficult to relate . . . Several months later, the real Bela Szecheny appeared . . . He was not Prince Charming, alas! He was only a handsome boy, nothing more.

He furiously sought the identity of the young usurper . . . And he learned that the usurper in question was his own sister, Terka.

. . . Sarolta and Prince Charming have never returned to Hungary. They are hiding in the depths of a Venetian castle or of a Florentine mansion. And sometimes they are seen, as one sees a vision of ideal tenderness, lovingly and chastely inter-twined.

KATHERINE MANSFIELD
LEVES AMORES

(1907)

I can never forget the Thistle Hotel.* I can never forget that strange winter night.

I had asked her to dine with me, and then go to the Opera. My room was opposite hers. She said she would come but – could I lace up her evening bodice, it was hooks at the back. Very well.

It was still daylight when I knocked at the door and entered. In her petticoat bodice and a full silk petticoat she was washing, sponging her face and neck. She said she was finished, and I might sit on the bed and wait for her. So I looked round at the dreary room. The one filthy window faced the street. She could see the choked, dust-grimed window of a wash-house opposite. For furniture, the room contained a low bed, draped with revolting, yellow, vine-patterned curtains, a chair, a wardrobe

* The text has been copied from a typescript lent to Claire Tomalin by Navin Sullivan, son of Vere Bartrick-Baker, who left it among her papers. It was printed for the first time in Claire Tomalin's *Katherine Mansfield: A Secret Life* (Viking, 1987).

with a piece of cracked mirror attached, a washstand. But the wallpaper hurt me physically. It hung in tattered strips from the wall. In its less discoloured and faded patches I could trace the pattern of roses — buds and flowers — and the frieze was a conventional design of birds, of what genus the good God alone knows.

And this was where she lived. I watched her curiously. She was pulling on long, thin stockings, and saying 'damn' when she could not find her suspenders. And I felt within me a certainty that nothing beautiful could ever happen in that room, and for her I felt contempt, a little tolerance, a very little pity.

A dull, grey light hovered over everything; it seemed to accentuate the thin tawdriness of her clothes, the squalor of her life, she, too, looked dull and grey and tired. And I sat on the bed, and thought: 'Come, this Old Age. I have forgotten passion, I have been left behind in the beautiful golden procession of Youth. Now I am seeing life in the dressing-room of the theatre.'

So we dined somewhere and went to the Opera. It was late, when we came out into the crowded night street, late and cold. She gathered up her long skirts. Silently we walked back to the Thistle Hotel, down the white pathway fringed with beautiful golden lilies, up the amethyst shadowed staircase.

Was Youth dead? . . . *Was* Youth dead?

She told me as we walked along the corridor to her room that she was glad the night had come. I did not ask why. I was glad, too. It seemed a secret between us. So I went with her into her room to undo those troublesome hooks. She lit a little candle on an enamel bracket. The light filled the room with darkness. Like a sleepy child she slipped out of her frock and then, suddenly, turned to me and flung her arms round my neck. Every bird upon the bulging frieze broke into song. Every rose upon the tattered paper budded and formed into blossom. Yes, even the green vine upon the bed curtains wreathed itself into strange chaplets and garlands, twined round us in a leafy embrace, held us with a thousand clinging tendrils.

And Youth was not dead.

H.D.

THE WISE SAPPHO

(*c.* 1916–18)

'Little, but all roses' is the dictate of the Alexandrine poet, yet I am inclined to disagree. I would not bring roses, nor yet the great shaft of scarlet lilies. I would bring orange blossoms, implacable flowerings made to seduce the sense when every other means has failed, poignard that glints, fresh sharpened steel: after the red heart, red lilies, impassioned roses are dead.

'Little, but all roses' – true there is a tint of rich colour (invariably we find it), violets, purple woof of cloth, scarlet garments, dyed fastening of a sandal, the lurid, crushed and perished hyacinth, stains on cloth and flesh and parchment.

There is gold too. Was it a gold rose the poet meant? But the gold of a girl-child's head, the gold of an embroidered garment hem, the rare gold of sea-grass or meadow-pulse does not seem to evoke in our thought the vision of roses, heavy in a scented garden.

'Little, but all roses.' I think, though the stains are deep on the red and scarlet cushions, on the flaming cloak of love, it is not warmth we look for in these poems, not fire nor sunlight, not heat in the ordinary sense, diffused, and comforting (nor is it light, day or dawn or light of sun-setting), but another element containing all these, magnetic, vibrant; not the lightning as it falls from the thunder cloud, yet lightning in a sense: white, unhuman element, containing fire and light and warmth, yet in its essence differing from all these, as if the brittle crescent-moon gave heat to us, or some splendid scintillating star turned warm suddenly in our hand like a jewel, sent by the beloved.

I think of the words of Sappho as these colours, or states rather, transcending colour yet containing (as great heat the compass of the spectrum) all colour. And perhaps the most obvious is this rose colour, merging to richer shades of scarlet, purple or Phoenician purple. To the superficial lover – truly – roses!

Yet not all roses – not roses at all, not orange blossoms even, but reading deeper we are inclined to visualize these broken sentences and unfinished rhythms as rocks – perfect rock shelves and layers of rock between which flowers by some chance may grow but which endure when the staunch blossoms have perished.

Not flowers at all, but an island with innumerable, tiny, irregular bays and fjords and little straits between which the sun lies clear (fragments cut from a perfect mirror of iridescent polished silver or of the bronze reflecting richer tints) or breaks, wave upon destructive passionate wave.

Not roses, but an island, a country, a continent, a planet, a world of emotion, differing entirely from any present-day imaginable world of emotion; a world of emotion that could only be imagined by the greatest of her own countrymen in the greatest period of that country's glamour, who themselves confessed her beyond their reach, beyond their song, not a woman, not a goddess even, but a song or the spirit of a song.

A song, a spirit, a white star that moves across the heaven to mark the end of a world epoch or to presage some coming glory.

Yet she is embodied – terribly a human being, a woman, a

personality as the most impersonal become when they confront their fellow beings.

The under-lip curls out in the white face, she has twisted her two eyes unevenly, the brows break the perfect line of the white forehead, her expression is not exactly sinister (sinister and dead), the spark of mockery beneath the half-closed lids is rather living destructive irony.

'What country girl bewitches your heart who knows not how to draw her skirt about her ankles?'

Aristocratic – indifferent – full of caprice – full of imperfection – intolerant.

High in the mountains, the wind may break the trees, as love the lover, but this was before the days of Theocritus, before the destructive Athenian satyric drama – we hear no praise of country girls nor mountain goats. This woman has still the flawless tradition to maintain.

Her bitterness was on the whole the bitterness of the sweat of Eros. Had she burned to destroy she had spent her flawless talent to destroy custom and mob-thought with serpent-tongue before the great Athenian era.

Black and burnt are the cheeks of the girl of the late Sicilian Theocritus, for says he, black is the hyacinth and the myrtle-berry.

But Sappho has no praise for mountain girls. She protrudes a little her under-lip, twists her eyes, screws her face out of proportion as she searches for the most telling phrase; this girl who bewitches you, my friend, does not even know how to draw her skirts about her feet.

Sophisticated, ironical, bitter jeer. Not her hands, her feet, her hair, or her features resemble in any way those of the country-bred among the thickets; not her garments even, are ill-fitting or ill-cut, but her manners, her gestures are crude, the bitterest of all destructive gibes of one sensitive woman at the favourite of another, sensitive, high-strung, autocratic as herself.

The gods, it is true, Aphrodite, Hermes, Ares, Hephaistos, Adonis, beloved of the mother of loves, the Graces, Zeus himself, Eros in all his attributes, great, potent, the Muses, mythical being and half-god, the Kyprian again and again are mentioned in these poems but at the end, it is for the strange almost petulant little phrases that we value this woman, this cry (against some simple unknown girl) of skirts and ankles we might think unnecessarily petty, yet are pleased in the thinking of it, or else the outbreak against her own intimate companions brings her nearer our own over-sophisticated, nerve-wracked era: 'The people I help most are the most unkind,' 'O you forget me' or 'You love someone better,' 'You are nothing to me,' nervous, trivial tirades. Or we have in sweetened mood so simple a phrase 'I sing' – not to please any god, goddess, creed or votary of religious rite – I sing not even in abstract contemplation, trance-like, remote from life, to please myself, but says this most delightful and friendly woman, 'I sing and I sing beautifully like this, in order to please my friends – my girl-friends.'

We have no definite portraits from her hands of these young women of Mitylene. They are left to our imagination, though only the most ardent heart, the most intense spirit and the most wary and subtle intellect can hope even in moments of ardent imagination to fill in these broken couplets. One reads simply this 'My darling,' or again 'You burn me.' To a bride's lover she says, 'Ah there never was a girl like her.' She speaks of the light spread across a lovely face, of the garment wrapped about a lovely body; she addresses by name two of these young women comparing one to another's disadvantage (though even here she temporizes her judgement with an endearing adjective), 'Mnasidika is more shapely than tender Gyrinno.' We hear of Eranna too. 'Eranna, there never was a girl more spiteful than you.'

Another girl she praises, not for beauty. Though they stand among tall spotted lilies and the cup of jacynth and the Lesbian iris, she yet extolls beyond Kypris and the feet of Eros, wisdom. 'Ah,' she says of this one, beloved for another beauty than that of perfect waist and throat and close-bound cap of hair and level brows, 'I think no girl can ever stand beneath the sun or ever will again and be as wise as you are.'

Wisdom — this is all we know of the girl, that though she stood in the heavy Graeco-Asiatic sunlight, the wind from Asia, heavy with ardent myrrh and Persian spices, was yet tempered with a Western gale, bearing in its strength and its salt sting, the image of another, tall, with eyes shadowed by the helmet rim, the goddess, indomitable.

This is her strength — Sappho of Mitylene was a Greek. And in all her ecstasies, her burnings, her Asiatic riot of colour, her cry to that Phoenician deity, 'Adonis, Adonis —' her phrases, so simple yet in any but her hands in danger of overpowering sensuousness, her touches of Oriental realism, 'purple napkins' and 'soft cushions' are yet tempered, moderated by a craft never surpassed in literature. The beauty of Aphrodite it is true is the constant, reiterated subject of her singing. But she is called by a late scholiast who knew more of her than we can hope to learn from these brief fragments, 'The Wise Sappho'.

We need the testimony of no Alexandrian or late Roman scholiast to assure us of the artistic wisdom, the scientific precision of metre and musical notation, the finely tempered intellect of this woman. Yet for all her artistic moderation, what is the personal, the emotional quality of her wisdom? This woman whom love paralysed till she seemed to herself a dead body yet burnt, as the desert grass is burnt, white by the desert heat; she who trembled and was sick and sweated at the mere presence of another, a person, doubtless of charm, of grace, but of no extraordinary gifts perhaps of mind or feature — was she moderate, was she wise? Savonarola standing in the courtyard of the Medici (some two thousand years later) proclaimed her openly to the assembled youthful laity and priests of Florence — a devil.

If moderation is wisdom, if constancy in love is wisdom, was she wise? We read even in these few existing fragments, name upon curious, exotic, fragrant name: Atthis — Andromeda — Mnasidika — Eranna — Gyrinno — more, many more than these tradition tells were praised in the lost fragments. The name of muse and goddess and of human woman merge, interspersed among these verses. 'Niobe and Leda were friends —' it is a simple statement – for the moment, Niobe and Leda are nearer, more human, than the Atthis, the Eranna who strike and burn and break like Love himself.

The wise Sappho! She was wise, emotionally wise, we suspect with wisdom of simplicity, the blindness of genius. She constructed from the simple gesture of a half-grown awkward girl, a being, a companion, an equal. She imagined, for a moment, as the white bird wrinkled a pink foot, clutching to obtain balance at the too smooth ivory of the wrist of the same Atthis, that Atthis had a mind, that Atthis was a goddess. Because the sun made a momentary circlet of strange rust-coloured hair, she saw in all her fragrance, Aphrodite, violet-crowned, or better still a sister, a muse, one of the violet wreathing. She imagined because the girl's shoulders seemed almost too fragile, too frail, to support the vestment, dragging a little heavily because of the gold-binding, that the same shoulders were the shoulders of a being, an almost disembodied spirit. She constructed perfect and flawless (as in her verse, she carved from current Aeolic dialect, immortal phrases) the whole, the perfection, the undying spirit of goddess, muse or sacred being from the simple grace of some tall, half-developed girl. The very skies open, were opened by these light fingers, fluffing out the under-feathers of the pigeon's throat. Then the wise Sappho clamours aloud against that bitter, bitter creature, Eros, who has once more betrayed her. 'Ah, Atthis, you hate even to think of me – you have gone to Andromeda.'

I love to think of Atthis and Andromeda curled on a sun-baked marble bench like the familiar Tanagra group, talking it over. What did they say? What did they think? Doubtless, they thought little or nothing and said much.

There is another girl, a little girl. Her name is Cleis. It is reported that the mother of Sappho was named Cleis. It is said that Sappho had a daughter whom she called Cleis.

Cleis was golden. No doubt Cleis was perfect. Cleis was a beautiful baby, looking exactly like a yellow flower (so her mother tells us). She was so extraordinarily beautiful, Lydia had nothing so sweet, so spiced; greatness, wealth, power, nothing in all Lydia could be exchanged for Cleis.

So in the realm of the living, we know there was a Cleis. I see her heaping shells, purple and rose-edged, stained here and there with saffron colours, shells from Adriatic waters heaped in her own little painted bowl and poured out again and gathered up only to be spilt once more across the sands. We have seen Atthis of yester-year; Andromeda of 'fair requital', Mnasidika with provoking length of over-shapely limbs; Gyrinno, loved for some appealing gesture or strange resonance of voice or skill of finger-tips, though failing in the essential and more obvious qualities of beauty; Eranna with lips curved contemptuously over slightly irregular though white and perfect teeth; angry Eranna who refused everyone and bound white violets only for the straight hair she herself braided with precision and cruel self-torturing neatness about her own head. We know of Gorgo, over-riotous, too heavy, with special intoxicating sweetness, but exhausting, a girl to weary of, no companion, her over-soft curves presaging early development of heavy womanhood.

Among the living there are these and others. Timas, dead among the living, lying with lily wreath and funeral torch, a golden little bride, lives though sleeping more poignantly even than the famous Graeco-Egyptian beauty the poet's brother married at Naucratis. Rhodope, a name redolent (even though we may no longer read the tribute of the bridegroom's sister) of the heavy out-curling, over-lapping petals of the peerless flower.

Little – not little – but all, all roses! So at the last, we are forced to accept the often quoted tribute of Meleager, late Alexandrian, half Jew, half Grecian poet. Little but all roses! True, Sappho has become for us a name, an abstraction as well as a pseudonym for poignant human feeling, she is indeed rocks set in a blue sea, she is the sea itself, breaking and tortured and torturing, but never broken. She is the island of artistic perfection where the lover of ancient beauty (shipwrecked in the modern world) may yet find foothold and take breath and gain courage for new adventures and dream of yet unexplored continents and realms of future artistic achievement. She is the wise Sappho.

Plato, poet and philosopher in the most formidable period of Athenian culture, looking back some centuries toward Mitylene, having perspective and a rare standard of comparison, too, speaks of this woman as among the wise.

You were the morning star among the living (the young Plato, poet and Athenian, wrote of a friend he had lost), you were the morning star before you died; now you are 'as Hesperus, giving new splendour to the dead'. Plato lives as a poet, as a lover, though the Republic seems but a ponderous tome and the mysteries of the Dialogues verge often on the didactic and artificial. So Sappho must live, roses, but many roses, for tradition has set flower upon flower about her name and would continue to do so though her last line were lost.

Perhaps to Meleager, having access to the numberless scrolls of Alexandria, there seemed 'but little' though to us, in a cheerless and more barren age, there seems much. Legend upon legend has grown up, adding curious documents to each precious fragment; the history of the preservation of each line is in itself a most fascinating and bewildering romance.

Courtesan and woman of fashion were rebuked at one time for not knowing 'even the works of Sappho'. Sophocles cried out in despair before some inimitable couplet, 'gods – what impassioned heart and longing made this rhythm'. The Roman Emperor, weary to death, left his wreathed drinking cup and said, 'It is worth living yet to hear another of this woman's songs.' Catullus, impassioned lyrist, left off recounting the imperfections of his Lesbia to enter a fair paradisal world, to forge silver Latin from imperishable Greek, to marvel at the praises of this perfect lover who needed no interim of hatred to repossess the loved one. Monk and scholar, grey recluse of Byzantium or Roman or medieval monastery, flamed to new birth of intellectual passion at discovery of some fatal relic until the Vatican itself was moved and deemed this woman fit rival to the seductions of another Poet and destroyed her verses.

The roses Meleager saw as 'little' have become in the history not only of literature but of nations (Greece and Rome and medieval town and Tuscan city) a great power, roses, but many, many roses, each fragment witness to the love of some scholar or hectic antiquary searching to find a precious inch of palimpsest among the funereal glories of the sand-strewn Pharaohs.

GERTRUDE STEIN
MISS FURR AND MISS SKEENE

(1922)

Helen Furr had quite a pleasant home. Mrs Furr was quite a pleasant woman. Mr Furr was quite a pleasant man. Helen Furr had quite a pleasant voice a voice quite worth cultivating. She did not mind working. She worked to cultivate her voice. She did not find it gay living in the same place where she had always been living. She went to a place where some were cultivating something, voices and other things needing cultivating. She met Georgine Skeene there who was cultivating her voice which some thought was quite a pleasant one. Helen Furr and Georgine Skeene lived together then. Georgine Skeene liked travelling. Helen Furr did not care about travelling, she liked to stay in one place and be gay there. They were together then and travelled to another place and stayed there and were gay there.

They stayed there and were gay there, not very gay there, just gay there. They were both gay there, they were regularly working there both of them cultivating their voices there, they were both gay there. Georgine Skeene was gay there and she was regular, regular in being gay, regular in not being gay, regular in being a gay one who was not being gay longer than was needed to be one being quite a gay one. They were both gay then there and both working there then.

They were in a way both gay there where there were many cultivating something. They were both regular in being gay there. Helen Furr was gay there, she was gayer and gayer there and really she was just gay there, she was gayer and gayer there, that is to say she found ways of being gay there that she was using in being gay there. She was gay there, not gayer and gayer, just gay there, that is to say she was not gayer by using the things she found there that were gay things, she was gay there, always she was gay there.

They were quite regularly gay there, Helen Furr and Georgine Skeene, they were regularly gay there where they were gay. They were very regularly gay.

To be regularly gay was to do every day the gay thing that they did every day. To be regularly gay was to end every day at the same time after they had been regularly gay. They were regularly gay. They were gay every day. They ended every day in the same way, at the same time, and they had been every day regularly gay.

The voice Helen Furr was cultivating was quite a pleasant one. The voice Georgine Skeene was cultivating was, some said, a better one. The voice Helen Furr was cultivating she cultivated and it was quite completely a pleasant enough one then, a cultivated enough one then. The voice Georgine Skeene was cultivating she did not cultivate too much. She cultivated it quite some. She cultivated and she would sometime go on cultivating it and it was not then an unpleasant one, it would not be then an unpleasant one, it would be a quite richly enough cultivated one, it would be quite richly enough to be a pleasant enough one.

They were gay where there were many cultivating something. The two were gay there, were regularly gay there. Georgine Skeene would have liked to do more travelling. They did some travelling, not very much travelling, Georgine Skeene would have liked to do more travelling, Helen Furr did not care about doing travelling, she liked to stay in a place and be gay there.

They stayed in a place and were gay there, both of them stayed there, they stayed together there, they were gay there, they were regularly gay there.

They went quite often, not very often, but they did go back to where Helen Furr had a pleasant enough home and then Georgine Skeene went to a place where her brother had quite some distinction. They both went, every few years, went visiting to where Helen Furr had quite a pleasant home. Certainly Helen Furr would not find it gay to stay, she did not find it gay, she said she would not stay, she said she did not find it gay, she said she would not stay where she did not find it gay, she said she found it gay where she did stay and she did stay there where very many were cultivating something. She did stay there. She always did find it gay there.

She went to see them where she had always been living and where she did not find it gay. She had a pleasant home there, Mrs Furr was a pleasant enough woman, Mr Furr was a pleasant enough man, Helen told them and they were not worrying, that she did not find it gay living where she had always been living.

Georgine Skeene and Helen Furr were living where they were both cultivating their voices and they were gay there. They visited where Helen Furr had come from and then they went to where they were living where they were then regularly living.

There were some dark and heavy men there then. There were some who were not so heavy and some who were not so dark. Helen Furr and Georgine Skeene sat regularly with them. They sat regularly with the ones who were dark and heavy. They sat regularly with the ones who were not so dark. They sat regularly with the ones that were not so heavy. They sat with them regularly, sat with some of them. They went with them regularly went with them. They were regular then, they were gay then, they were where they wanted to be then where it was gay to be then, they were regularly gay then. There were men there then who were dark and heavy and they sat with them with Helen

Furr and Georgine Skeene and they went with them with Miss
Furr and Miss Skeene, and they went with the heavy and dark
men Miss Furr and Miss Skeene went with them, and they sat
with them, Miss Furr and Miss Skeene sat with them, and there were
other men, some were not heavy men and they sat with Miss
Furr and Miss Skeene and Miss Furr and Miss Skeene sat with
them, and there were other men who were not dark men and
they sat with Miss Furr and Miss Skeene and Miss Furr and Miss
Skeene sat with them. Miss Furr and Miss Skeene went with
them and they went with Miss Furr and Miss Skeene, some who
were not heavy men, some who were not dark men. Miss Furr
and Miss Skeene sat regularly, then sat with some men. Miss
Furr and Miss Skeene went and there were some men with them.
There were men and Miss Furr and Miss Skeene went with
them, went somewhere with them, went with some of them.

Helen Furr and Georgine Skeene were regularly living where
very many were living and cultivating in themselves something.
Helen Furr and Georgine Skeene were living very regularly
then, being very regular then in being gay then. They did then
learn many ways to be gay and they were then being gay quite
regular in being gay, being gay and they were learning little
things, little things in ways of being gay, they were very regular
then, they were learning very many little things in ways of being
gay, they were being gay and using these little things they were
learning to have to be gay with regularly gay with then and they
were gay the same amount they had been gay. They were quite
gay, they were quite regular, they were learning little things, gay
little things, they were gay inside them and the same amount
they had been gay, they were gay the same length of time they
had been gay every day.

They were regular in being gay, they learned little things that
are things in being gay, they learned many little things that are
things in being gay, they were gay every day, they were regular,
they were gay, they were gay the same length of time every day,
they were gay, they were quite regularly gay.

Georgine Skeene went away to stay two months with her

brother. Helen Furr did not go then to stay with her father and her mother. Helen Furr stayed there where they had been regularly living the two of them and she would then certainly not be lonesome, she would go on being gay. She did go on being gay. She was not any more gay but she was gay longer every day than they had been being gay when they were together being gay. She was gay then quite exactly the same way. She learned a few more little ways of being in being gay. She was quite gay and in the same way, the same way she had been gay and she was gay a little longer in the day, more of each day she was gay. She was gay longer every day than when the two of them had been being gay. She was gay quite in the way they had been gay, quite in the same way.

She was not lonesome then, she was not at all feeling any need of having Georgine Skeene. She was not astonished at this thing. She would have been a little astonished by this thing but she knew she was not astonished at anything and so she was not astonished at this thing not astonished at not feeling any need of having Georgine Skeene.

Helen Furr had quite a completely pleasant voice and it was quite well enough cultivated and she could use it and she did use it but then there was not any way of working at cultivating a completely pleasant voice when it has become a quite completely well enough cultivated one, and there was not much use in using it when one was not wanting it to be helping to make one a gay one. Helen Furr was not needing using her voice to be a gay one. She was gay then and sometimes she used her voice and she was not using it very often. It was quite completely enough cultivated and it was quite completely a pleasant one and she did not use it very often. She was then, she was quite exactly as gay as she had been, she was gay a little longer in the day than she had been.

She was gay exactly the same way. She was never tired of being gay that way. She had learned very many little ways to use in being gay. Very many were telling about using other ways in being gay. She was gay enough, she was always gay exactly the same way, she was always learning little things to use in being gay, she was telling about using other ways in being gay, she was telling about learning other ways in being gay, she was learning other ways in being gay, she would be using other ways in being gay, she would always be gay in the same way, when Georgine Skeene was there not so long each day as when Georgine Skeene was away.

She came to using many ways in being gay, she came to use every way in being gay. She went on living where many were cultivating something and she was gay, she had used every way to be gay.

They did not live together then Helen Furr and Georgine Skeene. Helen Furr lived there the longer where they had been living regularly together. Then neither of them were living there any longer. Helen Furr was living somewhere else then and telling some about being gay and she was gay then and she was living quite regularly then. She was regularly gay then. She was quite regular in being gay then. She remembered all the little ways of being gay. She used all the little ways of being gay. She was quite regularly gay. She told many then the way of being gay, she taught very many then little ways they could use in being gay. She was living very well, she was gay then, she went on living then, she was regular in being gay, she always was living very well and was gay very well and was telling about little ways one could be learning to use in being gay, and later was telling them quite often, telling them again and again.

DJUNA BARNES

LADIES ALMANACK

(extract)

(1928)

LADIES ALMANACK

N ow this be a Tale of as fine a Wench as ever wet
Bed, she who was called Evangeline Musset and
who was in her Heart one Grand Red Cross for the
Pursuance, the Relief and the Distraction, of such Girls as
in their Hinder Parts, and their Fore Parts, and in whatsoever Parts did suffer them most, lament Cruelly, be it
Itch of Palm, or Quarters most horribly burning, which do
oft occur in the Spring of the Year, or at those Times when
they do sit upon warm and cozy Material, such as Fur, or
thick and Oriental Rugs, (whose very Design it seems,
procures for them such a Languishing of the Haunch and
Reins as is insupportable) or who sit upon warm Stoves,
whence it is known that one such flew up with an " Ah my
God ! What a World it is for a Girl indeed, be she ever
so well abridged and cool of Mind and preserved of Intention, the Instincts are, nevertheless, brought to such
a yelping Pitch and so undo her, that she runs hither
and thither seeking some Simple or Unguent which
shall allay her Pain ! And why is it no Philosopher of
whatever Sort, has discovered, amid the nice Herbage of
his Garden, one that will content that Part, but that
from the day that we were indifferent Matter, to this
wherein we are Imperial Personages of the divine human
Race, no thing so solaces it as other Parts as inflamed,
or with the Consolation every Woman has at her Finger
Tips, or at the very Hang of her Tongue ?"

For such then was Evangeline Musset created, a Dame

of lofty Lineage, who, in the early eighties, had discarded her family Tandem, in which her Mother and Father found Pleasure enough, for the distorted Amusement of riding all smack-of-astride, like any Yeoman going to gather in his Crops ; and with much jolting and galloping, was made, hour by hour, less womanly, "Though never", said she, "has that Greek Mystery occurred to me, which is known as the Dashing out of the Testicles, and all that goes with it !" Which is said to have happened to a Byzantine Baggage of the Trojan Period, more to her Surprise than her Pleasure. Yet it is an agreeable Circumstance that the Ages thought fit to hand down this Miracle, for Hope springs eternal in the human Breast.

It has been noted by some and several, that Women have in them the Pip of Romanticism so well grown and fat of Sensibility, that they, upon reaching an uncertain Age, discard Duster, Offspring and Spouse, and a little after are seen leaning, all of a limp, on a Pillar of Bathos.

Evangeline Musset was not one of these, for she had been developed in the Womb of her most gentle Mother to be a Boy, when therefore, she came forth an Inch or so less than this, she paid no Heed to the Error, but donning a Vest of a superb Blister and Tooling, a Belcher for tippet and a pair of hip-boots with a scarlet channel (for it was a most wet wading) she took her Whip in hand, calling her Pups about her, and so set out upon the Road of Destiny, until such time as they should grow to be Hounds of a Blood, and Pointers with a certainty in the

Butt of their Tails ; waiting patiently beneath Cypresses for this Purpose, and under the Boughs of the aloe tree, composing, as she did so, Madrigals to all sweet and ramping things.

Her Father, be it known, spent many a windy Eve pacing his Library in the most normal of Night-Shirts, trying to think of ways to bring his erring Child back into that Religion and Activity which has ever been thought sufficient for a Woman ; for already, when Evangeline appeared at Tea to the Duchess Clitoressa of Natescourt, women in the way (the Bourgeoise be it noted, on an errand to some nice Church of the Catholic Order, with their Babes at Breast, and Husbands at Arm) would snatch their Skirts from Contamination, putting such wincing Terror into their Dears with their quick and trembling Plucking, that it had been observed, in due time, by all Society, and Evangeline was in order of becoming one of those who is spoken to out of Generosity, which her Father could see, would by no Road, lead her to the Altar.

He had Words with her enough, saying : "Daughter, daughter, I perceive in you most fatherly Sentiments. What am I to do ?" And she answered him High enough, "Thou, good Governor, wast expecting a Son when you lay atop of your Choosing, why then be so mortal wounded when you perceive that you have your Wish ? Am I not doing after your very Desire, and is it not the more commendable, seeing that I do it without the Tools for the Trade, and yet nothing complain ?"

In the days of which I write she had come to be a witty and learned Fifty, and though most short of Stature and nothing handsome, was so much in Demand, and so wide famed for her Genius at bringing up by Hand, and so noted and esteemed for her Slips of the Tongue that it finally brought her into the Hall of Fame, where she stood by a Statue of Venus as calm as you please, or leaned upon a lacrymal Urn with a small Sponge for such as Wept in her own Time and stood in Need of it.

Thus begins this Almanack, which all Ladies
should carry about with them, as the Priest his
Breviary, as the Cook his Recipes,
as the Doctor his Physic, as
the Bride her Fears,
and as the Lion
his Roar !

JANUARY *hath 31 days*

THIS be the first Month of our Christian calendar, when the Earth is bound and the Seas in the grip of Terror. When the Birds give no Evidence of themselves, and are in the Memory alone recorded, when the Sap lies sleeping and the Tree knows nothing of it, when the bright Herbage and flourishing green things are only hope, when the Plough is put away with the Harrow, and the Fields give their Surface to a Harvest of Snow, which no Sickle garners, and for which no Grange languishes, and which never weighs the home-going Cart of the Farmer, but sows itself alone and reaps itself unrecorded.

Now in this Month, as it is with Mother Earth, so it will appear it is with all things of Nature, and most especially Woman.

For in this Month she is a little pitiful for what she has made of man, and what she has throughout the Ages, led him to expect, cultivating him indeed to such a Pitch that she is somewhat responsible.

Patience Scalpel was of this Month, and belongs to this Almanack for one Reason only, that from Beginning to End, Top to Bottom, inside and out, she could not understand Women and their Ways as they were about her, above her and before her.

She saw them gamboling on the Greensward, she heard them pinch and moan within the Gloom of many a stately Mansion; she beheld them floating across the Ceilings, (for such was Art in the old Days), diapered in *Toile de Jouy*, and welded without Flame, in one incalculable Embrace. "And what", she said, "the silly Creatures may mean by it is more than I can diagnose ! I am of my Time my Time's best argument, and who am I that I must die in my Time, and never know what it is in the Whorls and Crevices of my Sisters so prolongs them to the bitter End ? Do they not have Organs as exactly alike as two Peas, or twin Griefs; and are they not eclipsed ever so often with the galling Check-rein of feminine Tides ? So what to better Purpose than to sit the Dears on a Stack of Blotters, and let it go at that, giving them in their meantime a Bible and a Bobbin, and say with all Pessimism—they have come to a blind Alley ; there will be no Children born for a Season, and what matter it ?"

Thus her Voice was heard throughout the Year, as cutting in its Derision as a surgical Instrument, nor did she use it to come to other than a Day and yet another Day in which she said, "I have tried all means, Mathematical, Poetical, Statistical and Reasonable, to come to the Core of this Distemper, known as Girls ! Girls ! And can nowhere find where a Woman got the Account that makes her such a deft Worker at the Single Beatitude. Who gave her the Directions for it, the necessary Computation and Turpitude ? Where, and in what dark Chamber was the Tree so cut of Life, that the Branch turned to the Branch, and made of the Cuttings a Garden of Ecstasy ?"

Merry Laughter rose about her, as Doll Furious was seen in ample dimity, sprigged with Apple Blossom, footing it fleetly after the proportionless Persuasions of Señorita Fly-About, one of Buzzing Much to Rome !

"In my time", said Patience Scalpel, "Women came to enough trouble by lying abed with the Father of their Children. What then in this good Year of our Lord has paired them like to like, with never a Beard between them, layer for layer, were one to unpack them to the very Ticking ? Methinks", she mused, her

Starry Eyes aloft, where a Peewit was yet content to
mate it hot among the Branches, making for himself a
Covey in the olden Formula, "they love the striking
Hour, nor would breed the Moments that go to it.
Sluts !" she said pleasantly after a little thought, "Are
good Mothers to supply them with
Luxuries in the next Generation ;
for they them- selves will have no
Shes, unless some Her puts them
forth ! Well I'm not the Woman
for it ! They well have to pluck
where they may. My Daughters
shall go amarry- ing !"

FEBRUARY *hath 29 days*

THIS be a Love Letter for a Present, and when she is Catched, what shall I do with her ? God knows ! For 'tis safe to say I do not, and what we know

SAINTS DAYS

THESE are the Days on which Dame Musset was sainted, and for these things.

January

When new whelped, she

not, is our only proof of Him !

My Love she is an Old Girl, out of Fashion, Bugles at the Bosom, and theredown a much Thumbed Mystery and a Maze. She doth jangle with last Year's attentions, she is melted with Death's Fire ! Then what shall I for her that hath never been accomplished ? It is a very Parcel of Perplexities ! Shall one stumble on a Nuance that twenty Centuries have not pounced upon, yea worried and made a Kill of ? Hath not her Hair of old been braided with the Stars ? Her shin half-circled by the Moon. Hath she not been turned all ways that the Sands of her Desire know all Runnings ? Who can make a New Path where there be no Wilderness ? In the Salt Earth lie Parcels of lost Perfection—surely I shall not loosen her Straps a New Way, Love hath been too long a Time ! Will she unpack her Panels for such a Stale Receipt, pour out her Treasures for a

was found to have missed by an Inch.

February

When but five, she lamented Mid-prayers, that the girls in the Bible were both Earth-hushed and Jew-touched forever and ever.

March

When nine she learned how the Knee termed Housemaid's is come by, when the Slavy was bedridden at the turn of the scullery and needed a kneeling-to.

April

When fast on fifteen she hushed a Near-Bride with the left Flounce of her Ruffle that her Father in sleeping might not know of the oh !

May

When sweet twenty-one prayed upon her past Bearing she went to the Cockpit and crowed with the best, And at the Full of the Moon in Gaiters and Gloves mooed with the Herd, her Heels with their Hoofs, and in the wet Dingle hooted for hoot with the Quail on the Spinney, calling for Brides Wing and a Feather to flock with.

June

When well thirty, she, like

coin worn thin ? Yet to re-
nounce her were a thing as old ;
and saying "Go !" but shuts
the Door that hath banged a
million Years !

Oh Zeus ! Oh Diane ! Oh
Hellebore ! Oh Absalom ! Oh
Piscary Right ! What shall I
do with it ! *To have been the
First*, that alone would have
gifted me ! As it is, shall I
not pour ashes upon my Head,
gird me in Sackcloth, covering my Nothing and Despair
under a Mountain of Cinders,
and thus become a Monument
to No-Ability for her sake ?

Verily, I shall place me before
her Door, and when she cometh
forth I shall think she has left
her Feet inward upon the Sill
and when she enters in, I shall
dream her Hands be yet out-
ward upon the Door—for
therein is no way for
me, and Fancy is
my only Craft.

★

all Men before her, made a
Harlot a good Woman by
making her Mistress.

July

When forty she bayed up
a Tree whose Leaves had
no Turning and whose Name
was Florella.

August

When fifty odd and a day
she came upon that Wind
that is labelled the second.

Septembre

When sixty some, she
came to no Good as well as
another.

October

When Sixty was no lon-
ger a Lodger of hers, she
bought a Pair of extra far-
off, and ultra near-to Opera
Glasses, and carried them
always in a Sac by her Side.

November

When eighty-eight she said,
"It's a Hook Girl, not a
Button, you should know
your Dress better."

December

When just before her last
Breath she ordered a Pasty
and let a Friend eat it,
renouncing the World and
its Pitfalls like all Saints
before her, when she
had no longer
Room for them.
Prosit !

MARCH *hath 31 days*

A MONG such Dames of which we write, were two British Women. One was called Lady Buck-and-Balk, and the other plain Tilly-Tweed-In-Blood. Lady Buck-and-Balk sported a Monocle and believed in Spirits. Tilly-Tweed-In-Blood sported a Stetson, and believed in Marriage. They came to the Temple of the Good Dame Musset, and they sat to Tea, and this is what they said :

"Just because woman falls, in this Age, to Woman, does that mean that we are not to recognize Morals ? What has England done to legalize these Passions ? Nothing ! Should she not be brought to Task, that never once through her gloomy Weather have two dear Doves been seen approaching in their bridal Laces, to pace, in stately Splendor up the Altar Aisle, there to be United in Similarity, under mutual Vows of Loving, Honouring, and Obeying, while the One and the Other fumble in that nice Temerity, for the equal gold Bands that shall make of one a Wife, and the other a Bride ?

"Most wretchedly never that I have heard of, nor one such Pair seen later in a Bed of Matrimony, tied up in their best Ribands, all under a Canopy of Cambric, Bosom to Bosom, Braid to Braid, Womb to Womb ! But have, ever since the instigation of that Alliance, lain abed out of Wedlock, sinning in a double and similar Sin ; rising unprovided for by Church or Certificate ; Fornicating in an Evil so exactly of a piece, that the Judgement Call must be answered in a Trembling Tandem !"

"Therefore we think to bring the Point to the Notice of our Judges, and have it set before the House of Lords. For when a Girl falls in Love, with no matter what, should she not be protected in some way, from Hazard, ever attending that which is illegal ? And should One or the Other stray, ought there not to be a Law as binding upon her as upon another, that Alimony might be

Collected ; and that Straying be nipped in the Bud ?"

"Tis a thought" said the Good Musset. "But then there are Duels to take the place of the Law, and there's always a Way out, should one or both be found wanting. A strong Gauntlet struck lightly athwart the Buttock would bring her to the common Green, where with Rapier, or Fowling-Piece, she might demand and take her Satisfaction, thus ending it for both, in one way or another."

"It is not enough," said Lady Buck-and-Balk. "Think how tender are the Hearts of Women, at their toughest ! One small Trickle of Blood on that dear Torso (and here she starved toward her choice) and I should be less than any Man ! And I dare say Tilly would be as distracted were she to perceive in me one Rib gone astray, or one Wrist most horribly bleeding ! Nay, we could never come to a Killing, for women have not, like brutal Man," she concluded, "and Death between them, but Pity only, and a resuscitating Need ! Like may not spit Like, nor Similarity sit in Inquest upon Similarity !"

"I could do it with most disconcerting Ease," said Dame Musset, "but then there is in me no Wren's Blood or Trepidation. Why should a Woman be un-spit ? Love of Woman for Woman should increase Terror. I see that so far it does not. All is not as it should be !"

"Ah never, never, never," sighed a soft Voice, and the trio thus became aware of that touch of Sentiment known as Masie Tuck-and-Frill, erstwhile *Sage-femme* but now, because of the Trend of the Times, lamentably out of a Job, though it was said, nothing could cure her of her Longing, for though she was called to no Beds, but those of Sisters mingled in the Bond of no Relativity, nevertheless looked with a hoping Eye between the Sheets, and put a loving Hand at the Crook of every Arm, and between the Knees, though she found nothing ever requiring Attention, nor any small Voice saying "Where am I?" she still cherished a fond Delusion that in one Way or another, the Pretties would yet whelp a little Sweet, by fair Means or foul, and was heard in many a dim Corridor admonishing a Love of nine Months not to overtake her strength, and to be particularly careful not to slip in going down Stairs. "For", as she said, "Creation has ever been too Marvellous for us to doubt of it now, and though the Medieval way is still thought good enough, what is to prevent some modern Girl from rising from the Couch of a Girl as modern, with something new in her Mind? To stick to the old Tradition is Credulity, and Credulity has been worn to a Thread. A Feather", she said, "might accomplish it, or a Song rightly sung, or an Exclamation said in the right Place, or a Trifle done in the right Spirit, and then you would have need of me indeed!" and here she began to sing the first Lullaby ever cast for a Girl's Girl should she one day become a Mother. And with this as a Preface, every Woman of every sort, found her Everywhere. So it was that the Three saw her sitting among the Cushions sewing a fine Seam, and saying in the Wistful, lost Voice of those with a Trade too tender for Oblivion, "Women are a little this side of Contemplation, their Love has the Poignancy of all lost Tension. Men

are too early, Women too tardy, and Religion too late for Religion.

"Love in Man is Fear of Fear. Love in Woman is Hope without Hope. Man fears all that can be taken from him, a Woman's Love includes that, and then Lies down beside it. A Man's love is built to fit Nature. Woman's is a Kiss in the Mirror. It is a Farewell to the Creator, without disturbing him, the supreme Tenderness toward Oblivion, Battle after Retreat, Challenge when the Sword is broken. Yea, it strikes loudly on the Heart, for thus she gives her Body to all unrecorded Music, which is the Psalm."

"You speak," said Dame Musset, turning a charmed Eye upon her, "in the Voice of one who should be One of Us !"

"I speak", said Masie Tuck-and-Frill, "in that Voice which has been accorded ever to those who go neither Hither nor Thither ; the Voice of the Prophet. Those alone who sit in one Condition, their Life through, know what the plans were, and what the Hopes are, and where the Spot the two lie, in that Rot you call your Lives. Time goes with the Beast also, the Centuries fold him down, the Cry of his Young comes upward about him, the sigh of his Elders is as high as his Horns, yet above his Horns is also a Voice crying "Too hoo ! I would," she added, "that the Mind's Eye had not been so bent upon the Heart."

"It's a good Place," said Dame Musset in a Tone advertising her a Person well pleased a long time.

"A good place indeed," returned Masie Tuck-and-Frill, "but a better when seen Indirectly."

" I", said Lady Buck-and-Balk—for Spirits had made her a little Callous to Nuance, "would that we could do away with Man altogether !"

"It cannot be," sighed Tilly Tweed-in-Blood, "we need them for carrying of Coals, lifting of Beams, and things of one kind or another."

"Ah the dears !" said Patience Scalpel, that moment bounding in upon them, divesting herself of her furs, "and is there one hereabouts ?"

"Most certainly not !" cried Lady Buck-and-Balk in one Breath with Tilly Tweed-in-Blood, as if a large Mouse had run over their Shins, "What a thing to say !"

"Oh Fie, and why not !" said Patience sipping a cognac. "Were it not for them, you would not be half so pleased with things as they are. Delight is always a little running of the Blood in Channels astray !"

"When I wish to contemplate the highest Pitch to which Irony has climbed, and when I really desire to *wallow* in impersonal Tragedy", said Dame Musset, "I think of that day, forty years ago, when I, a Child of ten, was deflowered by the Hand of a Surgeon ! I, even I, came to it as other Women, and I never a Woman before nor since !"

"Oh my Darling !" wailed Tilly, in an Anguish on the sec-

ZODIAC

THIS is the part about Heaven that has never been told. After the Fall of Satan (and as he fell, Lucifer uttered a loud

ond. My poor, dear betrayed mishandled Soul ! To think of it ! Why I don't know whom to strike first ! But someone shall suffer for it I tell you. These Eyes shall know no Sleep until you are revenged !"

"Peace !" said Dame Musset, putting a Hand upon her Wrist, "I am my Revenge !"

"I had not thought of that," said Tilly happily, "You have, verily, hanged, cut down, and re-hung Judas a thousand times !"

"And shall again, please God !" said Dame Musset.

"That Man's Hand," said Patience Scalpel, "must drip more Agony and Regret than the Hand of Lady Macbeth, and must burn hotter than a Serpent's Tongue !"

"He mutters in his Sleep," said Tuck-and-Frill, "and turns from Side to Side, and finds no Comfort !"

"He be one Man," said Dame Musset peacefully, "who does not brag."

Cry, heard from one End of Forever-and-no-end to the other), all the Angels, Aries, Taurus, Gemini, Cancer, Leo, Virgo, Libra, Scorpio, Sagittarius, Capricornus, Aquarius, Pisces, all, all gathered together, so close that they were not recognizable, one from the other. And not nine Months later, there was heard under the Dome of Heaven a great Crowing, and from the Midst, an Egg, as incredible as a thing forgotten, fell to Earth, and striking, split and hatched, and from out of it stepped one saying "Pardon me, I must be going !" And this was the first Woman born with a Difference.

After this the Angels parted, and on the Face of each was the Mother look.

Why was that ?

★

*   *   *   *   *

DECEMBER *hath 31 days*

I N this cold and chill December, the Month of the
Year when the proof of God died, died Saint Musset,
proof of Earth, for she had loosened and come up-
rooted in the Path of Love, where she had so long flour-
ished. Nor yet with any alien Sickness came she to
her Death, but as one who had a grave Commission
and the ambassador recalled.

She had blossomed on Sap's need, and when need's Sap found such easy flowing in the Year of our Lord 19—what more was there for her to do ? Yet though her Life was completed, she has many Transactions for her end, so said she, lying on the flat of her Back, her good Beak of a nose yet more of a Pope's proportion, "I have heard somewhere that there be as many Burials, and as different, as there be Births, yea, even in excess of this, for a Babe is born one of two ways, Head or Foot, but a Corpse can go down all-in-one or bit by bit, sideways or lengthways or Shin to Chin. There is the Small-town Burial and the Burial of State, and the Burial of Harvest, and the Burial of Frost. There is cracking and crating as they understand it in the District of the Ganges, and there is the upright and the supine, and the Head to Heel, there is Urn Burial or Cremation, there is the Flesh-eating Stone, the Sarcophagus, there is embalming and stretching of the Gut, there is lamenting, and there is laughing, There are those buried in Trenches, and those in Tombs, and those on Hills and those in Dales, those buried of shallow and those of deep digging. Some are followed on Foot, and some are followed in Carriages, and some are followed in the Mind alone and some are not followed at all ; some have a Christian and some a Pagan rite, and some are swallowed up for an Hour in Churches, and others are accompanied with Wine and Song and covered with the Leaves of the Day, the while the Ass brays in the Market-place, and the sound of the Wine-press is like the Gush of a Girl's first Sorrow.

" Now I leave behind me, to those who shall follow, or
I much mistake my Prowess in these ripe Days of my
Life (she having reached a good ninety-nine), many Mourners of many Races and many Tempers, and as they
loved me differently in Life so I would have them plan
differently for me in Death. Think then of as many
manner of Rites of Interment and ending, burning and
cracking as there be ingenuity, only", she said in that logical Measure that had made her a great Politician all
the days of her Hour, "plan differently, for if you burn me
first, how shall you lay me out for shriving, and how, if
you drop me in Ocean, can you also bind me with Earth ?
Nay, you must come to the matter with Forethought
and no Jealousies, so that I stay not too long in that condition, which left to Nature, is most unseemly, like many
of her raw Tricks. Therefore provide a Council, and plan
with Fecundity, and bring about as good a Series as the
Wits of Women can devise."

So it was that when she came to die, there were many
so hard pressed with lamenting, and some so glut with
Vanity, and others so spoiled of Thought, that a wrang-
ling was heard for full forty-eight Hours, the while she
lay easily, as if she sensed in them a little old time Custom.

First forty Women shaved their Heads (all but
Señorita Fly-About who for no Woman, quick or dead,
would alter her Charm) and carried her through the City
on a monstrous Catafalque, and then in forty different
Heights these Women went down upon their knees in the
darkness of the Catholic Church, and then she was sealed

in a Tomb for many days, and the Women twittered about the Tomb like Birds about the Border of a Storm : and then they bore her to the Crossroads, and at every Crossway the Bier was laid down. And a Bird came, and in passing, crowed lamentably, though but that instant an Oat had descended into the dark of its Craw, and a little later at another Crossroad a Hare came, and standing upon the Lid, beat thrice with its custom of hind-foot Mating, and yet further on, a Mountain Goat that way going, threw its Beard up, and lamented bitterly from between its even row of Teeth that knew only the Grass going inward and no word over, and a little later, (there were many Forks going hither and thither, for the Spring in the Grass had seen many herds going four ways, and Love making a common pasture for a Season, what with moo and bray and Hoof and Heel stamping for tell tale), a Night-owl came and sat upon one end of the great and ebon Tassels, and said, or so the Parishioners aver, "Oh ! God !" as if it were his Heart's first Need, and still later a Ground thing, not to this day identified, came upward out of the Earth, and stood awhile, and still purblind and lidless, shook its Fur from Throat to Tail in one long, slow Undulation of Misery, and descended again. Now, a Tup, so new with Life that it walked on Waves came and raising its God's Gift of a Mouth, said "Baaaaa !" And so it was that they hurried on and laid her in the Earth of a little Village, and then they put her low in a great City, and some buried her shallow and some deep, and Women who had not told their Husbands everything, joined them. And there was veiled Face downcast, and bare Face upturned, and some lamenting sideways and some forward, and some who struck their Hands together, and some who carried them one on one. And they carved her many Tombs, and many sayings, and much Poetry was cast for her, and in the end they put her upon a great Pyre and burned her to the Heart, warming her Urn for her with their Hands, as a good Wine-bibber warms his Cup of Wine. And when they came to the ash that was left of her, all had burned but the Tongue, and this flamed, and would not suffer Ash, and it played about upon the handful that had been she indeed. And seeing this, there was a great Commotion, and the sound of Skirts swirled in haste, and the Patter of much running in feet, but Señorita Fly-About came down upon that Urn first, and beatitude played and flickered upon her Face, and from under her Skirts a slow Smoke issued, though no thing burned, and the Mourners barked about her covetously, and all Night through, it was bruited abroad that the barking continued, like the mournful baying of Hounds in the Hills, though by Dawn there was no sound, And as the day came some hundred Women were seen bent in Prayer. And yet a little later between them in its Urn on high, they took the Ashes and the Fire, and placed it on the Altar in the Temple of Love. There it is said, it flickers to this day, and one may still decipher the Line, beneath its Handles, "Oh ye of little Faith."

HERE I BE!
SAY ALAS!
FOR A PRESENT
BUT FOR MASS
STRUT A PHEASANT
SALT TO LEAVEN
CANDLES SEVEN
WHEN IVE RISEN
SAY THE PRAYER
WHERE MOUNT I
BE NO STAIR
BE NO ROPE
BE NO RUNG
MY WAY HUNG

MASS

VIRGINIA WOOLF
A ROOM OF ONE'S OWN
(Chapter 5)

(1928)

I had come at last, in the course of this rambling, to the shelves which hold books by the living; by women and by men; for there are almost as many books written by women now as by men. Or if that is not yet quite true, if the male is still the voluble sex, it is certainly true that women no longer write novels solely. There are Jane Harrison's books on Greek archaeology; Vernon Lee's books on aesthetics; Gertrude Bell's books on Persia. There are books on all sorts of subjects which a generation ago no woman could have touched. There are poems and plays and criticism; there are histories and biographies, books of travel and books of scholarship and research; there are even a few philosophies and books about science and economics. And though novels predominate, novels themselves may very well have changed from association with books of a different feather. The natural simplicity, the epic age of women's writing, may have gone. Reading and criticism may have given her a wider range, a great subtlety. The impulse towards autobiography may be spent. She may be beginning to use writing as an art, not as a method of self-expression. Among these new novels one might find an answer to several such questions.

I took down one of them at random. It stood at the very end of the shelf, was called *Life's Adventure*, or some such title, by Mary Carmichael, and was published in this very month of October. It seems to be her first book, I said to myself, but one must read it as if it were the last volume in a fairly long series, continuing all those other books that I have been glancing at – Lady Winchilsea's poems and Aphra Behn's plays and the novels of the four great novelists. For books continue each other, in spite of our habit of judging them separately. And I must also consider her – this unknown woman – as the descendant of all those other women whose circumstances I have been glancing at and see what she inherits of their characteristics and restrictions. So, with a sigh, because novels so often provide an anodyne and not an antidote, glide one into torpid slumbers instead of rousing one with a burning brand, I settled down with a notebook and a pencil to make what I could of Mary Carmichael's first novel, *Life's Adventure*.

To begin with, I ran my eye up and down the page. I am going to get the hang of her sentences first, I said, before I load my memory with blue eyes and brown and the relationship that there may be between Chloe and Roger. There will be time for that when I have decided whether she has a pen in her hand or a pickaxe. So I tried a sentence or two on my tongue. Soon it was obvious that something was not quite in order. The smooth gliding of sentence after sentence was interrupted. Something tore, something scratched; a single word here and there flashed its torch in my eyes. She was 'unhanding' herself as they say in the old plays. She is like a person striking a match that will not light, I thought. But why, I asked her as if she were present, are Jane Austen's sentences not of the right shape for you? Must they all be scrapped because Emma and Mr Woodhouse are dead? Alas, I sighed, that it should be so. For while Jane Austen breaks from melody to melody as Mozart from song to song, to read this writing was like being out at sea in an open boat. Up one went, down one sank. This terseness, this shortwindedness, might mean that she was afraid of something; afraid of being called 'sentimental' perhaps; or she remembers that women's writing has been called flowery and so provides a superfluity of thorns; but until I have read a scene with some care, I cannot be sure whether she is being herself or someone else. At any rate, she does not lower one's vitality, I thought, reading more carefully. But she is heaping up too many facts. She will not be able to use half of them in a book of this size. (It was about half the length of *Jane Eyre*.) However, by some means or other she succeeded in getting us all – Roger, Chloe, Olivia, Tony, and Mr Bigham – in a canoe up the river. Wait a moment, I said, leaning back in my chair, I must consider the whole thing more carefully before I go any further.

I am almost sure, I said to myself, that Mary Carmichael is playing a trick on us. For I feel as one feels on a switchback railway when the car, instead of sinking, as one has been led to expect, swerves up again. Mary is tampering with the expected sequence. First she broke the sentence; now she has broken the sequence. Very well, she has every right to do both these things if she does them not for the sake of breaking, but for the sake of creating. Which of the two it is I cannot be sure until she has faced herself with a situation. I will give her every liberty, I said, to choose what that situation shall be; she shall make it of tin cans and old kettles if she likes; but she must convince me that she believes it to be a situation; and then when she has made it she must face it. She must jump. And, determined to do my duty by her as reader if she would do her duty by me as writer, I turned the page and read . . . I am sorry to break off so abruptly. Are there no men present? Do you promise me that behind that red curtain over there the figure of Sir Chartres Biron is not concealed? We are all women you assure me? Then I may tell you that the very next words I read were these – 'Chloe liked Olivia . . .' Do not start. Do not blush. Let us admit in the privacy of our own society that these things sometimes happen. Sometimes women do like women.

'Chloe liked Olivia,' I read. And then it struck me how immense a change was there. Chloe liked Olivia perhaps for the first time in literature. Cleopatra did not like Octavia. And how completely *Antony and Cleopatra* would have been altered had she done so! As it is, I thought, letting my mind, I am afraid, wander a little from *Life's Adventure*, the whole thing is simplified, conventionalized, if one dared say it, absurdly. Cleopatra's only feeling about Octavia is one of jealousy. Is she taller than I am? How does she do her hair? The play, perhaps, required no more. But how interesting it would have been if the relationship between the two women had been more complicated. All these relationships between women, I thought, rapidly recalling the splendid gallery of fictitious women, are too simple. So much has been left out, unattempted. And I tried to remember any case in the course of my reading where two women are represented as friends. There is an attempt at it in *Diana of the Crossways*. They are confidantes, of course, in Racine and the Greek tragedies. They are now and then mothers and daughters. But almost without exception they are shown in their relation to men. It was strange to think that all the great women of fiction were, until Jane Austen's day, not only seen by the other sex, but seen only in relation to the other sex. And how small a part of a woman's life is that; and how little can a man know even of that when he observes it through the black or rosy spectacles which sex puts upon his nose. Hence, perhaps, the peculiar nature of woman in fiction; the astonishing extremes of her beauty and horror; her alternations between heavenly goodness and hellish depravity – for so a lover would see her as his love rose or sank, was prosperous or unhappy. This is not so true of the nineteenth-century novelists, of course. Woman becomes much more various and complicated there. Indeed it was the desire to write about women perhaps that led men by degrees to abandon the poetic drama which, with its violence, could make so little use of them, and to devise the novel as a more fitting receptacle. Even so it remains obvious, even in the writing of Proust, that a man is terribly hampered and partial in his knowledge of women, as a woman in her knowledge of men.

Also, I continued, looking down at the page again, it is becoming evident that women, like men, have other interests besides the perennial interests of domesticity. 'Chloe liked Olivia. They shared a laboratory together . . .' I read on and discovered that these two young women were engaged in mincing liver, which is, it seems, a cure for pernicious anaemia; although one of them was married and had – I think I am right in stating – two small children. Now all that, of course, has had to be left out, and thus the splendid portrait of the fictitious woman is much too simple and much too monotonous. Suppose, for instance, that men were only represented in literature as the lovers of women, and were never the friends of men, soldiers, thinkers, dreamers; how few parts in the plays of Shakespeare could be allotted to them; how literature would suffer! We might perhaps have most of Othello; and a good deal of Antony; but no Caesar, no Brutus, no Hamlet, no Lear, no Jaques – literature would be incredibly impoverished, as indeed literature is impoverished beyond our counting by the doors that have been shut upon women. Married against their will, kept in one room, and to one occupation, how could a dramatist give a full or interesting or truthful account of them? Love was the only possible interpreter. The poet was forced to be passionate or bitter, unless indeed he chose to 'hate women', which meant more often than not that he was unattractive to them.

Now if Chloe likes Olivia and they share a laboratory, which of itself will make their friendship more varied and lasting because it will be less personal; if Mary Carmichael knows how to write, and I was beginning to enjoy some quality in her style; if she has a room to herself, of which I am not quite sure; if she has five hundred a year of her own – but that remains to be proved – then I think that something of great importance has happened.

For if Chloe likes Olivia and Mary Carmichael knows how to express it she will light a torch in that vast chamber where nobody has yet been. It is all half lights and profound shadows like those serpentine caves where one goes with a candle peering up and down, not knowing where one is stepping. And I began to read the book again, and read how Chloe watched Olivia put a jar on a shelf and say how it was time to go home to her children. That is a sight that has never been seen since the world began, I exclaimed. And I watched too, very curiously. For I wanted to see how Mary Carmichael set to work to catch those unrecorded gestures, those unsaid or half-said words, which form themselves, no more palpably than the shadows of moths on the ceiling, when women are alone, unlit by the capricious and coloured light of the other sex. She will need to hold her breath, I said, reading on, if she is to do it; for women are so suspicious of any interest that has not some obvious motive behind it, so terribly accustomed to concealment and suppression, that they are off at the flicker of an eye turned observingly in their direction. The only way for you to do it, I thought, addressing Mary Carmichael as if she were there, would be to talk of something else, looking steadily out of the window, and thus note, not with a pencil in a notebook, but in the shortest of shorthand, in words that are hardly syllabled yet, what happens when Olivia – this organism that has been under the shadow of the rock these million years – feels the light fall on it, and sees coming her way a piece of strange food – knowledge, adventure, art. And she reaches out for it, I thought, again raising my eyes from the page, and has to devise some entirely new combination of her resources, so highly developed for other purposes, so as to absorb the new into the old without disturbing the infinitely intricate and elaborate balance of the whole.

But, alas, I had done what I had determined not to do; I had slipped unthinkingly into praise of my own sex. 'Highly developed' – 'infinitely intricate' – such are undeniably terms of praise, and to praise one's own sex is always suspect, often silly; moreover, in this case, how could one justify it? One could not go to the map and say Columbus discovered America and Columbus was a woman; or take an apple and remark, Newton discovered the laws of gravitation and Newton was a woman; or look into the sky and say aeroplanes are flying overhead and aeroplanes were invented by women. There is no mark on the wall to measure the precise height of women. There are no yard measures, neatly divided into the fractions of an inch, that one can lay against the qualities of a good mother or the devotion of a daughter, or the fidelity of a sister, or the capacity of a housekeeper. Few women even now have been graded at the universities; the great trials of the professions, army and navy, trade, politics, and diplomacy have hardly tested them. They remain even at this moment almost unclassified. But if I want to know all that a human being can tell me about Sir Hawley Butts, for instance, I have only to open Burke or Debrett and I shall find that he took such and such a degree; owns a hall; has an heir; was Secretary to a Board; represented Great Britain in Canada; and has received a certain number of degrees, offices, medals, and other distinctions by which his merits are stamped upon him indelibly. Only Providence can know more about Sir Hawley Butts than that.

When, therefore, I say 'highly developed', 'infinitely intricate' of women, I am unable to verify my words either in Whitaker, Debrett, or the University Calendar. In this predicament what can I do? And I looked at the bookcase again. There were the biographies: Johnson and Goethe and Carlyle and Sterne and Cowper and Shelley and Voltaire and Browning and many others. And I began thinking of all those great men who have for one reason or another admired, sought out, lived with, confided in, made love to, written of, trusted in, and shown what can only be described as some need of and dependence upon certain persons of the opposite sex. That all these relationships were absolutely Platonic I would not affirm, and Sir William Joynson Hicks would probably deny. But we should wrong these illustrious men very greatly if we insisted that they got nothing from these alliances but comfort, flattery and the pleasures of the body. What they got, it is obvious, was something that their own sex was unable to supply; and it would not be rash, perhaps, to define it further, without quoting the doubtless rhapsodical words of the poets, as some stimulus,

some renewal of creative power which is in the gift o
opposite sex to bestow. He would open the door of
room or nursery, I thought, and find her among her c
perhaps, or with a piece of embroidery on her knee – at an
the centre of some different order and system of life, and the
contrast between this world and his own, which might be the
law courts or the House of Commons, would at once refresh and
invigorate; and there would follow, even in the simplest talk,
such a natural difference of opinion that the dried ideas in him
would be fertilized anew; and the sight of her creating in a
different medium from his own would so quicken his creative
power that insensibly his sterile mind would begin to plot again,
and he would find the phrase or the scene which was lacking
when he put on his hat to visit her. Every Johnson has his
Thrale, and holds fast to her for some such reasons as these, and
when the Thrale marries her Italian music master Johnson goes
half mad with rage and disgust, not merely that he will miss his
pleasant evenings at Streatham, but that the light of his life will
be 'as if gone out'.

And without being Dr Johnson or Goethe or Carlyle or
Voltaire, one may feel, though very differently from these great
men, the nature of this intricacy and the power of this highly
developed creative faculty among women. One goes into the
room – but the resources of the English language would be
much put to the stretch, and whole flights of words would need
to wing their way illegitimately into existence before a woman
could say what happens when she goes into a room. The rooms
differ so completely; they are calm or thunderous; open on to
the sea, or, on the contrary, give on to a prison yard; are hung
with washing; or alive with opals and silks; are hard as horsehair
or soft as feathers – one has only to go into any room in any
street for the whole of that extremely complex force of femininity
to fly in one's face. How should it be otherwise? For women
have sat indoors all these millions of years, so that by this time
the very walls are permeated by their creative force, which has,
indeed, so overcharged the capacity of bricks and mortar that it

must needs harness itself to pens and brushes and business and politics. But this creative power differs greatly from the creative power of men. And one must conclude that it would be a thousand pities if it were hindered or wasted, for it was won by centuries of the most drastic discipline, and there is nothing to take its place. It would be a thousand pities if women wrote like men, or lived like men, or looked like men, for if two sexes are quite inadequate, considering the vastness and variety of the world, how should we manage with one only? Ought not education to bring out and fortify the differences rather than the similarities? For we have too much likeness as it is, and if an explorer should come back and bring word of other sexes looking through the branches of other trees at other skies, nothing would be of greater service to humanity; and we should have the immense pleasure into the bargain of watching Professor X rush for his measuring-rods to prove himself 'superior'.

Mary Carmichael, I thought, still hovering at a little distance above the page, will have her work cut out for her merely as an observer. I am afraid indeed that she will be tempted to become, what I think the less interesting branch of the species – the naturalist-novelist, and not the contemplative. There are so many new facts for her to observe. She will not need to limit herself any longer to the respectable houses of the upper middle classes. She will go without kindness or condescension, but in the spirit of fellowship, into those small, scented rooms where sit the courtesan, the harlot, and the lady with the pug dog. There they still sit in the rough and ready-made clothes that the male writer has had perforce to clap upon their shoulders. But Mary Carmichael will have out her scissors and fit them close to every hollow and angle. It will be a curious sight, when it comes, to see these women as they are, but we must wait a little, for Mary Carmichael will still be encumbered with that self-consciousness in the presence of 'sin' which is the legacy of our sexual barbarity. She will still wear the shoddy old fetters of class on her feet.

However, the majority of women are neither harlots nor

courtesans; nor do they sit clasping pug dogs to dusty velvet all through the summer afternoon. But what do they do then? and there came to my mind's eye one of those long streets somewhere south of the river whose infinite rows are innumerably populated. With the eye of the imagination I saw a very ancient lady crossing the street on the arm of a middle-aged woman, her daughter, perhaps, both so respectably booted and furred that their dressing in the afternoon must be a ritual, and the clothes themselves put away in cupboards with camphor, year after year, throughout the summer months. They cross the road when the lamps are being lit (for the dusk is their favourite hour), as they must have done year after year. The elder is close on eighty; but if one asked her what her life has meant to her, she would say that she remembered the streets lit for the battle of Balaclava, or had heard the guns fire in Hyde Park for the birth of King Edward the Seventh. And if one asked her, longing to pin down the moment with date and season, But what were you doing on 5 April 1868, or 2 November 1875, she would look vague and say that she could remember nothing. For all the dinners are cooked; the plates and cups washed; the children sent to school and gone out into the world. Nothing remains of it all. All has vanished. No biography or history has a word to say about it. And the novels, without meaning to, inevitably lie.

All these infinitely obscure lives remain to be recorded, I said, addressing Mary Carmichael as if she were present; and went on in thought through the streets of London feeling in imagination the pressure of dumbness, the accumulation of unrecorded life, whether from the women at the street corners with their arms akimbo, and the rings embedded in their fat swollen fingers, talking with a gesticulation like the swing of Shakespeare's words; or from the violet-sellers and match-sellers and old crones stationed under doorways; or from drifting girls whose faces, like waves in sun and cloud, signal the coming of men and women and the flickering lights of shop windows. All that you will have to explore, I said to Mary Carmichael, holding your torch firm in your hand. Above all, you must illumine your own soul with its profundities and its shallows, and its vanities and its generosities, and say what your beauty means to you or your plainness, and what is your relation to the ever-changing and turning world of gloves and shoes and stuffs swaying up and down among the faint scents that come through chemists' bottles down arcades of dress material over a floor of pseudo-marble. For in imagination I had gone into a shop; it was laid with black and white paving; it was hung, astonishingly beautifully, with coloured ribbons. Mary Carmichael might well have a look at that in passing, I thought, for it is a sight that would lend itself to the pen as fittingly as any snowy peak or rocky gorge in the Andes. And there is the girl behind the counter too – I would as soon have her true history as the hundred and fiftieth life of Napoleon or seventieth study of Keats and his use of Miltonic inversion which old Professor Z and his like are now inditing. And then I went on very warily, on the very tips of my toes (so cowardly am I, so afraid of the lash that was once almost laid on my own shoulders), to murmur that she should also learn to laugh, without bitterness, at the vanities – say rather at the peculiarities, for it is a less offensive word – of the other sex. For there is a spot the size of a shilling at the back of the head which one can never see for oneself. It is one of the good offices that sex can discharge for sex – to describe that spot the size of a shilling at the back of the head. Think how much women have profited by the comments of Juvenal; by the criticism of Strindberg. Think with what humanity and brilliancy men, from the earliest ages, have pointed out to women that dark place at the back of the head! And if Mary were very brave and very honest, she would go behind the other sex and tell us what she found there. A true picture of man as a whole can never be painted until a woman has described that spot the size of a shilling. Mr Woodhouse and Mr Casaubon are spots of that size and nature. Not of course that anyone in their senses would counsel her to hold up to scorn and ridicule of set purpose – literature shows the futility of what is written in that spirit. Be truthful, one would say, and the result is bound to be amazingly interesting.

Comedy is bound to be enriched. New facts are bound to be discovered.

However, it was high time to lower my eyes to the page again. It would be better, instead of speculating what Mary Carmichael might write and should write, to see what in fact Mary Carmichael did write. So I began to read again. I remembered that I had certain grievances against her. She had broken up Jane Austen's sentence, and thus given me no chance of pluming myself upon my impeccable taste, my fastidious ear. For it was useless to say, 'Yes, yes, this is very nice; but Jane Austen wrote much better than you do', when I had to admit that there was no point of likeness between them. Then she had gone further and broken the sequence – the expected order. Perhaps she had done this unconsciously, merely giving things their natural order, as a woman would, if she wrote like a woman. But the effect was somehow baffling; one could not see a wave heaping itself, a crisis coming round the next corner. Therefore I could not plume myself either upon the depths of my feelings and my profound knowledge of the human heart. For whenever I was about to feel the usual things in the usual places, about love, about death, the annoying creature twitched me away, as if the important point were just a little further on. And thus she made it impossible for me to roll out my sonorous phrases about 'elemental feelings', the 'common stuff of humanity', 'the depths of the human heart', and all those other phrases which support us in our belief that, however clever we may be on top, we are very serious, very profound and very humane underneath. She made me feel, on the contrary, that instead of being serious and profound and humane, one might be – and the thought was far less seductive – merely lazy-minded and conventional into the bargain.

But I read on, and noted certain other facts. She was no 'genius' – that was evident. She had nothing like the love of Nature, the fiery imagination, the wild poetry, the brilliant wit, the brooding wisdom of her great predecessors, Lady Winchilsea, Charlotte Brontë, Emily Brontë, Jane Austen, and George Eliot;

she could not write with the melody and the dignity of Dorothy Osborne – indeed she was no more than a clever girl whose books will no doubt be pulped by the publishers in ten years' time. But, nevertheless, she had certain advantages which women of far greater gift lacked even half a century ago. Men were no longer to her 'the opposing faction'; she need not waste her time railing against them; she need not climb on to the roof and ruin her peace of mind longing for travel, experience, and a knowledge of the world and character that were denied her. Fear and hatred were almost gone, or traces of them showed only in a slight exaggeration of the joy of freedom, a tendency to the caustic and satirical, rather than to the romantic, in her treatment of the other sex. Then there could be no doubt that as a novelist she enjoyed some natural advantages of a high order. She had a sensibility that was very wide, eager and free. It responded to an almost imperceptible touch on it. It feasted like a plant newly stood in the air on every sight and sound that came its way. It ranged, too, very subtly and curiously, among almost unknown or unrecorded things; it lighted on small things and showed that perhaps they were not small after all. It brought buried things to light and made one wonder what need there had been to bury them. Awkward though she was and without the unconscious bearing of long descent which makes the least turn of the pen of a Thackeray or a Lamb delightful to the ear, she had – I began to think – mastered the first great lesson; she wrote as a woman, but as a woman who has forgotten that she is a woman, so that her pages were full of that curious sexual quality which comes only when sex is unconscious of itself.

All this was to the good. But no abundance of sensation or fineness of perception would avail unless she could build up out of the fleeting and the personal the lasting edifice which remains unthrown. I had said that I would wait until she faced herself with 'a situation'. And I meant by that until she proved by summoning, beckoning, and getting together that she was not a skimmer of surfaces merely, but had looked beneath into the depths. Now is the time, she would say to herself at a certain moment, when without doing anything violent I can show the meaning of all this. And she would begin – how unmistakable that quickening is! – beckoning and summoning, and there would rise up in memory, half forgotten, perhaps quite trivial things in other chapters dropped by the way. And she would make their presence felt while someone sewed or smoked a pipe as naturally as possible, and one would feel, as she went on writing, as if one had gone to the top of the world and seen it laid out, very majestically, beneath.

At any rate, she was making the attempt. And as I watched her lengthening out for the test, I saw, but hoped that she did not see, the bishops and the deans, the doctors and the professors, the patriarchs and the pedagogues all at her shouting warning and advice. You can't do this and you shan't do that! Fellows and scholars only allowed on the grass! Ladies not admitted without a letter of introduction! Aspiring and graceful female novelists this way! So they kept at her like the crowd at a fence on the racecourse, and it was her trial to take her fence without looking to right or to left. If you stop to curse you are lost, I said to her; equally, if you stop to laugh. Hesitate or fumble and you are done for. Think only of the jump, I implored her, as if I had put the whole of my money on her back; and she went over it like a bird. But there was fence beyond that and a fence beyond that. Whether she had the staying power I was doubtful, for the clapping and the crying were fraying to the nerves. But she did her best. Considering that Mary Carmichael was no genius, but an unknown girl writing her first novel in a bed-sitting-room, without enough of those desirable things, time, money, and idleness, she did not do so badly, I thought.

Give her another hundred years, I concluded, reading the last chapter – people's noses and bare shoulders showed naked against a starry sky, for someone had twitched the curtain in the drawing-room – give her a room of her own and five hundred a year, let her speak her mind and leave out half that she now puts in, and she will write a better book one of these days. She will be a poet, I said, putting *Life's Adventure*, by Mary Carmichael, at the end of the shelf, in another hundred years' time.

RADCLYFFE HALL
MISS OGILVY FINDS HERSELF

(1934)

AUTHOR'S FORENOTE

This story, in which I have permitted myself a brief excursion into the
realms of the fantastic, was written in July 1926, shortly before I
definitely decided to write my serious study of congenital sexual
inversion, *The Well of Loneliness*.

Although Miss Ogilvy is a very different person from Stephen
Gordon, yet those who have read *The Well of Loneliness* will find in the
earlier part of this story the nucleus of those sections of my novel
which deal with Stephen Gordon's childhood and girlhood, and with
the noble and selfless work done by hundreds of sexually inverted
women during the Great War.

I

Miss Ogilvy stood on the quay at Calais and surveyed the
disbanding of her Unit, the Unit that together with the coming
of war had completely altered the complexion of her life, at all
events for three years.

Miss Ogilvy's thin, pale lips were set sternly and her forehead was puckered in an effort of attention, in an effort to memorize every small detail of every old war-weary battered motor on whose side still appeared the merciful emblem that had set Miss Ogilvy free.

Miss Ogilvy's mind was jerking a little, trying to regain its accustomed balance, trying to readjust itself quickly to this sudden and paralysing change. Her tall, awkward body with its queer look of strength, its broad, flat bosom and thick legs and ankles, as though in response to her jerking mind, moved uneasily, rocking backwards and forwards. She had this trick of rocking on her feet in moments of controlled agitation. As usual, her hands were thrust deep into her pockets, they seldom seemed to come out of her pockets unless it were to light a cigarette, and as though she were still standing firm under fire while the wounded were placed in her ambulances, she suddenly straddled her legs very slightly and lifted her head and listened. She was standing firm under fire at that moment, the fire of a desperate regret.

Some girls came towards her, young, tired-looking creatures whose eyes were too bright from long strain and excitement. They had all been members of that glorious Unit, and they still wore the queer little forage-caps and the short, clumsy tunics of the French Militaire. They still slouched in walking and smoked Caporals in emulation of the Poilus. Like their founder and leader these girls were all English, but like her they had chosen to serve England's ally, fearlessly thrusting right up to the trenches in search of the wounded and dying. They had seen some fine things in the course of three years, not the least fine of which was the cold, hard-faced woman who commanding, domineering, even hectoring at times, had yet been possessed of so dauntless a courage and of so insistent a vitality that it vitalized the whole Unit.

'It's rotten!' Miss Ogilvy heard someone saying. 'It's rotten, this breaking up of our Unit!' And the high, rather childish voice of the speaker sounded perilously near to tears.

Miss Ogilvy looked at the girl almost gently, and it seemed, for a moment, as though some deep feeling were about to find expression in words. But Miss Ogilvy's feelings had been held in abeyance so long that they seldom dared become vocal, so she merely said 'Oh?' on a rising inflection – her method of checking emotion.

They were swinging the ambulance cars in mid-air, those of them that were destined to go back to England, swinging them up like sacks of potatoes, then lowering them with much clanging of chains to the deck of the waiting steamer. The porters were shoving and shouting and quarrelling, pausing now and again to make meaningless gestures; while a pompous official was becoming quite angry as he pointed at Miss Ogilvy's own special car – it annoyed him, it was bulky and difficult to move.

'*Bon Dieu! Mais dépêchez-vous donc!*' he bawled, as though he were bullying the motor.

Then Miss Ogilvy's heart gave a sudden, thick thud to see this undignified, pitiful ending; and she turned and patted the gallant old car as though she were patting a well-beloved horse, as though she would say: 'Yes, I know how it feels – never mind, we'll go down together.'

II

Miss Ogilvy sat in the railway carriage on her way from Dover to London. The soft English landscape sped smoothly past: small homesteads, small churches, small pastures, small lanes with small hedges; all small like England itself, all small like Miss Ogilvy's future. And sitting there still arrayed in her tunic, with her forage-cap resting on her knees, she was conscious of a sense of complete frustration; thinking less of those glorious years at the Front and of all that had gone to the making of her, than of all that had gone to the marring of her from the days of her earliest childhood.

She saw herself as a queer little girl, aggressive and awkward because of her shyness; a queer little girl who loathed sisters and dolls, preferring the stable-boys as companions, preferring to play with footballs and tops, and occasional catapults. She saw herself climbing the tallest beech trees, arrayed in old breeches illicitly come by. She remembered insisting with tears and some temper that her real name was William and not Wilhelmina. All these childish pretences and illusions she remembered, and the bitterness that came after. For Miss Ogilvy had found as her life went on that in this world it is better to be one with the herd, that the world has no wish to understand those who cannot conform to its stereotyped pattern. True enough in her youth she had gloried in her strength, lifting weights, swinging clubs and developing muscles, but presently this had grown irksome to her; it had seemed to lead nowhere, she being a woman, and then as her mother had often protested: muscles looked so appalling in evening dress – a young girl ought not to have muscles.

Miss Ogilvy's relation to the opposite sex was unusual and at that time added much to her worries, for no less than three men had wished to propose, to the genuine amazement of the world and her mother. Miss Ogilvy's instinct made her like and trust men for whom she had a pronounced fellow-feeling; she would always have chosen them as her friends and companions in preference to girls or women; she would dearly have loved to share in their sports, their business, their ideals and their wide-flung interests. But men had not wanted her, except the three who had found in her strangeness a definite attraction, and those would-be suitors she had actually feared, regarding them with aversion. Towards young girls and women she was shy and respectful, apologetic and sometimes admiring. But their fads and their foibles, none of which she could share, while amusing her very often in secret, set her outside the sphere of their intimate lives, so that in the end she must blaze a lone trail through the difficulties of her nature.

'I can't understand you,' her mother had said, 'you're a very odd creature – now when I was your age . . .'

And her daughter had nodded, feeling sympathetic. There were two younger girls who also gave trouble, though in their case the trouble was fighting for husbands who were scarce enough even in those days. It was finally decided, at Miss Ogilvy's request, to allow her to leave the field clear for her sisters. She would remain in the country with her father when the others went up for the Season.

Followed long, uneventful years spent in sport, while Sarah and Fanny toiled, sweated and gambled in the matrimonial market. Neither ever succeeded in netting a husband, and when the Squire died leaving very little money, Miss Ogilvy found to her great surprise that they looked upon her as a brother. They had so often jibed at her in the past that at first she could scarcely believe her senses, but before very long it became all too real: she it was who must straighten out endless muddles, who must make the dreary arrangements for the move, who must find a cheap but genteel house in London and, once there, who must cope with the family accounts which she only, it seemed, could balance.

It would be: 'You might see to that, Wilhelmina; you write, you've got such a good head for business.' Or: 'I wish you'd go down and explain to that man that we really can't pay his account till next quarter.' Or: 'This money for the grocer is five shillings short. Do run over my sum, Wilhelmina.'

Her mother, grown feeble, discovered in this daughter a staff upon which she could lean with safety. Miss Ogilvy genuinely loved her mother, and was therefore quite prepared to be leaned on; but when Sarah and Fanny began to lean too with the full weight of endless neurotic symptoms incubated in resentful virginity, Miss Ogilvy found herself staggering a little. For Sarah and Fanny were grown hard to bear, with their mania for telling their symptoms to doctors, with their unstable nerves and their acrid tongues and the secret dislike they now felt for their mother. Indeed, when old Mrs Ogilvy died, she was unmourned except by her eldest daughter who actually felt a void in her life – the unforeseen void that the ailing and weak will not infrequently leave behind them.

At about this time an aunt also died, bequeathing her fortune to her niece Wilhelmina who, however, was too weary to gird up her loins and set forth in search of exciting adventure – all. she did was to move her protesting sisters to a little estate she had purchased in Surrey. This experiment was only a partial success, for Miss Ogilvy failed to make friends of her neighbours; thus at fifty-five she had grown rather dour, as is often the way with shy, lonely people.

When the war came she had just begun settling down – people do settle down in their fifty-sixth year – she was feeling quite glad that her hair was grey, that the garden took up so much of her time, that, in fact, the beat of her blood was slowing. But all this was changed when war was declared; on that day Miss Ogilvy's pulses throbbed wildly.

'My God! If only I were a man!' she burst out, as she glared at Sarah and Fanny, 'if only I had been born a man!' Something in her was feeling deeply defrauded.

Sarah and Fanny were soon knitting socks and mittens and mufflers and Jaeger trench-helmets. Other ladies were busily working at depots, making swabs at the Squire's, or splints at the Parson's; but Miss Ogilvy scowled and did none of these things – she was not at all like other ladies.

For nearly twelve months she worried officials with a view to getting a job out in France – not in their way but in hers, and that was the trouble. She wished to go up to the front-line trenches, she wished to be actually under fire, she informed the harassed officials.

To all her inquiries she received the same answer. 'We regret that we cannot accept your offer.' But once thoroughly roused she was hard to subdue, for her shyness had left her as though by magic.

Sarah and Fanny shrugged angular shoulders: 'There's plenty of work here at home,' they remarked, 'though of course it's not quite so melodramatic!'

'Oh . . .?' queried their sister on a rising note of impatience – and she promptly cut off her hair: 'That'll jar them!' she thought with satisfaction.

Then she went up to London, formed her admirable unit and finally got it accepted by the French despite renewed opposition.

In London she had found herself quite at her ease for many another of her kind was in London doing excellent work for the nation. It was really surprising how many cropped heads had suddenly appeared as it were out of space; how many Miss Ogilvies, losing their shyness, had come forward asserting their right to serve, asserting their claim to attention.

There followed those turbulent years at the front, full of courage and hardship and high endeavour; and during those years Miss Ogilvy forgot the bad joke that Nature seemed to have played her. She was given the rank of a French lieutenant and she lived in a kind of blissful illusion; appalling reality lay on all sides and yet she managed to live in illusion. She was competent, fearless, devoted and untiring. What then? Could any man hope to do better? She was nearly fifty-eight, yet she walked with a stride, and at times she even swaggered a little.

Poor Miss Ogilvy sitting so glumly in the train with her manly trench-boots and her forage-cap! Poor all the Miss Ogilvies back from the war with their tunics, their trench-boots, and their childish illusions! Wars come and wars go but the world does not change: it will always forget an indebtedness which it thinks it expedient not to remember.

III

When Miss Ogilvy returned to her home in Surrey it was only to find that her sisters were ailing from the usual imaginary causes, and this to a woman who had seen the real thing was intolerable, so that she looked with distaste at Sarah and then at Fanny. Fanny was certainly not prepossessing, she was suffering from a spurious attack of hay fever.

'Stop sneezing!' commanded Miss Ogilvy, in the voice that had so much impressed the Unit. But as Fanny was not in the least impressed, she naturally went on sneezing.

Miss Ogilvy's desk was piled mountain-high with endless

tiresome letters and papers: circulars, bills, months-old corre-
spondence, the gardener's accounts, an agent's report on some
fields that required land-draining. She seated herself before this
collection; then she sighed, it all seemed so absurdly trivial.

'Will you let your hair grow again?' Fanny inquired . . . she
and Sarah had followed her into the study. 'I'm certain the Vicar
would be glad if you did.'

'Oh?' murmured Miss Ogilvy, rather too blandly.

'Wilhelmina!'

'Yes?'

'You will do it, won't you?'

'Do what?'

'Let your hair grow; we all wish you would.'

'Why should I?'

'Oh, well, it will look less odd, especially now that the war is
over – in a small place like this people notice such things.'

'I entirely agree with Fanny,' announced Sarah.

Sarah had become very self-assertive, no doubt through having
mismanaged the estate during the years of her sister's absence.
They had quite a heated dispute one morning over the south
herbaceous border.

'Whose garden is this?' Miss Ogilvy asked sharply. 'I insist on
auricula-eyed sweet-williams! I even took the trouble to write
from France, but it seems that my letter has been ignored.'

'Don't shout,' rebuked Sarah, 'you're not in France now!'

Miss Ogilvy could gladly have boxed her ears: 'I only wish to
God I were,' she muttered.

Another dispute followed close on its heels, and this time it
happened to be over the dinner. Sarah and Fanny were living on
weeds – at least that was the way Miss Ogilvy put it.

'We've become vegetarians,' Sarah said grandly.

'You've become two damn tiresome cranks!' snapped their
sister.

Now it never had been Miss Ogilvy's way to indulge in acid
recriminations, but somehow, these days, she forgot to say:
'Oh?' quite so often as expediency demanded. It may have been

Fanny's perpetual sneezing that had got on her nerves; or it may have been Sarah, or the gardener, or the Vicar, or even the canary; though it really did not matter very much what it was just so long as she found a convenient peg upon which to hang her growing irritation.

'This won't do at all,' Miss Ogilvy thought sternly, 'life's not worth so much fuss, I must pull myself together.' But it seemed this was easier said than done; not a day passed without her losing her temper and that over some trifle: 'No, this won't do at all – it just mustn't be,' she thought sternly.

Everyone pitied Sarah and Fanny: 'Such a dreadful, violent old thing,' said the neighbours.

But Sarah and Fanny had their revenge: 'Poor darling, it's shell-shock, you know,' they murmured.

Thus Miss Ogilvy's prowess was whittled away until she herself was beginning to doubt it. Had she ever been that courageous person who had faced death in France with such perfect composure? Had she ever stood tranquilly under fire, without turning a hair, while she issued her orders? Had she ever been treated with marked respect? She herself was beginning to doubt it.

Sometimes she would see an old member of the Unit, a girl who, more faithful to her than the others, would take the trouble to run down to Surrey. These visits, however, were seldom enlivening.

'Oh, well . . . here we are . . .' Miss Ogilvy would mutter.

But one day the girl smiled and shook her blond head: 'I'm not – I'm going to be married.'

Strange thoughts had come to Miss Ogilvy, unbidden, thoughts that had stayed for many an hour after the girl's departure. Alone in her study she had suddenly shivered, feeling a sense of complete desolation. With cold hands she had lighted a cigarette.

'I must be ill or something,' she had mused, as she stared at her trembling fingers.

After this she would sometimes cry out in her sleep, living

over in dreams God knows what emotions; returning, maybe, to the battlefields of France. Her hair turned snow-white; it was not unbecoming yet she fretted about it.

'I'm growing very old,' she would sigh as she brushed her thick mop before the glass; and then she would peer at her wrinkles.

For now that it had happened she hated being old; it no longer appeared such an easy solution of those difficulties that had always beset her. And this she resented most bitterly, so that she became the prey of self-pity, and of other undesirable states in which the body will torment the mind, and the mind, in its turn, the body. Then Miss Ogilvy straightened her ageing back, in spite of the fact that of late it had ached with muscular rheumatism, and she faced herself squarely and came to a resolve.

'I'm off!' she announced abruptly one day; and that evening she packed her kit-bag.

IV

Near the south coast of Devon there exists a small island that is still very little known to the world, but which, nevertheless, can boast an hotel; the only building upon it. Miss Ogilvy had chosen this place quite at random, it was marked on her map by scarcely more than a dot, but somehow she had liked the look of that dot and had set forth alone to explore it.

She found herself standing on the mainland one morning looking at a vague blur of green through the mist, a vague blur of green that rose out of the Channel like a tidal wave suddenly suspended. Miss Ogilvy was filled with a sense of adventure; she had not felt like this since the ending of the war.

'I was right to come here, very right indeed. I'm going to shake off all my troubles,' she decided.

A fisherman's boat was parting the mist, and before it was properly beached, in she bundled.

'I hope they're expecting me?' she said gaily.

'They du be expecting you,' the man answered.

The sea, which is generally rough off that coast, was indulging itself in an oily ground-swell; the broad, glossy swells struck the side of the boat, then broke and sprayed over Miss Ogilvy's ankles.

The fisherman grinned: 'Feeling all right?' he queried. 'It du be tiresome most times about these parts.' But the mist had suddenly drifted away and Miss Ogilvy was staring wide-eyed at the island.

She saw a long shoal of jagged black rocks, and between them the curve of a small sloping beach, and above that the lift of the island itself, and above that again, blue heaven. Near the beach stood the little two-storeyed hotel which was thatched, and built entirely of timber; for the rest she could make out no signs of life apart from a host of white seagulls.

Then Miss Ogilvy said a curious thing. She said: 'On the south-west side of that place there was once a cave – a very large cave. I remember that it was some way from the sea.'

'There du be a cave still,' the fisherman told her, 'but it's just above highwater level.'

'A-ah,' murmured Miss Ogilvy thoughtfully, as though to herself; then she looked embarrassed.

The little hotel proved both comfortable and clean, the hostess both pleasant and comely. Miss Ogilvy started unpacking her bag, changed her mind and went for a stroll round the island. The island was covered with turf and thistles and traversed by narrow green paths thick with daisies. It had four rock-bound coves of which the south-western was by far the most difficult of access. For just here the island descended abruptly as though it were hurtling down to the water; and just here the shale was most treacherous and the tide-swept rocks most aggressively pointed. Here it was that the seagulls, grown fearless of man by reason of his absurd limitations, built their nests on the ledges and reared countless young who multiplied, in their turn, every season. Yes, and here it was that Miss Ogilvy, greatly marvelling, stood and stared across at a cave; much too near the crumbling edge for her safety, but by now completely indifferent to caution.

'I remember . . . I remember . . .' she kept repeating. Then: 'That's all very well, but what do I remember?'

She was conscious of somehow remembering all wrong, of her memory being distorted and coloured – perhaps by the endless things she had seen since her eyes had last rested upon that cave. This worried her sorely, far more than the fact that she should be remembering the cave at all, she who had never set foot on the island before that actual morning. Indeed, except for the sense of wrongness when she struggled to piece her memories together, she was steeped in a very profound contentment which surged over her spirit, wave upon wave.

'It's extremely odd,' pondered Miss Ogilvy. Then she laughed, so pleased did she feel with its oddness.

V

That night after supper she talked to her hostess who was only too glad, it seemed, to be questioned. She owned the whole island and was proud of the fact, as she very well might be, decided her boarder. Some curious things had been found on the island, according to comely Mrs Nanceskivel: bronze arrowheads, pieces of ancient stone celts; and once they had dug up a man's skull and thigh-bone – this had happened while they were sinking a well. Would Miss Ogilvy care to have a look at the bones? They were kept in a cupboard in the scullery.

Miss Ogilvy nodded.

'Then I'll fetch him this moment,' said Mrs Nanceskivel, briskly.

In less than two minutes she was back with the box that contained those poor remnants of a man, and Miss Ogilvy, who had risen from her chair, was gazing down at those remnants. As she did so her mouth was sternly compressed, but her face and her neck flushed darkly.

Mrs Nanceskivel was pointing to the skull: 'Look, miss, he was killed,' she remarked rather proudly, 'and they tell me that the axe that killed him was bronze. He's thousands and thousands of years old, they tell me. Our local doctor knows a lot about such things and he wants me to send these bones to an expert; they ought to belong to the Nation, he says. But I know what would happen, they'd come digging up my island, and I won't have people digging up my island, I've got enough worry with the rabbits as it is.' But Miss Ogilvy could no longer hear the words for the pounding of the blood in her temples.

She was filled with a sudden, inexplicable fury against the innocent Mrs Nanceskivel: 'You . . . *you* . . .' she began, then checked herself, fearful of what she might say to the woman.

For her sense of outrage was overwhelming as she stared at those bones that were kept in the scullery; moreover, she knew how such men had been buried, which made the outrage seem all the more shameful. They had buried such men in deep, well-dug pits surmounted by four stout stones at their corners – four stout stones there had been and a covering stone. And all this Miss Ogilvy knew as by instinct, having no concrete knowledge on which to draw. But she knew it right down in the depths of her soul, and she hated Mrs Nanceskivel.

And now she was swept by another emotion that was even more strange and more devastating: such a grief as she had not conceived could exist; a terrible unassuageable grief, without hope, without respite, without palliation, so that with something akin to despair she touched the long gash in the skull. Then her eyes, that had never wept since her childhood, filled slowly with large, hot, difficult tears. She must blink very hard, then close her eyelids, turn away from the lamp and say rather loudly:

'Thanks, Mrs Nanceskivel. It's past eleven – I think I'll be going upstairs.'

VI

Miss Ogilvy closed the door of her bedroom, after which she stood quite still to consider: 'Is it shell-shock?' she muttered incredulously. 'I wonder, can it be shell-shock?'

She began to pace slowly about the room, smoking a Caporal. As usual her hands were deep in her pockets; she could feel small, familiar things in those pockets and she gripped them, glad of their presence. Then all of a sudden she was terribly tired, so tired that she flung herself down on the bed, unable to stand any longer.

She thought that she lay there struggling to reason, that her eyes were closed in the painful effort, and that as she closed them she continued to puff the inevitable cigarette. At least that was what she thought at one moment – the next, she was out in a sunset evening, and a large red sun was sinking slowly to the rim of a distant sea.

Miss Ogilvy knew that she was herself, that is to say she was conscious of her being, and yet she was not Miss Ogilvy at all, nor had she a memory of her. All that she now saw was very familiar, all that she now did was what she should do, and all that she now was seemed perfectly natural. Indeed, she did not think of these things; there seemed no reason for thinking about them.

She was walking with bare feet on turf that felt springy and was greatly enjoying the sensation; she had always enjoyed it, ever since as an infant she had learned to crawl on this turf. On either hand stretched rolling green uplands, while at her back she knew that there were forests; but in front, far away, lay the gleam of the sea towards which the big sun was sinking. The air was cool and intensely still, with never so much as a ripple or bird-song. It was wonderfully pure – one might almost say young – but Miss Ogilvy thought of it merely as air. Having always breathed it she took it for granted, as she took the soft turf and the uplands.

She pictured herself as immensely tall; she was feeling immensely tall at that moment. As a matter of fact she was five feet eight which, however, was quite a considerable height when compared to that of her fellow-tribesmen. She was wearing a single garment of pelts which came to her knees and left her arms sleeveless. Her arms and her legs, which were closely tattooed with blue zig-zag lines, were extremely hairy. From a leathern thong twisted about her waist there hung a clumsily made stone weapon, a celt, which in spite of its clumsiness was strongly hafted and useful for killing.

Miss Ogilvy wanted to shout aloud from a glorious sense of physical well-being, but instead she picked up a heavy, round stone which she hurled with great force at some distant rocks.

'Good! Strong!' she exclaimed. 'See how far it goes!'

'Yes, strong. There is no one so strong as you. You are surely the strongest man in our tribe,' replied her little companion.

Miss Ogilvy glanced at this little companion and rejoiced that they two were alone together. The girl at her side had a smooth brownish skin, oblique black eyes and short, sturdy limbs. Miss Ogilvy marvelled because of her beauty. She also was wearing a single garment of pelts, new pelts, she had made it that morning. She had stitched at it diligently for hours with short lengths of gut and her best bone needle. A strand of black hair hung over her bosom, and this she was constantly stroking and fondling; then she lifted the strand and examined her hair.

'Pretty,' she remarked with childish complacence.

'Pretty,' echoed the young man at her side.

'For you,' she told him, 'all of me is for you and none other. For you this body has ripened.'

He shook back his own coarse hair from his eyes; he had sad brown eyes like those of a monk. For the rest he was lean and steel-strong of leg, broad of chest, and with features not too uncomely. His prominent cheekbones were rather high, his nose was blunt, his jaw somewhat bestial; but his mouth, though full-lipped, contradicted his jaw, being very gentle and sweet of expression. And now he smiled, showing his square, white teeth.

'You . . . woman,' he murmured contented, and the sound seemed to come from the depths of his being.

His speech was slow and lacking in words when it came to expressing a vital emotion, so one word must suffice and this he now spoke, and the word that he spoke had a number of meanings. It meant: 'Little spring of exceedingly pure water.' It meant: 'Hut of peace for a man after battle.' It meant: 'Ripe red berry sweet to the taste.' It meant: 'Happy small home of future generations.' All these things he must try to express by a word, and because of their loving she understood him.

They paused, and lifting her up he kissed her. Then he rubbed his large shaggy head on her shoulder; and when he released her she knelt at his feet.

'My master; blood of my body,' she whispered. For with her it was different, love had taught her love's speech, so that she might turn her heart into sounds that her primitive tongue could utter.

After she had pressed her lips to his hands, and her cheek to his hairy and powerful forearm, she stood up and they gazed at the setting sun, but with bowed heads, gazing under their lids, because this was very sacred.

A couple of mating bears padded towards them from a thicket, and the female rose to her haunches. But the man drew his celt and menaced the beast, so that she dropped down noiselessly and fled, and her mate also fled, for here was the power that few dared to withstand by day or by night, on the uplands or in the forests. And now from across to the left where a river would presently lose itself in the marshes, came a rhythmical thudding, as a herd of red deer with wide nostrils and starting eyes thundered past, disturbed in their drinking by the bears.

After this the evening returned to its silence, and the spell of its silence descended on the lovers, so that each felt very much alone, yet withal more closely united to the other. But the man became restless under that spell, and he suddenly laughed; then grasping the woman he tossed her above his head and caught her. This he did many times for his own amusement and because he knew that his strength gave her joy. In this manner they played together for a while, he with his strength and she with her weakness. And they cried out, and made many guttural sounds which were meaningless save only to themselves. And the tunic of pelts slipped down from her breasts, and her two little breasts were pear-shaped.

Presently, he grew tired of their playing, and he pointed towards a cluster of huts and earthworks that lay to the eastward. The smoke from these huts rose in thick straight lines, bending neither to right nor left in its rising, and the thought of sweet burning rushes and brushwood touched his consciousness, making him feel sentimental.

'Smoke,' he said.

And she answered: 'Blue smoke.'

He nodded: 'Yes, blue smoke – home.'

Then she said: 'I have ground much corn since the full moon. My stones are too smooth. You make me new stones.'

'All you have need of, I make,' he told her.

She stole closer to him, taking his hand: 'My father is still a black cloud full of thunder. He thinks that you wish to be head of our tribe in his place, because he is now very old. He must not hear of these meetings of ours, if he did I think he would beat me!'

So he asked her: 'Are you unhappy, small berry?'

But at this she smiled: 'What is being unhappy? I do not know what that means any more.'

'I do not either,' he answered.

Then as though some invisible force had drawn him, his body swung round and he stared at the forests where they lay and darkened, fold upon fold; and his eyes dilated with wonder and terror, and he moved his head quickly from side to side as a wild thing will do that is held between bars and whose mind is pitifully bewildered.

'Water!' he cried hoarsely, 'great water – look, look! Over there. This land is surrounded by water!'

'What water?' she questioned.

He answered: 'The sea.' And he covered his face with his hands.

'Not so,' she consoled, 'big forests, good hunting. Big forests in which you hunt boar and aurochs. No sea over there but only the trees.'

He took his trembling hands from his face: 'You are right . . . only trees,' he said dully.

But now his face had grown heavy and brooding and he started to speak of a thing that oppressed him: 'The Roundheaded-ones, they are devils,' he growled, while his bushy black brows met over his eyes, and when this happened it changed his expression which became a little subhuman.

'No matter,' she protested, for she saw that he forgot her and she wished him to think and talk only of love. 'No matter. My father laughs at your fears. Are we not friends with the Roundheaded-ones? We are friends, so why should we fear them?'

'Our forts, very old, very weak,' he went on, 'and the Roundheaded-ones have terrible weapons. Their weapons are not made of good stone like ours, but of some dark, devilish substance.'

'What of that?' she said lightly. 'They would fight on our side, so why need we trouble about their weapons?'

But he looked away, not appearing to hear her. 'We must barter all, all for their celts and arrows and spears, and then we must learn their secret. They lust after our women, they lust after our lands. We must barter all, all for their sly brown celts.'

'Me . . . bartered?' she queried, very sure of his answer otherwise she had not dared to say this.

'The Roundheaded-ones may destroy my tribe and yet I will not part with you,' he told her. Then he spoke very gravely: 'But I think they desire to slay us, and me they will try to slay first because they well know how much I mistrust them – they have seen my eyes fixed many times on their camps.'

She cried: 'I will bite out the throats of these people if they so much as scratch your skin!'

And at this his mood changed and he roared with amusement: 'You . . . woman!' he roared. 'Little foolish white teeth. Your teeth were made for nibbling wild cherries, not for tearing the throats of the Roundheaded-ones!'

'Thoughts of war always make me afraid,' she whimpered, still wishing him to talk about love.

He turned his sorrowful eyes upon her, the eyes that were sad even when he was merry, and although his mind was often obtuse, yet he clearly perceived how it was with her then. And his blood caught fire from the flame in her blood, so that he strained her against his body.

'You . . . mine . . .' he stammered.

'Love,' she said, trembling, 'this is love.'

And he answered: 'Love.'

Then their faces grew melancholy for a moment, because dimly, very dimly in their dawning souls, they were conscious of a longing for something more vast than this earthly passion could compass.

Presently, he lifted her like a child and carried her quickly southward and westward till they came to a place where a gentle descent led down to a marshy valley. Far away, at the line where the marshes ended, they discerned the misty line of the sea; but the sea and the marshes were become as one substance, merging, blending, folding together, and since they were lovers they also would be one, even as the sea and the marshes.

And now they had reached the mouth of a cave that was set in the quiet hillside. There was bright green verdure beside the cave, and a number of small, pink, thick-stemmed flowers that when they were crushed smelt of spices. And within the cave there was bracken newly gathered and heaped together for a bed; while beyond, from some rocks, came a low liquid sound as a spring dripped out through a crevice. Abruptly, he set the girl on her feet, and she knew that the days of her innocence were over. And she thought of the anxious virgin soil that was rent and sown to bring forth fruit in season, and she gave a quick little gasp of fear:

'No . . . no . . .' she gasped. For, divining his need, she was weak with the longing to be possessed, yet the terror of love lay heavy upon her. 'No . . . no . . .' she gasped.

But he caught her wrist and she felt the great strength of his rough, gnarled fingers, the great strength of the urge that leapt in his loins, and again she must give that quick gasp of fear, the while she clung close to him lest he should spare her.

The twilight was engulfed and possessed by darkness, which in turn was transfigured by the moonrise, which in turn was fulfilled and consumed by dawn. A mighty eagle soared up from his eyrie, cleaving the air with his masterful wings, and beneath him from the rushes that harboured their nests, rose other great birds, crying loudly. Then the heavy-horned elks appeared on the uplands, bending their burdened heads to the sod; while beyond in the forests the fierce wild aurochs stamped as they bellowed their love songs.

But within the dim cave the lord of these creatures had put by his weapon and his instinct for slaying. And he lay there defenceless with tenderness, thinking no longer of death but of life as he murmured the word that had so many meanings. That meant: 'Little spring of exceedingly pure water.' That meant: 'Hut of peace for a man after battle.' That meant: 'Ripe red berry sweet to the taste.' That meant: 'Happy small home of future generations.'

VII

They found Miss Ogilvy the next morning; the fisherman saw her and climbed to the ledge. She was sitting at the mouth of the cave. She was dead, with her hands thrust deep into her pockets.

COLETTE

NUITS BLANCHES

(1934)

Translated by Herma Briffault

In our house there is only one bed, too big for you, a little narrow for us both. It is chaste, white, completely exposed; no drapery veils its honest candour in the light of day. People who come to see us survey it calmly and do not tactfully look aside, for it is marked, in the middle, with but one soft valley, like the bed of a young girl who sleeps alone.

They do not know, those who enter here, that every night the weight of our two united bodies hollows out a little more, beneath its voluptuous winding sheet, that valley no wider than a tomb.

O our bed, completely bare! A dazzling lamp, slanted above it, denudes it even more. We do not find there, at twilight, the well-devised shade of a lace canopy or the rosy shell-like glow of a night lamp. Fixed star, never rising or setting, our bed never ceases to gleam except when submerged in the velvety depths of night.

Rigid and white, like the body of a dear departed, it is haloed with a perfume, a complicated scent that astounds, that one inhales attentively, in an effort to distinguish the blond essence of your favourite tobacco from the still lighter aroma of your extraordinarily white skin, and the scent of sandalwood that I give off; but that wild odour of crushed grasses, who can tell if it is mine or thine?

Receive us tonight, O our bed, and let your fresh valley deepen a little more beneath the feverish torpor caused by a thrilling spring day spent in the garden and in the woods.

I lie motionless, my head on your gentle shoulder. Surely, until tomorrow, I will sink into the depths of a dark sleep, a sleep so stubborn, so shut off from the world, that the wings of dream will come to beat in vain. I am going to sleep ... Wait only until I find, for the soles of my feet that are tingling and burning, a cool place ... You have not budged. You draw in long draughts of air, but I feel your shoulder still awake and careful to provide a hollow for my cheek ... Let us sleep ... The nights of May are so brief. Despite the blue obscurity that bathes us, my eyelids are still full of sunshine, and I contemplate the day that has passed with closed eyes, as one peers, from behind the shelter of a Persian blind, into a dazzling summer garden ...

How my heart throbs! I can also hear yours throb beneath my ear. You're not asleep? I raise my head slightly and sense rather than see the pallor of your upturned face, the tawny shadow of your short hair. Your knees are like two cool oranges ... Turn towards me, so that mine can steal some of that smooth freshness.

O, let us sleep! ... My skin is tingling, there is a throbbing in the muscles of my calves and in my ears, and surely our soft bed, tonight, is strewn with pine needles! Let us sleep! I command sleep to come.

I cannot sleep. My insomnia is a kind of gay and lively palpitation, and I sense in your immobility the same quivering exhaustion. You do not budge. You hope I am asleep. Your arm tightens at times around me, out of tender habit, and your charming feet clasp mine between them ... Sleep approaches, grazes me, and flees ... I can see it! Sleep is exactly like that heavy velvety butterfly I pursued in the garden aflame with iris.

Do you remember? What youthful impatience glorified this entire sunlit day! A keen and insistent breeze flung over the sun a smoke screen of rapid clouds and withered the too-tender leaves of the linden trees; the flowers of the butternut tree fell like brownish caterpillars upon our hair, with the flowers of the catalpas, their colour the rainy mauve of the Parisian sky. The shoots of the blackcurrant bush that you brushed against, the wild sorrel dotting the grass with its rosettes, the fresh young mint, still brown, the sage as downy as a hare's ear – everything overflowed with a powerful and spicy sap which became on my lips mingled with the taste of alcohol and citronella.

I could only shout and laugh, as I trod the long juicy grass that stained my frock ... With tranquil pleasure you regarded my wild behaviour, and when I stretched out my hand to reach those wild roses – you remember, the ones of such a tender pink – your hand broke the branch before I could, and you took off, one by one, the curved little thorns, coral-hued, claw-shaped ... And then you gave me the flowers, disarmed ...

You gave me the flowers, disarmed ... You gave me, so I could rest my panting self, the best place in the shade, under the Persian lilacs with their ripe bunches of flowers. You picked the big cornflowers in the round flower beds, enchanted flowers whose hairy centres smell of apricot ... You gave me the cream in the small jug of milk, at teatime, when my ravenous appetite made you smile ... You gave me the bread with the most golden crust, and I can still see your translucent hand in the sunshine raised to shoo away the wasp that sizzled, entangled in my curls ... You threw over my shoulders a light mantle when a cloud longer than usual slowly passed, towards the end of the day, when I shivered, in a cold sweat, intoxicated with the pleasure that is nameless among mankind, the innocent pleasure of happy animals in the springtime ... You told me: 'Come back ... Stop ... We must go in!' You told me ...

Oh, if I think of you, then it's goodbye to sleep. What hour struck just then? Now the windows are growing blue. I hear a murmuring in my blood, or else it is the murmur of the gardens down there ... Are you asleep? No. If I put my cheek against yours, I feel your eyelashes flutter like the wings of a captive fly ... You are not asleep. You are spying on my excitement. You protect me against bad dreams; you are thinking of me as I am thinking of you, and we both feign, out of a strange sentimental shyness, a peaceful sleep. All my body yields itself up to sleep, relaxed, and my neck weighs heavily on your gentle shoulder; but our thoughts unite in love discreetly across this blue dawn, so soon increasing.

In a short while the luminous bar between the curtains will brighten, redden ... In a few more minutes I will be able to read, on your lovely forehead, your delicate chin, your sad mouth, and closed eyelids, the determination to appear to be sleeping ... It is the hour when my fatigue, my nervous insomnia can no longer remain mute, when I will throw my arms outside this feverish bed, and my naughty heels are already preparing to give a mischievous kick.

Then you will pretend to wake up! Then I shall be able to take refuge in you, with confused and unjust complaints, exasperated sighs, with clenched hands cursing the daylight that has already come, the night so soon over, the noises in the street ... For I know quite well that you will then tighten your arms about me and that, if the cradling of your arms is not enough to soothe me, your kiss will become more clinging, your hands more amorous, and that you will accord me the sensual satisfaction that is the surcease of love, like a sovereign exorcism that will drive out of me the demons of fever, anger, restlessness ... You will accord me sensual pleasure, bending over me voluptuously, maternally, you who seek in your impassioned loved one the child you never had.

DOROTHY STRACHEY

OLIVIA
(Chapter 8)

(1949)

It was at this time that a change came over me. That delicious sensation of gladness, of lightness, of springing vitality, that consciousness of youth and strength and ardour, that feeling that some divine power had suddenly granted me an undreamt-of felicity and made me free of boundless kingdoms and untold wealth, faded as mysteriously as it had come and was succeeded by a very different state. Now I was all moroseness and gloom – heavy-hearted, leaden-footed. I could take no interest in my lessons; it was impossible to think of them. When, on Thursdays and Sundays, I sat with the other girls in our study where we were supposed to be writing our *devoirs*, I could not work. I sat for hours, my arms folded on the table in front of me, my head resting on them, plunged in a kind of coma.

'What on earth are you doing, Olivia?' a friend would ask. 'Are you asleep?'

'Oh, leave me alone,' I would cry impatiently. 'I'm thinking.'

But I wasn't thinking. I was sometimes dreaming – the foolish dreams of adolescence: of how I should save her life at the cost of my own by some heroic deed, of how she would kiss me on my deathbed, of how I should kneel at hers and what her dying word would be, of how I should become famous by writing poems which no one would know were inspired by her, of how one day she would guess it, and so on and so on.

At other times I wasn't even dreaming, but just a mass of physical sensations which bewildered me, which made me feel positively sick. My heart beat violently, my breath came fast and unevenly, with the expectation of some extraordinary event which was going to happen the very next minute. At the opening of every door, at the sound of the most casual footstep, my solar plexus shot the wildest stabs through every portion of my body, and the next minute, when nothing had happened, I collapsed, a pricked bladder, into flat and dreary quiescence. Sometimes I was possessed by longing, but I didn't know for what – for some vague blessing, some unimaginable satisfaction, which seemed to be tantalizingly near but which, all the same, I knew was unattainable – a blessing, which, if I could only grasp it, would quench my thirst, still my pulses, give me an Elysian peace. At other times, it was the power of expression that seemed maddeningly denied me. If only I could express myself – in words, in music, anyhow. I imagined myself a prima donna or a great actress. Oh, heavenly relief! Oh, an outlet for all this ferment which was boiling within me! Perilous stuff! If I could only get rid of it – shout it to the world – declaim it away!

Then there was a more passive, a more languorous state, when I seemed to myself dissolving, when I let myself go, as I phrased it to myself, when I felt as though I were floating luxuriously down a warm, gentle river, every muscle relaxed, every portion of me open to receive each softest caress of air and water, down, down, towards some unknown, delicious sea. My indefinite desire was like some pervading, unlocalized ache of my whole being. If I could only know, thought I, where it lies, what it is. In my heart? In my brain? In my body? But no, all I felt was that I desired something. Sometimes I thought it was to be loved in return. But that seemed to me so entirely impossible that it was really and truly unimaginable. I could not imagine *how* she could love me. *Like* me, be fond of me, as a child, as a pupil, yes, of course. But that had nothing to do with what I felt. And so I made myself another dream. It was a man I loved as I loved her, and then he would take me in his arms . . . and kiss me . . . I should feel his lips on my cheeks, on my eyelids, on my – No, no, no, that way lay madness. All this was different – hopeless. Hopeless! A dreadful word, but with a kind of tonic in it. I would hug it to my heart. Yes, hopeless. It was that that gave my passion dignity, that made it worthy of respect. No other love, no love of man and woman could ever be as disinterested as mine. It was I alone who loved – it was I alone whose love was an impossible fantasy.

And yet she sometimes showered me with marvellous kind-nesses. Often when she was reading aloud to me in the library, she would drop her hand into mine and let me hold it. Once when I had a cold, she visited me in my room, petted me, brought me delicacies from the table, told me stories that made me laugh, left me cheerful and contented. It was during my convalescence from that little indisposition that she put her head into my room one evening and said:

'I'm going out to dinner in Paris, but I'll look in on you when I get back and see how you are and say good-night to you.' Her good-night was gay and tender and the next day I was well.

A fortnight later she went out to dinner again. The last train from Paris reached the station at about half-past eleven and she used to be up at the house a little before twelve. How could I help keeping awake that night, half expecting her, listening for her? She had to pass my door to go to her room. Perhaps, perhaps she would come in again. Ah, straining ears and beating heart! But why was she so long? What could she be doing? Again and again I lit my candle and looked at my watch. Can she have passed the door without my having heard her? Impossible! At last, at last, the step came sounding down the long passage. Nearer, nearer. Would it stop? Would it go on? It stopped. A breathless pause. Would the handle turn? It turned. She came in in the dim light of the unshuttered room and stood beside my bed:

'I've brought you a sweet, you greedy little thing,' she said and pulled it out of her bag.

Oh yes, I was greedy, but not for sweets. Her hands were my possession. I covered them with kisses.

'There, there, Olivia,' she said. 'You're too passionate, my child.'

Her lips brushed my forehead and she was gone.

It was a little later that we had the usual Mardi Gras fancy-dress ball. Oh, yes, it was exactly like all other girls' school fancy-dress balls. There was a day's disorganization, while the dresses were being made and we were allowed to run about as we would into each other's rooms, chattering, laughing, trying on, madly sewing and pinning. And then came the excitement of the evening. The two ladies sat enthroned with the staff at one end of the music-room, which had been cleared for dancing; a march was played on the piano and we filed past them two and two, made our bows and our curtsies, were questioned, complimented and laughed at. Mlle Julie was in her element on such occasions. Tonight was no exception. There was something happier in the atmosphere, a relaxation of tension. Mlle Cara was smiling and cheerful; Mlle Julie's wit sparkled like her eyes; she was enjoying it all as much as anyone. We could see her curiosity, her interest in the different self that each girl revealed in her disguise, some betraying their secret longings and fantasies, some abandoning themselves recklessly to their own natural propensities.

So, it was Mary Queen of Scots that poor, plain Gertrude so pathetically aspired to be; Georgie's dark eyes burned mysterious and tragic beneath a top hat; with her false moustache and pointed beard, she made a marvellous romantic poet of 1830. On her arm hung Mimi, a charming little grisette in a poke bonnet, a shawl and a crinoline, and the two flirted outrageously to every one's delight. Madcap Nina was Puck himself, a torment and an amusement to the whole company. And I? I don't know what my dress revealed. It was a Parsee lady's dress which my mother had brought home from India. Very rich and splendid, I thought. The soft Oriental silk was of deep rose-colour and it had a gold band inwoven in the material round the edges of the sari and the part which made up the long skirt. I wore the sari over my head and managed the clinging folds well enough.

But there was no doubt who was the belle of the ball. Cécile, a lovely and complacent Columbia, swam with swan-like grace, a queen among us all. She was draped in the star-spangled banner. An audacious *décolletage* showed her beautiful shoulders and the rise of her breast. Diamond stars crowned her and sparkled round her long slim throat. She was radiantly beautiful.

I was giving her her due of compliments, when Mlle Julie came up.

'*La belle Cécile!*' she cried. 'You do us honour, *chère Amérique* – a beauty worthy of Lafayette's gallantry,' she went on, laughing. 'Turn round and let me look at you.'

She put her hands on Cécile's bare arms and as she twisted her round, bent down and kissed her shoulder. A long deliberate kiss on the naked creamy shoulder. An unknown pang of astonishing violence stabbed me. I hated Cécile. I hated Mlle Julie. As she raised her eyes from the kiss, she saw me watching her. Had she noticed me before? I don't know. Now, I thought, she was mocking me.

'Is Olivia jealous of so much beauty?' she said. 'No, Olivia, you'll never be beautiful, but you have your points,' appraising me, I thought angrily, as if I had been an animal at a cattle show. 'Pretty hands, pretty feet, a pretty figure, grace which is sometimes more than –' but then her voice trailed off into a murmur too low for me to hear. 'But even if I wanted to kiss you, fair Indian, how could I, wrapped as you are in all those veils? Come though, I'll tell you a secret.'

She drew me towards her, pulled back my sari, and whispered close, close in my ear, her lips almost touching me, her breath hot on my cheek:

'I'll come tonight and bring you a sweet.'

She was gone.

I remember that I felt as if my whole frame had been turned to water. My knees were giving way. I had to cling to a table and support myself till I recovered strength enough to get to a chair – she was coming – tonight – in a few hours – A paean sang in my heart. Had I been weak before? Now, exhilaration flowed through my veins. Why? Why? I didn't stop to think why. I only knew that there, in the immediate future, soon, soon, something was coming to me, some wild delight, some fierce anguish that my whole being called for. But I mustn't think of it. Now, I must dance. Just then Georgie passed me.

'Why are you so pale?' she asked and looked at me.

'Georgie,' I said, 'have you ever been in love?'

Georgie's dark eyes gloomed and glowed. I could see her breath quickening.

'Yes,' she answered sombrely, 'yes.'

'And what's it like?'

'Too horrible to speak of.' And then, as though some lovely memory were rising from the depths of her heart into the glowing eyes, they softened, melted, shone, behind a veil of tears – 'And too delicious – Come, let's dance!'

She put her arm round me and pressed me to her. There was comfort in the contact. Comfort, I felt, and pleasure for us both. She was stronger, taller than I. My head could rest on her shoulder; I was conscious of hers bending over me. Our steps, our limbs, harmonized, swayed, quickened, slackened to the music, as if one spirit informed them. I could trust myself to her guiding, I could abandon myself in a trance of ecstasy to the motion, to the rhythm, to the langours and the passions of the waltz.

That evening, we danced every waltz together (Georgie abandoned her grisette – 'she can't dance for twopence' –), but we knew well enough that we were not dancing with each other, that one of us was clasping, the other being clasped by the phantom of her own dreams.

It was the fashion to end every ball with what was called a

'galop'. I don't think this dance exists nowadays. It was the tempestuous conclusion in those Victorian days to evenings that had been filled with sentimentalities and proprieties – waltzes and Lancers – and people would rush into the frenzy of rapid motion with a fury of excitement. When the waltzes were over that night, Nina and I, sped by some magnetic impulse, shot madly into each other's arms for the final galop. Excitement was in the air. Fräulein, at the piano, caught it too and added to it by the *brio* of her playing. But no couple could compete with Nina and me. We rushed and whirled, faster and faster, more and more furiously, our hair, our draperies, streaming like Maenads' behind us, till at last the others gave out exhausted and we were left whirling alone, the only couple on the floor. It was the music that surrendered first, and as, at last, we dropped to the ground, laughing and breathless, all the watching girls applauded.

The evening was over. It was time to go to bed. I should have been glad for it to last longer. There was something coming that I dreaded as much as I longed for it. I was approaching an abyss into which I was going to fall dizzy and shuddering. I averted my eyes, but I knew that it was there.

After all the noisy good-nights, I was at last alone in my room. I tore off my veils impatiently. I must make haste. There was no time to be lost. I slipped into my schoolgirl's nightgown, high to the throat and buttoned to the wrists – and suddenly the vision of Cécile's creamy shoulder flashed upon me. I couldn't bear the hideous nightgown. I took out a clean day-chemise and put it on instead. That was better. My arms and neck at least were bare. I got into bed and blew out the candle.

What had she said? Pretty hands, pretty feet, a pretty figure. Yes, but in French, what strange expression does one use? '*Un joli corps.*' A pretty body. Mine, a pretty body. I had never thought of my body till that minute. A body! I had a body – and it was pretty. What was it like? I must look at it. There was still time. She wouldn't be coming yet. I lighted the candle, sprang out of bed and slipped off my chemise. The looking-glass – a small one – was over the wash-hand-stand. I could only see my face and shoulders in it. I climbed on to a chair. Then I could see more. I looked at the figure in the glass, queerly lighted, without head or legs, strangely attractive, strangely repulsive. And then I slowly passed my hands down this queer creature's body from neck to waist – Ah! – That was more than I could bear – that excruciating thrill I had never felt before. In a second my chemise was on again, I was back in bed.

And now, I listened, not thinking, not feeling any more, absorbed in listening. The noises gradually died away – slamming doors, footsteps, snatches of talk and laughter. The house was silent now. Not quite. I still heard from time to time a window or a shutter being closed or opened. Now. Yes, now it really was silent. Now was the time to hear a coming footstep, a creaking board. There! My heart beat, stood still, beat. No! A false alarm. How long she was! It must be getting late. How late! How late! And still she didn't come. She had never been as late as this before. I lighted my candle again and looked at my watch. One o'clock. And we had gone to bed at eleven. I crept to the door and opened it gently. I could see her room a little way off, on the opposite side of the passage. There was no light coming from the crack under the door. Nothing was stirring. Everything was wrapped in profound and deadly silence. I went heavily back to my bed. She had promised. She couldn't not come now. I must have faith in her. Or could anything have prevented her? Yet surely not for all this time. She knew I should wait for her. Ah! she was cruel. She had no right to promise and not to come. She had forgotten me. She didn't know whether I existed or not. She had other thoughts, other cares. Of course, of course. I was nothing to her. A silly schoolgirl. She liked Cécile better than she did me. Hark! A sound! Hope rose and died a dozen times that night. Even when I knew it was impossible – even when the late winter dawn was beginning to glimmer in the room, I still lay, tossing and listening. It must have been five o'clock before I fell asleep.

And yet I was to know other, bitterer vigils, during which I looked back on this one as happy – during which I realized she had never loved me, never would love me as well as on that night.

ISAK DINESEN
THE BLANK PAGE

(1957)

By the ancient city gate sat an old coffee-brown, black-veiled who made her living by telling stories.

She said:

'You want a tale, sweet lady and gentleman? Indeed I have told many tales, one more than a thousand, since that time when I first let young men tell me, myself, tales of a red rose, two smooth lily buds, and four silky, supple, deadly entwining snakes. It was my mother's mother, the black-eyed dancer, the often-embraced, who in the end – wrinkled like a winter apple and crouching beneath the mercy of the veil – took upon herself to teach me the art of story-telling. Her own mother's mother had taught it to her, and both were better story-tellers than I am. But that, by now, is of no consequence, since to the people they and I have become one, and I am most highly honoured because I have told stories for two hundred years.'

Now if she is well paid and in good spirits, she will go on.

'With my grandmother,' she said, 'I went through a hard school. "Be loyal to the story," the old hag would say to me.

"Be eternally and unswervingly loyal to the story." "Why must I be that, Grandmother?" I asked her. "Am I to furnish you with reasons, baggage?" she cried. "And you mean to be a story-teller! Why, you are to become a story-teller, and I shall give you my reasons! Hear then: Where the story-teller is loyal, eternally and unswervingly loyal to the story, there, in the end, silence will speak. Where the story has been betrayed, silence is but emptiness. But we, the faithful, when we have spoken our last word, will hear the voice of silence. Whether a small snotty lass understands it or not."

'Who then,' she continues, 'tells a finer tale than any of us? Silence does. And where does one read a deeper tale than upon the most perfectly printed page of the most precious book? Upon the blank page. When a royal and gallant pen, in the moment of its highest inspiration, has written down its tale with the rarest ink of all – where, then, may one read a still deeper, sweeter, merrier and more cruel tale than that? Upon the blank page.'

The old beldame for a while says nothing, only giggles a little and munches with her toothless mouth.

'We,' she says at last, 'the old women who tell stories, we know the story of the blank page. But we are somewhat averse to telling it, for it might well, among the uninitiated, weaken our own credit. All the same, I am going to make an exception with you, my sweet and pretty lady and gentleman of the generous hearts. I shall tell it to you.'

High up in the blue mountains of Portugal there stands an old convent for sisters of the Carmelite order, which is an illustrious and austere order. In ancient times the convent was rich, the sisters were all noble ladies, and miracles took place there. But during the centuries highborn ladies grew less keen on fasting and prayer, the great dowries flowed scantily into the treasury of the convent, and today the few portionless and humble sisters live in but one wing of the vast crumbling structure, which looks as if it longed to become one with the grey rock itself. Yet they are still a blithe and active sisterhood. They take much pleasure in their holy meditations, and will busy themselves joyfully with that one particular task which did once, long, long ago, obtain for the convent a unique and strange privilege: they grow the finest flax and manufacture the most exquisite linen of Portugal.

The long field below the convent is ploughed with gentle-eyed, milk-white bullocks, and the seed is skilfully sown out by labour-hardened virginal hands with mould under the nails. At the time when the flax field flowers, the whole valley becomes air-blue, the very colour of the apron which the blessed virgin put on to go out and collect eggs within St Anne's poultry yard, the moment before the Archangel Gabriel in mighty wing-strokes lowered himself on to the threshold of the house, and while high, high up a dove, neck-feathers raised and wings vibrating, stood like a small clear silver star in the sky. During this month the villagers many miles round raise their eyes to the flax field and ask one another: 'Has the convent been lifted into heaven? Or have our good little sisters succeeded in pulling down heaven to them?'

Later in due course the flax is pulled, scutched and hackled; thereafter the delicate thread is spun, and the linen woven, and at the very end the fabric is laid out on the grass to bleach, and is watered time after time, until one may believe that snow has fallen round the convent walls. All this work is gone through with precision and piety and with such sprinklings and litanies as are the secret of the convent. For these reasons the linen, baled high on the backs of small grey donkeys and sent out through the convent gate, downwards and ever downwards to the towns, is as flower-white, smooth and dainty as was my own little foot when, fourteen years old, I had washed it in the brook to go to a dance in the village.

Diligence, dear Master and Mistress, is a good thing, and religion is a good thing, but the very first germ of a story will come from some mystical place outside the story itself. Thus does the linen of the Convento Velho draw its true virtue from the fact that the very first linseed was brought home from the Holy Land itself by a crusader.

In the Bible, people who can read may learn about the lands of Lecha and Maresha, where flax is grown. I myself cannot read, and have never seen this book of which so much is spoken. But my grandmother's grandmother as a little girl was the pet of an old Jewish rabbi, and the learning she received from him has been kept and passed on in our family. So you will read, in the book of Joshua, of how Achsah the daughter of Caleb lighted from her ass and cried unto her father: 'Give me a blessing! For thou hast now given me land; give me also the blessing of springs of water!' And he gave her the upper springs and the nether springs. And in the fields of Lecha and Maresha lived, later on, the families of them that wrought the finest linen of all. Our Portuguese crusader, whose own ancestors had once been great linen weavers of Tomar, as he rode through these same fields was struck by the quality of the flax, and so tied a bag of seeds to the pommel of his saddle.

From this circumstance originated the first privilege of the convent, which was to procure bridal sheets for all the young princesses of the royal house.

I will inform you, dear lady and gentleman, that in the country of Portugal in very old and noble families a venerable custom has been observed. On the morning after the wedding of a daughter of the house, and before the morning gift had yet been handed over, the Chamberlain or High Steward from a balcony of the palace would hang out the sheet of the night and would solemnly proclaim: *Virginem eam tenemus* – 'We declare her to have been a virgin.' Such a sheet was never afterwards washed or again lain on.

This time-honoured custom was nowhere more strictly upheld than within the royal house itself, and it has there subsisted till within living memory.

Now for many hundred years the convent in the mountains, in appreciation of the excellent quality of the linen delivered, has held its second high privilege: that of receiving back that central piece of the snow-white sheet which bore witness to the honour of a royal bride.

In the tall main wing of the convent, which overlooks an immense landscape of hills and valleys, there is a long gallery with a black-and-white marble floor. On the walls of the gallery, side by side, hangs a long row of heavy, gilt frames, each of them adorned with a coroneted plate of pure gold, on which is engraved the name of a princess: Donna Christina, Donna Ines, Donna Jacintha Lenora, Donna Maria. And each of these frames encloses a square cut from a royal wedding sheet.

Within the faded markings of the canvases people of some imagination and sensibility may read all the signs of the zodiac: the Scales, the Scorpion, the Lion, the Twins. Or they may there find pictures from their own world of ideas: a rose, a heart, a sword – or even a heart pierced through with a sword.

In days of old it would occur that a long, stately, richly coloured procession wound its way through the stone-grey mountain scenery, upwards to the convent. Princesses of Portugal, who were now queens or queen dowagers of foreign countries, Archduchesses, or Electresses, with their splendid retinue, proceeded here on a pilgrimage which was by nature both sacred and secretly gay. From the flax field upwards the road rises steeply; the royal-lady would have to descend from her coach to be carried this last bit of the way in a palanquin presented to the convent for the very same purpose.

Later on, up to our own day, it has come to pass – as it comes to pass when a sheet of paper is being burnt, that after all other sparks have run along the edge and died away, one last clear little spark will appear and hurry along after them – that a very old highborn spinster undertakes the journey to Convento Velho. She has once, a long long time ago, been playmate, friend and maid-of-honour to a young princess of Portugal. As she makes her way to the convent she looks round to see the view widen to all sides. Within the building a sister conducts her to the gallery and to the plate bearing the name of the princess she has once served, and there takes leave of her, aware of her wish to be alone.

Slowly, slowly a row of recollections passes through the small, venerable, skull-like head under its mantilla of black lace, and it nods to them in amicable recognition. The loyal friend and confidante looks back upon the young bride's elevated married life with the elected royal consort. She takes stock of happy events and disappointments – coronations and jubilees, court intrigues and wars, the birth of heirs to the throne, the alliances of younger generations of princes and princesses, the rise or decline of dynasties. The old lady will remember how once, from the markings on the canvas, omens were drawn; now she will be able to compare the fulfilment to the omen, sighing a little and smiling a little. Each separate canvas with its coroneted name-plate has a story to tell, and each has been set up in loyalty to the story.

But in the midst of the long row there hangs a canvas which differs from the others. The frame of it is as fine and as heavy as any, and as proudly as any carries the golden plate with the royal crown. But on this one plate no name is inscribed, and the linen within the frame is snow-white from corner to corner, a blank page.

I beg of you, you good people who want to hear stories told: look at this page, and recognize the wisdom of my grandmother and of all old story-telling women!

For with what eternal and unswerving loyalty has not this canvas been inserted in the row! The story-tellers themselves before it draw their veils over their faces and are dumb. Because the royal papa and mama who once ordered this canvas to be framed and hung up, had they not had the tradition of loyalty in their blood, might have left it out.

It is in front of this piece of pure white linen that the old princesses of Portugal – worldly wise, dutiful, long-suffering queens, wives and mothers – and their noble old playmates, bridesmaids and maids-of-honour have most often stood still.

It is in front of the blank page that old and young nuns, with the Mother Abbess herself, sink into deepest thought.

ANAÏS NIN

CITIES OF THE INTERIOR
(extract)

(1959)

They had made contact then with the deepest aspect of themselves – Djuna with Lillian's emotional violence and her compassion for this force which destroyed her and hurled her against all
obstacles, Lillian with Djuna's power of clarification. They
needed each other. Djuna experienced deep in herself a pleasure
each time Lillian exploded, for she herself kept her gestures, her
feeling within an outer form, like an Oriental. When Lillian
exploded it seemed to Djuna as if some of her violent feeling, so
long contained within the forms, were released. Some of her
own lightning, some of her own rebellions, some of her own
angers. Djuna contained in herself a Lillian too, to whom she
had never given a moment's freedom, and it made her strangely
free when Lillian gave vent to her anger or rebellions. But after
the havoc, when Lillian had bruised herself, or more seriously
mutilated herself (war and explosion had their consequences)
then Lillian needed Djuna. For the bitterness, the despair, the
chaos submerged Lillian, drowned her. The hurt Lillian wanted
to strike back and did so blindly, hurting herself all the more.

And then Djuna was there, to remove the arrows implanted in Lillian, to cleanse them of their poison, to open the prison door, to open the trap door, to protect, to give transfusion of blood, and peace to the wounded.

But it was Lillian who was drowning, and it was Djuna who was able always at the last moment to save her, and in her moments of danger, Lillian knew only one thing: that she must possess Djuna.

It was as if someone had proclaimed: I need oxygen, and therefore I will lock some oxygen in my room and live on it.

So Lillian began her courtship.

She brought gifts. She pulled out perfume, and jewelry and clothes. She almost covered the bed with gifts. She wanted Djuna to put all the jewelry on, to smell all the perfumes at once, to wear all her clothes. Djuna was showered with gifts as in a fairy tale, but she could not find in them the fairy-tale pleasure. She felt that to each gift was tied a little invisible cord or demand, of exactingness, of debt, of domination. She felt she could not wear all these things and walk away, freely. She felt that with the gifts, a golden spider wove a golden web of possession. Lillian was not only giving away objects, but golden threads woven out of her very own substance to fix and to hold. They were not the fairy-tale gifts which Djuna had dreamed of receiving. (She had many dreams of receiving perfume, or receiving fur, or being given blue bottles, lamés, etc.) In the fairy tale the giver laid out the presents and then became invisible. In the fairy tales and in the dreams there was no debt, and there was no giver.

Lillian did not become invisible. Lillian became more and more present. Lillian became the mother who wanted to dress her child out of her own substance, Lillian became the lover who wanted to slip the shoes and slippers on the beloved's feet so he could contain these feet. The dresses were not chosen as Djuna's dresses, but as Lillian's choice and taste to cover Djuna.

The night of gifts, begun in gaiety and magnificence, began to thicken. Lillian had put too much of herself into the gifts. It was a lovely night, with the gifts scattered through the room like fragments of Miro's circus paintings, flickering and leaping, but not free. Djuna wanted to enjoy and she could not. She loved Lillian's generosity, Lillian's largeness, Lillian's opulence and magnificence, but she felt anxiety. She remembered as a child receiving gifts for Christmas, and among them a closed mysterious box gaily festooned with multicolored ribbons. She remembered that the mystery of this box affected her more than the open, exposed, familiar gifts of tea cups, dolls, etc. She opened the box and out of it jumped a grotesque devil who, propelled by taut springs, almost hit her face.

In these gifts, there is a demon somewhere; a demon who is hurting Lillian, and will hurt me, and I don't know where he is hiding. I haven't seen him yet, but he is here.

She thought of the old legends, of the knights who had to kill monsters before they could enjoy their love.

No demon here, thought Djuna, nothing but a woman drowning, who is clutching at me . . . I love her.

When Lillian dressed up in the evening in vivid colors with her ever tinkling jewelry, her face wildly alive, Djuna said to her, 'You're made for a passionate life of some kind.'

She looked like a white negress, a body made for rolling in natural undulations of pleasure and desire. Her vivid face, her avid mouth, her provocative, teasing glances proclaimed sensuality. She had rings under her eyes. She looked often as if she had just come from the arms of a lover. An energy smoked from her whole body.

But sensuality was paralyzed in her. When Djuna sought to show Lillian her face in the mirror, she found Lillian paralyzed with fear. She was impaled on a rigid pole of puritanism. One felt it, like a heavy silver chastity belt, around her soft, rounded body.

She bought a black lace gown like Djuna's. Then she wanted to own all the objects which carried Djuna's personality or spirit. She wanted to be clasped at the wrists by Djuna's bracelet watch, dressed in Djuna's kind of clothes.

(Djuna thought of the primitives eating the liver of the strong man of the tribe to acquire his strength, wearing the teeth of the elephant to acquire his durability, donning the lion's head and mane to appropriate his courage, gluing feathers on themselves to become as free as the bird.)

Lillian knew no mystery. Everything was open with her. Even the most ordinary mysteries of women she did not guard. She was open like a man, frank, direct. Her eyes shed lightning but no shadows.

One night Djuna and Lillian went to a night club together to watch the cancan. At such a moment Djuna forgot that she was a woman and looked at the women dancing with the eyes of an artist and the eyes of a man. She admired them, revelled in their beauty, in their seductions, in the interplay of black garters and black stockings and the snow-white frills of petticoats.

Lillian's face clouded. The storm gathered in her eyes. The lightning struck. She lashed out in anger: 'If I were a man I would murder you.'

Djuna was bewildered. Then Lillian's anger dissolved in lamentations: 'Oh, the poor people, the poor people who love you. You love these women!'

She began to weep. Djuna put her arms around her and consoled her. The people around them looked baffled, as passers-by look up suddenly at an unexpected, freakish windstorm. Here it was, chaotically upsetting the universe, coming from right and left, great fury and velocity – and why?

Two women were looking at beautiful women dancing. One enjoyed it, and the other made a scene.

Lillian went home and wrote stuttering phrases on the back of a box of writing paper: Djuna, don't abandon me; if you abandon me, I am lost.

When Djuna came the next day, still angry from the inexplicable storm of the night before, she wanted to say: are you the woman I chose for a friend? Are you the egotistical, devouring child, all caprice and confusion who is always crossing my path? She could not say it, not before this chaotic helpless writing on the back of the box, a writing which could not stand alone, but wavered from left to right, from right to left, inclining, falling, spilling, retreating, ascending on the line as if for flight off the edge of the paper as if it were an airfield, or plummeting on the paper like a falling elevator.

If they met a couple along the street who were kissing, Lillian became equally unhinged.

If they talked about her children and Djuna said: I never liked real children, only the child in the grown-up, Lillian answered: you should have had children.

'But I lack the maternal feeling for children, Lillian, though I haven't lacked the maternal experience. There are plenty of children, abandoned children right in the so-called grown-ups. While you, well you are a real mother, you have a real maternal capacity. You are the mother type. I am not. I only like being the mistress. I don't even like being a wife.'

Then Lillian's entire universe turned a somersault again, crashed, and Djuna was amazed to see the devastating results of an innocent phrase: 'I am not a maternal woman,' she said, as if it were an accusation. (Everything was an accusation.)

Then Djuna kissed her and said playfully: 'Well, then, you're a *femme fatale*!'

But this was like fanning an already enormous flame. This aroused Lillian to despair: 'No, no, I never destroyed or hurt anybody,' she protested.

'You know, Lillian, someday I will sit down and write a little dictionary for you, a little Chinese dictionary. In it I will put down all the interpretations of what is said to you, the right interpretation, that is: the one that is not meant to injure, not meant to humiliate or accuse or doubt. And whenever something is said to you, you will look in my little dictionary to make sure, before you get desperate, that you have understood what is said to you.'

The idea of the little Chinese dictionary made Lillian laugh. The storm passed.

But if they walked the streets together her obsession was to see who was looking at them or following them. In the shops she was obsessed about her plumpness and considered it not an attribute but a defect. In the movies it was emotionalism and tears. If they sat in a restaurant by a large window and saw the people passing it was denigration and dissection. The universe hinged and turned on her defeated self.

She was aggressive with people who waited on her, and then was hurt by their defensive abandon of her. When they did not wait on her she was personally injured, but could not see the injury she had inflicted by her demanding ways. Her commands bristled everyone's hair, raised obstacles and retaliations. As soon as she appeared she brought dissonance.

But she blamed the others, the world.

She could not bear to see lovers together, absorbed in each other.

She harassed the quiet men and lured them to an argument and she hated the aggressive men who held their own against her.

Her shame. She could not carry off gallantly a run in her stocking. She was overwhelmed by a lost button.

When Djuna was too swamped by other occupations or other people to pay attention to her, Lillian became ill. But she would not be ill at home surrounded by her family. She was ill alone, in a hotel room, so that Djuna ran in and out with medicines, with chicken soup, stayed with her day and night chained to her antics, and then Lillian clapped her hands and confessed: 'I'm so happy! Now I've got you all to myself!'

The summer nights were passing outside like gay whores, with tinkles of cheap jewelry, opened and emollient like a vast bed. The summer nights were passing but not Lillian's tension with the world.

She read erotic memoirs avidly, she was obsessed with the lives and loves of others. But she herself could not yield, she was ashamed, she throttled her own nature, and all this desire, lust, became twisted inside of her and churned a poison of envy and jealousy. Whenever sensuality showed its flower head, Lillian would have liked to decapitate it, so it would cease troubling and haunting her.

At the same time she wanted to seduce the world, Djuna, everybody. She would want to be kissed on the lips and more warmly and then violently block herself. She thrived on this hysterical undercurrent without culmination. This throbbing sensual obsession and the blocking of it; this rapacious love without polarity, like a blind womb appetite; delighting in making the temperature rise and then clamping down the lid.

In her drowning she was like one constantly choking those around her, bringing them down with her into darkness.

Djuna felt caught in a sirocco.

She had lived once on a Spanish island and experienced exactly this impression.

The island had been calm, silvery and dormant until one morning when a strange wind began to blow from Africa, blowing in circles. It swept over the island charged with torpid warmth, charged with flower smells, with sandalwood and patchouli and incense, and turning in whirlpools, gathered up the nerves and swinging with them into whirlpools of dry enervating warmth and smells, reached no climax, no explosion. Blowing persistently, continuously, hour after hour, gathering every nerve in every human being, the nerves alone, and tangling them in this fatal waltz; drugging them and pulling them, and whirlpooling them, until the body shook with restlessness – all polarity and sense of gravity lost. Because of this insane waltz of the wind, its emollient warmth, its perfumes, the being lost its guidance, its clarity, its integrity. Hour after hour, all day and all night, the body was subjected to this insidious whirling rhythm, in which polarity was lost, and only the nerves and desires throbbed, tense and weary of movement – all in a void, with no respite, no climax, no great loosening as in other storms. A tension that gathered force but had no release. It abated not once in forty-eight hours, promising, arousing, caressing, destroying sleep, rest, repose, and then vanished without releasing, without culmination . . .

This violence which Djuna had loved so much! It had become a mere sirocco wind, burning and shrivelling. This violence which Djuna had applauded, enjoyed, because she could not possess it in herself. It was now burning her, and their friendship. Because it was not attached to anything, it was not creating anything, it was a trap of negation.

'You will save me,' said Lillian always, clinging.

Lillian was the large foundering ship, yes, and Djuna the small lifeboat. But now the big ship had been moored to the small lifeboat and was pitching too fast and furiously and the lifeboat was being swamped.

(She wants something of me that only a man can give her. But first of all she wants to become me, so that she can communicate with man. She has lost her ways of communicating with man. She is doing it through me!)

When they walked together, Lillian sometimes asked Djuna: 'Walk in front of me, so I can see how you walk. You have such a sway of the hips!'

In front of Lillian walked Lillian's lost femininity, imprisoned in the male Lillian. Lillian's femininity imprisoned in the deepest wells of her being, loving Djuna, and knowing it must reach her own femininity at the bottom of the well by way of Djuna. By wearing Djuna's feminine exterior, swaying her hips, becoming Djuna.

As Djuna enjoyed Lillian's violence, Lillian enjoyed Djuna's feminine capitulations. The pleasure Djuna took in her capitulations to love, to desire. Lillian breathed out through Djuna. What took place in Djuna's being which Lillian could not reach, she at least reached by way of Djuna.

'The first time a boy hurt me,' said Lillian to Djuna, 'it was in school. I don't remember what he did. But I wept. And he laughed at me. Do you know what I did? I went home and dressed in my brother's suit. I tried to feel as the boy felt. Naturally as I put on the suit I felt I was putting on a costume of strength. It made me feel sure, as the boy was, confident, impudent. The mere fact of putting my hands in the pockets made me feel arrogant. I thought then that to be a boy meant one did not suffer. That it was being a girl that was responsible for the suffering. Later I felt the same way. I thought man had found a way out of suffering by objectivity. What the man called being reasonable. When my husband said: Lillian, let's be reasonable, it meant he had none of the feeling I had, that he could be objective. What a power! Then there was another thing. When I felt his great choking anguish I discovered one relief, and that was action. I felt like the women who had to sit and wait at home while there was a war going on. I felt if only I could join the war, participate, I wouldn't feel the anguish and the fear. All through the last war as a child I felt: if only they would let me be Joan of Arc. Joan of Arc wore a suit of armor, she sat on a horse, she fought side by side with the men. She must have gained their strength. Then it was the same way about men. At a dance, as a girl, the moment of waiting before they asked me seemed intolerable, the suspense, and the insecurity; perhaps they were not going to ask me! So I rushed forward, to cut the suspense. I rushed. All my nature became rushed, propelled by the anxiety, merely to cut through all the moment of anxious uncertainty.'

Djuna looked tenderly at her, not the strong Lillian, the overwhelming Lillian, the aggressive Lillian, but the hidden, secret, frightened Lillian who had created such a hard armor and disguise around her weakness.

Djuna saw the Lillian hidden in her coat of armor, and all of Lillian's armor lay broken around her, like cruel pieces of mail which had wounded her more than they had protected her from the enemy. The mail had melted, and revealed the bruised feminine flesh. At the first knowledge of the weakness Lillian had picked up the mail, wrapped herself in it and had taken up a lance. The lance! The man's lance. Uncertainty resolved, relieved by the activity of attack!

The body of Lillian changed as she talked, the fast coming words accelerating the dismantling. She was taking off the shell, the covering, the defenses, the coat of mail, the activity.

Suddenly Lillian laughed. In the middle of tears, she laughed: 'I'm remembering a very comical incident. I was about sixteen. There was a boy in love with me. Shyly, quietly in love. We were in the same school but he lived quite far away. We all used bicycles. One day we were going to be separated for a week by the holidays. He suggested we both bicycle together towards a meeting-place between the two towns. The week of separation seemed too unbearable. So it was agreed: at a certain hour we would leave the house together and meet half way.'

Lillian started off. At first at a normal pace. She knew the rhythm of the boy. A rather easy, relaxed rhythm. Never rushed. Never precipitate. She at first adopted his rhythm. Dreaming of him, of his slow smile, of his shy worship, of his expression of this worship, which consisted mainly in waiting for her here, there. Waiting. Not advancing, inviting, but waiting. Watching her pass by.

She pedaled slowly, dreamily. Then slowly her pleasure and tranquility turned to anguish: suppose he did not come? Suppose she arrived before him? Could she bear the sight of the desolate place of their meeting, the failed meeting? The exaltation that had been increasing in her, like some powerful motor, what could she do with this exaltation if she arrived alone, and the meeting failed? The fear affected her in two directions. She could stop right there, and turn back, and not face the possibility of disappointment, or she could rush forward and accelerate the moment of painful suspense, and she chose the second. Her lack of confidence in life, in realization, in the fulfillment of her desires, in the outcome of a dream, in the possibility of reality corresponding to her fantasy, speeded her bicycle with the incredible speed of anxiety, a speed beyond the human body, beyond human endurance.

She arrived before him. Her fear was justified! She could not measure what the anxiety had done to her speed, the acceleration which had broken the equality of rhythm. She arrived as she had feared, at a desolate spot on the road, and the boy had become this invisible image which taunts the dreamer, a mirage that could not be made real. It had become reality eluding the dreamer, the wish unfulfilled.

The boy may have arrived later. He may have fallen asleep and not come at all. He may have had a tire puncture. Nothing mattered. Nothing could prevent her from feeling that she was not Juliet waiting on the balcony, but Romeo who had to leap across space to join her. She had leaped, she had acted Romeo, and when woman leaped she leaped into a void.

Later it was not the drama of two bicycles, of a road, of two separated towns; later it was a darkened room, and a man and woman pursuing pleasure and fusion.

At first she lay passive dreaming of the pleasure that would come out of the darkness, to dissolve and invade her. But it was not pleasure which came out of the darkness to clasp her. It was anxiety. Anxiety made confused gestures in the dark, crosscurrents of forces, short circuits, and no pleasure. A depression, a broken rhythm, a feeling such as men must have after they have taken a whore.

Out of the prone figure of the woman, apparently passive, apparently receptive, there rose a taut and anxious shadow, the shadow of the woman bicycling too fast; who, to relieve her insecurity, plunges forward as the desperado does and is defeated because this aggressiveness cannot meet its mate and unite with it. A part of the woman has not participated in this marriage, has not been taken. But was it a part of the woman, or the shadow of anxiety, which dressed itself in man's clothes and assumed man's active role to quiet its anguish? Wasn't it the woman who dressed as a man and pedalled too fast?

ANN BANNON

I AM A WOMAN

(extract)

(1959)

EDITOR'S NOTE

At college Laura Landon fell in love with Beth. When Beth decides that she cannot live as a lesbian and abandons her lover to marry Charlie, Laura moves to New York and tries to forget her past. But there she shares a room with Marcie and eventually, goaded by the observations of her gay friend Jack, Laura is forced to admit to herself that she would rather share Marcie's bed.

Laura walked toward the subway station. All the way she noticed the women, as she never had before. She was at a loss to explain it. Before, she had always hurried, on her way somewhere, with a deadline to beat, somebody to meet, things on her mind. Now – perhaps it was the fatigue that made her slow – she sauntered, looking at the women.

Looking at their faces: sweet, fine-featured, delicate, some of them; others coarse, sensual, heavily female. They all appealed to her, with their soft skirts, their clicking heels, their floating hair. It caught in her throat, this aberration of hers, in a way it never had until that moment. It suffused her. She surrendered quietly to her feelings, walking slowly, looking without staring but with a warm pleasure that made her want to smile. She had trouble controlling her mouth.

God, I love them, she thought to herself, vaguely surprised. *I just love them. I love them all. I know I'm nuts, but I love them.* She stopped by a jewelry window where an exquisite girl was admiring a group of rings. She was all in gray, as fine and soft as twilight. Gray silk graced her slim legs, gray suede pumps with the highest heels were on her feet. A gray suit, impeccably tailored, terribly expensive – gray gloves – a tiny gray hat. Laura had never liked gray much before, but suddenly it was ideal on this cool dainty little creature, with her small nose and moist pink lips. She was extremely pretty. She looked up to find Laura gazing at her, collected herself with pretty confusion, and went off, pulling a recalcitrant gray poodle after her. Laura had not even noticed it till it moved. She looked after the girl for a minute with a foolish smile.

When she finally reached the subway she collapsed on a seat, exhausted. She wanted to get home and into bed so badly that she could hardly wait.

She was late getting home but even so, Marcie had not arrived. She wanted very much to see her, but there was no help for it. She would have to wait. She fell on her bed, meaning to rest for a minute before she took her bath. But so tired was she that before five minutes had passed she was asleep. She woke up to hear small sounds in the bedroom, and it seemed like perhaps half an hour had passed.

She opened her eyes and found herself all tangled up in her clothes, her shoes still on, her skirt wrinkled. There was a light on, the small table lamp between the beds. She pulled herself up and turned around. Marcie was standing in the bathroom door, with a frame of light around her, holding her toothbrush and smiling at Laura. She was all in white lace, in a short gown that barely reached her thighs. Laura smiled at her and blinked, shaking her head slightly.

'Know what time it is?' Marcie said.

'About seven.'

'Quarter of twelve.' Marcie laughed at her surprise. She walked over to her bed and stood beside her for a moment. She smelled gorgeous – intoxicating, sweet and clean, faintly powdered, warm and damp from her bath. She looked sleepy, soft, very feminine. Laura began to tremble, desperate to touch her, afraid even to look.

'You must have been awfully tired, Laur. You've been asleep for hours.'

'I could sleep till Monday and never wake up,' Laura murmured. She spoke without looking at Marcie. She couldn't. The scent of her was trouble enough.

'Burr and I went out for dinner. We didn't want to bother you.'

'Did you have a nice big fight?' Irresistibly Laura's eyes traveled up Marcie to her face.

Marcie sighed. 'We always have a nice big fight.'

'You must enjoy them.'

Marcie sat down beside her. 'Don't talk that way, Laur,' she said. 'I wish I could get interested in books, like you.'

Laura smiled at her, so close, so distant.

'Help me, Laura,' she said.

'How?' Laura felt herself on very shaky ground.

'I don't know how,' Marcie said impatiently. 'If I knew I could help myself. There must be something in life besides fights, Laur.'

'Don't call me Laur.'

Marcie looked at her in surprise. 'Why not?'

'Somebody else used to call me that. It still hurts a little.'

'I'm sorry. I remember, you told me about him.'

Laura felt confession working itself urgently into her thoughts. She wanted to clasp Marcie to her and say, 'Not "him". Her. *Her.* It was a girl I loved. As I love you.' *No, not as I love you. I can't love you that way, not even you.* To her sudden disgust the face of a handsome arrogant girl named Beebo came up in her mind. She frowned at her, trying not to see.

'What's the matter, Laur? Laura?' Marcie smoothed Laura's hair off her hot forehead. 'You must have loved him a lot.'

In a sudden convulsion of desire, Laura threw her arms around Marcie, pressing her hard, tight in her arms. Her need was terrible, and a sort of sob, half ache and half passion, came out of her. Marcie was frightened.

'Laura!' she said, pushing at her. Laura was always so docile; now suddenly she was strange and violent. 'Laura, are you all right?' Laura only clung to her the harder, wrestling against herself with all her strength.

For a moment, Marcie tried to calm her, whispering soothingly and rubbing her back a little. But this only aggravated Laura.

'Marcie, don't!' she said sharply. Panic began to well up in her. 'Oh, God!' she cried, and stood up abruptly, shaking all over. She covered her face with her hands, trying to force the tears back with them. Marcie watched her, astonished, from the bed.

With a little gasp Laura turned and ran out. Marcie rose to her feet and called after her, but it was too late. She heard the front door slam as she ran toward it. She pulled it open but Laura was in the elevator a floor below her and on her way out. Marcie stared into the black stairwell, feeling shocked and confused.

She slipped back into the apartment and into her bed, but she couldn't sleep. She simply sat there, her eyes wide and staring, oscillating between a fear of something she couldn't name and bewildered sympathy for Laura. For whatever it was that tortured her. She shivered everytime she thought of Laura's near-hysterical embrace, returning to it again and again. It gave her a reckless kick, a hint of shameless fun, like the night she kissed the bum in the park. She didn't know why it recalled that to her mind. But it did. Laura had scared her; yet now she felt like giggling.

Laura ran all the way to the subway station, three blocks off. She fell into a seat gasping, trembling violently. People stared at her but she ignored them, covering her face with her hands and sobbing quietly. She rode down to the Village and got off at Tenth Street. She had managed to control herself by this time, but she felt bewildered and lost, as if she didn't quite know what she was doing there. She stood for a moment on the platform, shivering with the chilly air. It was nearly the end of April, but it was still cold at night. She had run out in nothing but a blouse and skirt, with a light topper over them – the clothes she had fallen asleep in. She was aware of the cold, yet somehow didn't feel it.

Resolutely she began to walk, climbing the stairs and then starting down Seventh Avenue. She walked as if she had a goal, precisely because she had none and it frightened her. It was Friday night, and busy. People were everywhere. Young men turned to stare at her.

Within five minutes she was standing in front of The Cellar, rather surprised at herself for having found it so quickly. There was a strange tingling up and down her back and her eyes began to shine with a feverish luster. She walked down the steps and pulled the door open.

Almost nobody noticed her. It was too crowded, at this peak hour of one of the best nights of the week. She made her way through the crowd to the nearest end of the bar. She had to squeeze into a corner next to the juke box and it was work to get her jacket off. It was sweaty and close after the chill air outside.

Laura stood quietly in her corner, looking at all the faces strung down the bar like beads on a necklace. They were animated, young for the most part, attractive . . . There were a few that were sad, or old, or soured on life – or all three. Across the room the artist, with his sketch pad, was drinking with some friends.

Laura felt alone and apart from them all somehow. There were one or two faces she might have recognized from the night before, people Jack might have introduced her to, but she couldn't be sure. She had been too drunk to be sure of anything last night.

God, was it only last night? she wondered. It seemed like a thousand nights ago. She didn't really want to be noticed now. She only wanted to watch, to be absorbed in these gay faces, in the idioms, the milieu.

'What'll you have?' She realized the bartender was leaning stiff-armed on the bar, looking at her.

'Whiskey and water,' she said, wondering suddenly how much it would be. She pulled out a dollar and put it on the counter self-consciously. When he brought her the drink she gulped it anxiously. Marcie kept coming into her thoughts; Marcie's face, her shocked voice saying, 'Laura, are you all right?'

The bartender took her dollar and brought some change. It meant she could have another drink. Drinking your dinner. Where had she heard that? One of her father's friends, no doubt. She gazed at the ceiling. She wanted to talk to Jack, but she was ashamed to call him. She thought of her father again, and it gave her a sort of bitter satisfaction to imagine his face if he could see her now, alone and unhappy, disgracing him by drinking by herself, in a bar – a gay bar. Gay – that would strike him dead. She was sure of it. She smiled a little, but it was a mirthless smile.

After a moment, she ordered another drink. She counted her change fuzzily. There might be enough for a third. She slipped it back in her pocket and looked up to find a young man forcing himself into a place beside her.

Damn! she exclaimed to herself. *As if I didn't have enough on my mind.* Her slim arresting face registered subtle contempt and she turned away. It would have frozen another man, but this one only seemed amused.

'Hello, Laura,' he said.

At this, she looked at him. Her mind was a blank; she couldn't place him. 'Do I know you?' she said.

'No.' He grinned. 'I'm Dutton. This is for you.' He held out a piece of paper and she took it, curious. On it was a devilish reproduction of her own features mocking her from the white page.

'You're the artist,' she accused him suddenly.

'Thanks for the compliment.'

'I don't want it.'

'Keep it.'

'I won't pay for it.'

'You don't have to.' He laughed at her consternation. 'It's paid for, doll. Take it home. Frame it. Enjoy it.'

Laura stared at him. 'Who paid for it?'

'She said not to tell.' He laughed. 'You're a bitch to caricature. You know? Look me up sometime, I'll do a good one. I like your face.' And he turned and wriggled out of the crowd.

Laura was left standing at the bar with the cartoon of herself. She was suddenly humiliated and angry. She felt ridiculous standing there holding the silly thing, not knowing who paid for it. Her glance swept down the bar, looking for a face to accuse, but she recognized no one. No one paid her any attention.

She studied the sketch once more. It was clever, insolent; it made a carnival curiosity of her face. Quietly, deliberately, with a feeling of satisfaction, she tore the sketch in half. And in half again. And threw it down behind the bar where the bartender would grind it into the wet floor. Then she picked up her glass and finished her drink.

'What did you do that for?' said a low voice, so close to her ear that she jumped and a drop of whiskey ran down her chin. 'It was a damn good likeness.'

Laura looked up, gazing straight ahead of her, knowing who it was now and mad. She pulled a dime out of her pocket and smacked it on the bar in front of her.

'I owe you a dime, Beebo. There it is. Thanks for the picture. Next time don't waste your money.'

Beebo laughed. 'I always get what I pay for, lover,' she said. Laura refused to look at her, and after a pause Beebo said, 'What's the matter, Laura, 'fraid to look at me?'

Laura had to look then. She turned her head slowly, reluctantly. Her face was cold and composed. Beebo chuckled at her. She was handsome, like a young boy of fourteen, with her smooth skin and deep blue eyes. She was leaning on her elbows on the bar, and she looked sly and amused. 'Laura's afraid of me,' she said with a quick grin.

'Laura's not afraid of you or anybody else. Laura thinks you're a bitch. That's all.'

'That makes two of us.'

Under her masklike face Laura found herself troubled by the smile so close to her; the snapping blue eyes.

'Where's your guardian angel tonight?' Beebo said.

'I suppose you mean Jack. I don't know where he is, he doesn't have to tell me where he goes.' She turned back to the bar. 'He's not my guardian angel. I don't need one. I'm a big girl now.'

'Oh, excuse me. I should have noticed.'

Laura's cheeks prickled with embarrassment. 'You only see what you want to see,' she said.

'I see what I want to see right now,' Beebo said, and Laura felt her hand on the small of her back. She straightened suddenly.

'Go away,' she said sharply. 'Leave me alone.'

'I can't.'

'Then shut up.'

Beebo laughed softly. 'What's the matter, little girl? Hate the world tonight?' Laura wouldn't answer. 'Think that's going to make it any prettier?' Beebo pushed Laura's whiskey glass toward her with one finger.

'I'm having a drink for the hell of it,' Laura said briefly. 'If it bothers you, go away. You weren't invited, anyway.'

'Don't tell me you're drinking just because you like the taste.'

'I don't mind it.'

'You're unlucky in love, then. Or you just found out you're gay and you can't take it. That it?'

Laura pursed her lips angrily. 'I'm not in love. I never was.'

'You mean love is filth and all that crap? Love is dirty?'

'I didn't say that!' Laura turned on her.

Beebo shrugged. 'You're a big girl, lover. You said it yourself. Big girls know all about love. So don't lie to me.'

'I didn't ask you to bother me, Beebo. I don't want to talk to you. Now scram!'

'There she stands at the bar, drinking whiskey because it tastes good,' Beebo drawled, gazing toward the ceiling and letting the smoke from a cigarette drift from her mouth. 'Sweet sixteen and never been kissed.'

'Twenty,' Laura snapped.

'Excuse me, twenty. Your innocence is getting tedious, lover.' She smiled.

'Beebo, I don't like you,' Laura said. 'I don't like the way you dress or the way you talk or the way you wear your hair. I don't like the things you say and the money you throw around. I don't want your dimes and I don't want you. I hope that's plain because I don't know how to make it any plainer.' Her voice broke as she talked and toward the end she felt her own crazy tears coming up again. Beebo saw them before they spilled over and they changed her. They touched her. She ignored the hard words Laura spoke for she knew enough to know they meant nothing.

'Tell me, baby,' she said gently. 'Tell me all about it. Tell me you hate me if it'll help.'

For a moment Laura sat there, not trusting her, not wanting to risk a word with her, letting the stray tears roll over her cheeks without even brushing them away. Then she straightened up and swept them off her face with her long slim fingers, turning away from Beebo. 'I can't tell you, or anybody.'

Beebo shrugged. 'All right. Have it your way.' She dinched her cigarette and leaned on the bar again, her face close to Laura's. 'Try, baby,' she said softly. 'Try to tell me.'

'It's stupid, it's ridiculous. We're complete strangers.'

'We aren't strangers.' She put an arm around Laura and squeezed her a little. Laura was embarrassed and grateful at the same time. It felt good, so good. Beebo sighed at her silence. 'I'm a bitch, you're right about that,' she admitted. 'But I didn't want to be. It's an attitude. You develop it after a while, like a turtle grows a shell. You need it. Pretty soon you live it, you don't know any other way.'

Laura finished her drink without answering. She put it down on the bar and looked for the bartender. She wouldn't care what Beebo said, she wouldn't look at her, she wouldn't answer her. She didn't dare.

'You don't need to tell me about it,' Beebo went on. 'Because I already know. I've lived through it, too. You fall in love. You're young, inexperienced. What the hell, maybe you're a virgin, even. You fall, up to your ears, and there's nobody to talk to, nobody to lean on. You're all alone with that great big miserable feeling and she's driving you out of your mind. Every time you look at her, every time you're near her. Finally you give in to it – and she's straight.' She said the last word with such acid sharpness that Laura jumped. 'End of story,' Beebo added. 'End of soap opera. Beginning of soap opera. That's all the Village is, honey, just one crazy little soap opera after another, like Jack says. All tangled up with each other, one piled on top of the next, ad infinitum. Mary loves Jane loves Joan loves Jean loves Beebo loves Laura.' She stopped and grinned at Laura.

'Doesn't mean a thing,' she said. 'It goes on forever. Where one stops another begins.' She looked around The Cellar with Laura following her gaze. 'I know most of the girls in here,' she said. 'I've probably slept with half of them. I've lived with half of the half I've slept with. I've loved half of the half I've lived with. What does it all come to?'

She turned to Laura who was caught with her fascinated face very close to Beebo's. She started to back away but Beebo's arm around her waist tightened and kept her close. 'You know something, baby? It doesn't matter. Nothing matters. You don't like me, and that doesn't matter. Someday maybe you'll love me, and that won't matter either. Because it won't last. Not down here. Not anywhere in the world, if you're gay. You'll never find peace, you'll never find Love. With a capital L.'

She took a drag on her cigarette and let it flow out of her nostrils. 'L for Love,' she said, looking into space. 'L for Laura.' She turned and smiled at her, a little sadly. 'L for Lust and L for

143

the L of it. L for Lesbian. L for Let's – let's,' she said, and blew smoke softly into Laura's ear. Laura was startled to feel the strength of the feeling inside her.

It's the whiskey, she thought. *It's because I'm tired. It's because I want Marcie so much. No, that doesn't make sense.* She caught the bartender's eye and he fixed her another drink.

Beebo's arm pressed her again. 'Let's,' she said. 'How about it?' She was smiling, not pushy, not demanding, just asking. As if it didn't really matter whether Laura said yes or no.

'Where did you get that ridiculous name?' Laura hedged.

'My family.'

'They named you *Beebo?*'

'They named me Betty Jean,' she said, smiling. 'Which is even worse.'

'It's a pretty name.'

'It's a lousy name. Even Mother couldn't stand it. And she could stand damn near anything. But they had to call me something. So they called me Beebo.'

'That's too bad.'

Beebo laughed. 'I get along,' she said.

The bartender set Laura's glass down and she reached for her change. 'What's your last name?' she said to Beebo.

'Brinker. Like the silver skates.'

Laura counted her change. She had sixty-five cents. The bartender was telling a joke to some people a few seats down, resting one hand on the bar in front of Laura, waiting for his money. She was a dime short. She counted it again, her cheeks turning hot.

Beebo watched and began to laugh. 'Want your dime back?' she said.

'It's your dime,' Laura said haughtily.

'You must have left home in a hurry, baby. Poor Laura. Hasn't got a dime for a lousy drink.'

Laura wanted to strangle her. The bartender turned back to her suddenly and she felt her face burning. Beebo leaned toward him, laughing. 'I've got it, Mort,' she said.

'No!' Laura said. 'If you could just lend me a dime.'

Beebo laughed and waved Mort away.

'I don't want to owe you a thing,' Laura told her.

'Too bad, doll. You can't help yourself.' She laughed again. Laura tried to give her the change she had left, but Beebo wouldn't take it. 'Sure, I'll take it,' she said. 'And you'll be flat busted. How'll you get home?'

Laura went pale then. She couldn't go home. Even if she had a hundred dollars in her pocket. She couldn't stand to face Marcie, to explain her crazy behavior, to try to make herself sound normal and ordinary when her whole body was begging for strange passion, for forbidden release.

Beebo watched her face change and then she shook her head. 'It must have been a bad fight,' she said.

'You've got it all wrong, Beebo. It wasn't a fight. It was – I don't know what it was.'

'She straight?'

'I don't know.' Laura put her forehead down on the heel of her right hand. 'Yes, she's straight,' she whispered.

'Well, did you tell her? About yourself?'

'I don't know if I did or not. I didn't say it but I acted like a fool. I don't know what she thinks.'

'Then things could be worse,' Beebo said. 'But if she's straight, they're probably hopeless.'

'That's what Jack said.'

'Jack's right.'

'He's not in love with her!'

'Makes him even righter. He sees what you can't see. If he says she's straight, believe him. Get out while you can.'

'I can't.' Laura felt an awful twist of tenderness for Marcie in her throat.

'Okay, baby, go home and get your heart broken. It's the only way to learn, I guess.'

'I can't go home. Not tonight.'

'Come home with me.'

'No.'

'Well . . .' Beebo smiled. 'I know a nice bench in Washington Square. If you're lucky the bums'll leave you alone. And the cops.'

'I'll – I'll go to Jack's,' she said, suddenly brightening with the idea. 'He won't mind.'

'He might,' Beebo said, and raised her glass to her lips. 'Call him first.'

Laura started to leave the bar and then recalled that all her change was sitting on the counter in front of Beebo. She turned back in confusion, her face flushing again. Beebo turned and looked at her. 'What's the matter, baby?' And then she laughed. 'Need a dime?' She handed her one.

For a moment, in the relative quiet of the phone booth, Laura leaned against a wall and wondered if she might faint. But she didn't. She deposited the dime and dialed Jack's number. The phone rang nine times before he answered, and she was on the verge of panic when she heard him lift the receiver at last and say sleepily, 'Hello?'

'Hello, Jack? Jack, this is Laura.' She was vastly relieved to find him at home.

'Sorry, we don't want any.'

'Jack, I've got to see you.'

'My husband contributes to that stuff at the office.'

'Jack, please! It's terribly important.'

'I love you, Mother, but you call me at the Goddamnedest times.'

'Can I come over?'

'Jesus, no!' he exclaimed, suddenly coming wide awake.

'Oh, Jack, what'll I do?' She sounded desperate.

'All right now, let's get straightened out here. Let's make an effort.' He sounded as if he had drunk a lot and just gotten to sleep, still drunk, when Laura's call woke him up. 'Now start at the beginning. And make it quick. What's the problem?'

She felt hurt, slighted. Of all people, Jack was the one she had to count on. 'I – I acted like a fool with Marcie. I don't know what she thinks,' she half-sobbed. 'Jack, help me.'

'What did you do?'

'Nothing – everything. I don't know.'

'God, Mother. Why did you pick tonight? Of all nights?'

'I didn't pick it, it just happened.'

'*What* happened, damn it?'

'I – I sort of embraced her.'

There was a silence on the other end for a minute. Laura heard him say away from the receiver, 'Okay, it's okay. No, she's a friend of mine. A friend, damn it, a girl.' Then his voice became clear and close again. 'Mother, I don't know what to say. I'm not sure I understand what happened, and if I did I still wouldn't know what the hell to say. Where are you?'

'At The Cellar. Jack, you've just got to help me. Please.'

'Are you alone?'

'Yes. No. I've been talking to Beebo, but –'

'Oh! Well, God, that's it, that's the answer. Go home with Beebo.'

'No! I can't, Jack. I want to come to your place.'

'Laura, honey –' He was wide awake now, sympathetic, but caught in his own domestic moils. 'Laura, I'm – well, I'm entertaining.' He laughed a little at his own silliness. 'I'm involved. I'm fraternizing. Oh, hell, I'm making love. You can't come over here.' His voice went suddenly in the other direction as he said, 'No, calm down, she's not coming over.'

Then he said, 'Laura, I wish I could help, honest to God. I just can't, not now. You've got to believe me.' He spoke softly, confidentially, as if he didn't want the other to hear what he said. 'I'll tell you what I'll do, I'll call Marcie and get it straightened out. Don't worry, Marcie believes in me. She thinks I'm Jack Armstrong, the all-American boy. The four-square trouble-shooter. I'll fix it up for you.'

'Jack, please,' she whimpered, like a plaintive child.

'I'll do everything I can. You just picked the wrong night and that's the God's truth, honey. Where's Beebo? Let me talk to Beebo.'

Laura went out of the booth to get her, feeling half dazed, and found her way back to the bar. 'He wants to talk to you,' she said to Beebo, without looking at her.

Beebo frowned at her and then swung herself off her seat and headed for the phone. Laura sat down in her place, disturbed by the warmth Beebo left behind, twirling her glass slowly in her hand. She was crushed that Jack had turned her down.

Perhaps he had a lover, perhaps this night was so important to him that he couldn't give it up, even though she had all his sympathy. These things might be – in fact, were – true. But Laura could hardly discern them through her private pains.

Beebo came back in a minute and leaned over Laura, one hand on the bar, the other on Laura's shoulder. 'He says I'm to take you home,' she said, 'feed you aspirins, dry your tears, and put you to bed. And no monkey business.' She smiled as Laura looked slowly up into her face. It was a strong interesting face. With a little softness, a little innocence, it might have been lovely. But it was too hard and cynical, too restless and disillusioned. 'Come on, sweetie pie,' Beebo said. 'I'm a nice kid, I won't eat you.'

They walked until they came to a small dark street, and the second door up – dark green – faced right on the sidewalk. Beebo opened it and they walked down a couple of steps into a small square court surrounded by the windowed walls of apartment buildings. On the far side was another door with benches and play areas grouped in between on the court. Beebo unlocked the other door and led Laura up two flights of unlighted stairs to her apartment.

When they went inside a brown dachshund rushed to meet them and tried to climb up their legs. Beebo laughed and talked to him, reaching down to push him away.

Laura stood inside the door, her hands over her eyes, somewhat unsteady on her feet.

'Here, baby, let's get you fixed up,' Beebo said. 'Okay, Nix, down. Down!' she said sharply to the excited little dog, and shoved him away with her foot. He slunk off to a chair where he studied her reproachfully.

Beebo led Laura through the small living room to an even smaller bedroom and sat her down on the bed. She knelt in front of her and took her shoes off. Then, gently, she leaned against her, forcing her legs slightly apart, and put her arms around Laura's waist. She rubbed her head against Laura's breasts and said, 'Don't be afraid, baby.' Laura tried weakly to hold her off but she said, 'I won't hurt you Laura,' and looked up at her. She squeezed her gently, rhythmically, her arms tightening and loosening around Laura's body. She made a little sound in her throat and, lifting her face, kissed Laura's neck. And then she stood up slowly, releasing her.

'Okay,' she said. 'Fini. No monkey business. Make yourself comfortable, honey. There's the john – old, but serviceable. You sleep here. I'll take the couch. Here! Here, Nix!' She grabbed the little dog, which had bounded onto the bed and was trying to lick Laura's face, and picked him up in her arms like a baby. She grinned at Laura. 'I'll take him to bed, he won't bother you,' she said. 'Call me if there's anything you need.' She looked at Laura closely while Laura tried to answer her. The younger girl sat on the bed, pale with fatigue and hunger, feeling completely lost and helpless. 'Thanks,' she murmured.

Beebo sat down beside her. 'You look beat, honey,' she said.

'I am.'

'Want to tell me about it now?'

Laura shook her head.

'Well . . .' she said. 'Good night, Little Bo-peep. Sleep tight.' And she kissed her forehead, then turned around and went out of the bedroom, turning out the light on her way.

Laura had gotten off the bed without looking at her, but feeling Beebo's eyes on her. She shut the door slowly, until she heard the catch snap. Then she turned, leaning on the door, and looked at the room. It was small and full of stuff, with yellowed walls. Everything looked clean, although the room was in a state of complete confusion, with clothes draped over chairs and drawers half shut.

All of a sudden, Laura felt stronger. She undressed quickly, taking off everything but her nylon slip, and pulled down the bedclothes. She climbed in gratefully. She didn't even try to forget Marcie or what had happened. It would have been impossible. Mere trying would have made it worse. She relaxed on her back in the dark, her arms outflung, and waited for the awful scene to come up in her mind and torture her.

Her mind wandered. The awful embrace was awful no longer – only wrong and silly and far away. The damage was irreparable. She stared at the ceiling, invisible in the dark, and felt a soft lassitude come over her. She felt as if she were melting into the bed; as if she could not have moved if she tried.

Time flowed by and she waited for sleep. It was some time before she realized she was actually waiting for it. It didn't come. She turned on her side, and still it eluded her. Finally she snapped the light on to squint at her watch. It said five of four. She switched it off again, her eyes dazzled, and wondered what the matter was. And then she heard Beebo turn over in the next room, and she knew.

An old creeping need began to writhe in Laura, coming up suddenly out of the past and twisting itself around her innards. The pressure increased while she lay there trying to ignore it, becoming more insistent. It began to swell and fade with a rhythm of its own; a rhythm she knew too well and feared. Slowly the heat mounted to her face, the sweat came out on her body. She began to turn back and forth in bed, hating herself and trying to stop it, but helpless with it.

Laura was a sensual girl. Her whole being cried out for love and loving. It had been denied her for over a year and the effects were a severe strain on her that often brought her nerves to the breaking point. She pretended she had learned to live with it, or rather, without it. She even pretended she could live her whole life without it. But in her secret self she knew she couldn't.

Beebo turned over again in the living room and Laura knew she was awake, too. The sudden realization made her gasp, and she could fool herself no longer. She wanted Beebo. She wanted a woman; she wanted a woman so terribly that she had to put her hand tight over her mouth to stop the groan that would have issued from it.

For a few moments more she tossed feverishly on her bed, trying to find solitary release, but it wouldn't come. The thought of Beebo tortured her now, and not the thought of Marcie. Beebo – with her lithe body, her fascinating face, her cynical shell. There was so much of Beth there. At that thought, Laura found herself swinging her legs out of bed.

Moonlight glowed in two bright squares on the living room floor. Laura could see the couch, draped in blankets. She wondered whether Beebo had heard her and waited breathlessly for some sign. Nix lifted his head but made no sound, only watching her as she advanced across the room on her tiptoes, her white slip gleaming as she passed through the light.

Laura stood and hovered over the couch, uncertain what to do, her heart pounding hugely against her ribs, Beebo was on her side, turned toward Laura, apparently asleep. Nix was snuggled into the ditch between the back of Beebo and the back of the couch.

Beebo stirred slightly, but she didn't open her eyes. 'Beebo,' Laura whispered, dropping to her knees and supporting herself against the couch with her hands. 'Beebo?' she whispered again, a little louder. And then, sensing that Beebo had heard her she bent down and kissed her cheek, her hands reaching for her. Beebo was suddenly completely roused, coming up on her elbow and then falling back and pulling Laura with her.

'Laura?' she said huskily. 'Are you all right?' And then she felt Laura's lips on her face again and a shock of passion gripped her. 'Oh, God – Oh, baby,' she said, and her arms went around Laura hard.

'Hold me,' Laura begged, clinging to her, 'Oh, Beebo, hold me.'

Beebo rolled off the couch onto Laura and the abrupt weight of her body fired Laura into a frenzy. They rolled over each other on the floor, pressing each other tight, almost as if they wanted to fuse their bodies, and kissed each other wildly.

Laura felt such a wave of passion come up in her that it
almost smothered her. She thought she couldn't stand it. And
then she didn't think at all. She only clung to Beebo, half tearing
her pajamas off her back, groaning wordlessly, almost sobbing.
Her hands explored, caressed, felt Beebo all over, while her own
body responded with violent spasms – joyous, crazy, deep as her
soul. She could no more have prevented her response than she
could the tyrannic need that drove her to find it. She felt Beebo's
tongue slip into her mouth and Beebo's firm arms squeezing her
and she went half out of her mind with it. Her hands were in
Beebo's hair, tickling her ears, slipping down her back, over her
hips and thighs. Her body heaved against Beebo's in a lovely
mad duet. She felt like a column of fire, all heat and light,
impossibly sensual, impossibly sexual. She was all feeling, warm
and melting, strong and sweet.

It was a long time before either of them came to their senses.
They had fallen half asleep when it was over, still lying on the
floor, where Nix, after some trepidation, came to join them.
When Laura opened her eyes the gray dawn had replaced the
white moonlight. She was looking out the window at a mass of
telephone and electric wires. She gazed slowly downward until
she found Beebo's face. Beebo was awake, watching her – no
telling for how long. She smiled slightly, frowning at the same
time. But she didn't say anything and neither did Laura. They
only pulled closer together, until their lips touched. Beebo began
to kiss Laura over and over, little soft teasing kisses that kept
out of the way of passion, out of the way of Laura's own kisses
as they searched for Beebo's lips. Until it was suddenly imperative
that they kiss each other right. Laura tried feebly to stop it, but
she quickly surrendered. When Beebo relented a little it was
Laura who pulled her back, until Beebo was suddenly crazy for
her again.

'No, no, no, no,' Laura murmured, but she had asked for it. A
year and a half of abstinence was too much for her. At that
moment she was in bondage to her body. She gave in in spite of

herself, rolling over on Beebo, her fine hair falling over Beebo's breasts in a pale glimmering shower, soft and cool and bringing up the fire in Beebo again.

Once again they rested, half sleeping, turning now and then to feel each other, reassure themselves that the other was still there, still responsive. Now and then Beebo pushed Nix off Laura, or out from between them, where he was anxious to make himself a nest.

It was Saturday afternoon before they could drag themselves off the floor. It was Laura who pulled herself to her knees first by the aid of a handy chair, and squinted at the bright daylight. For a few moments she remained there, swaying slightly, trying to think straight and not succeeding. She felt Beebo's hand brush across her stomach and looked down at her. Beebo smiled a little.

An elusive feeling of shame slipped through Laura, disappeared, came back again, faded, came back. It seemed uncertain whether or not to stay. She swallowed experimentally, looking at Beebo. After a minute Beebo said, 'Who's Beth?'

'Beth?' Laura was startled.

'Um-hm. She the blonde?'

'No. That's Marcie.'

'Well, baby, seems to me like it's Beth you're after, not Marcie.'

Laura frowned at her. 'I haven't seen Beth for almost a year. She's married now. It's all over.'

'For her, maybe.'

'I won't discuss it,' she said haughtily, getting up and walking away from her, while Beebo lay on the floor admiring her body, her head propped comfortably on her hands. 'It happened long ago and I've forgotten it.'

'Then how come you called me Beth all night?'

Laura gasped, turning to look at her, and then her face went pink. 'I – I'm sorry, Beebo,' she said. 'I won't do it again.'

'Don't count on it.'

Laura stamped her foot. 'Damn you, Beebo!' she said. 'Don't talk to me as if I were an irresponsible child!'

Beebo laughed, rolling over and nearly crushing Nix, who reacted by licking her frantically and wagging his tail. Beebo squashed him in a hug, still laughing. Laura turned on her heel to leave the room, looking back quickly to grab her slip, and went into the bedroom, slamming the door. Within seconds it flew open again and Beebo leaned against the jamb, smiling at her. She sauntered into the room.

'Now, don't tell me you didn't enjoy yourself last night, Little Bo-peep,' she said.

Laura ignored her, moving speedily, suddenly embarrassed to be naked. In the heat of passion it was glorious, but in the morning, in the gray light, in the chill and ache of waking up, she hated it. Her own bare flesh seemed out of place. Not so with Beebo, who sprawled on the bed on top of the underwear Laura wanted to put on.

'Did you?' said Beebo. 'Enjoy yourself?'

'Get up, Beebo, I want to get dressed.'

'After all, it was your idea, baby.'

'Don't throw *that* in my face!' she exclaimed angrily, ashamed to remember it.

'Why not? It's true. Besides I'm not throwing it in your face, I'm just saying it.'

Laura turned away from her, unbearably conscious of her own slim behind, her dimpled rump, and her long limbs. She yearned to be shrouded in burlap. 'Beebo, I – I couldn't help myself last night.' She worked to control her voice, to be civilized about it. 'I needed – I mean – it had been so long.'

'Since Beth?'

Laura fought down a sudden impulse to strangle her. 'I was a fool,' she said, and her voice trembled. 'A fool with my room-mate and now with you. It got so I couldn't stand it at home. It got intolerable.'

'So you came down here. And I was a nice convenient safety valve.'

'I didn't mean that!' she flared.

'Doesn't matter what you mean, baby. It's a fact. Here you

were, desperate. And here was I, ready and willing. You knew I wouldn't turn you down.'

Laura's face began to burn. She had a wild idea that her back was blushing with her cheeks.

'What would you have done if I *had* turned you down, Laura?' Beebo spoke softly, insinuatingly, teasing Laura, enjoying herself.

But Laura was too humiliated to tease back. 'I don't know,' she exclaimed miserably. 'I don't know what I *could* have done.' And she covered her face with her hands.

'I'll tell you, then. You'd have begged me. You'd have gotten down on your knees and begged me. Sometime you will, too. Wait and see.'

Laura whirled toward her, insulted. 'That's enough!' she said harshly. She pulled her underthings forcibly from under Beebo, but Beebo caught the shoulder strap of her brassiere and hung on to it with both hands, her heels braced against the floor, laughing like a beautiful savage while Laura yanked furiously at it.

'You're going to get about half,' she said. 'If you're lucky. I'll get the other half. Half isn't going to hold much of you up, baby.'

Laura let go suddenly, and Beebo fell back on the bed, grinning at her.

'Laura hates me,' she said. 'Laura hates me.' She said it slowly, singsong, daring Laura to answer her.

Laura glared at her, defiant and fuming. 'You're an animal!' she hissed at her.

'Sure.' Beebo chuckled. 'Ask Jack. That's his favorite word. We're all animals.'

'You're nothing but a dirty animal!'

'What were you last night, Miss Prim? You were panting at me like a sow in rutting season.'

Laura's eyes went wide with fury. She grabbed the nearest thing – a hairbrush – and flung it violently at Beebo. Beebo ducked, laughing again at her young victim, and Laura turned and fled into the bathroom. She slammed the door so hard it bounced open and she had to shut it again. With frantic fingers she tried to turn the lock, but Beebo was already pushing on the other side. Laura heaved against it, but Beebo got it open and she fell back against the wall, suddenly frightened.

'Don't touch me!' she spat at her.

Beebo smiled. 'Why not? You didn't mind last night. I touched you all over. Did I miss anything?'

Laura shrank from her. 'Let me go, Beebo.'

'Let you go? I'm not even touching you.'

'I want to leave. I want to get out of here.' Laura tried to push past her but Beebo caught her, her strong hands pressing painfully into Laura's shoulders, and threw her back against the wall.

'You're not going anywhere, Bo-peep,' she said. And began to kiss her. Laura fought her, half sobbing, groaning, furious. Beebo's lips were all over her face, her throat, her breasts, and she took no notice of Laura's blows and her sharp nails. Laura grabbed handfuls of her hair, wanting to tear it out, but Beebo pulled her close, panting against her, her eyes hypnotically close to Laura's. And Laura felt her knees go weak.

'No,' she whispered. 'Oh, God no. Oh, Beebo.' Her hands caressed Beebo's hair, her lips parted beneath Beebo's. All the lonely months of denial burst like firecrackers between her legs. Once it had started her whole body begged for release. It betrayed her. She clung sweating and heaving to Beebo. They were both surprised at the strength and insistence of their feelings. They had felt the attraction from the first, but they had been unprepared for the crescendo of emotion that followed.

It was a long time before either of them heard the phone ringing. Finally Beebo stood up, looking down at Laura, watching her. Laura turned her face away, pulling her knees up and feeling the tears come. Beebo knelt beside her then, the hardness gone from her face.

'Don't cry, baby,' she said, and kissed her gently. 'Laura, don't cry. I know you don't want to make love to me, I know you *have* to. Damn that phone! It's not your fault. Laura, baby, you make beautiful love. God grant me a passionate girl like you just once in a while and I'll die happy.'

'Please don't touch me. Don't talk to me.' She was over-whelmed with shame.

'I have to. I can't help myself any more than you can. I had no idea you'd be like this – Jesus, so hot! You look so cool, so damn far above the rest of us. But you're not, poor baby. Better than some of us, maybe, but not above us.'

Laura turned her face to the wall. 'Answer the phone,' she said.

Beebo left her then and went into the living room. Laura could hear her voice when she answered.

'Hello?' she said. 'How are you, doll? Fine. Laura's fine. No, I didn't rape her. She raped me.' Laura sat straight up at this, her face flaming. Beebo was laughing. 'Tell her what? It's all fixed up? You mean I can send her home to Marcie?' Her voice became heavily sarcastic. 'Well, isn't that too sweet for words. Okay, Jack, I'll tell her. You what? ... With who? ... Oh, Terry! Yeah, I've seen him. You got a live one there, boy. Hang on to him, he's a doll ... Okay, don't mention it. It's been a pleasure. Most of it. She's lovely ... So long.'

When Beebo returned to the bathroom, Laura was standing at the washbowl, rinsing her face, trying to compose herself.

'What did he say?' she asked Beebo.

'It was Jack.'

'I heard.'

Beebo put her arms around Laura from behind, leaning a little against her, front to back, planting kisses in her hair while she talked. 'He says you're forgiven. He handed Marcie some psycho-logical hocus pocus about a neurosis. You are neurotic, love. As of now. As far as Marcie's concerned, you have attacks. She should have a few herself.'

'Don't be so sarcastic, Beebo. If you knew what I've been through – how scared I was –'

'Okay, no more sarcasm. For a few minutes at least. God,

you're pretty, Laura.' Like Jack, like Marcie, like many others, she realized it slowly. Laura's singular face fit no pattern. It had to be discovered. Laura herself had never discovered it. She didn't believe in it. She grew up convinced she was as plain as her father seemed to think, and when she looked into the mirror she didn't see her own reflection. She saw what she thought she looked like; a mask, a cliché left over from adolescence. It embarrassed her when people told her she was pretty.

'Don't flatter me,' she said sharply to Beebo. 'I hate it.'

Beebo shut her eyes and laughed in Laura's ear. 'You're nuts,' she said. 'You are *nuts*, Bo-peep.'

'I'm sane. And I'm plain. There's a poem for you. Now let me go.'

'There's no rush, baby.'

'There is. I want to get home.' She twisted away from Beebo, turning around to face her.

Beebo let her hands trail up the front of Laura. 'Home to Marcie?' she said, and let them drop suddenly. 'Okay. Go home. Go home, now that you can stand it for another couple of days. And when the pressure gets too great, come back down again. Come back to Beebo, your faithful safety valve.'

'You said you wouldn't be sarcastic.'

Beebo wheeled away, walking into the bedroom. 'What do you want me to do, sing songs? Write poems? Dance? Shall I congratulate you? Congratulations, Laura, you've finally found a way to beat the problem. Every time Marcie sexes you up, run down to Beebo's and let it off. Beebo'll fix you up. Lovely arrangement.'

She turned to Laura, her eyes narrowed. 'Laura gets loved up for free, Beebo gets a treat, and Marcie stays pure. Whatever happens, let's not dirty Marcie up. Let's not muss up that gorgeous blonde hair.'

'Don't talk about her!' Laura had followed her into the bedroom.

'Oh, don't get me wrong, Bo-peep. I'm not complaining. You're too good to me, you know. You give me your throw-away kisses. I get your cast-off passion. I'm your Salvation Army, doll, I get all the left-overs. Throw me a bone.' She was sitting on the edge of her rump on her dresser, legs crossed at the ankles, arms folded on her chest – a favorite stance with her.

Laura was suddenly ashamed of the way she had used Beebo. Beebo was hurt. And it was Laura's fault.

'Everything's my fault, Beebo,' she said. 'I'm sorry.' There was silence for a minute. Laura was acutely aware that 'I'm sorry' was no recompense for what she was doing to Beebo.

Beebo smiled wryly. 'Thanks,' she said.

'I am, Beebo. Really. I didn't come to you last night just because of Marcie.' It was suffocatingly hard to talk. She spoke in fits and starts as her nerve came and left her.

'No?' Beebo remained motionless with a 'tell-me-another' look on her face.

'No. I came – I came because –' She covered her face with her hands, stuck for words and ashamed.

'You came, baby. That's enough,' Beebo finished for her, relenting a little. 'You came and I'm not sorry. Neither are you, not really. The situation isn't perfect.' She laughed. 'But last night was perfect. It isn't like that very often, I can tell you.'

Laura looked at her again. Then she moved toward her clothes, afraid to stay naked any longer, afraid the whole thing would start over again.

Beebo came toward her, pulling the slip from her hand and dropping it on the floor. 'There's no hurry,' she said.

'I'm going, Beebo. Don't try to stop me.'

For a moment Beebo didn't answer. Then she scooped up some of Laura's clothes on her foot and flung them at her. 'Okay, baby,' she said. 'But next time, you don't get off so easily. Clear?'

'There won't be a next time.' Laura concentrated on dressing, on getting her body covered as quickly as possible. 'I'm grateful to you, but I'll never do it again. It isn't fair, not to you.'

Beebo laughed disagreeably. 'Don't worry about being fair to *me*, baby. It didn't bother you last night.'

'I couldn't think last night! You know that.'

'Yes. I know that. I'm glad. I hope I drive you out of your mind.' Beebo's eyes bored into her and made her rush and stumble. She was afraid to confront her, and when she had her clothes on she caught her jacket up with one hand and headed for the door without looking back.

Nix pranced after her. Before she got the front door open, Beebo caught her and turned her around. 'Goodby, Beebo,' she said stiffly.

Beebo smiled, upsetting Laura with her nude closeness. 'You'll be back, Little Bo-peep. You know that, don't you.' It was a statement, not a question.

I'll never come back, she told herself. *I'll never open this door again.*

And, confident that she meant what she said, she turned and walked away.

MONIQUE WITTIG

LES GUÉRILLÈRES

(extract)

(1969)
Translated by David Le Vay

GOLDEN SPACES LACUNAE
THE GREEN DESERTS ARE SEEN
THEY DREAM AND SPEAK OF THEM
THE IMMOBILE BIRDS OF JET
THE WEAPONS PILED IN THE SUN
THE SOUND OF THE SINGING VOICES
THE DEAD WOMEN THE DEAD WOMEN

CONSPIRACIES REVOLUTIONS
FERVOUR FOR THE STRUGGLE
INTENSE HEAT DEATH AND HAPPINESS
IN THE BREASTED TORSOS
THE PHOENIXES THE PHOENIXES
FREE CELIBATE GOLDEN
THEIR OUTSPREAD WINGS ARE HEARD

THE BIRDS THE SWIMMING SIRENS
THE TRANSLUCENT SPANS THE WINGS
THE GREEN SUNS THE GREEN SUNS
THE VIOLET FLAT GRASSLANDS
THE CRIES THE LAUGHS THE MOVEMENTS
THE WOMEN AFFIRM IN TRIUMPH THAT
ALL ACTION IS OVERTHROW

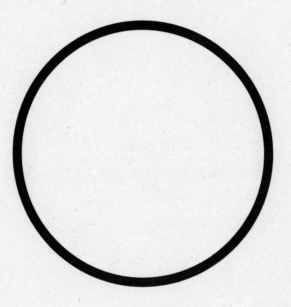

When it rains the women stay in the summer-house. They hear the water beating on the tiles and streaming down the slopes of the roof. Fringes of rain surround the summer-house, the water that runs down at its angles flows more strongly, it is as if springs hollow out the pebbles at the places where it reaches the ground. At last someone says it is like the sound of micturition, that she cannot wait any longer, and squats down. Then some of them form a circle around her to watch the labia expel the urine.

The women frighten each other by hiding behind the trees. One or other of them asks for grace. Then they chase each other in the darkness, ill-wishing the one who is caught. Or else they search gropingly, scenting the one whose perfume is to be honoured. Amomum aniseed betel cinnamon cubeb mint liquorice musk ginger clove nutmeg pepper saffron sage vanilla receive homage in turn. Then the wearers of these perfumes are chased in the dark as in blindman's-buff. Cries laughter sounds of falling are heard.

In dull weather the women may shed hot tears, saying that in the sunshine the roofs of the houses and the walls are of quite another colour. Mist spreads over the water over the fields about the houses. It penetrates through closed windows. Someone arrives to visit the house. She cannot see it. The huge paintings in vivid colours disappear behind orange vapours. Then she slumps to the ground demanding to be entertained. They tell her in great detail the story of the woman who, speaking of her vulva, used to say that thanks to that compass she could navigate from sunrise to sunset.

Some of the women swim letting themselves drift toward the last splashes of sunlight on the sea. At the most luminous spot when, dazzled, they try to move away, they say that they are assailed by an unbearable stench. Later they are seized with vomiting. Then they begin to moan as they strain their arms, swimming as fast as they can. At a certain point they collide

with the floating decaying carcase of an ass, at times the swell of
the sea reveals sticky shapeless gleaming lumps of indescribable
colour. They say that they shouted with all their might, shedding
many tears, complaining that no sea-breeze got up to drive away
the smell, supporting under the arms and groins one of them
who has fainted, while the vomit accumulates around them on
the surface of the water.

If anyone walks on the hillside she can hardly remain upright.
Through the hedges white colchicum and violets or pink-capped
mushrooms can be seen. The grass is not tall. Heifers stand in it,
in great number. The houses have been shuttered since the
autumn rains began. There are no little girls playing in the
gardens. There are no flowers in the flower-beds. A few toys lie
about, a painted wooden hoop a red and blue olisbos a white
balloon a lead rifle.

The women visit the market to obtain provisions. They pass by
the stalls of fruit vegetables bottles of pink blue red green glass.
There are piles of orange oranges ochre pineapples mandarines
walnuts green and pink mangos blue nectarines green and pink
peaches orange-yellow apricots. There are melons water-melons
paw-paws avocados green almonds medlars. There are cucumbers
aubergines cabbages asparagus white cassava red pimentos
gourds. Wasps coming and going settle on the bare arms of the
young women selling them.

The huntresses have dark maroon hats, and dogs. Hearing the
rifle-shots, Dominique Aron says that the bird is still flying, the
hare still running, the boar the deer the fox the wart-hog still
afoot. It is possible to keep a watch on the surroundings. If
some troop advances up the road raising a cloud of dust the
women watch its approach shouting to those within for the
windows to be closed and the rifles kept behind the windows.
Anne Damien plays, Sister Anne do you see anything coming, I
see only the grass growing green and the dusty road.

*

At evening a horse harnessed to a cart goes by. The cart carries a heap of cut beetroots or potatoes or grass for fodder. Long before and long after it passes the sound of the hooves striking the tarred road can be heard. The horse on its way is not being driven by anyone.

THAT WHICH IDENTIFIES THEM LIKE
THE EYE OF THE CYCLOPS,
THEIR SINGLE FORENAME,
OSEA BALKIS SARA NICEA
IOLA CORA SABINA DANIELA
GALSWINTHA EDNA JOSEPHA

Somewhere there is a siren. Her green body is covered with scales. Her face is bare. The undersides of her arms are a rosy colour. Sometimes she begins to sing. The women say that of her song nothing is to be heard but a continuous O. That is why this song evokes for them, like everything that recalls the O, the zero or the circle, the vulval ring.

By the lakeside there is an echo. As they stand there with an open book the chosen passages are re-uttered from the other side by a voice that becomes distant and repeats itself. Lucie Maure cries to the double echo the phrase of Phénarète, I say that that which is is. I say that that which is not also is. When she repeats the phrase several times the double, then triple, voice endlessly superimposes that which is and that which is not. The shadows brooding over the lake shift and begin to shiver because of the vibrations of the voice.

The women are seen to have in their hands small books which they say are feminaries. These are either multiple copies of the same original or else there are several kinds. In one of them someone has written an inscription which they whisper in each other's ears and which provokes them to full-throated laughter. When it is leafed through the feminary presents numerous blank pages in which they write from time to time. Essentially, it consists of pages with words printed in a varying number of capital letters. There may be only one or the pages may be full of them. Usually they are isolated at the centre of the page, well spaced black on a white background or else white on a black background.

After the sun has risen they anoint their bodies with oil of sandalwood curcuma gardenia. They steady one foot on a tree-trunk. Their hands rub each leg in turn, the skin glistening. Some of them are lying down. Others massage them with their fingertips. The bare bodies gleam in the strong morning light. One of their flanks is iridescent with a golden lustre. The rising sun does likewise when it sends its rays slanting across the erect rounded tree-trunks. The arcs of the circles so touched reflect a little of the light, their outlines are blurred.

There are peat-bogs above the hills. The mud they are made of has the colour of henna. They seethe, there are surface explosions, bubbles. A stick stirred around within them is caught by viscous soft bodies. It is not possible to fish these out. As soon as any pressure is exerted on them they slip away, they escape. The women say that at times the bursting of the bubbles is accompanied by groans murmurs. The sun dries up the bogs. The vapour that ascends then has a nauseating odour.

The gipsy women have a mummified corpse which they bring out when it is not raining, because of the smell of the body which is not quite dry. They expose it to the sun in its box. The dead woman is clothed in a long tunic of green velvet, covered with white embroidery and gilded ornaments. They have hung little bells on her neck, on her sleeves. They have put medallions in her hair. When they take hold of the box to bring it out the dead woman begins to tinkle everywhere. Every now and then someone goes out on to the three steps that lead up to the caravan to look at the clouds. When the sky is obscured two of them set about shutting the lid of the box and carrying it inside.

FLORA ZITA SAVA CORNELIA
DRAUPADI JULIENNE ETMEL
CHLOË DESDEMONA RAPHAELA
IRIS VERA ARSINOË LISA
BRENDA ORPHISE HERODIAS
BERENICE SIGRID ANDOVERA

The little girls search in the bushes and trees for the nests of goldfinches chaffinches linnets. They find some green canaries which they cover with kisses, which they hug to their breasts. They run singing, they bound over the rocks. A hundred thousand of them return to their houses to cherish their birds. In their haste they clasped them too tightly to themselves. They ran. They bent down to pick up pebbles which they cast far away over the hedges. They took no heed of their chirping. They climbed straight up to their rooms. They removed the birds from their garments, they found them lifeless, heads drooping. Then they all tried to revive them by pressing them to their mouths, letting their warm breath fall on them, lifting the limp heads, touching their beaks with a finger. They remained inert. Then a hundred thousand little girls bewailed the death of their green canaries in the hundred thousand rooms of the hundred thousand houses.

Whatever the time appointed to begin the work, they must hurry to get finished before sunset. The bottoms of the ladders are visible placed on the ground, the tops are hidden in the jumble of fruit and foliage. The baskets at the foot of the trees are filled at times to overflowing. There are *belles de Choisy* English cherries morellos marascas Montmorency cherries *bigaudelles* white-hearts. They are black white red translucent. Wasps hornets are busy around the baskets. Their buzzing can be heard in whatever part of the meadow one happens to be. The women climb into the trees, they descend arms laden with fruit. Some have baskets hooked to their belt. Some stand still at different heights on the rungs. Others move about among the branches. One sees them jump to the ground and get rid of their burden. The slanting rays of the sun glance over the leaves making them glitter. The sky is orange-coloured.

The women say that they expose their genitals so that the sun may be reflected therein as in a mirror. They say that they retain its brilliance. They say that the pubic hair is like a spider's web that captures the rays. They are seen running with great strides. They are all illuminated at their centre, starting from the pubes the hooded clitorides the folded double labia. The glare they shed when they stand still and turn to face one makes the eye turn elsewhere unable to stand the sight.

When the moon is full the drum is sounded on the main square. Trestle tables are erected. Glasses of every colour are put out and bottles containing differently coloured liquids. Some of these liquids are green red blue, they evaporate if they are not used as soon as the cork that seals them has been drawn. Everyone may drink until she falls dead-drunk or until she has lost her self-control. The odour of the drugs which have been allowed to escape from the bottles stagnates on the square, sickeningly sweet. Everyone drinks in silence standing or lying down on carpets unrolled in the street. Then they have the little girls brought out. They are seen standing half asleep bewildered hesitant. They are invited to try their strength on the whimpering outstretched bodies. The children go from one to the other trying to wake them up, using stones buckets of water, shouting with all their might, squatting down to be at the level of the ears of the sleeping women.

Marthe Vivonne and Valerie Céru make a report. They say that the river is rising up between its banks. The fields of flowers by its banks are swept away by the waters. Avulsed corollas, upside down, eddy capsized in the current. All along the river there is an odour of putrescence. A noise like that of a broken flood-gate is heard. Overturned boats drift by. Whole trees are carried away, their fruit-laden branches trailing in the water. Marthe Vivonne and Valerie Céru say they have not seen any corpses of animals. They say that for a long while on the way back they heard the rushing of the river, the shock of the current against its bed.

AIMEE POMA BARBA
BENEDICTA SUSANNA
CASSANDRA OSMONDA
GENE HERMINIA KIKA
AURELIA EVANGELINE
SIMONA MAXIMILIANA

The excursions with the glenuri on their leashes are not without difficulty. Their long filiform bodies are supported on thousands of feet. They constantly endeavour to move away to some place other than where they are. Their innumerable eyes are grouped round an enormous orifice that serves them as a mouth as well as taking the place of a head. It is filled by a soft extensile membrane that can become taut or relaxed, each of its movements producing a different sound. The harmony of the glenuri may be compared to fifes drums the croaking of toads the miaowing of rutting cats the sharp sound of a flute. The excursions with the glenuri are constantly being interrupted. This is because they systematically insinuate themselves into any interstice that affords passage to their bodies, for example the gates of public gardens, the grills of drains. They enter these backwards, they are stopped at a given moment by the size of their heads, they find themselves trapped, they begin to utter frightful shrieks. Then they have to be freed.

The women say that in the feminary the glans of the clitoris and the body of the clitoris are described as hooded. It is stated that the prepuce at the base of the glans can travel the length of the organ exciting a keen sensation of pleasure. They say that the clitoris is an erectile organ. It is stated that it bifurcates to right and left, that it is angled, extending as two erectile bodies applied to the pubic bones. These two bodies are not visible. The whole constitutes an intensely erogenous zone that excites the entire genital, making it an organ impatient for pleasure. They compare it to mercury also called quicksilver because of its readiness to expand, to spread, to change shape.

Daniela Nervi, while digging foundations, has unearthed a painting representing a young girl. She is all flat and white lying on one side. She has no clothes. Her breasts are barely visible on her torso. One of her legs, crossed over the other, raises her thigh, so concealing the pubis and vulva. Her long hair hides part of her shoulders. She is smiling. Her eyes are closed. She half leans on one elbow. The other arm is crooked over her head, the hand holding a bunch of black grapes to her mouth. The women laugh at this. They say that Daniela Nervi has not yet dug up the knife without a blade that lacks a handle.

Martha Ephore has made all the calculations. The engineers were mistaken. Or else the water arriving from the mountain slopes is insufficient to feed the lake beyond the barrage, even in time of spate. Or else they have been at fault over the position of the construction which they have sited too far upstream in relation to the junction of the water-courses. Every morning the engineers arrive at the dam which they patrol in all directions, marking the still fresh cement with the imprint of their feet, so that after they leave a team of masons have to busy themselves getting rid of them. Some of the women run with umbrellas held high, giving orders. Others walk about calm. By the shore of the lake or what ought to be the lake young girls in bermudas stroll about holding each other by the hand.

The women say that the goddess Eristikos has a pin head and yellow eyes. They say that the goddess Eristikos adores perfumes. In her honour they wear next the skin garments made of fragrant herbs. They set them on fire at nightfall by putting a light to each sprig. They are grouped in circles, their garments are incandescent in the darkness. They stand motionless, arms extended on either side of their bodies. The burning herbs crackle and give off an odour. Smoke clouds disperse. When the heat reaches the skin they savagely tear off their tunics and cast them in a heap. That is why they must continually manufacture new ones.

CALYPSO JUDITH ANNE
ISEULT KRISTA ROBERTA
VLASTA CLEONICE RENEE
MARIA BEATRICE REINA
IDOMENEA GUILHERMINA
ARMIDE ZENOBIA LESSIA

There exists a machine to record divergences. It is placed on an agate plinth. This is a parallelepipedon of low stature, at the centre of a meadow studded with daisies in spring, marguerites in summer, white and blue saffron in the autumn. The calculations taking place within the machine are continuously registered as clicks clicking high-pitched sounds as of tinkling bells, noises like those of a cash-register. There are lights that go out and come on at irregular intervals of time. They are red orange blue. The apertures through which they shine are circular. Every divergence is ceaselessly recorded in the machine. They are scaled to the same unit whatever their nature. The position in the field of the machine for recording divergences resembles that of a certain fountain guarded by young girls bearing flaming swords. But the machine is not guarded. It is easy of access.

The women recall the story of the one who lived for a long time where the camels pass. Bareheaded beneath the sun, Clemence Maïeul incessantly invokes Amaterasu the sun goddess, cutting her abundant hair, abasing herself three times on the ground which she strikes with her hands, saying, I salute you, great Amaterasu, in the name of our mother, in the name of those who are to come. Our kingdom come. May this order be destroyed. May the good and the evil be cast down. They say that Clemence Maïeul often drew on the ground that O which is the sign of the goddess, symbol of the vulval ring.

The women say that any one of them might equally well invoke another sun goddess, such as Cihuacoatl, who is also a goddess of war. Thus on the occasion of the death of one of their number they might use the song of mourning which is a glorious song. Then they sing in unison, Strong and warlike daughter, my well-beloved daughter/valiant and tender little dove, my lady/you have striven and worked as a valiant daughter/you have overcome, you have acted like your mother the lady Cihuacoatl/you have fought with valour, you have used shield and sword/arise my daughter/go to that good place which is the house of your mother the sun/where all are filled with joy content and happiness.

The women leap on the paths that lead to the village, shaking their hair, their arms laden with dog-faced baboons, stamping the ground with their feet. Someone stops, tears out a handful of her long hair and lets the strands go one by one with the wind. Like the balloons that little girls release on holidays, rising into the sky, light unsubstantial filiform and twisting, they are blown upward by the wind. Or perhaps the women sing in unison a song that includes these words, Who till now sucked at my nipple/a monkey. Then they throw down all the baboons and begin to run, chasing them into the shade of the wood until they have disappeared in the trees.

They say, how to decide that an event is worthy of remembrance? Must Amaterasu herself advance on the forecourt of the temple, her face shining, blinding the eyes of those who, prostrate, put their foreheads to the ground and dare not lift their heads? Must Amaterasu raising her circular mirror on high blaze forth with all her fires? Must the ray from her slanting mirror set fire to the ground beneath the feet of the women who have come to pay homage to the sun goddess, the greatest of the goddesses? Must her anger be exemplary?

IDO BLANCHE VALENTINA
GILBERTA FAUSTA MONIMA
GE BAUCIS SOPHIE ALICE
OCTAVIA JOSIANA GAIA
DEODATA KAHA VILAINE
ANGE FREDERICA BETJE

NICOLE BROSSARD

THE **S**E **S**OUR **S**MOTHERS

OR: THE DISINTEGRATING CHAPTER

(1977)

Translated by Barbara Godard

and the mother contracts at a distance . . .
HUGUETTE GAULIN

It's combat. The book. Fiction begins suspended mobile between words and the body's likeness to this *our* devouring and devoured mother

184

Fictive theory: words were used only in the ultimate embrace. The first word lips and sticky saliva on her breasts. Theory begins there when the breast or the child moves away. Strategic wound or suspended meaning.

I killed the womb. *My* life in summer the moon. *My* death. Thirty years separate me from life, thirty from death. My mother, my daughter. Mamma, Mam*elle*, Mamilla, a single life, mine. Clandestine system of reproduction. Anonymous matrix and matter.

the same day. One black sex, one white sex. One I caress, the other I wash. Cyprine juices, urine. Orgasm and labour as two sides of the same entity. Your bodies, lesbian lover and daughter. I write so I won't engulf and hurt your bodies and so as to find in them my void, my centre.

War measures. Interned by the matrix. The body of . . . like a missing link, found again in the water. Their industry of fantasies made her lose her sense of reality. The body of . . . rots. He retrieves the phantasm for his own ends. Recycled body.

another day. The alphabet. In the beginning. Desire brings me endlessly back to it and, my present . . . forward flight. What happens to a woman who recognizes this process and encounters its inexorability in fact, in age and in *his*tory, in body.

Each whirlpool had one facet. Each flake its geometry. One figure mine, one other, also different from you, another woman. Unspoken. Three-faced incest that refuses the lie yet whose eye nonetheless keeps all traces of it. The origin of Ah! From the depths of the throat. Chaos, our limbs afire. Maybe to burn out the fuse before the letter. To set our breasts ablaze. Sour milk. And the mamilla dyed green as in science fiction. Because the trial has begun. At last two generations of women have touched each other on the mouth and the sex and found their target. Each whirlpool with a different woman, because I had to go into black, water, blue and drown the acidity of white.

Cramp clutching the belly and clutching a male who cannot go in. Now none may enter the laboratory unless he is transformable. I have killed the womb and exploded the S^{ea}_{our} mother. Below the horizon in there alchemy, a prose of negotiation, is practised. As though to proliferate cells of desire when fascination ferments its violence. Great voracious fiction.

My mother is drinking her beer. I don't know what she expects from me. What could I expect from her, if not from myself. The sisterhood of women is the ultimate test of human solidarity laying itself open to another beginning of delusions of grandeur.

My mother is drinking her beer. She is writing while I wait for her to give me a cookie.

It's between her legs, sliding always a little more painfully for her, for me. A spurt of white. Panic. Between life and death. Blue funk.

she has breasts, pubic hair. Me pink. Her body, her texture makes my blood turn. She whispers. Her daughter-mother's lips. Shifty weather makes us die between two waters. A big white monkey puts his arms about her. I have split her soul in two: girl's sex. Humanity passes over us like a (c)rushing roller. Big neurotic primate. Gross anal. His-tory.

With a different woman, when we used to drink a lot, we didn't make love. We used to write, sitting facing each other. State of emergency. Don't let the battle break out between our bodies. Let the connection happen somewhere else. So that our bodies won't be mutilated immediately by the clasp of hands, by the warm embrace. No longer impressing each other mutually. Anarchy of the couple. Narrative cut around a/s motherly dependence. System of exchange and very precise code. We can support only one body at a time. Each her own. Let's make it clear.

there is always one body too many in one's life. Each mother. Each child. The same body.

If it weren't lesbian, this text would make no sense at all. Matrix, matter and production, all at once. In relation to. It constitutes the only plausible system to get me out of the belly of my patriarchal mother. And of distancing my eye from her enough so as to see her in a different way, not fragmented into her metaphoric parts. Crossing through the symbol while I am writing. An exercise in deconditioning that leads me to acknowledge my own legitimacy. The means by which every woman tries to exist: to be illegitimate no more.

Legality for a woman: not to be born from the womb of woman. That is what ruins them both. The womb of the species. Which is reproduced from generation to generation. Bitch and bastard. Equally illegitimate. Just look at the base of the cliff. The bloody sheet or the madwoman confronting the husband-psychiatrist couple who are putting their seals on her.

Between my mother and my daughter. Lesbian rather than incestuous text. Incest as an unconscious mode for the appropriation of the daughter-female by the father-male: an apt screen for justifying de-$^{\text{feat}}_{facto}$ rape. Mother-son incest propounding symbolic not factual castration. Symbol and carnal matter couple here like systems where the daughter-woman is already expiating the possible birth of a new being. To submit to the father (in body) or in representation (brother, lover, husband) brings every woman back to her illegitimacy. Her big belly. No waist, no stature, daughter.

And act$^{\text{ually}}_{\text{ed upon}}$ however, if she wants to survive, a woman must assert herself in reality and become recognized as symbolic mother: incestuous in power but inaccessible sexually for reproduction. She then completely fills the space of desire and so can appropriate for herself the work of the other. Strategic inversion: this symbolic woman-mother has lost her womb. But preserves the hues and stripes of her sex. Second mother, she can only be the cruel stepmother. Strong but entrenched within a patriarchy.

Every thirty years a girl is born. Nobody knows whether she will kill the womb and thus become the first and last legitimate woman. So putting an end to His-tory. To fiction: *putting out the last fantasy about women in heat and about beautiful schizophrenics laying the discrete charms of steel along their wrists.*

Inside the matter of her womb. Lotus head. Inverted image, I burn its eyes. Time at the heart of language, maternal cell. At intervals, there's vibration. I am captivated from within, this body. From which I break out. Neither pyramid, nor castle, nor skyscraper. This body has the gender of its brain: feminine as in the beginning.

Nothing in the motion of her hand on her hair can be conquered except my beautiful eye, unstitched like a button, which looks at her. Hanging on her breast.

Into what can she want to initiate me. Patriarchal mothers able only to initiate their daughters to a man. There is no confidence between us. Sold-out, at a loss. Split in two, multiplied, in the gaze a crystalline lens unsure of the closeness or remoteness of others. To write about it would be a woman's eye resting on others, on things. To create her own locus of desire. To find her own place at a distance. So as not to wither up under each caress. So as not to knock the caress away.

She who is writing in the present between barbed wires remembers her past. Maybe they've been forced to cut *the current*. She goes through.

I open her mouth with my thumb and index finger. The struggle begins in silence. The search. I part her lips: 'monster's chops' or 'angel's lips'. I have to see for my own ends. She lets me do it, I don't threaten any part of her true identity yet. She's my m ther, she knows it and I am supposed to know it just as well. Her mouth like an essential and vital egg, ambiguous. In the beginning. AAAAA. My thumb masters the lower jaw. Her breath is in my eyes. To know all about her breath. About the food she feeds herself. My m ther drinks her beer. Swallows. I have my index finger on her gum as if to give her an order. But it's only an image. She bares her teeth. Invades me with her laugh. For an initial act: the transfer of powers. Clipped words that I must pass through in order to conquer the flowing words that fecundated her through the ear. Sharp words, full of gaps, about my m ther that I work on as if I were arming myself. She drinks her beer. Amazon. Her identity is not single. The power she confers on my thumb is very different; more than just going into my mouth as a surrogate. If I suck it must be my whole body. And open her mouth for her. Speak to me. 'No. Mummy is near, she's writing, my lu llay.'

The relationship with this woman is biological, material. Hand to hand. Body against body. Nourishment. She could have pulled me back by the digestive tube and swallowed her child out of murderous hunger. Cannibalism of survival. Materialism. But she could not. Materialism is only reached by the symbolic route. I haven't yet become her *child*. She is not yet my *mother*. Not a word separates us. Several years later I'll call her my mother. I've lost *Mommy*. That could become a book.

Every morning I am called Mommy. I get up. I kiss her and I get her breakfast ready. We separate for the day. Because I have to write this book. As if to rid ourselves of a symbolic relationship or to begin to execute it: daughter-mother lesbians. But we still haven't got our mutual autonomy. Her way is littered with objects she cannot reach. I open the refrigerator door. I open the drawers. I cook the food. My time is fragmented by these same objects. I am stuck to matter. Things are what I touch. I can neither dream them nor estimate their exchange value. Just like me, things are useful to keep me as well as the child alive. 'I polish them unceasingly like fine bones'.*

* Translator's note: Anne Hébert, 'The Thin Girl', trans. by Alan Brown.

The only product a mother can use as a medium of exchange is her child. Her only enterprise: 50% of the primary matter (ovum), gestation (the uterus as tool, instrument), production (giving birth), marketing (her labouring strength: arms, legs, bearing down). But she cannot exchange her product. Entering the economic system as subject, she must also pass into the symbolic system as subject. Stuck in matter and to her child, she has no access to it whatsoever. Stammer. Stutter. Mmmme mess.

Prostitute, she would have found takers and profit. Finished product (her body) which she offers in a very exacting code of exchange. It's the whole factory she sells. The joint. Real estate. She really can't be *apprehended*. She knows how to *make herself useful* in the symbolic domain, neighbouring, bordering. Which touches her.

In appropriating for himself the entire symbolic domain, that is to say a vision, man has made sure of his control by laying hands on all the modes of energetic production of the female body (brain, uterus, vagina, arms, legs, mouth, tongue). In so far as woman's body is fragmented, woman cannot broach the global vision of man.

<u>I have murdered the womb and I am writing it.</u>

Of all women, the mother (and ideally for the whole of patriarchal society, thus for all women) is the one who earns no profit *in actual fact*. Defeated. Each woman can profit only to the extent that she becomes symbolic mother. That is when she stopped bearing children. The milk sours. Mona Lisa smiles.

I write my daughter is sick. Fever. High. Anxiety: I have killed the womb. Caught in the whirlpool, the wave, the dread, the pallor, I write. What if I didn't stop for hours. Bodies die. Feverish.

light out: grey like a brain in the room. She and I are drinking our beer. She has just dyed her hair. Black. Would madness be as radical as tightening around us, I write my love.

. . .

you whistle in the kitchen. I hear the water moving around your hands and over your black blouse you are washing and my pink brassière.

. . .

A Sunday morning listening to Edith Piaf. All three of us dance. I am in their arms. We whisper sounds to each other in our ears and on our mouths. We dance very close together. Pressedhard. Nobody here wants to be lost. Matter and words. The moment but also because we are speaking. Carnal interrogatives. Imperatives like shoulders in the tango. Mommy is there, stranger like a different woman, close like a beginning. I am trying to make us afraid of nothing, not them, nor me, nor her.

My mother by abstention, write so I abstain from you. The fever has dropped.

It is while caressing the body of another woman over its entire living surface that she kills the mother, that the identical woman is born. A ghost who gives her vision, which version?

It is not the mother's body which decays but that of every woman who has not found words to look at the bruised womb: the body of the mother as extended fiction. Matter. Our mother's bodies displaced, inverted as if the womb were to be found in place of the brain. Domesticated symbol. Entering the heart of the subject matter properly speaking, become materialist, in other words, to prepare one's capital on the maternal tomb. Ideological dead-end: word for word to escape the hand to hand, body against body. The biological mother isn't killed without a simultaneous explosion of fiction, ideology, utterance.

The dead mother laid out like a theoretical cloud above the mad eyes of Einstein's mother. (*Mère*) She covering (*mer*) sea like a perfect synthesis. Neo-realism.

Base of operations bankrupt: she can build a base on no one, she is her own safety device. But sabotaged by the words of smother, bitter death. Unacceptable. The only thing admissible is the labouring body of the daughter-mother. Since to go back up the current leads to the primal symmetry of the womb, that long blue line which on the body of the daughter-mother stretches out already like an ideological current – you shall bear children in pain – you shall give birth quite naturally. Every distinction which already takes away her body and her senses (the very expression on her face) by force of words keeps her at the other end, exiled, brought forth from him, aborted like a woman. He took possession of the child as of a word in the dictionary.

Her mother's daughter. A finger between my two lips close, as they say, as the bark and the tree, bringing about the ellipsis daughter-mother which makes the passing from one to the other without intermediary without interruption. Couple and generation at one and the same time. Instantaneity. Of death in its process. Blossoming: new cortex.

Before withdrawing. His-tory. She can only explode it, its passions, its parallels, its parameters. Bulging her belly one last time. For a girl.

To pass from one to the other. Which in itself eliminates all reproduction for the benefit of a single being. 'God is dead', the women pass from one to another through the very eye of the needle preparing the resistance. The final assault on the womb. Mutation. Uterus stitched up. 'Mother died today.'*

To experience bliss in the ultimate intercourse like two signifiers and metamorphose so mutually that they contain a single meaning, these women succeed in doing it.

In this region initiation between their mother's thighs makes sense to the daughters. Definite, these girls know then how to perform their own rite. They officiate. Blue words in the eyes. Nobody will infiltrate them, advance on them. Symbolic mothers, they have begun to spread. Nylon in hand. Since breasts will no longer smother anybody.

* Translator's note: Albert Camus, *The Outsider*, trans. Stuart Gilbert.

I am sitting on a bench in the park. My daughter is playing in the sand, right beside us. The other mothers who, we look at their children patiently. We don't speak a word to each other: what is there to exchange? A child. We could not do it. In silence we watch them disappear in the white bubble, the tear. At the sound of their cries. Fiction about us mothers, like great ostriches taking out little cookies and Kleenex so that the children will stop burrowing in the sand to get away from us.

Here is the clan of patriarchal mothers. Devoted to men. Raising their young. Who have nothing to say. To exchange a domestic silence. Enclosed.

Placed one after the other in contradiction. My daughter is playing in the sand, right beside us. The other mothers. The silence here is unbearable. Everything gravitates about a senseless grammar. I killed the womb too soon, alone and primitive in a park with for my entire vision, between a child's legs, brushing against the smooth flesh, the inaccuracy ageless, deliberate steps, the trampled grass.

All this time that she remains in the story, in his-tory, she can earn her living only by disturbing the symbolic field. Modifying the first clause, the instrument of reproduction, her only tool. The dissolution of forms, like an end of the world played on the stage of the flat belly. Her uterus set beside her like a backpack. That presupposes a reorganization of her whole body, her means of moving about. She has room to pass in front of the mirror. A space to reflect her living body on the gleaming ribs of the man, who . . . /she is silhouetted, potential touching two hemispheres at once like a callous body. Maternal matrix and materialist. She reorganizes her material: private and political life. An equation of life.

In peace time, in war time, she resorts to words.

About a woman's sex. Mythically covered by. Escorted away. 'There was an evening, there was a morning.' A story stretched out in the grass. Infernal coitus. Without mask, nor mask, without genitals, nor genitals, without woman, nor woman, nor words. Who could have withstood this stream of glowing embers around the anus, around the mouth. Like two cancerous deaths. Two theatres of men. The mother silhouetted between them. Writing. Embossed. Beside her posed like a girl, a woman.

To work myself into the grave over a body, to expiate all the symbols one by one, violence, like the stake, the witches, one by one. To have done with expiation. Inner torture. Madness. Among women we could liquidate madness, its fiction how it fascinates me, this power to excite me just like with another woman, there must be, this liquid in my spinal cord, an identity.

Like a large mark of tenacious lips on the clitoris, it moves, this historical orgasm, this one about the meeting of forces. Excitation through violence. Phantasm of the oppos-ite sex. The species, from murdered bodies.

a long time lo(u)nging our bodies two-gether to pass under cover of night. Mad and incompatible like two aborted heterosexuals who cannot penetrate each other. The scar must form. I put my mouth with your sex. Inner saliva. Eat and think as though there were no end.

The bodies of mothers entwined, in reality, it is also mine uneasy and enraptured by this heredity which takes shape inside the water drop, seaweed brushing eyelash. My form is no longer intact entwined with her body, but like a structure adorned for sexual bliss. Publicly fiction, publicly escapades, frescoes, multiple in the prism, the daughter-mothers cavalierly public and fantastic stretching out their arms like sexual intercessions in the political pages of the daily paper. The bodies of mothers entwined, in reality, is a truly beautiful expression.

JAYNE ANNE PHILLIPS
BLIND GIRLS, ACCIDENTS, SWIMMING

(1976 and 1979)

Blind Girls

She knew it was only boys in the field, come to watch them
drunk on first wine. A radio in the little shack poured out
promises of black love and lips. Jesse watched Sally paint her
hair with grenadine, dotting the sticky syrup on her arms. The
party was in a shack down the hill from her house, beside a field
of tall grass where black snakes lay like flat belts. The Ripple
bottles were empty and Jess told pornographic stories about
various adults while everyone laughed; about Miss Hicks the
home-ec teacher whose hands were dimpled and moist and
always touching them. It got darker and the stories got scarier.
Finally she told their favorite, the one about the girl and her
boyfriend parked on a country road. On a night like this with
the wind blowing and then rain, the whole sky sobbing potato
juice. Please let's leave, pleads girlie, It sounds like something
scratching at the car. For God's sake, grumbles boyfriend, and
takes off squealing. At home they find the hook of a crazed
amputee caught in the door. Jesse described his yellow face,
putrid, and his blotchy stump. She described him panting in the

grass, crying and looking for something. She could feel him smelling of raw vegetables, a rejected bleeding cowboy with wheat hair, and she was unfocused. Moaning in the dark and falsetto voices. Don't don't please don't. Nervous laughter. Sally looked out the window of the shack. The grass is moving, she said, Something's crawling in it. No, it's nothing. Yes, there's something coming, and her voice went up at the end. It's just boys trying to scare us. But Sally whined and flailed her arms. On her knees she hugged Jesse's legs and mumbled into her thighs. It's all right, I'll take you up to the house. Sally was stiff, her nails digging the skin. She wouldn't move. Jesse tied a scarf around her eyes and led her like a horse through fire up the hill to the house, one poison light soft in a window. Boys ran out of the field squawling.

Accidents

I'm not sure anymore when the first accident happened. Or if it was an accident. Now when I tell you about my accidents you are sympathetic and some of you fall in love with me. Men whose childhoods were slow and smooth want my strait jacket stories. My sugar is a panic that melts on your tongue and leaves a tiny hole in what you taste. Taste me Sugar, I'm fried around the edges. Mom used to say I was born with my eyes crossed. That was a joke she quit telling when I was old enough and wrapped up tight. You feel me spinning and the music's on too loud. You remember all the little dangers in your past. My body that long sleek car someone spun on curves, Hey you wanna drag? Yeah I'll do ya, and it degenerates. Six girls giggly drunk jumping out to run circles around an old Chevy at a red light. Hey wait a minute Honey, you dropped somthin. I keep dropping how things went, which story goes where. This week and next week and next week. Somewhere out there's a winner but I'm losing track. I try to stay home and turn the pages in my books. But the words are a dark crusted black that cracks. Black as wine or water. I keep wading out and the deep part is over my head. I wanna dance I wanna just wrap my legs around you like those rings are round the moon. Lemme press my mouth against you like the rain against the glass it's see-through. I can see clear out there to the end and I'm alone I'm burning like a fire fuel. I'm hot. I'm hot I'm a streak across the sky. You watch me, now bring me down hard and hold on. It doesn't matter if I tell one truth or another. I wanna feel a hand on my waist. He and I are through, why don't you come over? See, I hurt my head again. I hit it on the bed.

Swimming

Kay liked to dance with Jancy at slumber parties, whose breasts were already full and taut. The girls practised slow dancing to a crybaby voice, I'm just a soldier, a luh-honely soldier – Sometimes Kay stayed overnight at Jancy's. They would play 45s on the tinny record player and stand in front of the mirror, mouthing words and pretending to play guitars. Kay did this at home alone but was surprised to find that Jancy did it too. She wondered how many of the others did it. Neither of them ever told anyone they had done it together. Her mother said that Jancy was dirty, with her stringy hair and woman's breasts and sweaty crescents under her arms. When Kay was younger, her mother had bought her a doll that was three feet tall. Kay slept with the doll at night, embraced, kissing the plastic mouth. One night her mother saw the doll in her bed. What do you want to sleep with that thing for. The doll smelled like new soap. Its foot pressed against her cunt. When Jancy bent over to change the record she smelled ripe and dark and bitter. The smell came in subtle waves from her hair and neck. Kay went over to the bed and watched Jancy mime alone in front of the mirror. She felt miserable. She wished she could drown.

JOAN NESTLE

ESTHER'S STORY

(1987)

I had heard of Esther. She was tough, a passing* woman whose lover was a prostitute. Sea Colony talk. We all knew stories about each other, but like huge ice floes, we could occupy the same ocean without touching. This night we touched. She was sitting at the bar speaking a soft Spanish to Maria, the bartender from Barcelona. Amidst the noise and smoke, Esther sat straight and still, a small slim woman who dressed butch. Her profile was severe, grey hair rising from her forehead and waving back in the classic DA style. A small mole broke the tautness of her face. I do not remember how our contact began, but at some point I was standing between her legs as she sat with the lights of the bar at her back. Her knees jutted out around me like a sharp cove on a rocky shore. She joked with me, and I worried

---

* The word *passing* is used here to represent a lesbian who looked like a man to the straight world. She wore men's clothes and worked at what was considered a man's job, such as driving a taxi or clerking in a stockroom. Language here is inadequate, however. Neither *passing* nor *transvestism* explains the experience of the passing woman. Only she can.

that I could not hold her attention. I was not sure I wanted to. We were wary of each other, but an erotic need had flashed between us, and neither of us would let it go.

Later that night she offered to take me home. We agreed to go for a drive first. The night was dark, and Esther drove with ease, one hand on the wheel, the other holding her endless cigarette. She told me how she had left Ponce, Puerto Rico, her grown sons, and her merchant sailor husband, to come to America to live like she wanted. Her family had cursed her, and she had built a new family here in New York. Her life was hard. Her girlfriend gave her a lot of trouble; they both had struggled with drugs, but life was getting better now. She enjoyed driving the taxi, and because her customers thought she was a man, they never bothered her. I looked at her, at the woman in a neat white shirt and grey pants, and wondered how her passengers could be so deceived. It was our womanness that rode with us in the car, that filled the night with tense possibilities.

Our ride ended in a vast parking lot at Jones Beach. Spotted around the lot were other cars, far enough away from each other so that lovers could have privacy. We sat in silence for a while, with Esther's cigarette a sharp red circle moving in the car's darkness. She put out the light and turned toward me. I leaned into her, fearing her knowledge, her toughness – and then I realized her hands were trembling. Through my blouse, I could feel her hands like butterflies shaking with respect and need. Younger lovers had been harder, more toughened to the joy of touch, but my passing woman trembled with her gentleness. I opened to her, wanting to wrap my fuller body around her leanness. She was pared down for battle, but in the privacy of our passion she was soft and careful. We kissed for a long time. I pressed my breasts hard into her, wanting her to know that even though I was young, I knew the strength of our need, that I was swollen with it. Finally she pulled away, and we started the long drive home. She asked me if she could spend the night. I said no, because I had to get up to go to work in a couple of hours and because I could no longer balance my need for Esther and the fear that I was beginning something I could not control. She said she would call. She told me later that I was the first woman who had said no to her. She said it with admiration, and I felt dishonest. It was not femme purity that kept me from her that night.

A few weeks passed, and I was sitting in the back room of the Sea Colony waiting for Vicki to return from cruising in the front room. A Seven-and-Seven appeared on the table. 'Compliments of her,' the waitress said, gesturing to the corner. I turned to see Esther smile, constrained but amused. Later in the night, when all things were foggier, I heard a whisper in my ear, 'You will be mine.' I just saw the shadow of her face before she disappeared.

She called not long after, and I invited her to dinner. I knew I was testing my boundaries, and I think she was too. I was a young femme seeking the response of women I adored, needing their desire deep inside of me. I had brought several women home to my railroad apartment on East Ninth Street, but usually I was in control: I was sexually more expressive and on my own territory. From the first with Esther, I knew it would be different. I was twenty, and she was forty-five. I was out only two years, and she had already lived lifetimes as a freak. Her sexuality was a world of developed caring, and she had paid a dear price for daring to be as clearly defined as she was.

The day of our dinner dragged at work. I knew I would not have time to change from work clothes and cook dinner before she arrived. At least that was my excuse for staying in my heels, nylons, and dress. But the deeper reason was that I wanted her to see my competent femme self, self-supporting and sturdy, and then I wanted her to reach under my dress, to penetrate the disguise I wore in a world that saw me as having no sexuality because I had neither boyfriend nor husband.

I bought a steak and mushrooms on the way home, prepared a big salad, and set the oval table in the third room, the combined living and bedroom. This was a scene I had prepared many times before, my foreplay of giving. Each time I had felt fear and pride that two women could dare each other so. At seven-thirty she knocked. I opened the door breathlessly, as if I had run a long way. She walked past me and stood in the center of the living room, looking around, while I explained that I had not had time to change. She was wearing a white-on-white shirt with ruffles down the front, sharply creased black pants, and loafers. Her slimness shone clean and sharp. All of a sudden I felt everything in the apartment was too big: I was too big, the table was too full, my need was too big. Esther stood quietly, looking at the set table filled with my offerings.

'Can't I do something for you please,' she said. She examined the old apartment until she found a chair that needed fixing. 'I'll fix that for you.'

'No, no please, you don't have to.'

'I want to.'

She left and returned in a few minutes with some tools. She turned the chair upside down and repaired it. Only then would she allow herself to sit at my table. 'So much food.' We both ate very little, weighed down by the erotic tension in the room.

After dinner I asked if she would mind if I took a bath. Since I had started working at age thirteen, I had a need to break the work day from my own time by taking a bath. The hot water marked the border between my world and theirs. Tonight there was another reason as well. I knew we were going to make love and I wanted to be clean for her. Since my tub was in the kitchen and there were no doors between the rooms, it meant she could watch as I bathed. She did not. When I finished, I put on a robe and went to sit next to her. Joan Baez played on the phonograph, and we spoke half in English, half in Spanish about our lives. She asked me about my job, school; I asked her about her girlfriend, driving the taxi.

The room was dark. We always met in darkness it seemed. I knew that soon she would touch me and I was already wet with wanting her. Here, now, on the bed all the offerings would be tested. We both had power in our hands. She could turn from me and leave me with my wetness, my need – a vulnerability and a burden. I could close up, turn away from her caring and her expertise. But neither happened. With extreme tenderness she laid me down. We kissed for a few minutes, and soon her hands knew I was not afraid. She smiled above me. 'I know why you took that bath, to be clean for me.' We began caring but demanding love-making. As I rose to her, she said, '*Dámelo, Juanita, dámelo.*' I strained to take and give to her, to pour my wetness in gratitude upon her hands and lips. But another part of me was not moving. I was trying so hard to be good for her, to respond equally to her fullness of giving, that I could not come. She reached for pillows and put them under my hips. My legs opened wider. I held Esther's head in my hands as her tongue and fingers took my wetness and my need. I had never felt so beautiful. She reached deep into me, past the place of coming, into the center of my womanness. But I could do no more. I put my hand over her lips and drew her up along my body.

'Please, no more. It feels wonderful, and you have given me deep, deep pleasure.'

'Come home with me, I have things that will help.'

I knew she meant a dildo, and I wanted her to know it was not a lack of skill or excitement that was stopping me. It was her forty years of wisdom, her seriousness, her commitment to herself, and now her promising of it to me, that scared me. She lay still beside me; only her slenderness made lying on that small bed possible. I turned to touch her, but she took my hand away from her breast. 'Be a good girl,' she said. I knew I would have to work many months before Esther would allow me to find her wetness as she had found mine. The words, the language of my people, floated through my head – *untouchable, stone butch.* Yet it was Esther who lay beside me, a woman who trembled when she held me. Before she left she told me if I ever needed to reach her in the afternoons, she was next door sitting with an old woman, *una vieja*, a woman she had known for years who was now alone. She gave me the woman's number.

The next day was Saturday, and I spent the morning worrying about what I had done, my failure to perform. One-night stands are not simple events: sometimes in that risk-taking a world is born. I was washing my hair in the sink when I heard a knock at the door. Expecting a friend, I draped the towel around my naked shoulders and opened the door to an astonished delivery man. He thrust a long white box toward me as he turned his head. I took the box and closed the door. I had never had a messenger bring me a gift before. Twelve red roses lay elegantly wrapped in white tissue paper, a small square card snuggled between the stems:

> *Gracia, por todo anoche,*
> *De quien te puede amor profundamente*
> *Y con sinceridad* – Esther

For one moment the lower East Side was transformed for me: unheard of elegance, a touch of silk had entered my life. Esther's final gift. We never shared another night together. Sometimes I would be walking to work and would hear the beeping of a horn. There would be Esther rounding the corner in her cab with her passenger who thought she was a man.

MERRIL MUSHROOM

HOW TO ENGAGE IN COURTING RITUALS 1950s BUTCH-STYLE IN THE BAR

(1982)

You are sitting by yourself at the bar in the club you hang out at, legs wide, leaning on your elbow, holding your cigarette deep in the crotch of your fingers. There can be no doubt about the fact that you are a butch. You notice a woman you've never seen before sitting at a table, and you are attracted to her. She has short hair and is wearing some makeup, but she is not obviously femmie-looking. You are not sure if she is femme or butch – a critical issue – so you call over the bartender who is a friend of yours. You say, 'Don't be obvious, but see that new chick over there? Do you know who she is? Is she butch or femme?'

If the bartender knows, she will tell you, if she does not, she will venture a good guess. Trust her judgment. If the woman is a femme, you may proceed with the rituals. If the issue is uncertain, proceed as if she were a femme. If she is a butch, you can make a decision as to whether you want to forget it or try 'flipping' her.

Ritual #1
Cruising
You look at the woman, stare at her aggressively, arrogantly, trying to catch here eye. Does she look back at you? Does she look at you and then away? Does she not look at you? Any of these could be a sign of interest. Stare at her for a while. If she does not look back at you at all and you are getting impatient, proceed to ritual #2. If she glances at you and then looks away, you may want to skip to ritual #3. If she looks at you and smiles, proceed directly to ritual #4, and if she raises one eyebrow, go immediately to ritual #5. If she runs her tongue over her lips, ask her to go home without further ritual. If she looks at you and frowns, forget it.

Ritual #2
The Buying of the Drink

Call the bartender over. She is well practiced in these rituals and will be ready for your next question: 'What is she drinking?' The bartender will tell you, and you then say either, 'Send her over one from me,' or 'Send her over one but don't tell her it's from me.' Watch the woman's response as the drink is delivered to her. If she looks over at you and smiles, proceed directly to ritual #4. If she looks over at you and frowns, you may want to forget it. If she sends the drink back, really forget it. If she does not look at you, try to read her expression. If she seems to be bored, buy her another drink.

Ritual #3
The Playing of the Jukebox

This is an especially effective ritual if you are too shy to approach the woman directly, as it provides superficial contact and gives her a chance to get a good look at you. Be sure to pass her table on your way to the jukebox, no matter how devious a route you may have to fabricate; but be sure not to look at her yet. Lean on the jukebox with your arms straight in as butch a position as possible. Experiment at home with jukebox poses, and get a friend to tell you what angles you look best in against the light. Be extra casual and take a very long time making your selections, meanwhile trying to see out of the corner of your eye if she is watching you. You may, if you want to, look at her significantly before you press a button for a particular selection. When you are finished, straighten up and look directly at her. If she seems bored or annoyed, you may want to forget it. If she looks back at you, whether shyly, boldly, or arrogantly, smile at her. If she smiles back, immediately approach her and ask her to dance (ritual #6). If she does not smile back, proceed to ritual #4.

Ritual #4
The Approach

Walk over to where she is sitting. Be casual and swing your arms as you walk. Remain standing close to her, but be careful not to cause her to crane her neck into an uncomfortable position to look at you. If there is an extra chair, prop one foot up on it and lean over to talk to her, resting your forearms on your thighs. Look at her intensely, directly in the eye. If you are especially bold and confident, you can say, 'Hi, mind if I sit here?' as you slide your butt onto the seat. If you are not quite that aggressive, you can open with something like, 'Hi, are you WITH anyone?' or 'Hi, I've been watching you from the bar. Aren't you a friend of (make up any name here)'s?' or 'Didn't I see you at the (make up any place here)?' If the light where she's sitting is really dim and you want to get a better look at her, you can invite her to come sit at the bar with you 'where the air is a little better', or you can immediately ask her to dance. It's a good idea to exchange names and hold conversations on the dance floor, because it gives you something else to do while you are really seeing how your bodies fit.

Ritual #5
The Lighting of the Cigarette

The femme makes a motion toward her pack of cigarettes. You immediately grab your own pack from your breast pocket and extend it to her gracefully, snapping the pack so that three cigarettes shoot up a distance of $\frac{3}{4}''$, $\frac{1}{2}''$, and $1''$ respectively (this takes a lot of practice). Meanwhile, with your other hand, you smoothly slip your Zippo lighter out of your hip pocket, flip the lid open so that it rings, and slide the wheel along the leg of your denims so that you can present it to her with flame ready. This also takes practice, and until you become adept, you can use your thumb to flick the wheel. She plucks the tallest cigarette from the pack with the tips of her index and middle fingers, even if it isn't her brand, and deposits it firmly between her lips. If she is on the make, she will lick her lips slightly before closing her mouth around the filter tip. NEVER OFFER A FEMME A CIGARETTE THAT DOES NOT HAVE A FILTER TIP! Although the air in the bar is still, you cup your hand around the flame, touching her fingertips or brushing the back of her hand in the process. She either lowers her eyes or else looks at you intensely as she draws the smoke deep into her lungs, cupping her hand around yours and allowing the tips of her fingers to quiver slightly.

Ritual #6
The Asking to Dance

This shows definite interest – Butch: 'Wanna dance?' Femme: 'Sure.'

This shows lack of interest – Butch: 'Wanna dance?' Femme: 'Nope.' This sort of exchange should be followed by a return to and continuation of ritual #4.

This shows definite lack of interest, i.e. forget it – Butch: 'Wanna dance?' Femme: 'Fast or slow?' Butch: 'Slow.' Femme: 'No thanks.' Butch: 'Okay, fast, then.' Femme: 'No thanks.'

If she is sitting with other women, this shows interest – Butch: 'Anyone here wanna dance?' Femme: 'Whaddya mean, "anyone"?' This shows very blatant interest – Butch: 'Anyone here wanna dance?' Femme: 'Whaddya mean, "dance"?'

Ritual #7
The Dancing

This is one of the most important rituals and the most blatant form of foreplay. It often leads into ritual #8, the Going Home Together. Dancing in the 50s, whatever the style, always involved a great deal of body contact. Never forget that a butch ALWAYS leads when a couple dances, and a femme ALWAYS follows. If you get as far as the dance floor and the woman insists on trying to lead, forget it.

THE SLOW DANCE: Be sure to start with a simple foxtrot step, and don't hold your partner too close right at first. If you don't know how to fancy-dance, you can do a simple two-step or box-step. Lead with your right hand behind her back while she holds you around the neck with her left hand. You begin by holding hands on the other side (your left, her right), but if she seems receptive, you can ease your hands closer to your bodies until you manage to maneuver your left hand around her waist, pulling her right hand around her back. If she moves closer to you, you can begin a slow fish movement, rocking your pelvis, thighs, and breasts against hers in time to the music, with perhaps just a bit of syncopation every now and again. If she moves with you, you may breathe slightly on her neck. If she holds herself away from you or if you are too shy to get that close right away, you can converse while you are dancing. This keeps you both safe from having to get too phsyically close, because you have to lean your heads back in order to talk to one another. It also gives you something to pay attention to besides your bodies and how they feel together. If you can do fancy steps and she follows well, you can use whirls and dips in order to hold her more tightly. This is a good way to impress both her and onlookers, but be very careful not to get out of control through showing off and misstep, stumble, or, worst of all, drop her.

FAST DANCING: These were usually some form of the Lindy, Chicken, or Panama City Bop as well as line dances like the Madison and that famous outgrowth of the Madison, the Hully Gully. There is usually not a lot of body contact in fast dancing unless you do a Dirty Boogie. Fast dancing provides an excellent opportunity to show off. You can do a lot of fancy twirls and twists, and if you are strong enough, you can do lifts and swings. You can exchange names and immediate information while fast dancing, but usually there is no need for further conversation, since you really have to concentrate on breathing. Be sure to pace yourself so as not to run out of steam before the record is over and have to sit down.

If the dance ritual does not lead directly into ritual #8: The Going Home Together, be patient. You may get another date, or, at the least, you may have made a new friend.

Ritual #8
The Going Home Together

After you both have made perfectly clear to one another that neither of you goes for one-night stands, you leave the bar together. You may take her home to her place, whereupon she invites you in for a cup of coffee; or you may take her to your place for a cup of coffee before taking her home. In either case, the tension has built to the point that you both cling together and kiss the moment you step inside and close the door.

If you both are too hot to wait, you make your way to the bedroom while intertwined, shedding clothes as you go, until you fall together naked on the bed. If either of you is still a little shy, you may want to sit together on the sofa or the edge of the bed for a while, having conversation and, finally, a few tentative kisses.

Unlike the both of you, the coffee probably will not get made until the following morning.

REBECCA BROWN
BREAD

(1984)

For breakfast there were two kinds of rolls, white and wheat. We would get a basket of eight and there would be one, and sometimes – but only very rarely – two, wheat ones; the rest were white. The white ones were long and looked like short croissants straightened out with four or five sections. We could see where they were wrapped around. They were white with thin butter glazing that made them yellow or gold or brown on top. They were in sections and we could eat them in sections, tearing off a bite at a time and spreading a knot of butter on the soft open end we'd just pulled off. There was orange marmalade too, but I liked them more with only butter. The wheat ones were round around the top and sides, but flat on the bottom. They didn't have glaze but were rough and had specks of grain in them. They weren't as soft inside or in your mouth, or as sweet. We could just eat them; they weren't in sections and didn't have glazed caps to peel off or raisins to pick off. We could only tear them like a loaf of bread. They were small and fitted in one cupped palm.

There was only one different way to eat them and there was only one person who did it that way.

It was you.

You never talked about it and no one ever talked about it in front of you, but eveyone saw and no one dared do it like you. If someone else had started it, eveyone would maybe have done it or felt they could have done it. Probably no one would have noticed it as something special if any one else had done it. But you had started it. It was yours and it wasn't anyone else's.

Someone would bring the basket to the table and put it in the middle. Everyone would reach for a roll, a white one and, when everyone had one, there'd be one left; you'd take it. It was always the last one, the wheat one. You'd lean forward in your chair and reach your right arm over the basket and flex your whole hand around it and pick it up and put it on your plate and put your napkin in your lap. Then someone could start the butter around and we could eat.

You would slice the one brown wheat roll through the side like a knife into a stomach. You'd cut the top from the bottom and sometimes the knife would catch and there would be a pile-up of dough at the end where you split the top from the bottom. You sat at the end of the table with your back towards the window that looked out into the yard. Sometimes I could see steam rising from your just severed roll against the window. I'd watch you put the two portions on your plate, bottom and top down, the exposed, soft insides up. You'd slice a triangle of butter from the yellow rectangle on the common plate and press it to your plate, then a tiny spoon of marmalade. Then you'd pick up the bottom half of the roll in your right hand and butter it with the knife in your left. Then you'd put that half down, pick up the other, and spread marmalade on that. Then you'd put the knife down, pick up the bottom half in your left hand and put the two sides back together. Then you'd put it, assembled, back on your plate, wipe your hands on your napkin and pick it up and bite into it. Your teeth were straight, and slightly yellow.

*

If there was ever more than one wheat roll, we'd argue over it because it was special, but also because they were better. If there were two wheat rolls, we'd all, all of us except you rush to grab one of them. None of us ever dared touch both of them, because one was reserved for you. Whoever got the second one smiled and was smug and everyone else just took a white one. We took turns bringing the rolls to the table. Sometimes people would volunteer out of turn to get them so they could touch the extra wheat roll, if there was one, and claim it before anyone else at the table had a chance. But you never had to do that. You never went to bring the rolls. When there was another wheat one, whoever got it would eat it tearing off pieces bit by bit, like a white one. No one could eat them the way you did. It was your way.

Our table didn't talk at breakfast. We were usually one of the first tables dismissed because we finished quickly because we didn't talk. You didn't like to talk in the morning; we didn't either. Sometimes you would look up from where you were sitting by the window at another table across the room if someone was talking loud or a group was too energetic.

Once you stared over at two girls telling a story to the rest of their table. One girl was thin and blonde. Her fingers were like sticks and she kept snapping her skinny hands in the air to illustrate her story. She slapped the table and jumped around in her seat. Her friend was fat and very pale except for red cheeks. They interrupted each other, correcting each other and laughing. Their whole table was laughing with them. The fat one mimicked the accents of people in the story. She puffed out her cheeks and lowered her fat double chin into her neck and spoke in a drawl. The skinny blonde screeched a narration. People at other tables were looking at them and trying to listen. We did too. The fat girl slapped her hands to her chest above her breasts and swayed her shoulders back and forth in a parody of her character's gestures. It was a good story and everyone was watching. I turned to the girl to my left to ask her for the butter, but I didn't ask because when I turned, I saw you.

You were sitting perfectly still, your forearms solid on the table in front of you on either side of your plate. You were staring at the two girls at the table. You hadn't eaten but one bite of your wheat roll. Your face was completely still. You were utterly silent.

I was ashamed.

I nudged the girl on my left. She was smiling at the story and she smiled at me, almost leaning over to say something. But when she saw my face she quit smiling. She opened her mouth to say something to me but I nodded at you. She looked at you, then dropped her head and snatched up her soft white roll, snapped off a section and stuffed it in her mouth. She kept looking at her plate. She ate another bite before she realized she hadn't buttered it or put marmalade on. She buttered the next piece, but the knife slipped and she dropped it on her plate. It crashed and she grabbed it with both hands. Her hands were shaking. We all glanced at her, but everyone else turned back to the story.

I nudged the girl on my right and nodded at you. She looked at you and stopped listening to the story, too. She nudged the girl at the other end of the table and kicked the girl opposite her under the table. We stopped paying attention to the story.

The story went on. I tried not to hear it. I tried to listen to the inside of my ears, the crinkly sound when everything is quiet, or just the sound of my chewing. I tried not to hear the girls, but I did.

Our whole table had stopped looking at them. Some of us stole sideways looks at you. You were still staring at them. It was a long, loud story. The fat girl was getting louder and the blonde was getting more animated. They had the attention of the whole room.

Then you did it.

The skinny one threw her hands in front of her to punctuate a point and knocked a cup of coffee on herself. She jumped up and screeched. Everyone at her table flinched and moved. Two girls on either side of her put napkins on her hands and arms where the burning coffee hit. They rushed her out of the room. Everyone else in the room turned to their table and stared. People from different tables leapt up to get the head prefect and the Housemistress. Some other girls had gone to get the cleaning woman. Everyone looked up. Everyone flinched.

But you stayed still.

Our table stayed still.

Then, when everyone else was watching the aftermath of the accident, you began to eat again. You didn't say anything. You lifted your arms from the table, daubed your hands on the napkin in your lap and picked up your butter-marmalade wheat sandwich. You brought it to your mouth and bit.

At least one person from every other table went over to that table to ask what had happened and if everything was alright. But none of us did. We all tried to eat our rolls like you. We all looked at one another quickly. We looked at everyone at the table except you. You didn't look at anyone.

You willed the thing to happen. I knew. No one else knew, but I did. You knew I did.

We all felt ashamed.

I felt ashamed. I wanted to say, 'I didn't mean, none of us meant – '

After the coffee was cleaned up, things were quieter. You liked it more. You don't like conversation at breakfast and you never liked it if someone else started it.

We all felt ashamed. We all wanted to be forgiven by you. You didn't look at any of us.

That girl got blisters on her hand. After that, we were all more careful.

You sat at the end of the table. The seating was arbitrary. No one was assigned. We just established ourselves in time. Technically, one would think the other end, opposite you, was the head because it was in the center of the room and closer to the head table where the head prefect or the Housemistress sat, but the end you sat at was the head because you were there.

You sat at the end of the table in front of the window that overlooked the yard. I sat in the middle seat on the side of the table to your right. In the morning after breakfast the sun came in and lit you up from behind. Before someone put the lights on, and it was a little dark outside, your shadow went across the table a short way. When the lights came on, it disappeared.

One day there was a two-day period when there were no wheat rolls. You didn't eat white ones and we took the basket back at the end of breakfast with one white roll left in it. You didn't say anything about it. You just looked at the basket and didn't take a roll. No one else said anything about it in front of you. After breakfast, though, we talked among ourselves about it and made plans to go out and find wheat rolls for you if they didn't reappear soon.

We thought you were so strong to not even comment on their absence those two days. We talked about it for two days, then long afterwards. We admired your acceptance of the situation, but reasoned that the position of being the one to eat the wheat roll every day went with the ability to deal with its absence. You had something we hadn't. You knew how to deal with things.

You were our heroine.

Every day they'd give us either buns for morning break or biscuits. Bun days were better. You wouldn't touch biscuits; neither would any of us. Buns had raisins and were soft. There was a thin layer of shiny glaze on the top. They were soft and white around the sides but brown on the bottom from the tray and beige to brown to dark brown on the top like shellac. When we tore them open they were soft and white inside with raisins. We counted the raisins. We did it because one day you did it and the next day you suggested we all do it. We did it every bun day and started keeping tally, even when you weren't there. We reported to you when you came back, sometimes someone would cheat. No one ever told you about cheating. It wasn't your business, but it was an issue between us. But I know you knew about it anyway. I bet you were pleased with it.

What was good was to take a small bite from the edge and break the surface and make an opening and then, poking and folding one finger into the warm inside, pull out a thick wad of pure soft bread. We made shells; we hollowed out the insides with a finger and what was left was the shiny brown top and white sides and brown bottom and one hole in the side. Sometimes we found shells where someone had made one and left it.

We could also eat buns bit by bit eating the top first, because often there was a thin pocket between the brown shellacked top and the white inside. If there was a bubble in the top, we could put a fingernail in and peel it off and either eat it in pieces, or wait until the whole lid was peeled off then eat them together. Then we could eat the soft part or give it to someone who liked that part if we didn't.

You taught us these ways. Even if you didn't think of each of them, whoever did presented it to you and you dismissed or accepted it. If you accepted it, you'd teach it to us. You never said whose idea it was if it wasn't yours, and in your presence, no one ever said, 'That's my idea.' We didn't want to boast in front of you. But sometimes among ourselves, one of us would say, 'That was my idea.' But we didn't listen to anyone else. You were the person who mattered. You were the person we loved.

Before every meal we had prayer. After everyone was in the room and at their table, the head girl or the Housemistress would call on someone to say the prayer or say it herself.

The prayer was the same every meal. Only one person said it and no one had to say it with them. The prayer was, 'For what we are about to receive, may the Lord make us truly thankful.' Everyone said 'Amen' and sat down or rushed up to the counter to bring back the food. If it was breakfast, one person from every table went up to get the rolls and then someone from the kitchen, sometimes the fat girl, but usually her mother, wheeled out the cart with the pitchers of coffee. The coffee already had milk in it. They had it that way because without, it would make us nervous. One morning I got there early and was washing my hands in the kitchen and the fat girl smiled at me. She was pouring the milk into a big pot with the coffee in it. There was another pot with coffee without milk. I said, 'Can I have some?' She smiled at me and I picked up a cup from the counter and scooped it into the hot steaming pot. The cups were glass. There was no pattern on them. They were old. The glass was thick and I couldn't see through it. It was rough from so many washings. I scooped it into the hot steaming pot of black coffee. When I looked at the coffee through the cups, it was thin and brown. I tasted it and it burned my tongue. It was terrible coffee. She poured bottles of milk into the pots. She broke the silver circle seals on the bottle lips. She punched her fat thumb in the center and broke open one side of the seal, then she peeled it off and scooped the cream off with a spoon and put it into a dish. Then she poured the white milk into the coffee in the big silver pots. I threw the steaming terrible coffee into the sink and rinsed the cup and put it back on the counter. She picked up the cup and washed it with soap and water. She waited until the water from the faucet over the big stainless-steel sink got steamy then she got a dish-mop from the tray and scoured the cup. Her fingers got pink. I thanked her for the coffee. Then I left the kitchen and went into the dining-room and waited for breakfast.

We had prayer before every meal. The head girl or the Headmistress would say it herself or call on someone to say it. They could call on anyone. They did it that way to make sure everyone was paying attention to prayer. Some people didn't. Some people wouldn't listen or said it quickly to get through it. They rarely called our table, though. There was no need to. You were at our table.

It started this way.

One time she called on Philippa Rogers. Philippa Rogers did not believe. She skipped service each Sunday. When she got called on, the head girl said, 'Rogers –' and everyone bowed their head. Philippa Rogers said the prayer. She said, 'For what we are about to receive, may we all be truly thankful.' We heard people pause for a second before we scooted our chairs to sit down or rush to the basket of rolls.

You didn't sit down. Everyone began scooting their chairs and two people started from their tables to go and get their baskets of rolls. You stayed standing. You didn't move. You said out loud, 'That's not right.' Everyone stopped. Everybody looked at you.

You stood at your seat. Your left hand was open and your curved fingers were near the table and your fingernails tapped the edge of the table. The fingers of your left hand stretched and tapped the table 1–2–3–4 like a castanet player. Your right hand pressed the table. The fingers of your left hand tapped the table: little finger, ring finger, middle finger, index finger. Your right hand was clenched in a fist.

You only said it once. Everybody looked at you. Then everybody looked at their plates. You looked at Philippa Rogers. Your face was hard.

I heard you breathing.

You snapped your head back, then lowered it. You closed your eyes and everyone looked at you.

Two girls at our table lowered their heads. Three girls at the table in front of us lowered their heads. Two girls at Philippa Rogers's table lowered their heads. When everyone's head was bowed, we heard a scrape as Philippa Rogers leaned too heavily on her chair, lifting two of its legs off the floor, and it fell back to the floor. I looked down at my hands. My head was lowered and I saw my hands clenching and my knuckles going white. I tried to see around me without moving my head. The girl to my right was clutching her napkin. I closed my eyes and didn't see anything.

Philippa Rogers cleared her throat and said, 'For what we –' Then we heard her swallow. We heard the noise her neck made when the saliva went down from her mouth. She exhaled quickly through her nose then said, like she was out of breath, 'For what – for what we are about to receive, may the Lord make us truly thankful.'

No one moved.

Then we heard you slide your chair out. We raised our heads.

Your chair scraped across the floor and you sat down and scooted yourself in. You put your forearms on the table, on either side of your plate. You looked at the girl at our table whose turn it was to get the rolls. You smiled at her.

She jumped up quickly to get the rolls. We all sat down. When the rolls came we ate them quickly. During the meal someone at Philippa Rogers's table dropped a plate. You didn't look up. You ate your wheat marmalade roll. You were beautiful.

On Sundays we were required to go to church. We could go to whichever church we wanted to, but we had to go somewhere. The Housemistress or head pre would ask us where we'd been to make sure we'd gone. Also they would make spot checks at churches. They'd go to a different church every week to make sure people were where they said they were going to be. Christ Church was only two blocks away and St Philip's was three. There was also St James and Parish Church and all the denominations. People went to different ones to keep from being bored. We could go to the early service at 7.30 and be back for breakfast or go to the later service after breakfast at 10.30. Everyone went to the later service because Sunday breakfast was at 8.45, fifteen minutes later than the rest of the week, and we liked to sleep in.

On Saturday nights everyone would ask everyone else which church they were going to and make plans. Sometimes we took turns and four of us would sign out as though we were going to a church, but then only two of us would go and the other two would do something else like shopping or going to Devil's Chimney or the Sandwich Bar and if the head pre or Housemistress came to that church and asked where the other two were, the two in church would vouch for them and say they were sitting behind the pillar or in the bathroom. No one went to church by themselves.

Except you. You went to both services every Sunday. You went to St Gregory's 7.30 service every Sunday by yourself. St

Gregory's was far away and you had to take a cab. Every Sunday morning at 7.00 a black cab pulled up by the front door of our house and you were waiting for it. You stood inside the tall bay window to the left of the door coming in. You held the heavy beige curtain back with your left hand, your right hand holding your shoulder purse. Your fingernails shone. You did your nails the night before.

The cab drove into the driveway and stopped, but you were out in the driveway before he was even at the door and you'd wait for the cab driver to open the door for you and you'd get in. As you slid into the back seat, you tucked your coat in underneath your hips. You wore shiny black shoes with wide high heels. You never wore them any other time except to St Gregory's on Sunday.

One time I woke up early to go to the bathroom and when I stood over the sink by the window washing my hands, I looked out and saw you get into the cab.

Every Sunday after that I saw you from the bathroom window. I leaned on the white sink by the window to watch you. My feet were cold on the concrete. You wore your Sunday shoes. You never saw me.

From Monday to Friday from 8.00 to 4.45 we wore our uniforms, and from 8.00 a.m. to noon on Saturdays. At 4.45 class was over and we could change in the hour before we had to be back in the library to study or we could wait until right before dinner at 7.30 but we couldn't be in our uniform at dinner. If shoes were too high-heeled or not polished, we couldn't wear them. In the morning on the way into morning prayers, the pres stood at the door into the auditorium and looked at our shoes. They made sure they were polished. If they weren't polished, we were dismissed from prayers and docked an hour of free time or had to report to the Head Divinity Mistress for extra divinity lessons. We got the 1s and 2s to polish our shoes. They liked doing it for us and they'd compete for who got to do whose shoes. They tried to get the pres' first and everyone competed for the head girl. She awarded her shoes to different 1s and 2s from time to time, to give more of them a chance. She always had her shoes done the best because she had all of them compete for her. Her shoes were the best of anyone's.

Except yours.

You did your shoes yourself. At first the 1s and 2s competed for your shoes like they did for the head girl's. Then they stopped. No one else in our form did their own shoes. We were too old and the 1s and 2s wanted to do them for us. But you did. You did your shoes yourself. You did your shoes better than anyone.

To leave, we had to have it planned in advance and have our parents come or write permission and say where we were going. We had one weekend a month, plus half-term and Saturdays and Sundays. You were away more than anyone. No one else went as much as you. Your father came and got you every Saturday at 1.00. The first week of every month you spent the weekend at home. Every weekend after that you spent the day with him on Saturday and came back in the evening. On Sunday you went to church in the morning and sat in your room for the rest of the day. In the evening after supper, you came out and talked with us. You spoke with everyone the same.

One time you came back and had a huge white box. Your father left it in the calling room when he dropped you off. It was Saturday evening. The box was huge. The head pre called a house meeting. You opened the box and there was a huge Black Forest cake in it. It was at least three feet by two feet big. I'd never seen a Black Forest cake so big. I'd never seen a Black Forest cake half as big. It was gorgeous. Around the edge of the box on the inside I could see a rim of brown where the oil and cream had stained the white cardboard. There was dark brown and regular brown frosting. There were six rows of cherries. Someone from the kitchen brought a knife. You cut the cake. You asked someone from the kitchen for some napkins. She brought them. I was standing near you. She handed me the napkins. I put them on the table by the box. You picked up a piece of cake. I picked up a napkin and held it under your hand. You put the cake on the napkin. I handed the cake and napkin to the girl in front of me.

We did this for the whole house, thirty-six pieces of cake, plus two for the mistresses and three for the kitchen. We saved some pieces for people in the morning. You and I ate after everyone had their piece. The cake was good. The frosting was thick and smooth and creamy. The inside was brown sponge soaked with cherry liquid. Everything was moist and sweet and heavy. None of us had ever tasted anything so wonderful. All of us felt wonderful. No one asked you what it was for or where it came from.

We remembered that day for ever. The next day we told all the other houses about it. Some people from other houses said things to you, like they'd heard about it and wished they had been there, but no one asked you about it.

We talked about it for ever. Someone said your father owned a bakery. Most people disputed this; your father was too much of a gentleman. We didn't know why the cake had come.

Then the rumor started that it was your birthday. No one asked you and no one thought to ask the Housemistress. We didn't ask about your mysteries.

I started the rumor.

On Sundays I woke up early, every Sunday except the first Sunday of the month. I watched you from the bathroom window. I watched you with your shoulder purse. I thought of your shiny black shoes and your high black heels, getting into the cab on the way to St Greg's. My feet were chilly on the cold concrete. Then I went back to bed.

In the morning they rang a bell a half an hour before breakfast. I tried to be up earlier than the bell. I put on my robe and went to the bathroom. My robe was long and fake-velvet dark blue. It was soft and in a minute warm over me. I never put on slippers. If I was early, there was hardly anyone else in the bathroom. In the bathroom were four toilet stalls and five sinks with mirrors over them and windows between them. Next door was a room with four little rooms with bathtubs. I went to the bathroom and washed my face and brushed my teeth. By the time I was finishing, more people would be coming in and I would nod good morning if my mouth was full of toothpaste or say hello, and sometimes I wouldn't know who I was saying hello to if my eyes were closed under the soap. People were sleepy-looking and in their robes almost all buttoned up. Some people didn't talk at all because they'd just woken up and some people were in talkative moods.

When I finished in the bathroom, I went back to my room and got dressed. I undid my robe and it fell to the floor. I was usually very cold after that because sometimes the bathroom was warm because of the bath steam and I'd got used to my robe. Then I was naked. My uniform was hanging over the back of my chair by my desk. If it was cold I'd jump around and try to make my blood go faster with my hands and inhale through my teeth, a 'ssss' sound, and wring my hands. I put my shirt on first. It was white and long-sleeved and I buttoned it all the way up, even the sleeves. It was straight around the bottom with no tails. Then I pulled on my underpants. They were uniform, too. Always, ever and only white. Then I put on my skirt, thin if warm, thick if cold. It zipped up the side and was plain. Then I put on my tie. I stretched the tie in my arms over my head then put it behind my head on my shoulders. Then I dropped it and pulled my hair out from underneath it. I tied the tie. The tie was green with red stripes going down it diagonally. It was the house tie and I had a scarf to go with it too, red and green. It was very ugly. If it was too cold it took a long time for my hands to be loose enough to tie it. My hands were cold and sometimes they even looked blue. Then I put on my sweater. I almost always wore the thick one, not the thin one, because if it was really warm, I didn't wear one at all, but if it was cold at all, I wore the thick one, so I just pulled it on over my head. When it was on, I pulled my hair out from the sweater and straightened my tie and reached my hand up under my skirt to pull the shirt down and straighten it. Then I sat down on the bed. I picked up the socks on the chair and put them on. They were thick and soft and wonderful dark green. I liked them. I bunched them up over my hand and made a tight ball on my fist. I put my foot into the little opening at the end of my palm. My feet were freezing, even more than my hands, and sometimes I'd just hold on to my foot with my hand to try to make it warm. I put my foot in the sock and pulled the sock over my foot, then stretched it up my calf to my knee, smoothing and straightening the wool on the way up.

Then I put on my shoes. They were brown and plain and low. They were our uniform shoes.

I brushed my hair and tied it back. Then the bell was ringing and I went downstairs for breakfast.

For breakfast there were two kinds of rolls, white and wheat. There was butter and orange marmalade and pots of coffee. There was a box shelf on the wall by the door and everyone grabbed their napkin from the box and took it to the table. After the meal was over, we put them back. Everyone had their own box, their own napkin. They were white and stiff and rolled into a cylinder and stuffed in tiny boxes. We got them washed once a week with the laundry. By the end of the week the box was full of wilted, dirty napkins. There was only one napkin that was never wilted or dirty.

It was yours. Yours was always perfect.

On the Sundays when you were with your father, there was a wheat roll in the basket but you weren't there to eat it. On those Sundays, we'd rush to be the one to get the basket of rolls. We looked forward to the first Sunday of the month to see if we could get the wheat roll. Your seat at the head of the table was empty.

We talked a lot. We talked about you and wondered where you were and what you were doing. Then we just talked about where we were going to church and what everyone was doing. We were often very rowdy the first Sunday of the month.

The Night of the Cake we got to stay up half an hour later. The Housemistress smiled and said she realized we were all too keyed up to get to bed at the regular time, so she'd let us stay up until eleven, providing she didn't see too many tired faces in the morning, and if someone wanted to go to sleep before eleven, no one was to stop them. We finished eating our cake way before then, but we were all so thrilled we couldn't sleep or study. We just stood there in the calling room talking. When the Housemistress said we had to leave we went to our rooms and talked. We talked until 11.00 and then, even after she had called lights out and did her rounds, some people left their rooms and snuck into their friends' rooms and stayed up talking late. The next day everyone was in a particularly good mood, and some in a fake good mood because they were so tired but had to fake it for the Housemistress.

I went to bed at 11.00 and stayed in my room.

I lay in my bed with the lights out and looked outside. I saw the orange light of the street lamp through the dots of rainwater on the window. There was steam on the window from the cold outside. The leaves looked orange and bronze in the light of the street lamp and sent out shoots of orange into the air. I heard traffic going by and people walking and laughing quietly.

I thought about holding the napkins you put your cake on and everyone else eating theirs before we did. In my mind, I pretended we were doing it again. I wanted to tell someone, but someone different, not the people going to each other's rooms. I stayed in my room and looked at the bronze-leaved trees and listened to the traffic and people walking until I couldn't hear it any more. Then there was no noise coming in from the outside. I closed my eyes and fell asleep.

Sometimes I saw you in the bathroom before breakfast. You were always completely dressed. You never left your room without being completely dressed. You came to the bathroom completely dressed and washed your face and brushed your teeth in full uniform. Your shoes were always polished.

You were always perfect.

I was in love with you.

When they were taking people for a special scholarship, you were one of them. It meant you went away lots to be interviewed and look at schools. It meant you missed breakfast because you'd leave after lunch one day and go there, then come back the next day for lunch or supper. Your space was empty at the table. Your wheat roll just sat there. We were afraid there could be a mistake and you might just come in late and what would you do if you didn't have your wheat roll? We were very careful.

One time Fiona Donovan asked me if I would ask you something for her. Fiona Donovan had been raised poorly. She had no social sense. She wanted me to ask you if you would help her with her Applied Mathematics prep because she had been out for a week. Everyone knew you were the best at Applied Mathematics. I told Fiona Donovan she was a fool. I said you had better things to do with your time than help someone with their problems when she could get anyone to help her and what were teachers for anyway? Then she said, well couldn't I just ask you and I said, 'Why me?' and she said, 'You're the one who helped the Night of the Cake.' I said, 'Sure, but that's nothing.' She said, 'Everyone knows she told you it was her birthday the Night of the Cake.' I looked at Fiona Donovan. I didn't say anything. I had made it up. You hadn't told me anything. I said to Fiona Donovan, 'Yeah, well, so what? It's no big thing if it's your birthday. Why shouldn't she tell me?' I said it as nonchalantly as I could. I was thrilled. Fiona said, 'Well, she doesn't say things like that to anyone. You must be her friend.' I said, 'Well . . .' I tried to sound secretive and humble. I didn't look at Fiona. I was proud. Fiona said, 'Well, couldn't you just ask her –' I snapped my face up at her and said, 'Don't be so stupid.

She doesn't spend her time with just anyone, you know.' Then I walked away.

I pretended you had told me it was your birthday. I imagined you said my name. We were standing by the table holding our pieces of cake in our hands. You had cut a piece of cake and put it on the napkin I held. You said my name and then you said, 'Today is my birthday.' I listened to you and looked at you and you were beautiful and it was your birthday.

For breakfast, one person from each table went up after prayer to the counter and picked up a basket of rolls for the table. The person getting the rolls would put the bowl and plate into the basket and carry them back and put them on the table and take the bowl and plate out of the basket and put them on the table. We all got our rolls and passed the butter and marmalade around.

There was usually only one wheat roll and it was always yours.

One day – it was a Monday after you'd been to St Greg's – you weren't at breakfast. You were out somewhere looking at a school or being interviewed for a scholarship. We knew you wouldn't be there and your place was empty. I looked at your empty chair and the wheat roll sitting in the basket. We all ate our breakfast and at the end I took the basket back to the counter and the fat girl who poured coffee with her mother saw me and smiled. She saw the wheat roll and looked at me. I said not everyone was at our table. She looked at the wheat roll again. She shrugged her shoulders and picked up the wheat roll, then picked up the basket and turned to put the basket away. As she turned, I saw her pop the wheat roll into her mouth. She did it like it was nothing. My mouth fell open in awe. I stared at her.

The next day at breakfast you didn't come again. Someone brought the rolls to the table and there was one wheat roll and you weren't there. Everyone helped themselves to a roll. I was the last one. There was one white one left and the wheat one. I reached for my roll. Then I paused, hand in the air over the basket. I didn't turn my head, but I tried to look at everyone else. The butter was going around and people were eating. We didn't wait for everyone because you weren't there. I decided. I withdrew my hand and started again.

I leaned forward in my chair and reached my arm over the basket and flexed my hand around the wheat roll, and picked it up and put it on my plate. I put my napkin in my lap and someone passed me the butter.

I sliced the wheat roll through one side, cut the top from the bottom and put the two portions on my plate, bottom and top down, insides up. I sliced a triangle of butter from the yellow rectangle on the common plate and pressed it on to my plate, then a tiny spoon of marmalade. I picked up the bottom half of the roll and buttered it with the knife. I put that half down, picked up the other, and spread marmalade on it. Then I put the knife down, and put the two sides back together. I put it, assembled, back on my plate, and wiped my hands on my napkin. Then I picked it up with both my hands and bit.

I felt the tiny crunch as my teeth broke the surface and went into the soft inside. I tasted the warm brown taste and the knotty texture of the grains and specks of wheat. The texture was tougher than the plain white rolls. It didn't taste as sweet in my mouth, but did taste more full. I could feel the slick texture of the butter and the sweet one of the marmalade between the layers of bread. The marmalade was almost gritty it was so thick. The white rolls were bland compared to this. I was happy.

Then you were there. You stood directly opposite me. I saw you and stopped chewing. My mouth was full of roll but it felt dry like I was going to throw up. You stared at me for a second then passed on to your seat. You moved so gracefully, like your feet didn't touch the ground.

Everything in my mouth felt full. I felt like I had already thrown up and it was in my mouth. I looked around at everyone else. Some people were staring at me but most people were staring at their rolls or plates and wouldn't look at me. The girl to my right made a gesture to pass the basket of rolls to you. There was only one roll in the basket, a white one. I was eating the wheat one, your wheat one. You didn't shake your head, but almost. She took her hand back and put it into her lap. She didn't pass the rolls to you.

My mouth tasted like vomit. I swallowed. The roll sat on my plate with one bite taken out of it. I looked at my plate, then closed my eyes. Then I looked up at you. You drank your coffee and looked at nothing. Then you looked at me like nothing. Then you smiled.

You were so kind and forgiving.

Then you looked away and drank your coffee in silence, not looking at anyone.

I tried to drink my coffee, but I couldn't. I didn't try to eat the roll.

I took the basket back at the end of breakfast. The one white roll was left.

The next day at breakfast, after prayer, you touched the girl to your right, whose turn it was to get the rolls. You didn't need to say anything. She sat down. Everyone else did too. I wanted to say, 'No –' but I couldn't.

You went to get the rolls.

All of us were silent. You'd never been to get the rolls before.

You brought the rolls to the table. You took the plate and bowl and put them on the table. You stood at the corner of the table, two people away from me, the corner closest to the counter on the opposite side of the table from your seat. When you'd taken the plate and bowl out of the basket, you didn't put the basket on the table.

Here's what you did.

You offered the basket to the girl on your left, my right, and she took a roll. Then you offered the basket to the girl on your right, and she took a white roll. You moved around the table and offered everyone a roll, and everyone took a white one.

You'd started with the girl on my right. I was going to be the last one.

When you came to me, I reached up to take the last white one, but you pulled the basket back. I said, 'What are you doing?' You didn't answer. You reached your right hand over the white roll as if to take it out of the basket and put it on my plate, but you didn't. You took the white one out and held it in your hand. Then you turned the basket over on my plate. The wheat roll fell on its side, then fell upright. 'What are you doing?' I whispered.

You put the empty basket down in the center of the table. You sat down. You turned to the girl on your left and held out your hand. She passed you the butter. You had a white roll on your plate. It looked deformed, in front of you. You had never eaten a white roll before.

I looked at the white roll and felt spit in my mouth. I couldn't eat. My stomach felt hot like there was a bubble in it. My mouth was full of water.

The butter was going around and everyone was buttering their plates and their rolls. When the butter came to me, it stopped.

I looked at you and said, 'What are you doing to me?' I said, 'Why are you doing this to me?' You didn't look at me. You tore off sections of your white croissant roll. Everyone else looked at their plate or roll.

I looked at the girl across from me. I said, 'What is she doing?'

She didn't look at me. She looked at her white roll.

I looked at everyone. Everyone was eating white rolls. You were eating a white roll. No one looked at me. Nobody would look at me.

I sat there and I couldn't move. I closed my eyes.

Inside I saw the color of your St Greg's Sunday shoes.

JANE RULE

HIS NOR HERS

(1985)

The virtue of a reclusive husband is the illusion of freedom he may provide for his wife once the children are old enough for school and social lives of their own. Gillian's husband did not like her to be out as many evenings as she was, raising money and/or enthusiasm for one good cause or another. She irritated him also when she was at home, either being far too noisy and playful with their two daughters, already inclined to giggle, or busy at her typewriter clacking out right-minded letters to the editor, to her member of the legislative assembly, to the prime minister himself. But, when she asked him what he wanted her to do, he couldn't say. Gillian suggested that his image of a wife was a warm statue, breathing quietly in the corner of the couch, not even turning her own pages to disturb his reading. It was a far less offensive image to him than it was to her. A quiet presence was what a wife should be, but increasingly he had to settle for a quiet absence.

'Do you know where your daughters are half the time?' he asked her.

'Yes,' Gillian answered, for she knew what homes of friends they'd found more hospitable to their taste in music, their interest in their hair, their bursts of high-humoured silliness.

'Well, I don't. I don't know where you are half the time.'

'Only because you don't listen.'

How could he pay attention through all their mindless morning gossip simply for casually dropped clues to their whereabouts, he wanted to know.

'You can't, darling,' Gillian replied. 'And if we're all resigned to that, why can't you be?'

Sometimes, when he remembered to, he studied Gillian's clothes to decide whether or not she was dressing appropriately for where she said she was going. Since she inclined to suits without more adornment than a bright scarf at her throat, he thought it only fair to dismiss the idea of her being unfaithful to him. She was cooperative enough when it occurred to him to make love to her, and she had no cause to complain, as some women did, about an overly demanding husband. He had never been suspicious enough to try to check up on her. It would have seemed to him also somehow beneath him. He was not the kind of man to have married a woman he couldn't trust.

He wondered occasionally if he shouldn't have allowed her to take some sort of part-time job, something dignified and clearly low paying to indicate that it was an interest rather than a necessity. It might have used up some of her tireless and tiresome energy and made her more content to stay at home in the evening. But he was not the kind of man to marry a woman who wanted to work, and Gillian had never been forceful in such suggestions.

'It's good for your company image to have a wife active in the community,' Gillian reminded him.

Gillian had the taste to do nothing strident, like marching for abortion or peace. She raised money for the art gallery, lobbied for better education for handicapped children, for scholarships for the gifted, and she supported the little theatres. She never asked him for unreasonable donations, nor did she drag him, as so many other husbands were dragged, to the symphony or gallery openings.

'With your interest in the arts, why don't you want to stay at home and read a good book?'

'I'm a people person, darling. That's all.'

Clearly 'people' could not include him, the singular and solitary man that he was. But he had to admit that she never discouraged him from fishing or hunting, even encouraged him to take longer and more expensive sporting holidays than he could make up his mind about for himself since he did not like the idea of being selfish.

'You're not selfish. You're a very generous man. Why not occasionally be generous to yourself?'

Away from his wife and daughters, he could stop brooding about them, stop feeling left out of their lives, for which he had no taste to be included. Sometimes he wondered what it would have been like to have a son, but he was even less easy in the company of men if there were no business topic to preoccupy them. He fished and hunted alone. What he would have enjoyed was knowing that Gillian was back at whatever lodge or cabin waiting for him. Yet that sort of wife might complain about being lonely.

Sometimes when Gillian grew impatient with his complaints, she said to him, 'You have a good marriage and two lovely children. Why can't you just relax and be satisfied?'

Gillian believed what she said. Long-suffering was not on her list of virtues, nor did she think it should be. She complained neither to her husband nor about him. When she said of him, 'He has a difficult temperament; he's reclusive,' she was simply describing him to excuse his absence from plays, gallery openings – husbands weren't expected to be on committees. Gillian considered herself as good a wife as her husband could reasonably expect and a good deal better than he might have had.

He did not know that Gillian was not extravagant with his money because she had some of her own. She didn't think of herself as secretive about it so much as keeping her own counsel.

There was no need for him to appropriate what was hers as if it were some sort of dowry. She didn't ask him the particulars of his financial life, about which he was also inclined to keep his counsel. Unlike him, she never suspected that he might be unfaithful. She knew that he wasn't. He was far too fastidious a man to be involved in anything he would think of as messy.

Gillian's conscience about him was perfectly clear. She did do good works. She was a good mother. And she knew more clearly than he did that he would be just as irritated with her at home as he was with her for not being there, not because she was an irritating woman but because he was an irritable man.

Gillian did not know how long ago it had first occurred to her that she would one day leave him, after the girls were raised and safely settled. Simply gradually her illusion of freedom made her feel she would one day enjoy the real thing. Gillian would not leave him for anyone else. It would be unfair to involve a third party in divorce. Therefore, whenever a third party became at all pressing about time Gillian did not have, emotional support she could not offer, long before there was any question of commitment, Gillian retreated into being a wife and mother with, yes, some feeling of guilt about the deserted lover but with a sense, too, that it was for the best since she refused to burden any lover with the guilt of feeling responsible for a broken marriage. When Gillian decided to leave, she would deal with the problem of her outraged husband by herself, for outraged she knew he would be, no matter how much he complained about her inadequacies.

'Duplicity' was not the word Gillian would have used to describe her life, perhaps because she could move quite openly with a lover, go out to dinner, go to the theatre without causing a flicker of gossip. She could even invite one home, though she didn't very often, out of loyalty to her husband really because invariably a lover asked, 'How can you live with him?' For Gillian it wasn't all that difficult. She knew women who stayed with husbands who drank, who beat them, who didn't pay the bills. Her marriage in comparison was a solid, sane arrangement in which to raise children.

'But he's such an impossible person!' came the protest.

'Aren't we all,' Gillian would ask, 'one way or another?'

But she liked to avoid such discussions when she could. Her lovers almost always befriended her daughters, sometimes even became their confidantes. Gillian enjoyed being able to include the girls in her happiness. Sometimes she even took them with her on a holiday with a lover, for their father couldn't abide traveling with children but wouldn't begrudge them the experience. Occasionally, Gillian thought, the girls mourned the loss of a lover even more than she did, but the period between lost love and restored intimate friendship usually didn't last long. By now Gillian had what might almost be described as a community of ex-lovers who had become friends.

With men such an arrangement would not have been possible. If Gillian had been attracted to men, her life might have been full of tension and deceit. As it was, she never had to lie to her husband about whom she was with and only very occasionally about where she was going.

Only once her husband said, 'That friend of yours, Joan, I think she's a lesbian.'

'She may be,' Gillian said lightly, 'but she's great, good fun.'

'Doesn't your own reputation concern you?'

'Of course, but I'm not a bigot, and neither are you.'

In fact, Joan was only a good friend. Gillian's taste in women was for the feminine and sensitive. Her husband would never have suspected any of her lovers of being a lesbian. The idea would have offended his whole concept of womanhood. Her lovers might seem to him 'flighty' or 'neurotic' but never perverse.

It was Gillian's own behavior he would have suspected if he had ever seen her among her ex-lovers, for her bright scarf became an ascot, and she held her cigarette between her teeth when she lighted it. Her laughter was bold, and her eyes were direct and suggestive. Even the way she downed her beer, which she didn't touch at home, would have shocked him.

In this role, her daughters loved her best, for she was full of fun and daring. No matter what they were doing, there was the tension of excitement, which made them prance and whinny. They knew their mother was never like that around their father. They associated their mother's mood with themselves away from him rather than with her friends.

Gillian acknowledged the latent eroticism she felt for her daughters and they for her. It was one of the joys of mothering daughters. She would brook no criticism from her friends about it.

'Why should I mind if they grow up to be lesbians?'

But they were both growing up to be even crazier about boys than they were about their mother and her exciting friends. Gillian didn't worry about that either, though it made her sometimes restless, aware of how empty her particular nest would be when they were gone and she had no buffer between her and her irritable and isolated husband. For, though he was critical of the girls, they had grown very good at teasing and cajoling him when it was necessary.

Was it about this time, too, that the pattern of her relationships with other women shifted? Lynn, who had to be called Lynn Number Two or Lynn R. – it had gotten that bad, her friends teased her, such a string of women she'd had – instead of beginning to make unreasonable demands, was simply drifting away, busy when Gillian had a free night, not home at the hour she knew Gillian habitually called. Lynn finally confessed that there was someone else.

Gillian felt both bereft and betrayed. She had never left a lover for someone else, as she wouldn't leave her husband. There was something immoral about inflicting jealous pain.

'Pain is pain,' Lynn Number One, who resented this new designation, said to her. 'Don't you think I was jealous of your husband?'

'But why would you be?'

'You sleep with him, don't you?'

'Once a month.'

'You stay with him.'

'The children,' Gillian responded automatically.

'Gillian, you've always wanted your cake and to eat it, too. Face it: you're not getting any younger. What was in it for Lynn R.?'

'That's awfully calculating,' Gillian said.

She began to drink too much, to get maudlin with old lovers about the past beauty of their relationships, their lasting loyalty. (She wasn't speaking to Lynn R.) She often had to be forcibly sobered up before she was sent home, and she was later getting there than she had ever risked, even at the passionate height of an affair. The security of home, which she had never lost sight of in delight, seemed less meaningful to her in sorrow. Before, she could bring all her own nourished happiness in to brighten the gloom. Now, far more particularly miserable than her husband, she could not endure his bleak moods. When he approached her sexually, she turned him harshly away.

'You are *my wife*,' he said, more shocked than angry.

Gillian was shocked herself at how without generosity she was for him, how reckless of him. For she let him see how angry and out of control she was. She snatched up her coat and left the house.

She went to a lesbian bar where her friends had sometimes gone, a place too public for the way she arranged her life. There she picked up a young girl, hardly older than her own daughters, and took her to a hotel for the night.

'Won't you even tell me your name?' her young lover pleaded in the morning.

Gillian's terror overcame her remorse. She fled as cruelly as she had from her husband, revolting from what she had done. She was not that kind of woman, to take advantage of a mere child and to compound it with deserting her. If Gillian had had the presence of mind, she would have left money on the dresser.

Arriving home, Gillian expected to have the day to pull herself together and to figure out how to get back from the too far she had gone. Her husband had not gone to work. He sat in his chair in the living-room waiting for her. She put a surprised and guilty hand to her mouth. She had not made up her face, and his eyes were appraising her sternly.

'That is never to happen again,' he said, a thought-out new confidence in his voice. 'Nor are you ever going to go out in the evening more than one night a week. I have been a patient man, a far too patient man, and I've been taken advantage of.'

'I want a divorce,' Gillian said in a calm tone that masked hysteria.

'Don't be silly,' he said, as if she'd suggested something like a drink before breakfast.

'I'm not being silly. I've come to my senses,' Gillian said, first wondering what on earth that phrase meant, then frightened that she knew.

'If you call flinging yourself out of the house in the middle of the night . . .'

'Ten o'clock.'

'. . . sensible . . .'

'This is a discussion that is now finally over,' Gillian said. 'Our lawyers can deal with the details.'

'Gillian, we have been married for nineteen years. We have two still dependent children. What are you talking about? What's happened to you?'

'Because of the girls, I think you'd better be the one to move out,' Gillian said in a practical tone.

'This is *my* house!'

'It's *our* house, according to the law.'

'I will not tolerate this, Gillian!'

'I suggest you talk it over with your lawyer. That's what I'm going to do,' she said and turned to leave the room.

'Gillian!'

Halfway up the stairs, she heard the front door slam, and she sank right there, suddenly too weak to take another step. Though she had entertained the idea of leaving him for years, she had never considered the means of doing so. His lawyer was hers in so far as she had one. Legally, she didn't know what 'marriage breakdown' was. She did know that humanly hers had, and whatever irrationality and self-destructiveness had led her into this circumstance, there was now no going back.

Slowly Gillian got up and went to the phone in their bedroom. The first call she made was to a locksmith, ordering the locks on all the doors to be changed by four o'clock.

At six o'clock that evening, Gillian and her daughters sat at the dinner table, listening to a pounding fist on the front door, then on the back, not speaking to each other until they heard the slamming of the car door and the starting up of an engine.

'Are you afraid of him, Mother?' her youngest daughter asked timidly.

'I never have been,' Gillian said.

'Is it legal?' her older daughter asked.

'It will be,' Gillian said. 'This evening you can play any music you want as loudly as you want, and you can invite your friends over.'

But that evening the house was quieter than it would have been if the master of gloom had been home, his forced absence even more palpable than his presence.

Gillian overheard her younger daughter say, 'I don't really like Daddy, but I'm used to him.'

'He's our father,' the older replied, but casually.

Ugly days stretched into ugly weeks in which Gillian often felt a prisoner in her own fortress. She had given up all her committees since her real interest in them had never been strong. They had been little more than a screen behind which she could lead her personal life. Now she had neither a personal life nor a husband to deceive, for he was now nothing but an enemy into whose hands she was determined not to fall. She saw none of the women who had been her intimates for so many years. Any hint of impropriety now would irreparably damage her case in court, leave her not only without a fair financial settlement but even without her daughters.

In the end, her husband behaved as Gillian had counted on him to, not generously but with scrupulous fairness. She could live in the house until the girls left home, at which time it would be sold, the proceeds divided between them. There was generous child support until the girls either reached twenty-one or finished college. For her own support, Gillian was responsible. The money her husband had never known she had made looking for a job less urgent than it should have been for Gillian's state of mind.

'Mother,' her oldest daughter finally said to her, 'even when Daddy was around, you used to have fun.'

'You're right,' Gillian admitted.

'Well, it's time you started having fun again.'

It wasn't that simple. Gillian was more than ever at risk, the custody of her daughters the price she could pay for any visibility in the bars. The cohesiveness of her old friends, which she had once prized, excluded her as long as she could not behave as she'd expected others to behave, resigned to loss and open to new adventures of the heart. Gillian simply could not forgive Lynn Number Two her betrayal. There was something else, too. As long as she had been married, the limitations of any other relationship were clear. Now, when she tired of someone – supposing that woman were not as untrustworthy as Lynn Number Two – Gillian could see no way out, no iron-clad and moral excuse for waning interest. Could there be a woman so remarkable as to hold Gillian's interest for the rest of her life? She had never thought of a woman in those terms.

Gillian's husband enjoyed his perfect solitude no more than Gillian enjoyed her freedom. After his outrage had worn itself out, erupting only occasionally at some convenience or familiar object lost to him, he suffered from simple loneliness, which he had no social skills to combat. Even his sporting trips, which he had made sure he could still afford, were not the escapes from domestic irritation which they had once been and lost their savor.

His daughters dutifully lunched with him, but he knew he bored them with his complaints, which would be repeated to their mother in a tone not sympathetic to him. He was not even sure what kind of sympathy he was asking for. He had been too deeply humiliated by Gillian's treatment of him to imagine that he wanted her back even on his own terms, which she would never agree to. He wanted back what he could not have, the illusion of Gillian as his wife.

And Gillian also wanted back what she could not have, not her husband, but the illusion of freedom he had given her.

ANNA LIVIA
5½ CHARLOTTE MEWS

(1986)

'Base to Lizzy. Base to Lizzy. Over.'

Middle of New Oxford Street. Damn the bloody radio. Impossible to stop now. Have to edge into the kerb, just when she'd achieved the right-hand lane.

'Base to Lizzy. Base to Lizzy. Crackle. Lizzy, Lizzy, Lizzy. If you hear me, love, give us a couple of rogers. Over.'

Left foot on pavement. Right arm round parcel.

'Lizzy to Base. Lizzy to Base. Over.'

'Lizzy did you pick up at Tiger?'

'Roger. Parcel On Board. Over.'

'POB? Ace. Pick up: Terracotta; Drop: Charlotte Mews.'

'Pick up: Roger. Crackle, crackle Mews?'

'Proceed to pick up, then RTB. Over.'

'Roger rog. Over and out.'

Damn and blast. Lizzy did not want to RTB. Not yet. Must be more traffic somewhere. Her daysheet counted thirteen drops total. You needed at least fifteen for breakeven. Kit, the controller, was paying her back. Lizzy was sure of it. Yesterday Lizzy'd totalled twenty-six drops, no cancellations, no returns, no wait-ing. Twenty was average for the men, though the longterms expected thirty. That's how Fast Buck made money. Kept the multidrops for the longterms, metered the rest out to the bleeps: rarely more than fifteen a day. Breakeven. The odd lucky streak thrown in to make you go on playing. Keep your body out of the doorways. Just another way of using it, really. Course you weren't meant to know you were being metered. Meant to accept you weren't fast enough, unfamiliar with the streets. Then there was the bleep problem. All you knew was that somebody, somewhere wanted a drop. But to find the pick up you had to dismount, locate a functional phone box, wait your turn in the consequent queue, and ring base. The radios just coasted to the kerb and called in. But a complete set cost £200 so was only allocated to the over twenties. Neat.

Yesterday Lizzy had raced wildly for ten hours in the oozing rain. When you stay wet long enough your rubbers mush, your fingers are anyway too cold to pull the levers and your toes cramp permanently in their clips. Water no longer falls from the sky, but seeps up out of the treacherous earth. Lizzy had crashed reds, let alone ambers; shortcut pavements; been smacked in the mug by a taxi-driver for burning the Wardour one-way. She had literally not stopped all day. Ate a Mars bar at Paddington Red Star, but that's all there'd been time for. She wanted to break the twenty a day barrier and achieve a radio. Get up to thirty like the longtermers. Prove she could do it.

Most of the bleeps were women. Fast Buck was an Equal Opportunity Employer. Besides, some firms preferred a pretty packet. Handed you three skimpy slide boxes and asked sweetly, 'Can you manage? We were expecting ... someone bigger.' Loaded you down with so many videos you thought the Times bag would split, then shoved their latest catalogue at you. 'Might as well take this while you're at it. Saves paying twice.' They liked to think of you weighted down by video nasties, labouring up narrow flights, dropping to their client, a sweating, panting face sandwiched between *Lesbian Lusts* and *Meat Cleaver*

Fever. Cinema drops were the worst. As you chained up you saw the women in hot pants and goose pimples, dancing in doorways as if they'd just been walking past, heard the music and were bopping along. While you waited on the buzzer, you could hear them talking to men.

'How bout some fun, honey? Want a good time? What do you like? Black, huh, you like black? We got black, we got white, got allsorts. Got anything you want.'

The bleeps rarely mentioned it to each other, but it must happen to all of them. They all had to drop to Soho. Lizzy smiled at the woman dancing. A ghastly smile, knowing that's where she'd end up if she failed at the fifteen a day; that's where many of the bleeps came from. Jiggling in a doorway. Though the greenfield drops lent you the ambiguous respectability of the suburbs, when you dragged yourself panting up the steep stairs of Windmill Street, you got to be part of it anyway. That kind of place.

And it slowed you down. 'Lucky little saddle.' 'Try this for thighs.' 'You do go all the way?' 'Nice firm crossbar there between your legs.' Lizzy ignored it, but it slowed you down. Couldn't do a racing start with the men jeering about throwing a leg over. She was fast though. When Kit turned excitedly from the phones and announced, 'Okay, everybody. Seven minute drop. BJ, you on?' Lizzy was sure she could have done it. Beat a lot of the men anyway on the flat, plus she was a Londoner and hers was a racer. Even the quickest amongst them took ten minutes on a puncture. Lizzy had replaced her wheels with sprints so when she got a flat she just ripped off the old tube and stretched on a new. Two mins max. Spent the evenings sewing up tyres, but it made the job more lucrative.

The other bleeps were more ladylike than Lizzy. Weren't going to push themselves. Smiled when the longterms asked, 'How many today? Reached double figures?' You got an extra quid waiting time over ten mins. The joke went that bleep wages were made up entirely of waiting time. So it was a point of honour not to charge it. Lizzy had sat for over half an hour in an enormous brown leather, open fire office off Saint Jameses for a bloke to sign his own cheque. Lost two drops just sitting there. 'Mark it down, mark it down,' the secretary hissed as Lizzy scowled. 'Your young men add on at least a quid for every delivery they make.' Lizzy told the other bleeps of her discovery, but they were loth to lose face. The women in Soho still danced in the doorways. Lizzy couldn't see any face to lose. It was a point of honour, also, to earn as much money as possible. Ever since, Lizzy systematically added a quid per drop.

And now she'd earned a radio. Though there were still problems. The men cut in and ripped off each other's jobs, pretending they'd heard their own name called. More serious, unless she dropped at least twenty today, Lizzy might forfeit the radio. Thirteen down. Another seven to go.

She shot into Percy, dropped the Tiger, leaving her wheels unchained. Should lock up, but no time. Rain'd most probably put them off. Damp saddle. Wet bottom. On to the Terracotta pick up and . . . where was the drop? She could not remember. Mind blank. Panic. Have to radio Base. They'd all hear and Kit would laugh, 'Der, where I am going please, Miss?' in her hoarse whisky voice.

When Lizzy first rang for a job, she was convinced Kit was a man. Then that she was a dyke. Such a deep voice. She must mean to have such a voice.

'So you wanna work for Fast Buck?' Kit had asked. 'How long you been riding?'

'Since I was four.'

'Long time. How well d'you know London? The Soho parallelogram?'

'Enough to know it's not one.'

'Unparalleled, huh? Name?'

'Anne Smith.'

'Got one of those already. You'll need a name for the radio.'

Not that Kit planned to give her a radio. Just a new name. It was her thought up 'Lizzy', 'Lizzy Longacre'. Which, for a ten hour a day rider, has its little sarcasm.

Kit was a bloody good controller. Six phones at once, twenty riders and never fucked up.

'And if I do, I admit it. That's the first thing. Send the next rider out with a big bottle of whisky and apologize abjectly. Like this is absolutely unprecedented in the annals of the firm.'

Lizzy wondered why Kit offered her these tips. She was sure as hell never going to work up to controller. Not unless she married, position of trust like that. But at first Kit clearly singled Lizzy out to talk to. Smoothed Lizzy's short, spikey hair so the bristles rubbed her palms silkily; called her hedgehog; told her she was hyper and that was a good thing.

'They say I'm hyper. Only way to be if you got a job to do, and I got six.'

Lizzy liked Kit. If she worked ten hours, Kit worked fourteen. She was there doing the accounts, billing clients, working out daysheets, long after the riders had left. She personally checked the radios, recharged batteries, replaced faulty sets. And she knew the London one-ways like the veins in her wrist. 'Down Dean, up Wardour,' she would remind Lizzy, when Lizzy was offering to burn them, 'ain't you got no pride?' She never told you wrong addresses, and she always knew what floor. If she and Lizzy had fallen out, it was not because Kit metered jobs.

Kit used to help Lizzy. Gave her returns, which doubled your takings if not your prestige. Got her doing paperwork in the slack to round up the pounds. Told her about the old country where it was hot and light. Slowly Lizzy's totals had crept up. Thirteen, fifteen, nineteen. So, unlike many bleeps, she didn't pack up the first month in despair.

Then came That Friday. Friday was always worst, because of the weekend looming. Rushes to take to labs, bank drafts to deliver, even contracts to get signed. The funny drops: a piece of liver for the ICA, green test tubes for Regent's Park zoo, always seemed to come on a Wednesday, but Friday was one endless scurry. No one took Friday off, not even the newest, most despairing bleep. That Friday was full of panicking bosses sending manic memos to Ms Smith across town, pick ups from one firm only two floors above the drop, but none of their staff could be spared the lift time. Multidrops of urgent minutes going out to sixty Members of the Board. The later it got, the angrier and more abusive were the clients. Lizzy delivered a manilla envelope to an editing firm only to have it ripped up in front of her.

'Tell him it can't be done. It's not reasonable. He simply can't use me like this. Offer a seven day service, they want it tomorrow. Offer twenty-four hours, they want it yesterday.'

'Oh they all want it yesterday,' agreed Lizzy philosophically, sensing a return and even a wait, during which she could eat her cheese roll.

'Well it's not possible!' shrieked the client in a rage, stamping his foot on the shredded envelope. A comic figure, a clown to amuse other clients with, but Lizzy knew a moment of terrible fear as she glanced at the intercom, checking she knew how to let herself out, away from the crazy.

'Will that be all?' she asked politely, edging for the door. But the man had calmed down, rang whoever and arranged to do the job if Lizzy would wait. Lizzy had now no desire to wait whatsoever, but it looked like the only chance she'd have to sit down all day. To refuse a drop was tantamount to resignation, and the more tired you were, the less likely to look out for side streets, homicidal maniacs, motorbikes cutting you up, the more likely to kiss a juggernaut. The man went off to deal with the editing and Lizzy sank into a deep green sofa, soft enough to cajole the most important deal; helped herself to filter coffee and read advertising awards. She gained an hour and a half, only rider to get any break at all, consequently the only one with any speed left in her. Kit's voice on the phone was hoarser and deeper than ever.

About 7 p.m. it began to calm down. Kit sent a couple of longterms out to get crates of beer for the riders. 'Thank you everyone,' she said warmly, 'we've all had one helluva day and I think we've deserved these.' The men knocked back the beer in approval, fizzed it up and frothed it out in a merry shower.

Neither Kit nor Lizzy touched the stuff. Kit looked exhausted. On the phone for fifteen hours non-stop. Responsible for twenty riders. Hundreds of drops.

'You look dead beat,' said Lizzy, looking at her.

'I am, love, I am,' said Kit, looking back.

'Tough job.'

'Tough cookie!' Kit laughed. 'Could do with a rest yourself.'

'I know,' said Lizzy, 'I'm going greenfields with my girlfriend this weekend.'

And that's when it changed. Kit with the husky voice, would flirt with Lizzy, of the bristly hair, but if Lizzy was a real dyke Kit didn't wanna know. Or maybe Kit wanted to be butch and Lizzy's sympathy galled. Was it butch to ride flat out and flex your thighs; femme to control the riders, send out for beer for the lads? Sounded right. Only Kit was tall, strong, loud-mouthed and unemotional. Lizzy was little, lithe, nervy and squeaky-voiced. Well, maybe Kit was pissed off Lizzy already had a lover. Not that that should have worried her. They hadn't lasted the weekend. But Kit never said. Just stopped giving Lizzy any but the longest drops, at the end of an underpass with a shortcut via the motorway.

On her first day with a radio, Lizzy did not want to call base for a repeat transmission. She'd done the Tiger, picked up from Terracotta and now where? Oh shit. Return to Base. No chance of another job for half an hour. Put her out of the running. But surely there'd been an address given out before the crackles. Had one of the men cut in on her? Useless, as she was POB and they weren't. Lizzy hated to think Kit liked the slimy creatures; called them 'Yes, my sweet,' and 'Yes, my love.' Aberrant: that big, husky woman with the cheekbones and the jaw chatting up men, of all people. The motorbikes in the leather and zips were femme; the pedals, with black tights and condor vests were clearly butch. They were the ones with muscles and a penchant for raw steak. Or perhaps Lizzy'd got it wrong again. Couldn't work out butch and femme for women, let alone them.

It was no good. Charlotte Street already and she could not remember the drop.

'Lizzy to Base. Lizzy to Base. Come in Base. Over.'

'Crackle. Crackle. Nyarrzzemd.'

'Lizzy POB in Charlotte Street. Lizzy, Charlotte Street, Parcel on Board.'

'Nyarzz. Static. Splutter.'

'Lizzy? Base here. 5½ Charlotte Mews.'

'Repeat. Repeat drop. Sounded like Charlotte Mews? Over.'

But the radio was dying, if not dead. Trust Kit to give her flat batteries. And she had trusted Kit. Pathetic. But taking directions from Kit used to be pure joy. So beautifully accurate, lyrical almost. 'South along Berwick. West Noel. South Poland. East Darblay. Right at Portland Mews. Yellow doorway, left arch, top buzzer. And return via Hyde. It's hot and you'll like the water fountain.'

Lizzy twiddled the buttons. White noise, more static, then:

'Okay everybody. Well I'm very pleased to introduce myself: I'm Nyarrzzemd and I shall be one of your four encouragers during your time at Charlotte Mews. This is what you might call an "orientation speech", in which I shall introduce a few basic concepts, which may be of use to you in your journey. If you do not feel you can use any encouragement at the present moment, please do not hesitate to turn off. Invert journeyings can be as productive as out and outs.'

Lizzy reckoned she could do with some encouragement. She stayed tuned.

'As you already know, and as we must repeat, our knowledge of your journey is sketchy in the extreme. We cannot advise you concretely, except in terms of how best to pit yourselves against adversity. We do not know, however, what constitutes adversity for you. We will ask you to push your muscles to, through, and past breaking point and not break, so that at every moment you are both aching and sinking into pain, transcending pain. You will run till your lungs can no longer gasp, your legs no longer pound nor your feet feel the ground under you. You will swim till your back longs to become a dolphin, or at least a hinge, till the battle to breast the water is almost lost. You will ride till your hands shake and your fingers twitch from clutching, till the ball muscles in your calves harden into marble and your thighs are long, lean tendons of pushing. Only you will know whether you can go on or not, because, when you go forth, only you will be able to secure yourselves from danger. We will urge you to continue. You must be strong enough to tell us to stop.

'You must prepare yourselves for tremendous depression, also, lethargy, fear, misery, confusion and here we can offer you only exercises in extreme sensory deprivation of a kind you have hitherto not imagined. From what little we know of the journey you are about to undertake, from those few survivors willing to testify, the place to which you are going seems almost to emanate anguish from its roots. These emanations are, of course, traceable to concrete causes by one qualified to judge. You will not be so qualified.

'I hope the following illustrations will give you some idea what to expect of the exercise at least, if not the reality beyond. You are lying in bright sunlight beneath a cloudless sky, the flowers around you the usual mix of azalea translucent and lush tropical. You are thirsty and stand up in search of a glass of water. You go into the house and it's so dark in there, after the light outside, that you are blinded by the gloom. You can see nothing, but walk through the room with your fingertips. Slowly your eyes become used to the dimness and pick out the shadowy outline of familiar objects, begin almost to see a certain beauty in a comparison of greys. Now, hold still at that point. Your eyes, used to the dark, will lose their capacity to appreciate bright colours, will think them gaudy and shy away. Will no longer distinguish between the fresh lime, the deep viridian and the flashing emerald of our native hills. Will call them simply green, tolerate them at dusk only.

'Again, you are lying in bright sunlight beneath a cloudless sky, the sun swarms over your naked body suffusing it with warmth. You feel a slight tightening in your cunt from the simple caress of the sun's rays lazily playing upon it. You do not wish to burn, so reach out for some light garment beside you.

Slowly, you dress. And with each article of clothing you feel colder and colder and pile on more clothes in search of warmth till, finally, you are muffled under thick sweaters and woollen vests, enormous overcoats and fur-lined gloves, boots on your feet making your steps heavy and awkward, your ears covered in a long knitted scarf so you can scarcely hear. Gone are the bare toes skipping lightly on sand, running luxurious in velvet grass. Now you walk sombrely, and others like you, bumping against each other, hardly hearing, and with no idea even of the shape of your own bodies.

'Once more you are lying in bright sunlight beneath a cloudless sky, you are eating peaches. Peaches and cherries, nectarines, plums, tangerines and grapes. They are firm, sweet, soft, juicy, wet. You spit out pips with strong teeth and much laughter. You reach for another. There are none left. There is only custard. Cold custard. Cold, long-congealed and slightly burnt, slightly powdery, as though with lumps of mixture not smoothed in. You say you don't like custard. Then there is tinned tomatoes, raw chick peas. You stand up to dance at least, if you cannot eat. The band plays a waltz, sweet, old-fashioned. You like to waltz, but your partner does not keep time and will not touch you, will only jerk spasmodically with grim heroism, hands in pockets. Frantically you look at the pictures on the walls for some soothing symmetry, a flash of energy, a hint of purpose. They are hung slightly crooked. For no reason. It would have been as easy to hang them straight. But they are not. The colours do not clash, they edge uneasily away from one another. There is no vigour in the brush strokes but an apologetic, helpless dash from place to place which peters out ineffectually.

'Finally, across the room you glimpse an old friend, a close friend with whom you have spent long, intense hours talking, persuading, earnestly, happily. You make your way towards her through the heavy, muffled figures in the gloom. You will tell her how it is always cold here, how, when the sun shines, it is brief and watery, the colours muted and everything tastes of cold, wet custard, slightly sweet. How women dance out of time, the graphics slope off-centre and even the purples and oranges do not clash but sidle. Everything will be bearable if only you two can agree on the clammy, spongelike awfulness. She tells you to cheer up and make the best of it, the cold is not so much harsh as bracing. You'll get used to it, you may even go swimming, give your body to the waves. She giggles. She never used to giggle. She says she likes cold custard, that grey's a very subtle taste, co-ordinates so well with pink. You look out bleakly at the oily sea. She puts a sympathetic hand on your shoulder and tells you, you must try to enjoy it a little. You must not feel so passionately, this is a world of men, a world where women care for men, and for men it is neither possible, nor advisable, to feel passion.

'Well, this has just been an introductory presentation and I feel it is only fair to ask you all, if only for formality's sake, whether any of you are the least put off by what you have heard. Do please speak now, your niggling doubts, your slightest uncertainties. No one is obliged to go on the journey. So, are you all still committed?'

Crackle. Splutter. Criik. Whoosh. Sh, sh.

Then another voice began to speak, and another, till there came the sound of many voices speaking together.

'No. No. We're not. Sounds terrible. Perfectly dreadful. Who in her right mind would want to go to a place like that? No wonder they go crazy.'

Then the first voice came back.

'I fully accept your reasoning. Your sentiments are mine exactly. But every generation we have to put the question, in case anyone tunes in and feels something is being kept from her.'

Crackle. Crackle. Static interference. And Lizzy's radio fell silent.

'Base to Lizzy. Base to Lizzy. Come in please. Over.'

'Lizzy here. Over,' called Lizzy, dazed at the sound of Kit's voice.

'Current location? You were told to RTB. Over.'

'Sorry, I . . . I . . . Kit, didn't you hear that broadcast?'

'What broadcast? Specify. Over.'

'From Charlotte Mews.'

'Repeat transmission station. Over.'

'5½ Charlotte Mews. It was . . .'

'I know what it was! Message received and understood. So they're back on air. Has it been that long? There was just a chance with you, but you seemed more concerned with drops, I wasn't sure.'

'Unsure of what? Specify uncertainty. Over.'

'That they'd get through to you.'

'To me? They were transmitting to each other. Whole different system. Over.'

'You got tuned, believe me.'

'How do you know? Specify certainty. Over.'

'This journey they were talking about. That's here. I took it.'

'You mean it's not like this there? Weather conditions hot, light, sunny, permanent fixture? Over.'

'Affirmative.'

'So why the hell did you leave, Kit? Weren't taken in by that transcending pain shit?'

'Negative. Kept receiving Outside Broadcasts. Sounded like a lot of power men had. Deciding, striding, conquering. Hot stuff. Never occurred to me I'd have to be a woman. Over.'

'Women in the Mews don't have power? Over.'

'Affirmative power. Negative work ethic. Over.'

'Negative work ethic? They got no traffic? Over.'

'Double affirmative. Traffic but no deadlines. Love affairs instead. Over.'

'Could speed em up. Good love affair.'

'Possibility.'

'Want to try it?'

'Meet you down there, darling.'

'Message received and understood. Proceeding Charlotte Mews. Estimated arrival time 2½ mins. Weather conditions fair to exuberant. Over and Out.'

SARA MAITLAND

LULLABY FOR MY DYKE AND HER CAT

(1987)

The immediate problem is to think of some way to explain it to the boys; for their sake as much as mine – though I can't cope with them peering at me lovingly for the next few weeks and suggesting that perhaps I need a nice rest – which I do of course, but that is another story. And I'm not the sort of person who functions well on Valium, it doesn't suit my style and I think it would be dangerous for the baby. I can hardly use postnatal depression which I thought of at first, because my son is over a year now and having sailed through the whole thing so far I think it would lack credibility. I did consider telling them I had been experimenting with hallucinogenic drugs, but I doubt if they'd believe that either, and the consequences might prove even more complicated than the reality.

Reality is an odd word to use in this context. You see, I thought my son was turning into a cat. Only for a moment or two, and he wasn't anyway, so it doesn't really matter a lot.

When I tell Liz it will make her laugh. At least I hope to God it does. I think it probably will.

I'm not sure if I've ever told you about Liz; she's my best friend. We go back a long way together; as a matter of fact – although this is so corny that we don't often mention it – we met at an anti-Vietnam-War demo in Grosvenor Square in 1968. Neither of us was being particularly heroic, I should say, but we were both with people who knew each other, and then of course it turned out that we were both at college together, so really we had met before though we just hadn't noticed. And if you remember how it was, one thing led to another, and then we were best friends, and before long there was feminism and we discovered that together and fought about it together – both against each other and together against others and we were better friends still. You know people put down the sixties now, it's become trendy to be blasé and dismissive about it, but I go on believing that there was really something there, something important and that those of us who failed to sustain the vision that we had then have something to answer for; and how to know this and hold on to it and still not succumb to the cosiness of Liberal Guilt is a question well worth asking, but one doesn't too often because it is all a bit painful; and we have not been rewarded with the joyfulness and richness that we so optimistically believed in. Or perhaps all I want to say is that those were incredibly happy days for me and I look back on them with nostalgia and regret and the certain knowledge that I blew it and yet totally uncertain as to quite how or when. And a large part of that happiness was having Liz as my best friend and – to be crude – getting the benefit of her extraordinary acute and eccentric mind. And then to everyone's surprise except mine, and possibly Dr Turner's (who was our tutor in our final year and knew damn well that mine was show-off and Liz's was solid) she got an incredibly fancy degree and a research fellowship and I went off to Devon to teach my aphasic children and we did not see each other so much: because she was hardly one to brave the countryside, of which she radically disapproved; and because I was so into hearing those silenced voices and playing with ideas about language and the social construction of the self that I never went away. And then, listening to them so hard, I couldn't take the right line on abortion and we squabbled about that; and she went off to the States for a year and you would have thought that our friendship had come to an end.

But it didn't. I started to write stuff and woke up one morning and realized that, for the moment, the kids didn't have anything more to teach me – I'd never thought that I'd had much to teach them and being them they never made guilt inducing demands for gratitude so I said good-bye and came to London. Then when I was finishing my second book I suddenly realized how much of it I owed to Liz as well as to the children and the school and I put that in the acknowledgements as a good feminist ought and the week *before* it was published the telephone rang and this unforgettable voice said, 'How *dare* you bracket me with brain-damaged infants?'

And I laughed from pure joy. Then she said, 'It's not bad at all and you always did have a way with words but . . .' and with concision and no indulgence she listed thirty-seven real problems with the text. Now it is always flattering to have that degree of attention paid to your work, and also she was enormously knowledgeable – and it wasn't even her subject – but if anyone else I hadn't seen for five years had done that to me I would probably have killed them. As it was, within twenty minutes I had leapt on my bike and was pedalling merrily off to Victoria Park where she was living and where we fell into each other's arms and we were best friends – still or again? I do not know and I do not care.

This is all narrative, it tells nothing, except narrative. And I'm not good at 'the well-rounded character', that stand-by of Western prose literature. I don't know how, within the limits of a short story, to show the way our lives fitted into a much larger web or mesh of friendships and work connections: that is what I want to tell, and also I want to describe her – because I assure you all this does have a lot to do with my present dilemma about explaining to the men I live with how it was that I came to think that my son was turning into a cat. But narrative is not the answer – or not at least to the questions that I want to ask.

Apart from linear narrative there is also anecdote. (There is also analysis, of course, but I think that it is cheating to tell the reader what she has to think about something unless you also tell her the something she is meant to be thinking about: for instance, I can tell you that one of the most delightful things about Liz was that she was extremely witty – faster on her verbal toes than anyone I've ever met, and that at times she would sacrifice anything, truth, friendship and innocent people's social comfort, for a good line – but unless I can give you concrete examples of this, which is difficult because all the best jokes come so totally out of context which is long and elaborate and often inaccessible to anyone else, it is not fair on you. You might, like many others, find her humour not charming at all but unnerving and sadistic and why should you have to take it from me?) Anyway anecdote:

Once she and I were having supper with some people one of whom was a friend of mine who dislikes Liz rather a lot; and the two of us – Liz and I – were showing off rather, and the friend said crossly, bad timing, suddenly heavy, 'For God's sake, you two; stop being each other's *alter egos* and behave yourselves, the way you two go on isn't natural.' Well, I would just have said yeah and let it go at that, but Liz launched into an elaborate though completely accurate description of the reproductive cycle of the coriantis, the bucket orchid; and then another about the horsehair worm. (I don't know if you know about either of these natural phenomena, but they both have life-cycle patterns which are so far-fetched, arbitrary and ridiculous that they boggle the mind, make one wonder if Darwin can actually be right, or whether in fact and after all there isn't a delightfully humorous and whimsical old man with a beard up there running the whole show for the amusement of a bunch of angels. You can read about the horsehair worm, if you want, in a wonderful book which practically comes to this conclusion called *Pilgrim at*

Tinker's Creek which is written by a woman called Annie Dillard. But I'm getting off the point again.) Liz gave this lecture with great *élan* and brilliance, if somewhat excessive length. She didn't like this friend any more than the friend liked her. 'Nothing, in nature,' she concluded, 'is remotely natural. Why should our relationship be?'

Once when we were very much younger, I got into a terrible temper and smashed thirty-seven empty milk bottles against the wall of our kitchen. Liz swept up all the broken glass, gave me a hug and never mentioned it again until, over ten years later, when we were talking on the telephone as I described above and she finished her current list of criticisms of my book, she said, 'You see, one for each milk bottle; I've been longing to punish you for that idiotic tantrum.'

Once quite recently we were rather drunk at a large and noisy party; Liz was dancing on the other side of the room and some man – not a very nice one – asked me some question about Liz's early career, and Liz detached herself from the arms of her partner at once and crossed the room and touched his sleeve and said, 'It's not fair to ask Meg those sorts of questions; she's the only woman around who knew me before I was invented.' She went right back to her dancing and I said to the man, 'That's the loveliest compliment I've ever been paid.' And he clearly thought the pair of us were entirely mad.

Once when it was the middle of an extremely cold winter I went round to visit her and, despite several degrees of frost and a howling wind, her cat door was tied open with the lace from her tennis shoes. Shivering I asked her why and she told me that she was afraid that having to push on the icy glass would hurt the cat's nose.

Once. You see, it doesn't work. I've also just remembered that I've forgotten to mention something extremely important about Liz; or rather extremely important to the story that, despite all these digressions, I'm trying to tell you. Well, to be honest, I didn't really forget, I just was not sure at what point to put it in: either in terms of politics, or in terms of artistry. Now of course I've left it so late that it has far more force than I really wanted it to; I feel it to be a fact about her just as the colour of her hair (pale mouse) or her stately bosom and tiny ankles. She's a lesbian. And once, a long time ago, when we were younger, we . . . well, that bit isn't very important. Now I often think that difference helps and sustains our friendship: once we were talking on the phone about whether or not we wanted to go into analysis and she said, 'My problem is when I'm in a room on my own I don't know if I'm alive.' And I said, 'Whereas when I'm in a room on my own I can't understand why I'm not alone.' And this made us laugh with considerable pleasure. I didn't go into analysis as it turned out, but she did: she's quite a lot braver than me in many ways. However, be this as it may, I'm not making very good progress with this story about thinking my son was turning into a cat.

Liz has a cat; her cat is black with a few grey hairs (not dissimilar from mine now I think about it), and quite small and is called Mog. Not directly from Moggie as you might think, but because there are these children's books about a witch called Meg and her cat Mog: they're rather fine books actually and are written in a children's lower-case script rather than proper print. So when I gave Liz a kitten when I first went to Devon and she to Essex and we stopped sharing a flat, she called her Mog because of my name being Meg. People come and go in Liz's domestic life, but Mog stays. She's got old of course and a bit arthritic, and less inclined to frolic; but if you go to Liz's there she will be, as often as not curled around Liz's shoulder and drooped across what we unkindly call 'The Continental Shelf': a wide soft plain created by Liz's breasts.

Liz really loves Mog, in a very simple and pure relationship which I find inexhaustibly touching – a fact which I, like most of her friends, express by mockery and cynicism. When I was first pregnant I went to tell her about it – for some reason I felt extraordinarily nervous about doing so, though I have looked to her and received support in many far less promising ventures – and she looked faintly disgusted. (This did not altogether surprise me, she has the most bizarrely naïve views about the facts of life; once when she wanted to find out what heterosexuality was about she asked if she could borrow my cap and was amazed when I told her (a) that this freaked me out and (b) that it wouldn't work.) Then she sighed thoughtfully and said, 'God another damn case of sublimation.' 'What?' I said, startled. 'You know,' she said. 'Another poor heterosexual woman trying to substitute for the fact that she cannot achieve the one perfect relationship in this sad world: the relationship between a dyke and her cat. Haven't you noticed it? Here we all are pushing forty and having to settle for what we can get; and you're all getting babies because you know you can't have what we've got.' Then she collapsed on the sofa in fits of giggles with Mog in her arms. Later she twanged my bra strap rather over-enthusiastically – because I never wore one until I got pregnant when it hurt not to – and said that at least we now had something in common. Later still she bought some beautiful scarlet and black wool and knitted the most wonderful pram suit you have ever seen covered with cabbalistic designs and said if it was a girl would I please keep her in pristine purity until she was sixteen and then hand her over for the traditional *droit de seigneuresse*? After that she did not talk about the pregnancy very much, but the morning that Noah was born she came to visit us both with him still so new that he looked like a tiny interplanetary voyager trying to disguise himself as a human being. And, despite the forbidding notices all over the place, she picked him up and hugged him and said he was nearly as lovely as Mog. But when Paul arrived she swapped bawdy jokes with him about deliveries and knife-crazed surgeons until I felt quite pissed off with the pair of them.

So that is sort of the background; except that I've completely left Paul out of all this somehow. He is the bloke I live with; he and I share a slightly grotty little house with another good friend called David – and it is to them, and now Noah as well of course, that I am referring when I say 'the boys'. I feel a bit overwhelmed to be honest about the number of males there are in my habitation; I had sort of planned on having a daughter to even things out a bit but David and Paul are very old friends and it would be asking a bit much to suggest that David left and there isn't any room for anyone else so there you are. Or rather, there I am, and by and large pretty pleased with it.

So. Last night I had a panicked call from Liz. Mog was sick. Liz was in tears. I have not seen her cry for years; the last time was when I . . . well that would be another long anecdote and I really must get on with this, especially as the anecdotes don't seem to help much. So I chucked the supper-filled Noah at his dad, ignored both their whingeings about it and rode off as fast as I could to Liz's flat, pausing only at an off-licence to buy a large bottle of brandy.

The vet had sent Mog home to die. She had had what seemed to be a twisted gut and the vet had opened her up and discovered that she was riddled with feline cancer. He had suggested putting her down and Liz had refused, refused point blank. The vet had got annoyed with her, said there was nothing more he could do and sent Liz and Mog home. There was nothing we could do either. We sat on Liz's bed with Mog laid out on her Continental Shelf with her eyes slitting up, and we drank the brandy steadily, while Liz petted the dankening fur and I periodically petted Liz. Sometime about two in the morning Mog died. A while later I said as gently as I knew how, 'Liz, she's dead.' And Liz said, 'No, no,' in a little kid's voice. So I took them both in my arms and we just sat there a whole lot longer, and Liz cried and cried and cried, and then she didn't cry any more, she just sat in my arms and held on to Mog. Later still we finished what was left of the brandy, and at about five I said I would have to go because of getting home before Noah woke up and did she want to come? And she said that she didn't, so I said I would take the day off work and come back later with Noah and she said, 'Thank you.'

I admit that bicycling home I realized I was a bit smashed, but not that smashed and it was the darkest night I had been out in for some time and quite windy and spooky, and I'm not a great night person and it is rare to put it mildly that I am out and about at so late and weird an hour. When I arrived the house was silent and dark. I brought the bike in and locked up behind me and went upstairs, suddenly very tired and longing for my bed. At the top of the stairs is Noah's little room; it was more a reflex of tenderness and tiredness that made me go in to look at him than anything else. He sleeps with a night-light on which gives the room a faint and sweet glow. I leaned over the cot as I often do, expecting to be reassured by his sound and total sleep. He was lying as usual on his front with his nappied bottom sticking up in the air and his paw in his mouth, and his whiskers slicked out elegantly; where his sleeper poppers had come undone a little of his soft ginger fur poked out. I thought vaguely that we must get him out of nappies before the summer because it would be too hot for his tail when I realized what was happening. My baby was turning into a cat. And I was so shit scared that I created the most amazing rumpus; screaming and screaming. And Noah woke up and joined in and Paul and David appeared shocked and sleep-hagged, and even in my panic I noticed that David was actually wearing the most preposterous pair of bright yellow silk pyjamas that I had given him for his last birthday and for some reason this did not comfort me. As soon as I had Noah in my arms I realized that it was nothing, nothing at all, a trick of the light, or my tiredness, and he was just my little boy, nearly eighteen months old and only as softly furred as all small human beings are, his face warm and pink and whisker-free. The boys were both concerned and cross. Paul took Noah and settled him down again, and David offered to make some hot chocolate, and I just wanted to be in bed, alone.

You see, I wasn't scared because I thought that Noah was turning into a cat, but because I thought that if he was it meant I was becoming a lesbian and for a tiny moment I felt so relieved. It had been stupid, stupid, and there is no way I can explain it to Paul. I mean it was just a moment of madness, and drunkenness and lateness, wasn't it?

So why am I curled up alone in my bed with some lovely hot chocolate and a unique promise to do Noah's breakfast and crying and crying?

JEWELLE GOMEZ
DON'T EXPLAIN

(1987)

Boston 1959

Letty deposited the hot platters on the table, effortlessly. She slid one deep-fried chicken, a club-steak with boiled potatoes and a fried porgie platter down her thick arm as if removing beaded bracelets. Each plate landed with a solid clink on the shiny Formica, in its appropriate place. The last barely settled before Letty turned back to the kitchen to get Bo John his lemonade and extra biscuits and then to put her feet up. Out of the corner of her eye she saw Tip come in the lounge. His huge shoulders, draped in sharkskin, barely cleared the narrow door frame.

'Damn! He's early tonight!' she thought but kept going. Tip was known for his generosity, that's how he'd gotten his nickname. He always sat at Letty's station because they were both from Virginia, although neither had been back in years. Letty had come up to Boston in 1946 and been waiting tables in the 411 Lounge since '52. She liked the people: the pimps were limited but flashy; the musicians who hung around were unpredictable in their pursuit of a good time and the 'business' girls were generous and always willing to embroider a wild story.

After Letty's mother died there'd been no reason to go back to Burkeville.

Letty took her newspaper from the locker behind the kitchen and filled a large glass with the tart grape juice punch for which the cook, Mabel, was famous.

'I'm going on break, Mabel. Delia's takin' my station.'

She sat in the back booth nearest the kitchen beneath the large blackboard which displayed the menu. When Delia came out of the bathroom Letty hissed to get her attention. The reddish-brown skin of Delia's face was shiny with a country freshness that always made Letty feel a little warm.

'What's up, Miss Letty?' Her voice was soft and saucy.

'Take my tables for twenty minutes. Tip just came in.'

The girl's already bright smile widened, as she started to thank Letty.

'Go 'head, go 'head. He don't like to wait. You can thank me if he don't run you back and forth fifty times.'

Delia hurried away as Letty sank into the coolness of the overstuffed booth and removed her shoes. After a few sips of her punch she rested her head on the back of the seat with her eyes closed. The sounds around her were as familiar as her own breathing: squeaking Red Cross shoes as Delia and Vinnie passed, the click of high heels around the bar, the clatter of dishes in the kitchen and ice clinking in glasses. The din of conversation rose, levelled and rose again over the juke box. Letty had not played her record in days but the words spun around in her head as if they were on the turntable:

> . . . right or wrong don't matter
> when you're with me sweet
> Hush now, don't explain
> You're my joy and pain.

Letty sipped her cool drink; sweat ran down her spine soaking into the nylon uniform. July weather promised to give no breaks and the fans were working overtime like everybody else.

She saw Delia cross to Tip's table again. In spite of the dyed red hair, no matter how you looked at her, Delia was still a country girl: long and self-conscious, shy and bold because she didn't know any better. She'd moved up from Anniston with her cousin a year before and landed the job at the 411 immediately. She worked hard and sometimes Letty and she shared a cab going uptown after work, when Delia's cousin didn't pick them up in her green Pontiac.

Letty caught Tip eyeing Delia as she strode on long, tight-muscled legs back to the kitchen. 'That lounge lizard!' Letty thought to herself. Letty had trained Delia: how to balance plates, how to make tips and how to keep the customer's hands on the table. She was certain Delia would have no problem putting Tip in his place. In the year she'd been working Delia hadn't gone out with any of the bar flies, though plenty had asked. Letty figured that Delia and her cousin must run with a different crowd. They talked to each other sporadically in the kitchen or during their break but Letty never felt that wire across her chest like Delia was going to ask her something she couldn't answer.

She closed her eyes again for the few remaining minutes. The song was back in her head and Letty had to squeeze her lips together to keep from humming aloud. She pushed her thoughts on to something else. But when she did she always stumbled upon Maxine. Letty opened her eyes. When she'd quit working at Salmagundi's and come to the 411 she'd promised herself never to think about any woman like that again. She didn't know why missing Billie so much brought it all back to her. She'd not thought of that time or those feelings for a while.

She heard Abe shout a greeting at Duke behind the bar as he surveyed his domain. That was Letty's signal. No matter whether it was her break or not she knew white people didn't like to see their employees sitting down, especially with their shoes off. By the time Abe was settled on his stool near the door, Letty was up, her glass in hand and on her way through the kitchen's squeaky swinging door.

'You finished your break already?' Delia asked.

'Abe just come in.'

'Uh oh, let me git this steak out there to that man. Boy he sure is nosey!'

'Who, Tip?'

'Yeah, he ask me where I live, who I live with, where I come from like he supposed to know me!'

'Well just don't take nothing he say to heart and you'll be fine. And don't take no rides from him!'

'Yeah, he asked if he could take me home after I get off. I told him me and you had something to do.'

Letty was silent as she sliced the fresh bread and stacked it on plates for the next orders.

'My cousin's coming by, so it ain't a lie, really. She can ride us.'

'Yeah,' Letty said as Delia giggled and turned away with her platter.

Vinnie burst through the door like she always did, looking breathless and bossy. 'Abe up there, girl! You better get back on station. You got a customer.'

Letty drained her glass with deliberation, wiped her hands on her thickly starched white apron and walked casually past Vinnie as if she'd never spoken. She heard Mabel's soft chuckle float behind her. She went over to Tip who was digging into the steak like his life depended on devouring it before the plate got dirty.

'Everything alright tonight?' Letty asked, her ample brown body towering over the table.

'Yeah, baby, everything alright. You ain't workin' this side no more?'

'I was on break. My feet can't wait for your stomach, you know.'

Tip laughed. 'Break! What you need a break for, big and healthy as you is!'

'We all gets old, Tip. But the feet get old first, let me tell you that!'

'Not in my business, baby. Why you don't come on and work for me and you ain't got to worry 'bout your feet.'

Letty sucked her teeth loudly, the exaggeration a part of the game they played over the years. 'Man, I'm too old for that mess!'

'You ain't too old for me.'

'Ain't nobody too old for you! Or too young neither, looks like.'

'Where you and that gal goin' tonight?'

'To a funeral,' Letty responded dryly.

'Aw woman get on away from my food!' The gold cap on his front tooth gleamed from behind his greasy lips when he laughed. Letty was pleased. Besides giving away money Tip liked to hurt people. It was better when he laughed.

The kitchen closed at 11.00 p.m. Delia and Letty slipped out of their uniforms in the tiny bathroom and were on their way out the door by 11.15. Delia looked even younger in her knife-pleated skirt and white cotton blouse. Letty did feel old tonight in her slacks and long-sleeved shirt. The movement of car headlights played across her face, which was set in exhaustion. The dark green car pulled up and they slipped in quietly, both anticipating tomorrow, Sunday, the last night of their work week.

Delia's cousin was a stocky woman who looked forty, Letty's age. She never spoke much. Not that she wasn't friendly. She always greeted Letty with a smile and laughed at Delia's stories about the customers. 'Just close to the chest like me, that's all,' Letty often thought. As they pulled up to the corner of Columbus Avenue and Cunard Street, Letty opened the rear door. Delia turned to her and said, 'I'm sorry you don't play your record on your break no more, Miss Letty. I know you don't want to, but I'm sorry just the same.'

Delia's cousin looked back at them with a puzzled expression but said nothing. Letty slammed the car door shut and turned to climb the short flight of stairs to her apartment. Cunard Street was quiet outside her window and the guy upstairs wasn't blasting his record player for once. Still, Letty lay awake and restless in her single bed. The fan was pointed at the ceiling, bouncing warm air over her, rustling her sheer nightgown.

Inevitably the strains of Billie Holiday's songs brushed against her, much like the breeze that fanned around her. She felt silly when she thought about it, but the melodies gripped her like a solid presence. It was more than the music. Billie had been her hero. Letty saw Billie as big, like herself, with big hungers, and some secret that she couldn't tell anyone. Two weeks ago, when Letty heard that the Lady had died, sorrow enveloped her. A refuge had been closed that she could not consciously identify to herself or to anyone. It embarrassed her to think about. Like it did when she remembered Maxine.

When Letty first started working at the 411 she met Billie when she'd come into the club with several musicians on her way back from the Jazz Festival. There the audience, curious to see what a real, live junkie looked like, had sat back waiting for Billie to fall on her face. Instead she'd killed them dead with her liquid voice and rough urgency. Still, the young, thin horn player kept having to reassure her: 'Billie you were the show, the whole show!'

Once convinced, Billie became the show again, loud and commanding. She demanded her food be served at the bar and sent Mabel, who insisted on waiting on her personally, back to the kitchen fifteen times. Billie laughed at jokes that Letty could barely hear as she bustled back and forth between the abandoned kitchen and her own tables. The sound of that laugh from the bar penetrated her bones. She'd watched and listened, certain she saw something no one else did. When Billie had finished eating and gathered her entourage to get back on the road she left a tip, not just for Mabel but for each of the waitresses and the bartender. 'Generous just like the "business" girls,' Letty was happy to note. She still had the two one dollar bills in an envelope at the back of her lingerie drawer.

After that, Letty felt even closer to Billie. She played one of the few Lady Day records on the juke box every night during her break. Everyone at the 411 had learned not to bother her when her song came on. Letty realized, as she lay waiting for sleep, that she'd always felt that if she had been able to say or do something that night to make friends with Billie, it might all have been different. In half sleep the faces of Billie, Maxine and Delia blended in her mind. Letty slid her hand along the soft nylon of her gown to rest it between her full thighs. She pressed firmly, as if holding desire inside herself. Letty could have loved her enough to make it better. That was Letty's final thought as she dropped off to sleep.

Sunday nights at the 411 were generally mellow. Even the pimps and prostitutes used it as a day of rest. Letty came in early and had a drink at the bar and talked with the bartender before going to the back to change into her uniform. She saw Delia through the window as she stepped out of the green Pontiac, looking as if she'd just come from Concord Baptist Church. 'Satin Doll' was on the juke box, wrapping the bar in cool nostalgia.

Abe let Mabel close the kitchen early on Sunday and Letty looked forward to getting done by 10.00 or 10.30, and maybe enjoying some of the evening. When her break time came Letty started for the juke box automatically. She hadn't played anything by Billie in two weeks; now, looking down at the inviting glare, she knew she still couldn't do it. She punched the buttons that would bring up Jackie Wilson's 'Lonely Teardrops' and went to the back booth.

She'd almost dropped off to sleep when she heard Delia whisper her name. She opened her eyes and looked up into the girl's smiling face. Her head was haloed in tight, shiny curls.

'Miss Letty, won't you come home with me tonight?'

'What?'

'I'm sorry to bother you, but your break time almost up. I wanted to ask if you'd come over to the house tonight . . . after work. My cousin'll bring you back home after.'

Letty didn't speak. Her puzzled look prompted Delia to start again.

'Sometime on Sunday my cousin's friends from work come over to play cards, listen to music, you know. Nothin' special, just some of the girls from the office building down on Winter

Street where she work, cleaning. She, I mean we, thought you might want to come over tonight. Have a drink, play some cards . . .'

'I don't play cards much.'

'Well not everybody play cards . . . just talk . . . sitting around talking. My cousin said you might like to for a change.'

Letty wasn't sure she liked the last part: 'for a change,' as if they had to entertain an old aunt.

'I really want you to come, Letty. They always her friends but none of them is my own friends. They alright, I don't mean nothin' against them, but it would be fun to have my own personal friend there, you know?'

Delia was a good girl. Those were the perfect words to describe her, Letty thought smiling. 'Sure honey, I'd just as soon spend my time with you as lose my money with some fools.'

They got off at 10.15 and Delia apologized that they had to take a cab uptown. Her cousin and her friends didn't work on Sunday so they were already at home. Afraid that the snag would give Letty an opportunity to back out Delia hadn't mentioned it until they were out of their uniforms and on the sidewalk. Letty almost declined, tempted to go home to the safe silence of her room. But she didn't. She stepped into the street and waved down a Red and White cab. All the way uptown Delia apologized that the evening wasn't a big deal and cautioned Letty not to expect much. 'Just a few friends, hanging around, drinking and talking.' She was jumpy and Letty tried to put her at ease. She had not expected her first visit would make Delia so anxious.

The apartment was located halfway up Blue Hill Avenue in an area where a few blacks had recently been permitted to rent. They entered a long, carpeted hallway and heard the sounds of laughter and music ringing from the rooms at the far end.

Once inside, with the door closed, Delia's personality took on another dimension. This was clearly her home and Letty could not believe she ever really needed an ally to back her up. Delia stepped out of her shoes at the door and walked to the back with her same, long-legged gait. They passed a closed door, which Letty assumed to be one of the bedrooms, then came to a kitchen ablaze with light. Food and bottles were strewn across the pink and gray Formica top table. A counter opened from the kitchen into the dining-room, which was the center of activity. Around a large mahogany table sat five women in smoke-filled concentration, playing poker.

Delia's cousin looked up from her cards with the same slight smile as usual. Here it seemed welcoming, not guarded as it did in those brief moments in her car. She wore brown slacks and a matching sweater. The pink, starched points of her shirt collar peeked out at the neck.

Delia crossed to her and kissed her cheek lightly. Letty looked around the table to see if she recognized anyone. The women all seemed familiar in the way that city neighbors can, but Letty was sure she hadn't met any of them before. Delia introduced her to each one: Karen, a short, round woman with West Indian bangles up to her pudgy elbow; Betty, who stared intently at her cards through thick eyeglasses encased in blue cat-eye frames; Irene, a big, dark woman with long black hair and a gold tooth in front. Beside her sat Myrtle who was wearing army fatigues and a gold Masonic ring on her pinky finger. She said hello in the softest voice Letty had ever heard. Hovering over her was Clara, a large red woman whose hair was bound tightly in a bun at the nape of her neck. She spoke with a delectable southern accent that drawled her 'How're you doin' into a full paragraph that was draped around an inquisitive smile.

Delia became ill-at-ease again as she pulled Letty by the arm toward the French doors behind the players. There was a small den with a desk, some books and a television set. Through the next set of glass doors was a living-room. At the record player was an extremely tall, brown-skinned woman. She bent over the wooden cabinet searching for the next selection, oblivious to the rest of the gathering. Two women sat on the divan in deep conversation, which they punctuated with constrained giggles.

'Maryalice, Sheila, Dolores . . . this is Letty.'

They looked up at her quickly, smiled, then went back to their preoccupations: two to their gossip, the other returning to the record collection. Delia directed Letty back toward the foyer and the kitchen.

'Come on, let me get you a drink. You know, I don't even know what you drink!'

'Delia?' Her cousin's voice reached them over the counter, just as they stepped into the kitchen. 'Bring a couple of beers back when you come, OK?'

'Sure, babe.' Delia went to the refrigerator and pulled out two bottles. 'Let me just take these in. I'll be right back.'

'Go 'head, I can take care of myself in this department, girl.' Letty surveyed the array of bottles on the table. Delia went to the dining-room and Letty mixed a Scotch and soda. She poured slowly as the reality settled on her. These women were friends, perhaps lovers, like she and Maxine had been. The name she'd heard for women like these burst inside her head: bulldagger. Letty flinched, angry she had let it in, angry that it frightened her. 'Ptuh!' Letty blew air through her teeth as if spitting the word back at the air.

She did know these women, Letty thought, as she stood at the counter smiling out at the poker game. They were oblivious to her, except for Terry. Letty remembered that was Delia's cousin's name. As Letty took her first sip, Terry called over to her. 'We gonna be finished with this game in a minute Letty, then we can talk.'

'Take your time,' Letty said, then went out through the foyer door and around to the living-room. She walked slowly on the carpet and adjusted her eyes to the light, which was a bit softer. The tall woman, Maryalice, had just put a record on the turntable and sat down on a love seat across from the other two women. Letty stood in the doorway a moment before the tune began:

> Hush now, don't explain
> Just say you'll remain
> I'm glad you're back
> Don't explain . . .

Letty was stunned, but the song sounded different here, among these women. Billie sang just to them, here. The isolation and sadness seemed less inevitable with these women listening. Letty watched Maryalice sitting with her long legs stretched out tensely in front of her. She was wrapped in her own thoughts, her eyes closed. She appeared curiously disconnected, after what had clearly been a long search for this record. Letty watched her face as she swallowed several times. Then Letty moved to sit on the seat beside her. They listened to the music while the other two women spoke in low voices.

When the song was over Maryalice didn't move. Letty rose from the sofa and went to the record player. Delia stood tentatively in the doorway of the living-room. Letty picked up the arm of the phonograph and replaced it at the beginning of the record. When she sat again beside Maryalice she noticed the drops of moisture on the other woman's lashes. Maryalice relaxed as Letty settled on to the seat beside her. They both listened to Billie together, for the first time.

DOROTHY ALLISON
A LESBIAN APPETITE

(1988)

Biscuits. I dream about baking biscuits, sifting flour, baking powder, and salt together, measuring out shortening and butter-milk by eye, and rolling it all out with flour-dusted fingers. Beans. I dream about picking over beans, soaking them over-night, chopping pork fat, slicing onions, putting it all in a great iron pot to bubble for hour after hour until all the world smells of salt and heat and the sweat that used to pool on my mama's neck. Greens. Mustard greens, collards, turnip greens and poke – can't find them anywhere in the shops up north. In the middle of the night I wake up desperate for the taste of greens, get up and find a twenty-four hour deli that still has a can of spinach and a half a pound of bacon. I fry the bacon, dump it in the spinach, bring the whole mess to a boil and eat it with tears in my eyes. It doesn't taste like anything I really wanted to have. When I find frozen collards in the Safeway, I buy five bags and store them away. Then all I have to do is persuade the butcher to let me have a pack of neck bones. Having those wrapped packages in the freezer reassures me almost as much as money in the bank. If I wake up with bad dreams there will at least be something I want to eat.

Red beans and rice, chicken necks and dumplings, pot roast with vinegar and cloves stuck in the onions, salmon patties with white sauce, refried beans on warm tortillas, sweet duck with scallions and pancakes, lamb cooked with olive oil and lemon slices, pan-fried pork chops and red-eye gravy, potato pancakes with applesauce, polenta with spaghetti sauce floating on top – food is more than sustenance; it is history. I remember women by what we ate together, what they dug out of the freezer after we'd made love for hours. I've only had one lover who didn't want to eat at all. We didn't last long. The sex was good, but I couldn't think what to do with her when the sex was finished. We drank spring water together and fought a lot.

I grew an ulcer in my belly once I was out in the world on my own. I think of it as an always angry place inside me, a tyranny that takes good food and turns it like a blade scraping at the hard place where I try to hide my temper. Some days I think it is the rightful reward for my childhood. If I had eaten right, Lee used to tell me, there would never have been any trouble.

'Rickets, poor eyesight, appendicitis, warts, and bad skin,' she insisted, 'they're all caused by bad eating habits, poor diet.'

It's true. The diet of poor southerners is among the worst in the world, though it's tasty, very tasty. There's pork fat or chicken grease in every dish, white sugar in the cobblers, pralines, and fudge, and flour, fat, and salt in the gravies – lots of salt in everything. The vegetables get cooked to limp strands with no fiber left at all. Mothers give sidemeat to their toddlers as pacifiers and slip them whiskey with honey at the first sign of teething, a cold, or a fever. Most of my cousins lost their teeth in their twenties and took up drinking as easily as they put sugar in their iced tea. I try not to eat so much sugar, try not to drink, try to limit pork and salt and white flour, but the truth is I am always hungry for it – the smell and taste of the food my mama fed me.

Poor white trash I am for sure. I eat shit food and am not worthy. My family starts with good teeth but loses them early. Five of my cousins bled to death before thirty-five, their stomachs finally surrendering to sugar and whiskey and fat and salt. I've given it up. If I cannot eat what I want, then I'll eat what I must, but my dreams will always be flooded with salt and grease, crisp fried stuff that sweetens my mouth and feeds my soul. I would rather starve death than myself.

In college it was seven cups of coffee a day after a breakfast of dry-roasted nuts and Coca-Cola. Too much grey meat and reheated potatoes led me to develop a taste for peanut butter with honey, coleslaw with raisins, and pale, sad vegetables that never disturbed anything at all. When I started throwing up before classes, my roommate fed me fat pink pills her doctor had given her. My stomach shrank to a stone in my belly. I lived on pink pills, coffee, and Dexedrine until I could go home and use hot biscuits to scoop up cold tomato soup at my mama's table. The biscuits dripped memories as well as butter: Uncle Lucius rolling in at dawn, eating a big breakfast with us all, and stealing mama's tools when he left; or Aunt Panama at the door with her six daughters, screaming, *That bastard's made me pregnant again just to get a son*, and wanting butter beans with sliced tomatoes before she could calm down. Cold chicken in a towel meant Aunt Alma was staying over, cooking her usual six birds at a time. *Raising eleven kids I never learned how to cook for less than fifteen.* Red dye stains on the sink was a sure sign Reese was dating some new boy, baking him a Red Velvet Cake my stepfather would want for himself.

'It's good to watch you eat,' my mama smiled at me, around her loose teeth. 'It's just so good to watch you eat.' She packed up a batch of her biscuits when I got ready to leave, stuffed them with cheese and fatback. On the bus going back to school I'd hug them to my belly, using their bulk to remind me who I was.

*

When the government hired me to be a clerk for the social security administration, I was sent to Miami Beach where they put me up in a crumbling old hotel right on the water while teaching me all the regulations. The instructors took turns taking us out to dinner. Mr McCullum took an interest in me, told me Miami Beach had the best food in the world, bought me an order of Oysters Rockefeller one night, and medallions of veal with wine sauce the next. If he was gonna pay for it, I would eat it, but it was all like food seen on a movie screen. It had the shape and shine of luxury but tasted like nothing at all. But I fell in love with Wolfe's Cafeteria and got up early every morning to walk there and eat their danish stuffed with cream cheese and raisins.

'The best sweet biscuit in Miami,' I told the counter man.

'*Nu?*' he grinned at the woman beside me, her face wrinkling up as she blushed and smiled at me.

'*Nischt,*' she laughed. I didn't understand a word but I nodded anyway. They were probably talking about food.

When I couldn't sleep, I read Franz Kafka in my hotel room, thinking about him working for the social security administration in Prague. Kafka would work late and eat Polish sausage for dinner, sitting over a notebook in which he would write all night. I wrote letters like novels that I never mailed. When the chairman of the local office promised us all a real treat, I finally rebelled and refused to eat the raw clams Mr McCullum said were 'the best in the world'. While everyone around me sliced lemons and slurped up pink and grey morsels, I filled myself up with little white oyster crackers and tried not to look at the lobsters waiting to die, thrashing around in their plastic tanks.

'It's good to watch you eat,' Mona told me, serving me dill bread, sour cream, and fresh tomatoes. 'You do it with such obvious enjoyment.' She drove us up to visit her family in Georgia, talking about what a great cook her mama was. My mouth watered, and we stopped three times for boiled peanuts. I wanted to make love in the back seat of her old DeSoto but she was saving it up to do it in her own bed at home. When we arrived her mama came out to the car and said, 'You girls must be hungry,' and took us in to the lunch table.

There was three-bean salad from cans packed with vinaigrette, pickle loaf on thin sliced white bread, American and Swiss cheese in slices, and antipasto from a jar sent directly from an uncle still living in New York City. 'Deli food,' her mama kept saying, 'is the best food in the world.' I nodded, chewing white bread and a slice of American cheese, the peanuts in my belly weighing me down like a mess of little stones. Mona picked at the pickle loaf and pushed her ankle up into my lap where her mother couldn't see. I choked on the white bread and broke out in a sweat.

Lee wore her hair pushed up like the whorls on scallop shells. She toasted mushrooms instead of marshmallows, and tried to persuade me of the value of cabbage and eggplant, but she cooked with no fat; everything tasted of safflower oil. I loved Lee but hated the cabbage – it seemed an anemic cousin of real greens – and I only got into the eggplant after Lee brought home a basketful insisting I help her cook it up for freezing.

'You got to get it to sweat out the poisons.' She sliced the big purple fruits as she talked. 'Salt it up so the bitter stuff will come off.' She layered the salted slices between paper towels, changing the towels on the ones she'd cut up earlier. Some of her hair came loose and hung down past one ear. She looked like a mother in a Mary Cassatt painting, standing in her sunlit kitchen, sprinkling raw seasalt with one hand and pushing her hair back with the other.

I picked up an unsalted wedge of eggplant and sniffed it, rubbing the spongy mass between my thumbs. 'Makes me think of what breadfruit must be like.' I squeezed it down, and the flesh slowly shaped up again. 'Smells like bread and feels like it's been baked. But after you salt it down, it's more like fried okra, all soft and sharp-smelling.'

'Well, you like okra, don't you?' Lee wiped her grill with peanut oil and started dusting the drained eggplant slices with flour. Sweat shone on her neck under the scarf that tied up her hair in back.

'Oh yeah. You put enough cornmeal on it and fry it in bacon fat and I'll probably like most anything.' I took the wedge of eggplant and rubbed it on the back of her neck.

'What are you doing?'

'Salting the eggplant.' I followed the eggplant with my tongue, pulled up her T-shirt, and slowly ran the tough purple rind up to her small bare breasts. Lee started giggling, wiggling her ass, but not taking her hands out of the flour to stop me. I pulled down her shorts, picked up another dry slice and planted it against her navel, pressed with my fingers and slipped it down toward her pubic mound.

'Oh! Don't do that. Don't do that.' She was breathing through her open mouth and her right hand was a knotted fist in the flour bowl. I laughed softly into her ear, and rocked her back so that she was leaning against me, her ass pressing into my cunt.

'Oh. Oh!' Lee shuddered and reached with her right hand to turn off the grill. With her left she reached behind her and pulled up on my shirt. Flour smeared over my sweaty midriff and sifted down on the floor. 'You. You!' She was tugging at my jeans, a couple of slices of eggplant in one hand.

'I'll show you. Oh you!' We wrestled, eggplant breaking up between our navels. I got her shorts off, she got my jeans down. I dumped a whole plate of eggplant on her belly.

'You are just running salt, girl,' I teased, and pushed slices up between her legs, while I licked one of her nipples and pinched the other between a folded slice of eggplant. She was laughing, her belly bouncing under me.

'I'm gonna make you eat all this,' she yelled.

'Of course.' I pushed eggplant out of the way and slipped two fingers between her labia. She was slicker than peanut oil. 'But first we got to get the poison out.'

'Oh you!' Her hips rose up into my hand. All her hair had come loose and was trailing in the flour. She wrapped one hand in my hair, the other around my left breast. 'I'll cook you . . . just you wait. I'll cook you a meal to drive you crazy.'

'Oh honey.' She tasted like frybread – thick, smoked, and fat-rich on my tongue. We ran sweat in puddles, while above us the salted eggplant pearled up in great clear drops of poison. When we finished, we gathered up all the eggplant on the floor and fried it in flour and crushed garlic. Lee poured canned tomatoes with basil and lemon on the hot slices and then pushed big bites onto my tongue with her fingers. It was delicious. I licked her fingers and fed her with my own hands. We never did get our clothes back on.

In South Carolina, in the seventh grade, we had studied nutrition. 'Vitamin D,' the teacher told us, 'is paramount. Deny it to a young child and the result is the brain never develops properly.' She had a twangy midwestern accent, grey hair, and a small brown mole on her left cheek. Everybody knew she hated teaching, hated her students, especially those of us in badly fitting worn-out dresses sucking bacon rinds and cutting our names in the desks with our uncle's old pocketknives. She would stand with a fingertip on her left ear, her thumb stroking the mole, while she looked at us with disgust she didn't bother to conceal.

'The children of the poor,' she told us, 'the children of the poor have a lack of brain tissue simply because they don't get the necessary vitamins at the proper age. It is a deficiency that cannot be made up when they are older.' A stroke of her thumb and she turned her back.

I stood in the back of the room, my fingers wrapping my skull in horror. I imagined my soft brain slipping loosely in its cranial cavity shrunk by a lack of the necessary vitamins. How could I know if it wasn't too late? Mama always said that smart was the only way out. I thought of my cousins, big-headed, watery-eyed, and stupid. VITAMIN D! I became a compulsive consumer of vitamin D. Is it milk? We will drink milk, steal it if we must. *Mama, make salmon stew. It's cheap and full of vitamin D.*

If we can't afford cream, then evaporated milk will do. One is as thick as the other. Sweet is expensive, but thick builds muscles in the brain. Feed me milk, feed me cream, feed me what I need to fight them.

Twenty years later the doctor sat me down to tell me the secrets of my body. He had, oddly, that identical gesture, one finger on the ear and the others curled to the cheek as if he were thinking all the time.

'Milk,' he announced, 'that's the problem, a mild allergy. Nothing to worry about. You'll take calcium and vitamin D supplements and stay away from milk products. No cream, no butterfat, stay away from cheese.'

I started to grin, but he didn't notice. The finger on his ear was pointing to the brain. He had no sense of irony, and I didn't tell him why I laughed so much. I should have known. Milk or cornbread or black-eyed peas, there had to be a secret, something we would never understand until it was too late. My brain is fat and strong, ripe with years of vitamin D, but my belly is tender and hurts me in the night. I grinned into his confusion and chewed the pink and grey pills he gave me to help me recover from the damage milk had done me. What would I have to do, I wondered, to be able to eat pan gravy again?

When my stomach began to turn on me the last time, I made desperate attempts to compromise – wheat germ, brown rice, fresh vegetables and tamari. Whole wheat became a symbol for purity of intent, but hard brown bread does not pass easily. It sat in my stomach and clung to the honey deposits that seemed to be collecting between my tongue and breastbone. Lee told me I could be healthy if I drank a glass of hot water and lemon juice every morning. She chewed sunflower seeds and sesame seed candy made with molasses. I drank the hot water, but then I went up on the roof of the apartment building to read Carson McCullers, to eat Snickers bars and drink Dr Pepper, imagining myself back in Uncle Lucius's Pontiac inhaling Moon Pies and R.C. Cola.

*

'Swallow it,' Jay said. Her fingers were in my mouth, thick with the juice from between her legs. She was leaning forward, her full weight pressing me down. I swallowed, sucked between each knuckle, and swallowed again. Her other hand worked between us, pinching me but forcing the thick cream out of my cunt. She brought it up and pushed it into my mouth, took the hand I'd cleaned and smeared it again with her own musky gravy.

'Swallow it,' she kept saying. 'Swallow it all, suck my fingers, lick my palm.' Her hips ground into me. She smeared it on my face until I closed my eyes under the sticky, strong-smelling mixture of her juice and mine. With my eyes closed, I licked and sucked until I was drunk on it, gasping until my lungs hurt with my hands digging into the muscles of her back. I was moaning and whining, shaking like a newborn puppy trying to get to its mama's tit.

Jay lifted a little off me. I opened stinging eyes to see her face, her intent and startling expression. I held my breath, waiting. I felt it before I understood it, and when I did understand I went on lying still under her, barely breathing. It burned me, ran all over my belly and legs. She put both hands down, brought them up, poured bitter yellow piss into my eyes, my ears, my shuddering mouth.

'Swallow it,' she said again, but I held it in my mouth, pushed up against her and clawed her back with my nails. She whistled between her teeth. My hips jerked and rocked against her, making a wet sucking sound. I pushed my face to hers, my lips to hers, and forced my tongue into her mouth. I gripped her hard and rolled her over, my tongue sliding across her teeth, the taste of all her juices between us. I bit her lips and shoved her legs apart with my knee.

'Taste it,' I hissed at her. 'Swallow it.' I ran my hands over her body. My skin burned. She licked my face, growling deep in her throat. I pushed both hands between her legs, my fingertips opened her and my thumbs caught her clit under the soft sheath of its hood.

'Go on, go on,' I insisted. Tears were running down her face. I licked them. Her mouth was at my ear, her tongue trailing through the sweat at my hairline. When she came her teeth clamped down on my earlobe. I pulled but could not free myself. She was a thousand miles away, rocking back and forth on my hand, the stink of her all over us both. When her teeth freed my ear, I slumped. It felt as if I had come with her. My thighs shook and my teeth ached. She was mumbling with her eyes closed.

'Gonna bathe you,' she whispered, 'put you in a tub of hot lemonade. Drink it off you. Eat you for dinner.' Her hands dug into my shoulders, rolled me onto my back. She drew a long, deep breath with her head back and then looked down at me, put one hand into my cunt, and brought it up slick with my juice.

'Swallow it,' Jay said. 'Swallow it.'

The year we held the great Southeastern Feminist Conference, I was still following around behind Lee. She volunteered us to handle the food for the two hundred women that were expected. Lee wanted us to serve 'healthy food' – her vegetarian spaghetti sauce, whole-wheat pasta, and salad with cold fresh vegetables. Snacks would be granola, fresh fruit, and peanut butter on seven-grain bread. For breakfast she wanted me to cook grits in a twenty-quart pan, though she wasn't sure margarine wouldn't be healthier than butter, and maybe most people would just like granola anyway.

'They'll want donuts and coffee,' I told her matter-of-factly. I had a vision of myself standing in front of a hundred angry lesbians crying out for coffee and white sugar. Lee soothed me with kisses and poppyseed cake made with gluten flour, assured me that it would be fun to run the kitchen with her.

The week before the conference, Lee went from church to campus borrowing enormous pots, colanders, and baking trays. Ten flat baking trays convinced her that the second dinner we had to cook could be tofu lasagna with skim milk mozzarella and lots of chopped carrots. I spent the week sitting in front of the pool table in Jay's apartment, peeling and slicing carrots, potatoes, onions, green and red peppers, leeks, tomatoes, and squash. The slices were dumped in ten-gallon garbage bags and stored in Jay's handy floor-model freezer. I put a tablecloth down on the pool table to protect the green felt and made mounds of vegetables over each pocket corner. Every mound cut down and transferred to a garbage bag was a victory. I was winning the war on vegetables until the committee Lee had scared up delivered another load.

I drank coffee and chopped carrots, ate a chicken pot pie and peeled potatoes, drank iced tea and sliced peppers. I peeled the onions but didn't slice them, dropped them in a big vat of cold water to keep, I found a meat cleaver on the back porch and used it to chop the zucchini and squash, pretending I was doing karate and breaking boards.

'Bite-sized,' Lee told me as she ran through, 'it should all be bite-sized.' I wanted to bite her. I drank cold coffee and dropped tomatoes one at a time into boiling water to loosen their skins. There were supposed to be other women helping me, but only one showed up, and she went home after she got a rash from the tomatoes. I got out a beer, put the radio on loud, switching it back and forth from rock-and-roll to the country-and-western station and sang along as I chopped.

I kept working. The only food left in the apartment was vegetables. I wanted to have a pizza delivered but had no money. When I got hungry, I ate carrots on white bread with mayonnaise, slices of tomatoes between slices of raw squash, and leeks I dipped in a jar of low-sodium peanut butter. I threw up three times but kept working. Four hours before the first women were to arrive I took the last bushel basket of carrots out in the backyard and hid it under a tarp with the lawn mower. I laughed to myself as I did, swaying on rubbery legs. Lee drove up in a borrowed pickup truck with two women who'd come in from Atlanta and volunteered to help. One of them kept talking about the no-mucus diet as she loaded the truck. I went in the bathroom, threw up again, and then just sat on the tailgate in the sun while they finished up.

'You getting lazy, girl?' Lee teased me. 'Better rev it up, we got cooking to do.' I wiped my mouth and imagined burying her under a truckload of carrots. I felt like I had been drinking whiskey, but my stomach was empty and flat. The blacktop on the way out to the Girl Scout camp seemed to ripple and sway in the sunlight. Lee kept talking about the camp kitchen, the big black gas stove and the walk-in freezer.

'This is going to be fun.' I didn't think so. The onions still had to be sliced. I got hysterical when someone picked up my knife. Lee was giggling with a woman I'd never seen before, the two of them talking about macrobiotic cooking while rinsing brown noodles. I got the meat cleaver and started chopping onions in big raw chunks. 'Bite-sized,' Lee called to me, in a cheerful voice.

'You want 'em bite-sized, you cut 'em,' I told her, and went on chopping furiously.

It was late when we finally cleaned up. I hadn't been able to eat anything. The smell of the sauce had made me dizzy, and the scum that rinsed off the noodles looked iridescent and dangerous. My stomach curled up into a knot inside me, and I glowered at the women who came in and wanted hot water for tea. There were women sitting on the steps out on the deck, women around a campfire over near the water pump, naked women swimming out to the raft in the lake, and skinny, muscled women dancing continuously in the rec room. Lee had gone off with her new friend, the macrobiotic cook. I found a loaf of Wonder bread someone had left on the snack table, pulled out a slice and ate it in tiny bites.

'Want some?' It was one of the women from Atlanta. She held out a brown bag from which a bottle top protruded.

'It would make me sick.'

'Naw,' she grinned. 'It's just a Yoo-hoo. I got a stash of them in a cooler. Got a bad stomach myself. Only thing it likes is chocolate soda and barbecue.'

'Barbecue,' I sighed. My mouth flooded with saliva. 'I haven't made barbecue in years.'

'You make beef ribs?' She sipped at her Yoo-hoo and sat down beside me.

'I have, but if you got the time to do slow pit cooking, pork's better.' My stomach suddenly growled loudly, a grating, angry noise in the night.

'Girl,' she laughed. 'You still hungry?'

'Well, to tell you the truth, I couldn't eat any of that stuff.' I was embarrassed.

My new friend giggled. 'Neither did I. I had peanuts and Yoo-hoo for dinner myself.' I laughed with her. 'My name's Marty. You come up to Atlanta sometime, and we'll drive over to Marietta and get some of the best barbecue they make in the world.'

'The best barbecue in the world?'

'Bar none.' She handed me the bottle of Yoo-hoo.

'Can't be.' I sipped a little. It was sweet and almost warm.

'You don't trust my judgement?' Someone opened the porch door, and I saw in the light that her face was relaxed, her blue eyes twinkling.

'I trust you. You didn't eat any of those damn noodles, did you? You're trustworthy, but you can't have the best barbecue in the world up near Atlanta, 'cause the best barbecue in the world is just a couple of miles down the Perry Highway.'

'You say!'

'I do!'

We both laughed, and she slid her hip over close to mine. I shivered, and she put her arm around me. We talked, and I told her my name. It turned out we knew some of the same people. She had even been involved with a woman I hadn't seen since college. I was so tired I leaned my head on her shoulder. Marty rubbed my neck and told me a series of terribly dirty jokes until I started shaking more from giggling.

'Got to get you to bed,' she started to pull me up. I took hold of her belt, leaned over, and kissed her. She kissed me. We sat back down and just kissed for a while. Her mouth was soft and tasted of sweet, watery chocolate.

'Uh huh,' she said a few times, 'uh huh.'

'Uh huh,' I giggled back.

'Oh yes, think we gonna have to check out this barbecue.' Marty's hands were as soft as her mouth, and they slipped under the waistband of my jeans and hugged my belly. 'You weren't fixed on having tofu lasagna tomorrow, were you?'

'Gonna break my heart to miss it, I can tell you.' It was hard to talk with my lips pressed to hers. She licked my lips, the sides of my mouth, my cheek, my eyelids, and then put her lips up close to my ears.

'Oh, but think . . .' Her hands didn't stop moving, and I had to push myself back from her to keep from wetting my pants. '. . . Think about tomorrow afternoon when we come back from our little road trip hauling in all that barbecue, coleslaw, and hush puppies. We gonna make so many friends around here.' She paused. 'They do make hush puppies at this place, don't they?'

'Of course. If we get there early enough, we might even pick up some blackberry cobbler at this truck stop I know.' My stomach rumbled again loudly.

'I don't think you been eating right,' Marty giggled. 'Gonna have to feed you some healthy food, girl, some *healthy* food!'

Jay does karate, does it religiously, going to class four days in a week and working out at the gym every other day. Her muscles are hard and long. She is so tall people are always making jokes about 'the weather up there.' I call her Shorty or Tall to tease her, and Sugar Hips when I want to make her mad. Her hips are wide and full, though her legs are long and stringy.

'Lucky I got big feet,' she jokes sometimes, 'or I'd fall over every time I stopped to stand still.'

Jay is always hungry, always. She keeps a bag of nuts in her backpack, dried fruit sealed in cellophane in a bowl on her dresser, snack-packs of crackers and cheese in her locker at the gym. When we go out to the women's bar, she drinks one beer in three hours but eats half a dozen packages of smoked almonds.

Her last girlfriend was Italian. She used to serve Jay big batches of pasta with homemade sausage marinara.

'I need carbohydrates,' Jay insists, eating slices of potato bread smeared with sweet butter. I cook grits for her, with melted butter and cheese, fry slabs of cured ham I get from a butcher who swears it has no nitrates. She won't eat eggs, won't eat shrimp or oysters, but she loves catfish pan-fried in a batter of cornmeal and finely chopped onions. Coffee makes her irritable. Chocolate makes her horny. When my period is coming and I get that flushed heat feeling in my insides, I bake her Toll House cookies, serve them with a cup of coffee and a blush. She looks at me over the rim of the cup, sips slowly, and eats her cookies with one hand, the other hooked in her jeans by her thumb. A muscle jumps in her cheek, and her eyes are full of tiny lights.

'You hungry, honey?' she purrs. She stretches like a big cat, puts her bare foot up, and uses her toes to lift my blouse. 'You want something sweet?' Her toes are cold. I shiver and keep my gaze on her eyes. She leans forward and cups her hands around my face. 'What you hungry for, girl, huh? You tell me. You tell mama exactly what you want.'

Her name was Victoria, and she lived alone. She cut her hair into a soft cloud of curls and wore white blouses with buttoned-down collars. I saw her all the time at the bookstore, climbing out of her baby-blue VW with a big leather book bag and a cane in her left hand. There were pictures up on the wall at the back of the store. Every one of them showed her sitting on or standing by a horse, the reins loose in her hand and her eyes focused far off. The riding hat hid her curls. The jacket pushed her breasts down but emphasized her hips. She had a ribbon pinned to the coat. A little card beneath the pictures identified her as the steeplechase champion of the southern division. In one picture she was jumping. Her hat was gone, her hair blown back, and the horse's legs stretched high above the ground. Her teeth shone white and perfect, and she looked as fierce as a bobcat going for prey. Looking at the pictures made me hurt. She came in once while I was standing in front of them and gave me a quick, wry grin.

'You ride?' Her cane made a hollow thumping sound on the floor. I didn't look at it.

'For fun, once or twice with a girlfriend.' Her eyes were enormous and as black as her hair. Her face looked thinner than it had in the pictures, her neck longer. She grimaced and leaned on the cane. Under her tan she looked pale. She shrugged.

'I miss it myself.' She said it in a matter-of-fact tone, but her eyes glittered. I looked up at the pictures again.

'I'll bet,' I blushed, and looked back at her uncomfortably.

'Odds are I'll ride again.' Her jeans bulged around the knee brace. 'But not jump, and I did love jumping. Always felt like I was at war with the ground, allied with the sky, trying to stay up in the air.' She grinned wide, and a faint white scar showed at the corner of her mouth.

'Where you from?' I could feel the heat in my face but ignored it.

'Virginia.' Her eyes focused on my jacket, the backpack hanging from my arm, and down to where I had my left hip pushed out, my weight on my right foot. 'Haven't been there for a while, though.' She looked away, looked tired and sad. What I wanted in that moment I will never be able to explain – to feed her or make love to her or just lighten the shadows under her eyes – all that, all that and more.

'You ever eat any Red Velvet Cake?' I licked my lips and shifted my weight so that I wasn't leaning to the side. I looked into her eyes.

'Red Velvet Cake?' Her eyes were friendly, soft, black as the deepest part of the night.

'It's a dessert my sister and I used to bake, unhealthy as sin and twice as delicious. Made up with chocolate, buttermilk, vinegar and baking soda, and a little bottle of that poisonous red dye number two. Tastes like nothing you've ever had.'

'You got to put the dye in it?'

'Uh huh,' I nodded, 'wouldn't be right without it.'

'Must look deadly.'

'But tastes good. It's about time I baked one. You come to dinner at my place, tell me about riding, and I'll cook you up one.'

She shifted, leaned back, and half-sat on a table full of magazines. She looked me up and down again, her grin coming and going with her glance.

'What else would you cook?'

'Fried okra maybe, fried crisp, breaded with cornmeal. Those big beefsteak tomatoes are at their peak right now. Could just serve them in slices with pepper, but I've seen some green ones, too, and those I could fry in flour with the okra. Have to have white corn, of course, this time of the year. Pinto beans would be too heavy, but snap beans would be nice. A little milk gravy to go with it all. You like fried chicken?'

'Where you from?'

'South Carolina, a long time ago.'

'You mama teach you to cook?'

'My mama and my aunts.' I put my thumbs in my belt and tried to look sure of myself. Would she like biscuits or cornbread, pork or beef or chicken?

'I'm kind of a vegetarian.' She sighed when she said it, and her eyes looked sad.

'Eat fish?' I was thinking quickly. She nodded. I smiled wide.

'Ever eat any crawfish pan-fried in salt and Louisiana hot sauce?'

'You got to boil them first.' Her face was shining, and she was bouncing her cane on the hardwood floor.

'Oh yeah, 'course, with the right spices.'

'Sweet Bleeding Jesus,' her face was flushed. She licked her lips. 'I haven't eaten anything like that in, oh, so long.'

'Oh.' My thighs felt hot, rubbing on the seams of my jeans. She was beautiful, Victoria in her black cloud of curls. 'Oh, girl,' I whispered. I leaned toward her. I put my hand on her wrist above the cane, squeezed.

'Let me feed you,' I told her. 'Girl . . . girl, you should just let me feed you what you really need.'

I've been dreaming lately that I throw a dinner party, inviting all the women in my life. They come in with their own dishes. Marty brings barbecue carried all the way from Marietta. Jay drags in a whole side of beef and gets a bunch of swaggering whiskey-sipping butch types to help her dig a hole in the backyard. They show off for each other, breaking up stones to line the firepit. Lee watches them from the porch, giggling at me and punching down a great mound of dough for the oatmeal wheat bread she'd promised to bake. Women whose names I can't remember bring in bowls of pasta salad, smoked salmon, and Jell-o with tangerine slices. Everybody is feeding each other, exclaiming over recipes and gravies, introducing themselves and telling stories about great meals they've eaten. My mama is in the kitchen salting a vat of greens. Two of my aunts are arguing over whether to make little baking powder biscuits or big buttermilk hogs-heads. Another steps around them to slide an iron skillet full of cornbread in the oven. Pinto beans with onions are bubbling on the stove. Children run through sucking fatback rinds. My uncles are on the porch telling stories and knocking glass bottles together when they laugh.

I walk back and forth from the porch to the kitchen, being hugged and kissed and stroked by everyone I pass. For the first time in my life I am not hungry, but everybody insists I have a little taste. I burp like a baby on her mama's shoulder. My stomach is full, relaxed, happy, and the taste of pan gravy is in my mouth. I can't stop grinning. The dream goes on and on, and through it all I hug myself and smile.

PAT CALIFIA

THE VAMPIRE

(1988)

Purgatory was fairly crowded that night. About sixty men and a
score of women had assembled in the tiny club by one o'clock in
the morning. Most of the women (other than one who was
naked and being led around on a leash) were clad in the high
fashion of the bizarre – leather skirts, spike heels, PVC corsets,
thigh-high boots, studded wristbands or belts, black latex
evening gowns. A handful of scruffy lesbians, dressed like
destitute bikers, kept to themselves around a low set of stairs
along one wall, covered with carpet and meant to be sat upon.
The men (other than a few slumming, well-built leathermen)
were in casual, even sloppy street clothes. The mistresses stood
by the bar, under track lights, impassive and unapproachable,
each one giving out some ominous signal – perhaps toying with
a whip around her waist or keeping time to the music with a
riding crop in her gloved hand. No one but Teddy, the bartender,
spoke to the few expensively attired tourist couples who walked
around clinging to one another, wearing fixed, exaggerated
smiles which were belied by the tight grip they kept on each
other.

Solitary male submissives prowled around the dance floor and the two large bondage frames in the corner, up the stairs to the bathroom, down the stairs, toward the back and down the hall which opened into half a dozen tiny cubicles with plywood walls, back to the dance floor and up to the bar, to the well-lit women, and then stood humbly, wistfully, heads down, for long minutes until hope ran out and they moved off again to make another restless circuit of the premises. Occasionally a dominatrix would focus her gaze on a particular man and beckon him forward to kneel, get her a drink, light her cigarette, answer some insulting question, and kneel again.

A young man, perhaps more confident because he was better looking than the older, slack-bellied submissives, accosted a dark-haired, dignified mistress and asked if he might give her a foot massage. She acquiesced, and they adjourned to the carpeted stairs, where he sat on the floor, lovingly removed one of her high heels and kissed it. He cradled her stockinged foot in his lap and polished the sole with his thumbs. The leather dykes had made room for them, and one leaned over to offer the dominatrix a joint. She shook her head, but held it down for the submissive man to take a toke. He smiled and said, 'Thank you, Mistress,' and wondered why the act he was performing gave him so much pleasure. Would she, he wondered, let him remove her stockings and actually kiss her feet, lick them? She took the joint away from him and passed it up the stairs, then rested the foot that was still shod upon his crotch. 'Do you like my shoes?' she asked. He nearly fainted as the spike pressed between his balls, and the sole threatened to flatten the shaft of his hardening penis. This was a very lucky night.

Back at the bar, someone noticed this spontaneous interaction and felt jealousy gnaw at his heart. He was one of a gaggle of submissives dancing attendance upon a very lovely, very young professional who styled herself The Goddess Domina. For a moment, he stopped competing for her attention and watched the mistress seated on the stairs grind her heel into the boy's crotch while he leaned back, yielding to her, suffering written all over his face. She was older and plainer than Domina, but she was calm and self-assured, handling her young man with such understanding, easily claiming him for her service. Domina, on the other hand, was already drunk, a criminal waste of the small fortune in cocaine she had snorted before coming to Purgatory. Her jealous submissive knew exactly how much coke there had been because that was the price of being brought to this club with her. Why did he always have to pay? He told himself that Domina was the best-looking woman in the club. The other submissives must surely be jealous of him because he belonged to such a gorgeous bitch-goddess. Why, then, did he want to keep watching the foot-slave and his newly found mistress instead of keeping track of Domina's tiresome antics and pretending it was a privilege to light her cigarettes?

His Goddess was uncoiling a short bullwhip, only four feet long, and ordering one of her submissives to crawl away from her. She tried to hit him as he scuttled away and wound up tangling the end of her whip in the taps behind the bar. Before anything could get broken, Teddy plucked it from her hands. 'Domina,' he said sharply, 'you know we don't allow bullwhips in here. The club just isn't large enough.' The rebuke was administered in a way intended to save her face. After all, he had not told her what he really thought, which was that she was an incompetent alcoholic who ought not to be allowed to hit anyone with so much as a feather duster. She gave him an evil look anyway, the ungrateful, spoiled twit. Let her sulk, Teddy told himself.

'Let's go to the Mine Shaft,' one of the leathermen urged his partner, slapping his gloves against one palm. He was wearing a shiny, custom-made leather jacket and chaps that were so new, they creaked. His cover was an American attempt to imitate the Muir motorcycle cap. It was decorated with cheap chain and a badly cast American eagle. He wore his keys on the left, and they jangled as he rocked from one boot to the other.

'Mmm, we will,' said the other man absently. His head (as was fitting) was bare, and he kept his hair short, to make the small bald spot look like a tonsure. He wore his keys on the right, where they had, over time, left an impression, an indent in the chaps that cushioned them, kept them quiet. His leathers were not as fancy or as shiny as his companion's. The completely broken-in latigo hugged his burly body. 'Who just came in?' he said, lifting his head to stare toward the door. 'Oh, this is a treat, Howard.'

Howard couldn't see what the fuss was about. 'Huh?' he said. It was just a skinny little boy, wearing *brown* leather, no less, with a Muir, which of course was black. The tight pants were tucked into knee-high boots, the sleeves on the leather shirt were rolled up in concession to the summer night, and the peaked cap was ornamented with a silver skull and crossbones on the front. The leather was the color of dried blood. The boy had short, black hair and an olive complexion. A cat-o'-nine-tails and two flails were threaded through the large key ring on his left hip. There was a dagger stuck in his belt behind his right hip and another, smaller, tucked in his right boot. 'I didn't know you were into chicken, Gil.'

Gil sighed. 'That's Kerry,' he explained. 'Have you ever seen her work?'

Her? This became even less exciting. Why had they left all the hot men at the Spike to come to this weird hangout?

'We should stick around, Howard.'

Now it was Howard's turn to sigh. There was usually no arguing with Gil when he used that tone of voice. 'Get me another beer, boy,' he ordered sharply.

'Yes, sir,' Gil said courteously, and went at his own pace to obey.

Iduna overheard this interaction (her hearing was very sharp) and chuckled. She was in her usual place at one end of the bar, where she could play dice with Teddy. For most of the night, she stood, but Teddy kept a stool there in case she wanted to sit down. None of the regulars sat there, even if she was not in that night. Teddy would warn away tourists who made the mistake of trying to occupy her spot if he thought they had potential to become members of the scene. If he wanted to get rid of them, he let nature take its course. Helping people to see themselves as others saw them was Iduna's greatest gift.

Tonight, she was wearing a long, black dress with spaghetti straps. It was very low-cut, but a short jacket with long sleeves was worn over the dress, and concealed everything except a white diamond of cleavage. A brilliant red stone carved in the shape of a skull glittered between her breasts. Beneath the jacket, the waist of the dress was reinforced with whalebone stays, giving her a wasp waist and a very straight back. It also shaped her ample ass and made it swell out invitingly, but her imperious manner made it quite clear that you would lose your hand if you touched her. She had long, blonde hair, and she was drinking a glass of red wine.

None of the submissive men approached this lady, but they kept track of her out of the corner of their eyes. So did the leather dykes and the dominatrices. This was easy to do, because her complexion was so pale it was luminous. In the dark, she almost seemed to glow. Anyone who had gotten close enough would have seen that there was something odd about her skin. It seemed to lack pores or wrinkles. The few people who did get that close to her were usually too busy with their own troubles to make note of her peculiarities. But they did notice that it was difficult to tell how old she was. No one would have mistaken her for a youngster, but she was not middle-aged, either. It was as if her biological clock was not set to the human year.

'Teddy,' Domina said breathily, 'here's my riding crop.'

'What?' For one glad moment, he thought she was asking to be thrashed with it. Then she deigned to explain.

'Keep it behind the bar,' she snapped, and tried to stalk away.

'Domina!'

She came back, piqued. Teddy held out her crop. 'I don't have room back here for this,' he said brusquely, and began to lift glasses and swab underneath them.

Iduna smiled. Her cane, with its red-and-black leather handle, was neatly racked above Teddy's bottles, along with a handful of implements that belonged to other mistresses he had honored. Teddy would have been glad to provide a similar service for Kerry, but she never let any of her whips out of her hands.

Then Iduna realized that the show Gil had promised Howard was about to happen. Kerry had ordered a bottle of beer and stood with her back to the rest of the room, one foot up on the bar rail. She drank with intense concentration, like a thirsty animal. It looked as if she were oblivious to everything except the beer gurgling down her throat. But when a largish, clumsy-looking man lumbered toward her, she turned around and snarled at him before he could touch her. The noise was uncanny. There were no words, but you would have to be crazy not to understand that it meant, 'Keep away – or pay the price.' No wonder he jumped away from her. But Domina snickered at him, and Iduna thought, oh dear, now he'll have to get angry and prove something.

'The name's Bill,' he said heartily, shoving his hand at Kerry. She looked at it as if it were leprous. There was a long silence. She regarded him from behind her mirrored shades. No telling what she thought. Iduna looked lovingly at that full mouth and the two tiny puckers in it over the prominent canine teeth. She was sure no one else could have spotted these minute irregularities, or known why there were two places where Kerry's lips could not quite meet.

Finally, the leatherwoman spoke. 'Can I help you?' she said softly, speaking each word slowly and precisely. It was not a question. Ooh, Iduna squealed to herself, massacre alert, massacre alert!

'Wall, Ah don't know what a little bitty thang like yew could do fer me,' he drawled. An out-of-towner, Iduna thought. But that was no excuse. She was an out-of-towner herself, and she knew better.

Kerry smiled. On her face, this expression signified the opposite of its usual meaning.

The fool kept on talking. 'Why Ah don't reckon yew could even make a dent in my hide,' he chuckled. 'Probably be a waste of time. Ah kin take quite a lot, yew know. Wouldn't want ta embarrass a lil gal like yew – yew are a gal, ain'tcha?'

Then the fatuous ass pronounced his own sentence: 'Ah kin take anythin' yew kin dish out, sister.'

It took one well-placed kick to take him down. Iduna was the only one who could follow the swiftness of that booted foot. Once down, he stayed down, and Kerry kicked him in the direction she wanted him to go. The pointed toe of her boot made a crunching noise when it hit his buttocks and ribs. She hustled him to the foot of a large ladder that stood in one corner of the dance floor. Then she put her boot on the back of his neck and pushed him flat. She bent down to speak to him. What she told him made him keep very still, then shudder and hide his head beneath his arms. Eventually, she lifted him up off the floor – literally lifted him, with one hand – and hauled him up to face the whipping ladder.

A revolving ball with mirrored facets spun a dizzy procession of colored lights over the scene. The ball was part of the special effects for the disco music played on other nights of the week. This club had a different name then, and catered to vanilla swingers. But Kerry, a master of her craft, was not distracted. She knew you must practice this despised art where you can, and disregard what is tawdry or unclean – or learn to love the dirt, the sleaze, because it represents your membership in the elite.

Now she had him remove his shirt and grab a rung far above his head. He was stretched on his tiptoes in front of her. She asked him a question that only Iduna could hear. 'Ah don't want no bondage,' he said loudly. Iduna and Teddy shared a brief, unpleasant laugh. Even planarians can learn.

Even Howard sat up and took notice when Kerry began to work on Bill's naked back with a short, suede flail. Hanging from her belt, it looked homemade, innocuous. In her hand, it was a weapon. She whirled it so quickly that there was no apparent difference between the sound it made swinging through the air and the sound it made striking skin. It was one continuous, ominous tone, a single voice that became a duet when the man began to scream. However, he did not let go. Gil leaned toward Howard and whispered that he had seen some people cut and run at this stage. Howard was still skeptical, but now he was keeping an open mind.

Everyone watched. It was what you did at the club when someone hung by their cold and sweating palms and took a beating. Granted, not all of them approved. By tomorrow night, rumor would have it that Kerry had half-killed someone. Heavy S/M is not popular with most of the adherents of light bondage and discipline. Unless you love pure pain, for its own sake, it is difficult to see that deliberately administered, controlled agony retains its own severe sensuality. Iduna rocked on her bar stool, separating her legs enough to let the edge of it press across the middle of her cunt. Teddy spared a glance for her and smiled at her flushed cheeks, then ran a hand along his own erection. It had been a long time since he had played with Kerry. She hadn't been in for a while. Maybe Iduna would take a quick stint behind the bar.

The leatherwoman had switched to a longer flail. It was not suede, and the tails had knots in them. Bill's broad back was now an evenly raised mass of bruises. Kerry danced behind him, side to side, quick as a cat, cruel and exact. He was crying out continuously, twisting from side to side. He seemed to have forgotten he could let go of the ladder. Iduna swallowed a mouthful of wine and thought, how delicious, it would take only one good stroke to split that wide open. And of course this is what Kerry (wielding the braided cat now) did. Nine narrow tails whistled through the air, and the skin divided, rent, bled. She shifted her weight to the other hip and reversed the motion, criss-crossing the previously inflicted lashes.

Bill let go of the ladder and turned around as soon as the first stroke drew blood, but the woman behind him was so fast, she inflicted a dozen times nine crimson and overflowing welts, each bleeding bouquet placed an even distance from its mates, before he could get out of her way. As he turned to face her, she continued to flog him overhand, catching his shoulders, then changed direction and came down hard across both of his tits. The welts were instantly visible, even in the club twilight.

'Jesus,' Iduna heard Howard say, 'this is a bit sick.' Gil sighed again.

'I'm sorry!' Bill screamed, falling to the filthy concrete floor. 'Please stop, please stop, please stop!' She jerked her arm back, and the incomplete stroke came back into her own stomach. He was crawling back now, reaching for her hand. Despite being an out-of-towner, he must have heard enough of Kerry's legend to know that she allowed select victims to kiss her ring. But Iduna knew he would never receive that boon, even after taking all that punishment. He had promised her he could take *anything*, and then he had tried to get away. Kerry didn't like it when they moved, let alone tried to get away.

Indeed, a boot in the face stopped his progress, and its owner removed her silver shades to give him one hard stare that shut his whining mouth. There was something funny about this, since she wasn't even looking into his face. She was looking at the blood that ran in thin but eager trickles to the floor. In the middle of his renewed and tearful apologies, she spun on her heel and made for the door, tucking the blood-stained cat beside its fellows. 'Shit!' Teddy said, and slammed his beer down on the bar. He turned to complain to Iduna, but she was not there.

Kerry was not pleased to be intercepted between the coatcheck and the door by her personal, self-appointed voyeur, wine glass in hand. She made quite a provocative picture, this full-bosomed, very pale woman in her black dress, but she was in the way and a nuisance. Then she became impertinent. She tilted the glass to her lips and let a half-swallow of wine run out of the corner of her mouth. It was just a little too purple to be blood, that tiny rivulet, the few drops clinging to her lips.

Kerry snarled and went sideways to get by, angry, almost pushing the woman who had arranged this strange tableau for her. A man who had behaved that way might have gotten a broken jaw for his bad manners. But she was known for her chivalry. It was part of a code she thought all true leathermen (regardless of gender) should obey. Let women make do with their feminine wiles and plots and foibles. She did not want to become entangled in them. This creed of Kerry's took a form that dismayed many of the heavier masochists in the scene: she could rarely be persuaded to treat women like sides of beef. Only men were usually that stupid or lucky. In her lofty unconcern with women's untidy minds and manipulative ways, Kerry had somehow omitted to learn who this impudent blonde (whom she had certainly seen many times before) was. Ignorance is bliss, but we are rarely allowed to remain in that happy state.

There was another club, Roissy, just three blocks away, closer to the docks. That was where Kerry headed now, whips swinging at her hip, the knife scabbard bumping the small of her back, her boot heels making a satisfying tempo on the pavement, a rhythm that confirmed that she was in motion, making progress, getting away from those thin scarlet streams, the smell of life that made her mouth water and her jaws ache.

She knew immediately that she was being followed. She also had no trouble detecting that the person behind her was wearing spike-heeled shoes, and so she knew who was following her. The why of it bothered her, and the notion that anybody in spikes could keep up with (let alone catch or combat) someone in boots amused her.

She cut through an alley, thinking, 'Let's see if the bitch will come into the darkness and teeter around in the trash and rubble for the sake of a closer look at me.' Besides, it was a shortcut to Roissy.

Surprise! There at the mouth of the alley was her pursuer, somehow ahead of her and once again blocking her way. She was wearing a satin cloak with a red lining, and a sudden gust of wind (uncharacteristic for the season) lifted it and spread it out until it fluttered about her like wings. Her breasts gleamed like alabaster, even in the absence of street lights and moonlight.

Kerry had reached for her boot and belt and unhitched her blades the second she realized she was being followed, despite her contempt for the mettle of her opponent. She did not consciously plan to use them on the other woman. She was sure she could take her with her bare hands, if a physical contest was necessary. But that seemed unlikely. No, the blades were for others, stronger and more dangerous, who might come upon them and interrupt their tête-à-tête.

Silence poured into the space between them, filled it up, then spilled over into speech.

'Why are you running away?' purred the woman in the black dress, red flames playing all around her. She was very sure of herself.

Startled, Kerry blurted, 'What the hell are you talking about?' then bit her lip and repented not keeping silent. She knew she was about to be laughed at.

She was. The laugh was rich, full of private enjoyment and secret knowledge. It was not mocking, but it was too intimate, and it made her hate the intrusive blonde whose name she wished she could remember, so she could chew her out properly.

'You haven't fed for months now. You still draw blood, but you don't allow yourself to taste it.'

This time, Kerry held her tongue, put her hand onto her dagger, and watched to make sure the other did not come any closer. If she had spoken, she wondered if she would be able to hear herself talking over the noise that her blood was making, roaring in her ears. This was starting to feel like her worst-case scenario, hardly a fair price to pay for a little mayhem at a braggart's expense.

'I think I'm the only one who's noticed. It's so much a part of your legend, this penchant you have for flaying someone with your cat-o'-nine-tails until the walls and innocent bystanders are spattered with blood, or using your knife to release the hot, sticky, salty fuel that feeds the heart, the lungs and the brain. It appalls everyone so much that they don't realize you've ceased to put your lips to the wound, to swallow what you've set free, or clean your blade with your tongue. But I do. I do. And I wonder why. Would you like to tell me why?'

The leatherwoman shook her head so hard that the gesture

looked painful. The nerve! What could they possibly have to talk about? She owed no one any explanations. When she spoke, it was not to the point: 'Stay right where you are.'

'I'm not here to assault you!' The tone was hurt surprise. 'I'm not going to approach you without permission. I just want to have a little chat. I may want you to come to me, later, when we understand one another better. But I promise I won't move one step from this spot, no matter what happens.'

Was this some crazy kind of come-on, then, from a dominant who wanted to bottom for her? Kerry had received many invitations like these. Perhaps she was being paranoid. But if that was the case, her rule was that the other must make an explicit request. It would be insulting to anticipate such needs in a colleague. So they watched each other in renewed silence, taking measurements, making calculations.

Like most women, the blonde did not seem to be able to hold her tongue. Kerry braced herself when she saw that whorishly lipsticked mouth, with its bee-stung lower lip, open. But the woman only said, 'I was in such a hurry to catch up with you that I left my cigarettes at the bar. Would you happen to have one?'

A pack was extracted from a leather shirt pocket and went flying toward Iduna, closely followed by a silver lighter. She caught them both in the same hand, took a cigarette, lit it, and tossed both pack and lighter back. They were caught and returned to the breast pocket. Kerry waited two heartbeats, then relented and fished them out again and lit a cigarette for herself. Iduna smiled. It was a minor triumph, a small victory, to have them share even this much common ground – a quiet smoke together in a dark alley, with rats just out of eyeshot, telling each other their tribal stories about eating garbage and tormenting human babies, fucking their mothers and devouring their own succulent children.

Smoke curled around her fingers as she resumed talking. 'I have been an archivist of your legend ever since I came to the city. In fact, your legend is what brought me here.' Kerry gave her a brief nod, accepting this as her due. 'I've been collecting all the stories about you, verifying what I can, making observations of my own. I'm always interested in legends even if the people who inspire them are not really of mythic proportions. But when I realized just how legendary you truly are, I began to keep very close track of you. As far as I know, James was your last . . . shall we say, completely satisfying experience? It's a little less cold than calling him a meal. He says you tied him down, took a scalpel, exposed an artery in his thigh and partially sutured it, slit it between the sutures and drank nearly a pint of his blood before you pulled the stitches tight and closed the incision with butterflies of surgical tape. All with his permission, of course, and he says it made you quite sick to have that much at once. He was close to passing out, so he may have been hallucinating. But I don't think so. Was his blood bad? Is that what stops you now? A fear of tainted blood? Disease, perhaps? Or did you get enough from him to last you all this while?'

Now they both knew the game, her question and the answer, and Iduna saw the mirrored shades removed for her benefit, saw herself regarded by cold eyes, eyes surrounded by darkness, eyes that already saw her dead in six different positions. 'James,' said Kerry hoarsely, 'talks too much.'

'Don't be hasty,' Iduna cautioned, smiling and blowing smoke up at the moonless sky. 'Surely you haven't lived this long by being rash and impulsive.'

Now it was her turn to be laughed at. After all her casual conversation about other people's blood, it was horrid to feel her own turn to cold sludge, stop running through her veins, then freeze solid, liable to break like glass and cut her to pieces inside if she moved.

Well, but . . . Iduna had been in some very dangerous places, and she always spoke to the people she met there. Otherwise, life would turn into an ordeal instead of an adventure. Now, she spoke as if to her lover, which of course is the most dangerous audience of all.

'Wouldn't you like to know how I figured it out?' The

question was a caress. She made herself wait for the curt, reluctant nod before she continued. 'To begin with, there is your name. It means "son of the dark one."' She paused for that to sink in, then said politely, 'You have not asked, but my name is Iduna. In ancient Norse mythology, Iduna guarded the golden apples of immortality.' 'But in our case, my love, the apples are the brightest, truest red imaginable,' she thought, but did not say.

Kerry twitched. But Iduna felt like being a little ruthless. It was rude, forcing someone to make their own introduction. 'You have trouble remembering your age and your birthday. You've told some people you're twenty-two and other people you're thirty-five. There are certain historic periods you are very fond of, and when you speak about them, you occasionally lapse into the first person and the present tense. You speak several languages; however, none of them (with the exception of your American English) is contemporary. I am enough of a linguist to recognize nineteenth-century French when I hear it, and your German is full of colloquialisms from the 1930s. You say you were born here, but there is no birth certificate on file for you in any of the five boroughs of New York City.' In the process of investigating Kerry, Iduna had figured out how to dummy up this basic ID for herself. 'You need some help,' she thought. 'It's dangerous to fall behind the times.'

'You are photophobic. You don't even like the brightly lit area of the bar where all the other S&M dominants stand and model. You wait for your prey in shadows. You have unusual strength, you are preternaturally quick, and you have an ability to see in the dark and hear things no one else can hear. Your sense of smell is also very keen. I've traced some of your employment, and much of it is at places where you can handle blood or blood products. All of these jobs have been abruptly terminated for mysterious reasons, and you have not had one for quite some time. You do not have sex, ever, with anyone that I've been able to locate and, given your reputation, I would imagine that someone who had come close enough to even lie about it would have claimed they had made love with you by now.'

Kerry shuddered delicately. 'Sex with a victim,' she said with great distaste, 'is out of the question.'

Iduna ignored this aside. 'All of this could simply mean you are an adventurer, a liar, a psychopath, a soldier of fortune, or a celibate, amateur hematologist, but I don't think any of these explanations are logical. So many of the stories about . . . your people are idle fantasy or vicious gossip motivated by religious bigotry, but I know enough not to expect you to run away from crosses. Your kind is far older than Christianity. You love garlic, and you have a perfectly good reflection in a mirror. But I don't need evidence as crude as that to recognize you for what you are. You are a predator, and human beings are your natural prey. Humans like to believe that they are the ultimate predators, at the top of the food chain. They sleep secure in the belief that nobody stalks them. It is only their deep need for this illusion that keeps people from recognizing you, running away from you, and screaming their fool heads off.'

A grin matched the skull on Kerry's cap. 'Ah, but people do run from me, screaming.'

'When you are partially unveiled, yes. During the epiphany, then they scream and escape if they can.'

'But you have not screamed. Or tried to run. You came after me, Iduna.'

Her own name spoken in Kerry's cold voice made her shiver. 'Perhaps it's because, despite all my circumstantial evidence, I'm still not sure just who or what you are. And there is only one way for me to be sure, isn't there?' She put her hands to her bodice and touched the ruby skull. 'This dress has a built-in corset, a very old-fashioned one, of a seventeenth-century pattern,' she said. 'The jacket covers the laces so most people don't notice. It has a busk in the front. That was the earliest form of stay, you know. Only my busk is rather special.' From between her breasts she pulled a very slim blade. The grinning jewel was its pommel.

Before it was fully exposed, Kerry had a knife in her hand, poised for use. Iduna ignored this, put the thin steel between her teeth, and removed her black jacket. The long sleeves were quite tight, and she had to turn the damn thing inside out to get it off.

'Have you ever noticed my veins? Probably not. You haven't been watching me the way I've been watching you, and anyway, I don't expose a lot of skin in the clubs. I like to show cleavage and nothing else, not even my forearms or my calves.' Kerry was staring at her décolletage. Iduna knew that her breasts were very prominent and was always amused by men and women who were so attracted to them that they talked to her tits rather than to her face. It was appropriate, in a way, because breasts were symbolic of nurturance. 'But the nourishment I provide,' she thought, 'is not milk, but a different humor.'

She continued her pedantic, distracting speech. 'My skin is very pale, almost transparent. It looks fragile, but I heal very quickly. My veins are close to the surface, easy to get to. See how thick and blue they are? I never have any trouble giving blood. The needle just pops right in, and out it spurts. Easy as sin.'

She was picking at her wrist with the point of the blade, then caressing the inside of her elbow. 'All it would take is a little more pressure, and we'd have a fountain here. A scarlet fountain, pouring onto the dirty ground, completely wasted, unless . . . unless someone had a use for it. Unless someone caught it in their mouth before it hit the ground. Caught it and drank it, took life from it, rolled it around their tongue and palate and described the vintage to me, swallowed and swallowed as if they would never get enough. Look, my pulse is beating right here.'

The arm held out was steady, not shaking. A glinting edge pressed against old scars along the vein, hard enough to make an indentation but not to break the skin. The sight made Kerry's leather-clad hips jerk, just once, but Iduna saw it and was immediately excited. How interesting, to see a reflexive response there, in the crotch, instead of just the jaws and hands. What possibilities it opened up . . . but the words the leatherwoman spoke next shattered her erotic fantasies.

'You will bleed to death if you cut yourself there, that way,' said she. It might have been a report on the temperature and time of day.

'Don't you want it? Need it? Wouldn't you like to smell it, falling through the air? The wind is behind me. It would bring the scent to you at once, fresh and abundant.'

The other shook her head. 'No.'

'No?'

'No. Why are you surprised? Even if this mad story you've concocted is true, you yourself said I've already gone without it for months.'

Iduna made the mistake of arguing. 'Then the need must be intense right now. You must be hungry. I don't think you'll die without blood, but it must make you feel a little sick to be deprived. A little less powerful than usual, a little less energetic. Distracted. Frustrated. Off.'

Iduna had never had someone pay so much attention to her with such a look of utter indifference on their face. She had not anticipated this much resistance. This was even more difficult than locating her quarry in the first place. Clearly, the offer of her wrist was not enough. Perhaps scars annoyed them. She thought they had a heat-seeking sense, like rattlesnakes. She imagined that scars would be like cold streaks in the hot aura that radiated through the skin, making the marked person less appealing than someone with a smooth body. Perhaps this one was just fastidious about unzipping an old scar, thought of it as drinking from a glass someone else had already used.

She probed again, looking for the weak spot, the turning point, the breaking point. 'Do you prefer men, is that it? Is it because women are weaker, smaller, and too quickly drained? But then, I've never heard of you leaving anyone bloodless and dead. So why should it matter? I know most of you don't need as much blood as the stories say you do. Too many of those legends are about the stupid and greedy ones, the ones so unrelentingly selfish they get caught. Or the ones who unfortunately can't live on anything other than human blood. Why are you denying yourself this pleasure?' She dared to allow compassion to creep into her voice. 'You must have had to develop an enormous amount of self-control and get awfully good at living in a constant state of deprivation. Is that why you stopped after James, to prove that you could do without it if you had to? But it's not necessary now. I want you to have me.'

The stony face of the other said, 'Don't try to cozen me. In a thousand years, you could never understand what I am, where I have been, what living has done to me.'

Iduna despaired. Her head drooped, and Kerry almost felt sorry for her. Then inspiration struck. 'Or could it be that you would rather drink your life from a woman, hold her in your arms, slit her throat with your teeth, then eagerly gulp down what wells up around your mouth – yet you refuse to let yourself have me because you would enjoy it too much and then want it and need it again? Are you afraid you would lose control if you got what you really want?'

There was no change in the other's fighting stance and icy expression. The air between them simply became busier, hummed like a high-voltage wire, stank of ozone, seemed to turn an even darker shade of midnight blue.

Now or never. It was the moment that would decide the outcome of the hunt. Iduna stared into Kerry's eyes, covered with the reflecting aviators, and used the tiny portrait in them to guide her hand while she made two slashes at the place where her breasts came together, a little 'v' that fit into her cleavage. The blood immediately started to rill and she cupped her hands under her breasts to help her corset push them close enough together to gather it and keep it in a pool.

She knew that she was as beautiful then as she ever would be – her head tossed back, her mass of curly, blonde hair being rearranged by a breeze, her white throat, shoulders and breasts exposed, and the red color of the thread of blood just barely distinguishable from the ebony of her dress in the darkness.

She thought for a moment that her adversary had disappeared, because she suddenly was not where she had been. But then muscular hands dug into her back, claws bent and held her. There was a tongue lapping between her breasts, but what was there was quickly consumed, and then there were sharp teeth biting, and warm, soft, strong lips pressing around them, sucking. The pain disappeared as soon as her blood mingled with the fluids in the other's mouth. Of course there's no pain while they're feeding, she thought sleepily. It's an adaptive trait, evolutionarily speaking . . . The hands moved to her breasts and began to knead them, like nursing kittens, and she writhed from the sudden pleasure it brought her. Apparently she moved too much, because one of the hands left her breast and took her by the hair. Steel fingers kept her bent back in a perfect bow, the bleeding part of her uppermost, taut, an available feast.

She could smell her own blood. It was sickening and yet very satisfying, familiar, comforting. The scent of fresh blood was nicer than menstrual fluid, though it was always pleasant to bleed. The body over her moved convulsively, paying heed only to what it was drawing in from her, taking care only that she would not escape until she had given satisfaction, satiation, quieted all hunger. She was painfully aware of her heart beating in her left bosom, and realized that was the breast that the brutal hand kept milking and bruising, as if to keep the heart pumping, as if to squeeze its contents directly into the waiting mouth full of razors.

Iduna slipped on the gravel, and immediately the hand left her breast and a strong arm was wedged between her legs, the hand clasping the small of her back, holding her the way a mother holds an infant. She realized by the mushy feel of her panties against Kerry's leather sleeve that she was wet down there, as wet as the mouth that fed on her. Her assailant realized it, too, because she ripped at her panties, literally clawed them to pieces, and then she was being crammed full, opened terribly, spread far too wide, almost lifted off her feet by the force of the fucking, and it hurt so much for so long that she came, came even as the canines sank another notch into her cuts and drank fresh blood from the deepened wound. Which penetration made her come? She did not know.

Then she was being picked up, cradled. Adults are usually not lucky enough to re-experience this infantile pleasure. Even she had not guessed just how strong Kerry really was. A face was close to hers, familiar for its wolfish features, unfamiliar for its look of peace. The teeth in that smile were stained, and the tongue was cupped. The mouth came toward hers, and she opened her mouth, and the tongue slid into her and fed her a mouthful of her own blood. They kissed around it, neither one swallowing, keeping the blood between them to taste, play with, and savor for as long as possible, until their mouths were so full of saliva they had to swallow or let it run down their chins. Then Kerry bent down and took more, and offered it to her again, and this time Iduna leaped for it, bit at it, then worried the mouth that spit blood into hers. Now there were words being spoken in between the kisses, words that said, 'Be careful. Are you really sure you want some of *my* blood?'

Iduna almost wept with gladness. So there was love here, or at least need – a need to keep her available for another feeding. It is only when they become indifferent or vengeful that the undead make their victims like themselves, immortal predators and thus useless and untouchable. When passion returned, she was careful not to bite the other's lips or tongue.

'Take me with you,' she whispered, and her bearer did not ask her where or when, just carried her away in a rush of black and silent wind. Oh, how she had missed being transported this way, effortlessly, in the grip of something far more powerful than herself, so powerful that it was pointless to worry about the destination or what would happen once they arrived there. The venom that had prevented her blood from clotting and closing the wound sang now in her veins, making her see colors behind her closed eyelids, making her warm inside and simultaneously relaxed and alert. No other drug could ever duplicate this ecstasy, this calm. She should know, she had had long enough to search for a substitute. Her thighs trembled, needing to be separated, and the arms around her tightened, hurt her and reassured her.

Her arms full, but under no strain, Kerry felt amazed, disgusted with herself, hopeful, but terribly afraid. She had a low tolerance for ambiguity. It slowed her down too much, made her angry. She had succumbed to temptation, and that was a dangerous weakness. She had not kept her secret, which must mean she had been careless. If one woman could ferret it out, someone else could. Furthermore, she had not slain her discoverer. This was surely stupidity. The code had been violated beyond repair. It was time for another change, another sleep, another decade, another name.

But this blood – whose? Her name was . . . Iduna – Iduna's blood had been very good. She had never had it offered this way, seductively, with persistence and determination, or felt it being given up with joy. But should the pleasure of feeding be mutual? It made her uneasy, no matter how many times she had imagined it and craved it. Now, of course, she wanted it again, and how she resented that! Would there be more nourishment, more pleasure from this source? Or would the woman wake up sweating with the fear of death and the devil, sick of what she had done, and repudiate it and try to make her terror public? What did it mean, to be offered blood by a mortal who claimed to know what she was doing? Could anyone who was not like herself really know what it meant? Had any of her kind ever felt this way, asked themselves these questions? Perhaps it would be better to allow her own veins to be opened, briefly become prey, and turn this taking heifer into a hated peer. That image brought too much shame, hostility, and desire (yes, desire) to be tolerated for long. What had she done?

She wrapped Iduna's cloak more snugly about her, to shut out the cold, transparent fingers of the wind, hugged her newly opened vessel to her breast, then took her deeper into darkness. The Eyrie was still far away. The slut moaned, twisted, and exposed her throat. She wanted it again. It was going to be difficult to avoid draining her completely before dawn. *What had she done?*

Safe, at home in the inhuman arms, Iduna dabbled her fingers in her still-oozing wound and thought, 'After the long hunt, the desperate search, the years of doing without, being alone and bereft, with no wings to shelter me, no sharp teeth in any of the mouths that kissed me, I have you. You are no dream, no fantasy. Finally, my treasure, my pet, my lord, I will make you my beloved. Your strength, your magic, my death and your immortality – I have it all within my reach.'

This rare and beautiful creature did not know how happy she was going to make her, how much she would change her life. Iduna assumed she would never know how Kerry really felt about her, if only because she was so ignorant about her own emotions. The first one, the almost-forgotten one, so needy and yet powerful, had been that way, and Kerry seemed younger, less experienced than it. But Kerry would always need her because her blood was so sweet. Evolutionarily speaking, it was an adaptive trait. And she knew how to make it interesting to take. She had been well schooled.

How old are you, Iduna wondered, and how old am I? Will you ever bother to ask me the kind of questions I've been asking about your kind for these countless lonely, crazy years? Is my blood, precious as it is to me, enough to pay for the wonder and contentment I feel in your presence?

She twined one arm around her captor's neck and reached with the other hand for the leather seam that accentuated, pulled up and divided Kerry's genitals. The curve was like a ripe peach pushed into her hand. It rubbed insistently against her palm. Kerry made the same noise she had made to warn the man in Purgatory to keep his distance, but Iduna only smiled. Abstinence is the mother of shameless lust.

'Sex doesn't seem to be out of the question after all, does it?' the vampire said.

FRANCES GAPPER

THE SECRET OF SORRERBY RISE
A Tale of Mysterious Perils and Hazardous Adventure, Leading to an Astonishing Discovery

(1991)

I was born in the southern county of —shire, a place of gently swelling hills, mild summer skies, clear flowing rivers and trees gracefully waving in the warm caressing winds. A place 'quiet as milk', as the country people say. My mother was a gentlewoman, cast off and abandoned by her rich hard-hearted relatives and yet bearing herself bravely in reduced and poverty-stricken circumstances. She took care to instil in me all the true female virtues – generosity, wisdom of mind and heart, love of all God's creatures and my own body. Above all, she encouraged my natural boldness and spirit of adventure. When I could scarce walk, she taught me my letters and so acquainted me at a tender age with the works of Mrs Radcliffe and Sir Horace Walpole.

My mother's beloved lifelong companion, whom I regarded with near-equal filial affection and respect, was one Miss Louisa Amersham. Sweet, loving spirit, may I ever continue to honour and bless thy memory! Louisa lingered on this earth only three days after my mother's death and they were buried together in one grave, in the little country churchyard, by the old grey church. Inseparable in death, as in life – their gravestone bears the following inscription:

> Stranger, below this sod together rest
> A matchless pair, and one another's Best.
> Two female Friends, with but a single Heart,
> who met, were joined, and never now shall part.
> Cruel Ignorance begrudged their Love reward.
> Nature and Truth united to Applaud.

I now determined to seek my fortune in the world. For though I took pleasure in solitude, and the healthy, well-regulated life of an independent countrywoman – quiet mornings devoted to study and philosophical reflection, the remainder of the day to hill-walking, sketching, cultivating my small vegetable garden, a spot of pugilism with the village lads, or fencing practice – yet this was not enough, could never be enough. My nature, ever warm and impulsive, demanded adventure, romance, passion. Destiny beckoned, and I must heed her call.

I decided to go north. Louisa's birthplace was in the northern county of —shire, and I had often heard her speak with enthusiasm of the beauty of the —shire moors and dales.

While still laying plans for my departure, I went one evening to scatter flowers and shed tears on my dear mother's grave. Spring was then unfolding her brightest glories in field and woodland and by the murmuring brook, and I must linger to praise and exclaim; so the hours slipped away unnoticed and it was near midnight by the time I reached my destination.

The moon was full and sailing high among fast-blowing clouds; trees cast flickering shadows over the white gravestones, like a multitude of ghosts gathering and fleeing at my approach. It was a romantic scene, worthy of a painter's hand – unluckily, I had left my sketchbook behind in the cottage.

As I stood in pensive silence, cursing my lack of forethought, I was arrested by an unexpected vision. A solitary figure was standing in a grassy clearing, beside my mother's grave. From his bearing and attire he appeared a gentleman of means, and of advanced years. He had removed his hat and was standing with his white head bowed, in the attitude of one recently bereaved, and deeply shaken by grief. I drew closer, though hesitant to disturb his sorrowful meditations, but with the helpful intention of re-directing him to the right grave.

'Old Sir —' I began. With a start, he turned, and gazed upon me like one thunderstruck.

'Maria!' he uttered, in a croak. 'Maria, my dearest daughter! My long lost child!'

'Nay, Sir, you are mistaken. My name is not Maria, but Abigail. Maria was my mother's name. There she lies' — I pointed to the grave — 'at rest, in the arms of Louisa, her be-loved.'

'You are her daughter, then?'

'I am.'

'My dear child —' He touched my face, with a trembling hand. 'You bear a remarkable resemblance to her. Those dark eyes — yet clear, and shining with the pure light of angelic goodness and unbending, courageous love. The sweetness of your expres-sion withal — and your bearing, graceful and womanly. Heavenly angel!' he cried, falling to his knees. 'You are indeed her child — Maria, my own daughter, whom to my eternal regret I banished from her parental home and deprived of her rightful inheritance. She was a young widow then, with an infant clinging to her breast, and her affectionate friendship with Louisa Amersham appeared to be transgressing all bounds of propriety. But oh, that I had stopped my ears to the scandalous rumours of spiteful gossip-mongers! My dearest treasure is forever lost to me. Too late now to beg her forgiveness, to offer recompense! She is dead, and by my hand, as surely as if I had killed her myself. Poverty destroyed her spirit — destitution brought her to an early grave . . .'

During all this time I had been attempting to persuade the poor old man to rise, and at last succeeded. I then represented to him earnestly, and with all the descriptive power at my command, what my mother's life had been — her happiness with Louisa, the rock she leaned upon in times of adversity, their love of Nature and the countryside, their busy, active and useful lives, their devoted friends. I described my mother's artistic achievements and many successfully executed commissions. I touched, with heartfelt gratitude, on her tender care of myself; and concluding with the recollection of her steadfastness, courage and fortitude, even as the end drew near, I assured him that, whatever my mother's sufferings, she was incapable of bearing a grudge towards any fellow being, or feeling even the smallest trace of bitterness: he might therefore be confident of her complete and loving forgiveness.

By degrees, as I talked, I saw his anguish lose its initial sharpness, to be replaced by a more gentle melancholy. He stood watching while I scattered flowers from my basket o'er the grave. Then – 'Dear daughter!' he exclaimed, 'for may I so call you? Come with me to London, to my house in St James's Square. There, I can promise you a life of ease, security and good social standing. Solace my few remaining years and I will bequeath to you my entire fortune . . .'

I thanked him courteously for this offer, but instantly declined it. Inwardly, I shrank with horror at the prospect. Was my free, exultant soul to be thus bound in servitude, in the petty round of London masques, routs and balls, the paying of half-hour visits to Lady So-and-so and the Misses Such-and-such, the leaving of cards and the making of social chit-chat, not to speak of *men* and their unwelcome attentions? No! I had better things to do with my life. Though scarce eighteen, I had formed some knowledge of my own nature. Above all things, I longed for a Friend, a true and lasting companion, such as I was unlikely ever to discover in that false and artificial world.

Upon further inquiry, I discovered that my grandfather was returning to the Great Capital that very night. He readily agreed to give me a lift to the nearest town, King's Ditchly, from whence I might catch a stagecoach to the North. Grasping this heaven-sent opportunity, I ran back to the cottage, packed my few modest belongings – principally my sketchbook, two changes of clothes, my sword and a treasured locket containing daguerrotypes of Louisa and my mother – then hastened to the village outskirts, where his carriage awaited me.

As we clattered through the narrow and twisting country lanes, overhung by the towering hedgerows, I was filled with excited apprehension and strove with difficulty to calm the wild beating of my heart. What might the future hold in store for me? Would I find adventure, happiness, love? In all events, I was determined against ever becoming a children's governess, that well-trodden path followed by so many other heroines before me.

At King's Ditchly, I descended from the carriage into a muddy cobbled street, and bade farewell to my grandfather, whose settled melancholy had by now dispersed like the dawn clouds, giving way to a more philosophical optimism – by morning, no doubt, he would be in fine spirits. Thus – transient and shallow – are men's feelings. He pressed upon me a small hamper of food and a bag of gold sovereigns. I thought it wisest to accept, having forgotten, in my haste, to bring any money with me.

There followed several days and nights of hard travelling, in broken-down, iron-seated stagecoaches, from town to town, between flea-ridden inns. This time is blurred and confused in my recollection, and I pass quickly over it – only to say that I was forced several times to repel coarse advances from men, and my opinion of the sex did not improve.

At length, weary and travel-stained, I reached the fringes of —shire, and commanded a room in a modest but clean hostelry, run by an honest-seeming woman and her husband. Having dined excellently on roast parsnips and elderberry wine – eschewing the capons and sirloin of beef, in accordance with my strictest principles – I was shown by candlelight to a bedchamber above, where a cheerful fire was already lit. I bent over it with pleasure, holding my hands out to the leaping flames, and sinking on to a stool, I let the blissful warmth steal through my numbed and chilled limbs. (Accustomed from birth to the gentle and clement weather of the south of England, I had failed to anticipate the sterner northern climate, its bitter winds and harsh driving rains.)

Thus I remained, lost in reverie, until the fire was reduced to glowing coals and a clock chimed midnight in the hallway. Then of a sudden, I heard voices from the adjoining chamber, raised in altercation, and a woman's protest, followed by a scream. Without pausing to consider further, I grabbed my sword and rushed into the corridor. The next door was fast closed; I rattled the handle and shouted, but received no answer. Drawing back a little way, I hurtled with all possible force at the locked door, which burst open, precipitating me into the room.

Instantly, I found myself measuring swords with a man of middle age – thirty or so – in a curled and oiled wig, with cold grey eyes and a face marked by dissipation. Decidedly, a villain. Behind him shrank a young maiden of bewitching beauty, her blonde hair tumbling in disarray around her heaving bosom and her blue eyes filled with imploring terror.

After staring at me a few moments, the villain slowly lowered his sword and returned it to the sheath, his lip curling in a disdainful half-smile. 'Your pardon, Madam – from your manner of entrance, I took you for some common cut-throat or highway-man. I pray you, put up your sword – it becomes you ill, and I have no desire to murder a lady. No doubt you have misapprehended – this young woman is my niece, and I am accompanying her to London, to her father's house.'

'He lies!' cried the girl energetically. 'Lend no ear to these vile falsehoods! I am not this man's niece, nor ever will be – merely his third, fourth, or perchance even fifth cousin – and he has no natural authority, nor any rights over me. Were it not that I foolishly, without consideration – that I –' whereupon she burst into a shower of tears.

Her honour was clearly at stake, and mine also; for I took some pride in my swordsmanship, and was enraged by the man's insults. 'Never fear!' I cried. 'I am your sister, and will defend you to the death, if need be. Sir, I challenge you!' I thrust forward, ripping open his waistcoat. He flinched back in surprise, his eyes narrowing, and emitted a sound not unlike a hiss from between clenched teeth. We fought up and down the room, our swords flashing in the candlelight. I had the initial advantage of surprise, but was hampered by my dress; nevertheless, I had benefited from Louisa's instruction, and she was an excellent swordswoman. I was beginning to gain the upper hand, when he leapt behind a small table, kicking it towards me so that I stumbled over it – then, while I was still regaining my balance, he pinked me in the arm.

I fought on bravely with my left hand, and at length, with a cunning twist, sent his sword spinning across the room. 'Mercy!' he cried, falling on his knees before me.

'You deserve none,' I answered. 'But nevertheless, I will spare your life – on condition that you first apologize to this lady, for attempting to force your unwelcome attentions upon her, and then leave this place instantly . . .'

With a sideways glance in her direction, he muttered something below his breath, the substance of which I construed as an apology, although the words were impossible to distinguish – then rose heavily and stumbled from the room. I kicked the door shut behind him.

Then turned.

Her eyes were heavenly blue, like summer skies, her skin so astonishingly fair and clear, it seemed almost transparent, her hair loosened of its bindings seemed to float around her like a shining golden mist. Her dress was of sprigged muslin, caught under her breasts with a ribbon, accentuating their soft fullness. Her mouth was like a cherry. Her nose was simple but charming. The speaking blood rose to her cheeks as I gazed upon her, imparting to them a delicate tinge, like a white rose flushed with the faintest hue of pink. A rose, I thought, just unfurled from the bud – with the fresh early morning dew not yet evaporated from her soft, velvety petals – fragrant, innocent, untouched. As I stood captured by admiration, she sighed and spoke. Her voice was clear and musical, yet low, and it thrilled me to the depths, to the very marrow, to my innermost soul. The precise words at first escaped me, so entranced was I, but at length I absorbed them.

'Now I suppose you, too, have fallen in love with me!' she exclaimed, in disconsolate, impatient tones. 'Oh yes, don't trouble to deny it. I perceive the signs already – your moonstruck eyes and that foolish expression upon your face. Oh, why does this always . . .'

Her voice was drowned by a loud commotion from the yard below – the snorting and alarmed neighing of horses, clattering on the cobbles, and a man's voice – that of my former opponent – uttering a string of voluble curses. 'Damn you, Horace, let go! You'll ruin the creature's mouth! Here, take this!'– the sharp ringing of coins on stone.

My companion rushed to the window, and leaning out, cried 'Stop him! Landlord, I charge you!' – then, as the sound of hooves faded, she uttered a despairing cry. 'Oh God, he has stolen her! My dearest Belinda!'

She fell back, and threw herself on the bed, in a fury of impatient anguish.

'Who is Belinda?' I inquired.

'My horse, my sweet horse!'

'Are you very fond of her, then?'

'Oh, you have no conception! She means everything to me! She has all my heart! And now Roland – my wicked cousin – has ravished her from me!' And she burst once more into hysterical tears.

I made inarticulate sounds of sympathy, for her distress could not but move me, although personally I never had much of a fondness for horses. She raised her head and gazed at me, her eyes like drowned violets in a lake of milk. 'I entreat you, go after him! Pursue him, the dastard! We must lose no time. Every second is precious – I am sure the landlord, honest Horace, would willingly lend you one of his horses . . .'

The room faded and grew dim, and my ears were filled with an immense roaring, like the sea or like wind sweeping over the hills. 'Your pardon — at this moment I cannot —' I heard my voice coming as if from a long way off, and her dismayed exclamation — 'Oh God, what is it? Your sleeve is soaked with blood! You are wounded!' Then I lost consciousness.

When I awoke, I was lying on a soft bed, near a shuttered window. I could see bright sunlight between the slats, and birds were singing musically outside. 'Where am I?' was my first thought, then as memory flooded back, 'and where is she? How long have I been lying here, unconscious, and what has transpired in the interval? Has that villain returned to abduct her, to force her against her will? Has he killed her? Alas the day!'

I struggled to rise, and at once sank back, overcome by dizziness. My arm was tightly bandaged, past the elbow, so I could scarcely move it; even my hand felt numb. Gazing round me, I saw my dress and undergarments laid over a chair. A clock ticked on the mantelpiece, above a fireplace heaped with grey ashes. A moment later, I heard a soft tread; the door-handle turned and the innkeeper entered. A smile spread across her face on seeing me; approaching, she laid a cool hand on my forehead.

'How are you faring?' she inquired.

'Madam, I beseech you tell me, how long have I been lying here?'

'Three days and more. The fever has passed, thanks be.'

'Where is the young lady who —'

'Whish, settle back now. She's long gone. She paid her account and rushed away like the wind in a great hurry — I doubt you'll ever catch up with her. But stay — now I recall, she left a letter for you—'

Stepping out of the room, she returned a moment later, holding a sealed document, tied up with ribands; this she extended towards me at arm's length and with a somewhat doubtful air. 'Pray, fold back the shutters . . .' I implored. She did so, and the morning sunlight flooded in. I tore open the letter and eagerly devoured it, although the hand was near indecipherable: but at length I made out the following:

My dear Friend,

Forgive my discourtesy towards you: it was ill judged. The desper-
ation of my predicament having raised my emotions to fever pitch, I
can hardly be held responsible in the circumstances for what, in an
unguarded moment, I may have ejaculated, although if it wounded
your sensibilities I am sorry for it, but forsooth, let it pass, I am
eternally grateful to you and should we ever meet again, I will endeavour to behave more kindly. I am now setting forth in search of Belinda,
my beloved Horse, but first, to prove that I am not by nature heartless
and insensible, let me relate to you the sorrowful story of my past life.

I was born the sole child of affectionate – too affectionate, alas! –
parents. My father was a wealthy tradesman, who having achieved
worldly success and prosperity early in his career was content to
purchase an estate in the county of —shire and retire there. My mother
willingly complied, being fatigued with the exigencies of London life,
no longer in her first youth and somewhat depressed in spirits.

She and my father were both good people, and by all appearances
seemed ideally suited: neither was bookish or had any odd freaks; in
affairs of religion and politicks, their opinions exactly coincided. Yet
they could not love one another. God knows by what miracle I came
into the world at last, for certainly I never saw them embrace, or even
touch. As the years passed, disinclination and coldness grew into a
positive distaste for one another's company: no longer conversing, they
kept separate rooms within the same house, my father in the east wing,
my mother in the west. To hear either of them speak, you would think
the other was no more than a distant, unfavoured relative.

Meanwhile I grew to girlhood, the helpless object of all their wasted,
unspent affection; showered in equal measure by each with embraces,
confidences and gifts. The more unhappy I became, it seemed, the
greater their enthusiasm. I developed coughing and choking fits, which
only increased their attentions. Their love was the very air I breathed,
an element unsuited to my nature. Yet other children would crave such
parental fondness. I felt as if I were drowning in a silver river, while
those around me were dying of thirst . . .

But this, though bad enough, was not the limit of my sorrowful
predicament. Scarce twelve years old, I was acknowledged universally

as a Beauty, and receiving homage from all sides. Everybody I met seemed to fall in love with me – one gentleman, madly enamoured and attempting to scale the wall to my bedchamber, fell from a drainpipe and was killed; another, a melancholic, drowned himself; several were slain or horribly injured in duels; and so on. By my fifteenth year, I had received three times that many proposals of marriage, and suffered countless insults and indecent suggestions.

And not only from men! Nay, though innocently I had fled for protection and safety to the female sex, I soon discovered the naïvety of my conceptions. One governess after the other had to be dismissed without a character – cooks and kitchenmaids likewise. Even my aunt, a highly respectable married woman, made advances to me in the shrubbery, when she and I were sheltering from a rainstorm.

At last, my only place of refuge was the stables, where the groom and stable lad were happily enamoured only of one another; and there I first encountered my beloved Belinda. Horses are in every way preferable to human beings, I consider: their odour is sweeter, their intelligence more sensitive and refined; above all they are utterly indifferent to foolish aesthetic considerations. Belinda has no notion of my being beautiful or charming: she likes me because I feed her with apples and keep a light hand on the reins. I honour her judgement. She herself is a peculiarly ugly horse; but no words of mine can describe the sweetness and gaiety of her spirit. I cannot help but shed a tear, remembering. Forgive the brevity of this communication. I must depart instantly, in pursuit of Roland, my wicked cousin, for I feel sure he intends harm to Belinda.

Adieu – Marianne.

Having perused the foregoing epistle, I refolded it with a sigh, and fell back. 'Well, there is no use in following her, even if I were capable of doing so. Marianne!' – I breathed the lovely name aloud.

'Marianne!' echoed a mocking voice, behind me. I turned sharply, and saw to my utter astonishment and confusion, standing by my bedstead, a man! Though apparently a mere stripling, not more than eighteen, his manner was self-assured and easy –

he seemed not in the least discomfited by my horrified gaze.

In stature he was of middle height, and slim. His hair was a light reddish brown, tied back with a riband and powdered. He wore a brown velvet coat, with darker lacing, and a cambric shirt, with a lace neck-cloth, falling in lavish ruffles. This modish style of dress gave him a somewhat foppish air, belied by the sword fastened neatly at his side. Also the swiftness of his movements – for before I knew it, he was gone from behind me and arranging himself comfortably on the broad window seat. His shapely legs were clad in white stockings and buckled shoes.

'Who is Marianne? Your sister, cousin, friend, mistress?'

A pang shot to my heart at the latter suggestion, but I bit my lip and strove to maintain a stony expression. 'I wonder, Sir, that you should make it your business to inquire. Marianne is – a stranger to me – I encountered her but recently, and we parted not half an hour after meeting.'

'Is that so?' His brow lifted and his gaze rested upon me, thoughtfully. 'And will you – ah – encounter her again, in the foreseeable future?'

'How should I tell?' was my irritable rejoinder.

'I merely wondered.'

'And I can only repeat, what business may it be of yours?'

'None at all – unless I should perchance take an interest in your affairs, and choose to involve myself therein.'

'Pray desist from doing so. I would rather you left me – and my affairs – entirely alone.' Unwisely, I made an abrupt movement, and winced.

'That arm is dressed very clumsily – no wonder it pains you. I understand something of physic – will you allow me –?' Before I could protest, he was at my side, untying the bandage. A faintness overcame me and my sight was dimmed for a moment: I heard his sharply indrawn breath on seeing the wound. 'This must be cleaned, and the dressing renewed.'

'No, I pray you –' I protested, weakly.

'My dear girl, you can trust my discretion, calm yourself.'

'But I would rather have a woman –'

'I admire your discrimination. However, this is hardly the time to be debating the merits of the sexes . . .'

These were the last words I heard; then I must have lapsed into unconsciousness, for when I next opened my eyes, he was gone.

I had slept deeply, and was filled with the sweetest sensation of peace, as if rocked gently and hushed in my own dear mother's arms. It was evening, and the moon cast down her luminous beams, suffusing my chamber with a soft radiance. Instantly I rose and walked to the window. My arm was loosely bound and no longer troubled me, although I was greatly weakened by the fever, and somewhat dazed by the rapid passing of recent events. 'That extraordinary young man – who was he, I wonder? Did I dream of him, or does he exist in truth? Sure, I could never have imagined such a vision!' I smiled, remembering. 'Despite his discourtesy, I liked him. He amused me and he was charming, unlike other men. I wonder if . . .'

I settled myself in the broad window enclosure, gazing out across the moonlit fields; and sighed deeply. 'How ignorant I am! I understand nothing of man, or woman either. My own heart is an entire mystery to me. I have travelled far, yet for no good cause, and to no perceptible end – my destination becomes increasingly uncertain, ever retreating as I advance. Where shall I find true happiness? Am I wrong in settling my hopes on that elusive object – should I not rather strive to curb and restrain my perhaps too impulsive, too eager nature; by turning inwards, to rely ever more upon myself, establishing a surer foundation of self-knowledge and moral strength? Since I am now alone in the world, with none to care for me and nobody to love, and no reason to expect any change in this most painful predicament. Nay, since I fall in love so easily and on such slender acquaintance, it may be that I am incapable of forming any lasting attachment . . .'

Thus besieged by melancholy thoughts, and plunging ever deeper into self-induced despondency, I sat and wept; till of a sudden, some other influence, of relief, of comfort, seemed to enter my soul. I lifted my eyes and saw before me a vision – the face of a woman, old and wise – neither Louisa nor my mother, yet with something of each in her countenance.

'Arise, my daughter!' she exclaimed. 'Forgo these bitter doubts and needless self-recriminations. Never doubt your capacity to love, and that you will receive abundant love in return. There is one who needs you and who is in peril of her life. You alone have the power to save her. Take courage, therefore, and struggle onward . . .'

Her face shimmered and vanished. I was left alone, gazing at the blank and rounded full moon. Yet in spirit I was no longer alone – no longer despairing or wrought upon by the false phantoms of tremulous conscience. 'So be it!' I exclaimed. 'Great Mother of All, how can I choose but obey you, and follow rejoicing wherever you direct me?' And I passed several moments in silent thankfulness.

Pangs of hunger then assailed me, and recollecting that I had eaten nothing for nigh on three days, I dressed myself and hastened downstairs. I could discover little of sustenance in the larder, saving a number of dry biscuits, which I consumed with an eager appetite. Then, throwing a thick cloak over my shoulders, I drew the bolts of a side door, and stepped into the cobbled courtyard.

Dawn was then stretching her yellow fingers across the eastern horizon, and the joyous calling of birds rang clearly on the still air. A cock crew; a dog barked; deep sighs and impatient blowing noises came from the nearby stables. Taking a circuit of the building, I admired how the hillside rose up steeply and majestically behind; the little inn seeming to nestle in its depths, like a chick folded under her mother's wing. This situation would account, I reflected, for the extreme dampness of the structure, and the resultant gloomy and dank atmosphere of the lower rooms – 'it be all thikky up the walls', as my countrymen would say.

Well, I had reached the North, and was already enchanted by it. Life moved here at an exhilarating pace; the very air seemed infused with passion and adventure; soon I hoped to make acquaintances less transient, or even friends. Though doubtless many of these —shire folk, as in other remote country places, would be dour and distrustful of strangers. On this point, I determined to interrogate my good hostess, whom by her quaint accents and turn of speech I judged a —shire woman born and bred. A moment later, I heard a stirring within the house and she emerged, throwing a bucket of slops into the courtyard.

She greeted me, though with a sober mien, and an air of heaviness – I hardly recognized my comforter of the previous morning. Without further preamble, she began, 'You'll not have heard – and the tidings will hardly touch thee, being a foreigner –'

'What, I pray you?'

She drew closer to me, lowering her voice and casting a nervous glance back over her shoulder, as if wary of intruders. 'A man was killed last night, crushed to death by a falling rock, as he was riding homewards, along by Carransfell . . .'

A cold chill struck to my heart, recalling my visitor, that young man of the lace ruffles and exquisite manners. I described him to my hostess, and she regarded me with astonishment. 'Know you not who that was? 'Twas Lord Courtenay de L'Isle. From the concern he showed over thee, I felt sure he must be thy cousin or some other relative. No, 'twas not he, but —, a well-to-do farmer of this district . . .'

On further inquiry, I elicited the following sensational information: it appeared that this part of —shire was greatly infested with foot robbers; the roads being narrow and not seldom overhung by steep ledged outcrops of rock, these desperados would leap down from above on passing carriages; then, having disabled the coachmen and stripped those within of money and valuables, they would scatter and vanish into the surrounding hills.

However, the terrain was in general bare and bleak, offering few hiding places; or it turned quickly from rocky crags to open moorland. To forestall pursuers, the robbers had lately adopted a most cruel and dastardly practice. One of their number would remain above, overlooking the scene, and on a pre-arranged signal, would send rocks of a massive size tumbling and bouncing down the hillside. These would oftentimes hurt or kill innocent travellers, or else fright the horses, causing them to bolt; or set off a landslide, crushing all below and blocking the road for many days hence.

As my hostess was talking the sun rose clear of the eastern horizon, bathing the fields in dewy light. It was a scene of awesome beauty, and moved me deeply; yet admiration mingled strangely in my heart with sensations of pity and horror, resultant on my landlady's revelations. 'This beautiful landscape, which appears with the freshness and untouched glory of Eden, is yet tainted by human evil,' I reflected. 'Nature nurses a viper in her bosom, a wilful and vicious son at her breast. Oh, that Man could be wiped from this earth!'

My thoughts reverted to Marianne – had she succeeded in overtaking that odious brute, Roland, and recapturing Belinda, without further hazard or mischance? Surely the villain would let slip no opportunity to insult her afresh – and she defenceless, unprotected . . . Meanwhile my hostess was still talking, being clearly of a voluble disposition, and before long, to my great astonishment, began to expound on this very subject. She informed me that Marianne was now safe, that – wonder of wonders! – Lord de L'Isle himself had pursued Roland and recaptured Belinda, giving Roland a large sum of money in exchange – further, that Marianne was Lord de L'Isle's ward, and that he owned most of the land thereabouts. This was strange indeed!

'But is not Lord de L'Isle very young?' I ventured. 'If he is the gentleman who recently accosted me in my bedchamber – he seemed a mere stripling, in the very bloom of youth, the lightest of down upon his cheek . . .'

'Nay – he looks young, I grant ye, but he is thirty. His parents died when he was just come of age, bequeathing him all their wealth, and a great castle on Sorrerby Rise; you may just glimpse its turrets, beyond that wood ... He travels much abroad, but in the intervals of his journeying, he has made great improvements to the estate and the village – building cottages for the poor and a new schoolhouse. Blessings on him! He is loved by all hereabouts, and deservedly so. 'Tis our dearest wish that he should marry, and produce an heir – otherwise, should he by some sad accident chance to die, the estate would fall by default to that villainous cousin of his, that Mr Roland Hooker Waller' – my hostess pronounced this name with a fine disdain.

'Mr Hooker Waller – the gentleman I crossed swords with, three nights past?'

'Aye, the very same, excepting he's no gentleman. "Sewer rat" would be a more fitting description, for he's most vicious and corrupt – even to speak of him, it brings the bile swimming in my throat' – in eloquent proof of which, she spat on the cobbles.

'Is Mr Hooker Waller then universally disliked?'

'Aye, in these parts. He only hangs around here to cause mischief – otherwise he's mostly in London, gambling and frittering away his fortune – I should rather say, my Lord's fortune.'

'How!' I exclaimed. 'Is Lord de L'Isle then so blind to his cousin's faults – so easily deluded by him – so readily imposed upon? Does he bestow money freely upon this unworthy object – thus condoning, by implication, Mr Hooker Waller's debauched and vicious lifestyle?'

'I fear 'tis so,' she replied. 'Nothing is more mysterious, for Lord de L'Isle has as sharp and good a wit as any man, yet in this matter he appears befuddled and inconstant. Mr Hooker Waller comes and goes as he pleases, partaking frequently of Lord de L'Isle's hospitality – my lord keeps a fine cellar and the covers are laid each night, as befits his rank . . .'

She continued talking thus, digressing proudly on the subject of my lord's wealth, nobility, condescension, and so on, but I heard no more; my head was in a whirl of new conceptions. So Mr Hooker Waller was a regular guest at the Castle – at Marianne's place of residence – and invited, nay even welcomed there by her so-called guardian, her supposed protector! What could be the meaning of this? Instantly I was filled with burning resolution – I must seek out Marianne and if possible rescue her from the dread Castle, or at least offer her my service and protection – my heart, my sword, my life!

With this confirmed intent, I set out later that day, by foot, across the fields, and following the bank of a pleasant meandering river, soon arrived at the western boundary of Lord de L'Isle's estate. Here I paused – for the day was exceeding hot – to splash my face and dabble my feet in the clear running water. Impatient with constriction, I untied my bonnet and loosened my hair, so it tumbled free. Now truly I felt a daughter of Nature – like to some river naiad, or a dryad of the nearby woods. Sadly tanned and freckled, my hands roughened by country labour, I possessed nothing of Marianne's fair and ethereal beauty – yet my own body pleased me well enough. Sure, I would never wish to be a boy!

It was midday, and the sun having attained her zenith, the heat and glare were near insupportable. Instead of approaching the main gate of the Castle, therefore, I decided to walk through the woods, trusting to my luck and sense of direction, and hoping not to fall into any concealed mantraps. The beechwood was cool, well shaded and pleasant, though unexpectedly deep; an hour or so later, I was completely lost, and doubted my chances of emerging before nightfall.

It was then I heard voices nearby; familiar voices; one low and well modulated, the other raised in sneering deprecation. Lord de L'Isle and Mr Hooker Waller! I crept forward, and before long found myself on the edge of a wide clearing.

The greensward was closely mown, and marble statues were disposed here and there, representations of goddesses and the heroines of classical mythology. In the centre stood Lord de L'Isle, a slim and upright figure, now dressed in satin small clothes and a coat of excellent tailoring, fitting tightly across the shoulders. As I perceived him, my heart seemed to miss a beat, or several, and my breath quickened, yet recollecting the brevity

341

of our connection and the kindness he had hitherto shown me, I strove to calm myself. Surely I had no reason to fear the man – if I were discovered, it was unlikely he would do me any harm, or even reprove me for trespassing on his land. Mr Hooker Waller, at a few yards' distance, lounged indolently against a statue of Atalanta, smoking a cheroot.

'My dear cousin, pray cease to trouble yourself thus needlessly. I meant no harm to the girl, nor to that – one may scarce call it a horse – to that animal. I beg you will forget the whole disastrous episode – believe me, it is of very little significance.'

'Not to you, perhaps,' Lord de L'Isle replied, evenly. 'But you may recollect, Roland, that Marianne is my ward. Her parents being dead, I am now entrusted with her safe keeping – a duty which, believe me, I take seriously.'

'But how delightful for you. Mixing duty with pleasure, so to speak.'

'My task has so far proved the very opposite of delightful, or pleasurable. As you are well aware – and mainly due to your own interference –'

'My dear sweet coz, how can this be? I strive only to please you, in all things.'

'You would please me best by keeping your distance – by continuing to reside in London, as I think we agreed, and confining yourself to twice-yearly visits.'

'Ah yes, but then the air here is so invigorating, the prospects so charming, and despite having a monthly income – your most generous settlement, dear coz – somehow I find myself continually short of money . . .'

'Due to foolish extravagance.'

'Possibly . . .' Mr Hooker Waller finished his cheroot and threw it on the ground, grinding it with his heel.

'At all events, let me entreat you . . .'

'Let us postpone your so-elegant entreaties to some future time; as you are aware, I dislike being lectured' – he took out a pocket watch – 'and I am engaged to be in London tomorrow night, so if you will excuse me' – and sweeping a low, mocking bow, he withdrew. I now perceived that the clearing formed the central meeting place of three wide and majestic avenues. Mr Hooker Waller sauntered away down the furthest of these, which I assumed led back to the house.

Left alone, Lord de L'Isle exhibited every sign of irritable exhaustion and despondency. He struck his forehead, and aimed several kicks at a statue of Venus reclining at her toilet; then sinking into a conveniently placed bench, of curious and ornate design, he rested his head despairingly in both hands, and moaned aloud.

It was scarcely possible to remain any longer in concealment. I could not thus stand by as witness to the distress and suffering of a fellow human being, without seeking in some way to alleviate it; and besides, I owed this particular gentleman a debt of kindness; so I walked forward. He remained unconscious of my presence till I was but a yard away; then a twig cracked, and he looked up in surprise. Recognition dawned in his eyes, followed swiftly by another expression, of glad interest.

'If I am disturbing you, my Lord, I crave your pardon, but I – I –' My voice faltered and died.

'You are not,' he replied, gently. 'Pray sit down – I am happy to see you again, even at such a time as this. How much did you overhear of what just passed?'

'Hardly anything.' I sat down beside him, feeling confused and somewhat shy. He was so elegant! – unlike anybody I had ever known. His well-manicured nails and long white fingers, his lightly powdered hair, the intricate fall of his necktie – all bespoke a gentleman of high breeding. Even his skin seemed to waft a faint perfume . . . How could *I* have anything in common with someone so infinitely civilized?

'Marianne is then your ward?' I ventured.

'Yes – and I owe you an apology, for my former behaviour. I was not quite open with you – for you see, I suspected you of being involved in my cousin's conspiracy.'

'How!' I exclaimed in astonishment, 'Me, conspiring with Mr Hooker Waller to abduct your ward?'

'Believe me, where Marianne is concerned, anything is possible – she attracts abductors, lovers, what you will, as a honey pot attracts flies. And do you then deny – did you never feel –' His eyes held mine, and I felt the blood rise to my cheeks. 'Never mind,' he said, quickly. 'I will not question you.'

We sat for some while in silence. I perceived with dismay the full awkwardness of my position – for had it not indeed been my professed object in coming here to abduct Marianne, in the guise of a rescuer and supposedly in her interests? The arrows of self-accusation struck to my heart and remained there, quivering; I was o'erspread with shame's mantle.

My companion meanwhile had recommenced speaking, thanking me with sincerity for my protection of Marianne, and regretting my wound. Observing my confusion, he let the subject lapse and began instead to ply me with questions concerning my past life – where was my birthplace and what my parentage? I replied at first with hesitancy, but gradually gaining confidence, told him something of my mother and of Louisa.

He regarded me with wonder. 'And is it so?' he cried at last. 'Did these two women spend their lives together in happy and enduring love, faithful even unto the grave? And were these your parents?'

'My father died when I was a babe,' I replied. 'Louisa was my loving guardian, friend, sister and teacher; to my mother, all these and more, far more. They were happy indeed – and as for me, I should count myself fortunate to find a Friend of one tenth Louisa's worth.'

'I believe you,' he returned, warmly 'and I wish that I had known your stepmother, your guardian – she sounds a remarkable woman and an example to her Sex. I should have valued her acquaintance.'

'But she would scarcely have valued *yours*, for she greatly mistrusted and despised all *men*.' I spoke without thinking, and instantly regretting my words, wished that I had stayed silent – yet indeed, I had spoken nothing but truth.

He smiled faintly. 'And did she so? I have known other Ladies of that persuasion – friends of mine, whose judgement I approve entirely. Yet these Ladies, though despising my Sex in general, have made an exception for me.'

'Why so?'

'I cannot say. You will have to ask them. As it happens, they will be arriving here tonight, bringing a large party from London – they find my house a convenient place for dances and soirées. I could procure you an invitation, if you are willing to stay. I believe it is a coming-out ball.'

While he was speaking, the sky had darkened rapidly, and soon huge drops of rain were falling here and there, in certain promise of a storm. We moved quickly to shelter, and taking my hand, he led me after him through the woods, until soon we came to a small roofed pavilion or summer-house, at a vantage point above the landscape.

It was a most glorious scene. From where we stood, the smooth green hillside swept down unhindered to a vast lake, which curved in serpentine fashion into the distance, giving the illusion of a winding river. In more clement, bright weather, I could imagine how the lake surface would glitter with a thousand sparkling lights; but now overhung by tumultuous grey clouds, it conveyed an awesome and sombre majesty. At some distance, I could see a foaming Cascade; near to it, the ruins of an Abbey; and on a far hillside, the entrance to what must be a network of underground Caves. Above all, I admired how clumps of trees stood here and there, most pleasing in their arrangement and drawing the eye towards distant prospects. The entire scene possessed all the splendour of an Italian painting; an effect unspoilt by the driving rain, now moving in sheets across the land.

'And did Nature do all this?' I exclaimed.

'She did little – although all was done in her Name,' replied Lord de L'Isle. 'The main part was contrived by Alice Brown, also known as Possibility Brown, a landscaper of consummate genius, though small fame – her brother takes all the credit for her work.

'And there is my house' – he pointed to the right. There at half a mile's distance against the grey sky I saw a huge castle with crenellated battlements, its every window blazing with light. A number of carriages were visible, drawn up outside the main gates.

'My guests have arrived,' he added. A smile crossed his lips, yet in his eyes lingered an indefinable expression of sadness. Watching him, I realized that despite his noble birth, his great wealth and fashionable friends, Lord de L'Isle was yet unhappy – even lonely. For a moment I glimpsed his true self, behind the mask. I wished to speak, yet dared not – and the next instant, he turned towards me.

As our eyes met, my heart seemed to dissolve into liquid silver, and for a moment I was near fainting. I could no longer deceive myself – I was stricken with dismay – surely it could not be that I loved a Man! Nothing in my upbringing had prepared me for such a horrible eventuality – it ran contrary to all my former inclinations and against all my most fervently held principles.

Turning aside, I strove to regulate my emotions and compose my features – happily, it was still raining, and my distress concealed, so I hoped, by the more general atmospheric turmoil.

At that moment, I heard the calling of a sweetly familiar voice, and Marianne appeared over the hill, in company with another Female – both were clad in voluminous riding capes, ample protection against the Elements. Marianne was leading a horse, whom by the simple plainness of her countenance and her cross-eyed squint, I assumed to be Belinda.

Marianne made exclamations of surprised pleasure on catching sight of me and saluted me on both cheeks, in sisterly fashion; I gladly returned the embrace. Meanwhile, the other female was shaking hands with Lord de L'Isle. She was a large woman, and in her manner and bearing, reminded me somewhat of Louisa, for though she wore no ornaments and was far from the ideal of female beauty – her greying hair was bound back severely, her nose a forbidding beak – yet she was obviously of high birth and accustomed to command. Soon she accosted me with a friendly air, made inquiry of my name and demanded an account of my past life and present journey; I answered her honestly, as seemed best.

While I was speaking, she and Lord de L'Isle exchanged several glances; and I thought he looked steadily at me, though I could not, for fear, meet his gaze.

'My dear,' she said at length, 'I am Melissa Cheverel. I knew your stepmother, Louisa, in her youth, and loved her well – indeed I may say that I owe everything to her good offices, for she encouraged and by example aided my Conversion, leading me to escape from the miserable constrictions of family and stultifying respectability. Through her I first encountered the author and foundation of all my present happiness, Amaryllis, to whom I will introduce you this evening. I assume you are coming to the Ball?'

I knew not how to reply, for though her kindness touched me and I was pleased to make her acquaintance, yet I was hardly in a mood for festivity. Besides, what would this great Lady think of me, when her clear gaze penetrated, as it surely would, the turmoil of my heart – when she discovered my perverted affection for Lord de L'Isle, which I could hardly yet admit even to myself? Surely she would turn from me in revolted scorn?

The rain lessening, our party began to descend the hillside. Belinda's pace was uneven, as she would often pause to crop the fresh verdure; so the others drew ahead, while Marianne, taking my arm, proceeded to discourse with animation on the superior wisdom of Animals. I attended with a heavy heart.

'Oh!' she exclaimed 'that human beings would only cultivate Natural Understanding – taking our example from such as my dear Horse. Our true needs are indeed very few and easily satisfied – principally for shelter and sustenance. Passionate love is a disorder of the natural emotions, resulting oftentimes in madness, and certainly antagonistic to Right Living. I am a subscriber to the New Philosophy of Mrs M. Humphry Allenby – if you are curious, I will gladly lend you her two most recent publications, the *Rediscovery of Happiness* and the *Return to Innocence*. Mrs Allenby's character is wholly admirable, and her writings would persuade even the –'

With a sudden access of spleen, I interrupted her. 'No doubt – but Marianne, whatever the extraordinary virtues of Mrs M. Humphry Allenby – whatever higher state this lady may happily have attained – *you* are still susceptible to passionate error; for but a few days past, I seem to recall, you consented foolishly to elope with Mr Hooker Waller.'

'No indeed! You are wholly mistaken on that score. Roland cunningly deluded me – I believed his intentions to be entirely honourable.'

'How! You thought he would offer marriage?'

'No – but he promised to accompany me to the horse fair at Mickleton Cross, which I had a great desire to see. Pray do not berate me – indeed, I deeply regret my naïvety on that occasion, especially as my dear guardian was forced to pay for it.'

Again we paused, for Belinda to savour an especially nourishing piece of vegetation. Lord de L'Isle and Miss Cheverel were now lost to view, having passed through the Castle gates.

But why, I wondered, should Lord de L'Isle have given money to Mr Hooker Waller – wherefore such craven behaviour towards a traitorous and despicable villain? Was this not strange? I expressed my bewilderment to Marianne, and she flushed.

'My guardian has a – a secret, which I am not at liberty to reveal. It explains All – and yet for his own safety, it must remain closely guarded. Perhaps if you ask him – I note he has a fondness for you . . .'

My heart gave a lurch. A fondness! Yes, he was fond of me – no more than fond. As for love – no. Perhaps he loved Marianne – or perhaps Mr Hooker Waller! Yes, that was surely the explanation: Mr Hooker Waller had spurned Lord de L'Isle's advances and was now blackmailing him, threatening to reveal his secret passion to the world! My mind moved with a marvellous rapidity, building conjecture upon conjecture. Thus engaged, to the exclusion of all else, I took absent-minded leave of

Marianne in the stable courtyard and wandered into the great entrance hall of the Castle.

All around was bustle and movement – here a chambermaid scurried past carrying a pile of bed linen, and another with silver branched candlesticks; there two cooks, in animated discussion; and here a deputation of gardeners, bringing baskets of earthy vegetables and orchard fruits. All were women – a peculiarity that failed to strike me at the time, for I was admiring the vastness of the hall, with its flagstoned floor and huge pillars soaring to a fan-vaulted ceiling.

The housekeeper came forward, seemingly unsurprised by my arrival, and welcomed me kindly, introducing herself as Mrs Weston. She led me up a broad red-carpeted staircase and along a corridor hung with portraits; then, selecting a key from the bundle at her waist, she unlocked a door and opened it.

On entering the chamber, I exclaimed aloud with delight; for besides being nobly furnished, with a majestic four poster bed and ornately framed pictures and looking glasses on the walls, it was decked throughout with the most beautiful flowers. They were principally roses – roses of the deepest red and the purest white, and of heavenly scent. As I stood captivated, several chambermaids entered, carrying jugs of steaming hot water, which they poured into a tub, standing on feet fashioned like animal paws.

Mrs Weston turned to me. 'My Lord gave instructions, Miss, that you would need dry stockings and shoes and a gown for tonight's ball. Everything is provided here, as you will find . . .' She unlocked the closet and left it a little ajar, then curtseyed and withdrew.

All was peaceful, save for occasional sounds of laughter, and women's voices below the windows: Lord de L'Isle's guests, I presumed, now taking exercise in the gardens, following the passing of the storm. Glancing down, I saw my garments were sodden with rain and liberally splashed with mud. I undid my gown and stepped out of it; then thought it best to uncover my long-forgotten wound, which proved to be near healed.

Curious to view my reflection, I walked forward to the nearest glass; and to my surprise, found that I looked almost beautiful. My eyes, darker and more open, my parted lips, the burning summer in my cheeks – all betrayed what I would fain conceal.

In the ensuing silence, I heard a rose drop her velvet petals, one by one; some fell on the carpet, and others into my bath water, where they floated and idly drifted.

I bathed with pleasure, and emerged from the water in good spirits.

Opening the closet, I found a dress of yellow silk and brocade, heavy and richly patterned, with a hooped petticoat and another of silver lace. Ranged on a shelf below were a great many shoes – I liked best a pair of yellow satin, which happily fitted me exactly. Rejecting a fan of painted chicken skin with ivory sticks, I picked another of gilded paper.

The day was fading and a maid entered carrying a taper, to light the candles in my room. She was very young and herself appeared surrounded by a soft radiance of golden light – it seemed she might have kindled the candles just with her fingertips. She stayed to help me with my hair, and from time to time gave a gentle sigh.

'What ails you?' I demanded. She made no answer, but her eyes, meeting mine in the glass, told all. Love is indeed the finest melancholy, spilling over in sighs and tears. 'Will you meet her tonight?' I asked.

She nodded. 'But first I must light all the candles, and help the ladies to dress . . .'

I took the comb from her hand and pushed her towards the door. 'Go now,' I said. 'Leave your taper; I shall light the candles. The ladies can dress themselves, I dare say.'

Instruments were being tuned below and would occasionally break into a waltz or quadrille. I felt a growing excitement. This would be my first ball! – and perhaps if I drank enough negus or ratafie, I might put Lord de L'Isle from my thoughts and find my affections turning towards a more suitable object.

I went down the corridor, knocking and entering at every door. Some of the bedchambers were empty; in others I encountered a lady at her toilet, or several of them together, laughing and talking. I received some curious glances, but lit the candles and was gone before any could question me.

Having crossed the stairwell, I came to an oaken door of imposing dimensions. I tried the handle; it opened easily and I entered carrying my taper before me.

The room was huge and made sombre by the deepening dusk. I could descry a bay window at the far end, and bookcases lining the two long walls and reaching to the ceiling – itself an impressive specimen of ornate plasterwork. I walked forward incautiously, prompted by my desire to examine the books; nearest were a number of bound calfskin volumes of Shakespeare's plays and the collected works of Mr Pope; but I got no further, for a shadowy figure moved with heart-stopping suddenness from an alcove and strong fingers closed around my wrist. I gasped for fright and nearly dropped the taper – but he took it from me in time. It was Lord de L'Isle!

Keeping his eyes steady upon mine, he moved back a pace; then turned to light a branch of candles, standing in a niche. Our shadows danced and stretched up to the ceiling like giants.

He was dressed in grey satin with old lace at his wrists and throat, a light dress sword fastened by his side, and broad diamond buckles on his shoes.

'Did you hope to avoid me?' he said, lightly.

'I – I – no,' I stammered. 'I had no such desire – I am honoured to be your guest.'

'Yet your expression indicates a certain displeasure. Pray tell me, have I disgusted you in any way – or insulted you?'

'No – no –'

'Then why . . .?'

The blood rose to my face in a burning tide. My wrist still ached sorely from his clasp and I rubbed at it with a sense of grievance – it would very likely bruise. In sudden anger, I exclaimed, 'I need not tell you my thoughts – you have no right to interrogate me. *You* keep your own secrets – then let me keep mine!'

A window was opened beneath. Sweet strains of music floated out on the evening air, and then a woman's voice singing:

> Whoe'er she be
> That not impossible She
> That shall command my heart and me;
>
> Where'er she lie,
> Lock'd up from mortal eye
> In shady leaves of destiny:
>
> – Meet you her, my Wishes
> Bespeak her to my blisses,
> And be ye call'd, my absent kisses . . .

Feeling a little giddy headed, I sank into the window seat. 'Have you eaten?' he inquired.

'Not since this morning . . .'

'There is a cold collation laid out below – but if we are to exchange heart's confidences, it had best not be in a crowded ballroom. Besides, your descent is eagerly awaited – I would scarce have you to myself a moment. Let me order a tray to be brought up.' He tugged the bellpull.

'By the way, you know it is a masked ball this evening. I have always been greatly interested in masks. When I was young, I spent a year in Venice, where the mask-makers ply their trade, by the Bridge of Sighs. Of these the most famous was Bartolomeo de San Servino, who had begun his career by casting the death masks of great noblemen and poets. His masks were so like real faces, you would believe they smiled sometimes, or grew melancholy. I saw a mask he made of the moon, that was said to confer immortality upon its owner: but you would have to accustom yourself to waxing and waning. One young married lady of my acquaintance sold her beautiful pearl ring and her emerald brooch to buy his mask of a female wolf. She was advised not to wear this until after her pregnancy was past, but the Carnivale falling in her sixth month, she could not resist – the results were exactly as predicted. Her husband ordered the child to be drowned.

'As for me, I was twenty-one, my parents had just died, I was unable to sleep at nights. When I entered the mask shop, Bartolomeo himself came forward to the counter: he looked not more than twenty, though I believe in that year he was 102. He refused to serve me, informing me that it was not advisable to place one mask on top of another. "That you wear," he said, pointing in my face, "is already in a way to killing you."

'In the next week, made bold by terror, I revealed my secret to a number of friends; then I felt the mask loosen its grip; I gained a little breathing space. Otherwise, I do believe it would have suffocated me. For you see, it is one of those dead men's faces. I had a twin brother and he was the heir to my parents' estate; when we were ten years old and my mother past childbearing age, he died. Anxious to secure the succession – for the estate, like most, was entailed in favour of a male heir – they determined that I should be a boy – that I should be, in effect, my brother. So they gave it out, 'twas the girl that died.

'And now, since I have told you my secret, can you trust me with yours?'

Mrs Weston had answered the bell, and brought us a number of little dishes on a tray, and gone away again, before I was anywhere near speaking.

'And Mr Hooker Waller?' I managed at last. 'Is he aware of – of what you have just told me?'

'If he were, the whole of Society would also know it within a day or two, and Roland would be installed in his rightful place, as Master of this estate. He would be Lord de L'Isle – and I, plain Cordelia Beaufort. He senses his power over me, none the less, and makes use of it. I expect he will find out eventually – then I shall be forced to flee the country and live abroad – the estate will go to rack and ruin under his ownership, for he would care naught, either for the land or for its people. You may well think me an unsuitable protector for Marianne –

possessing a borrowed past and no future, living ever in the uncertain present – but at least I provide a home for her. Her parents entrusted her to me, knowing all. If you love her indeed, I give you leave to hazard your suit, though you have not much chance of success, I warn you – others have tried –'

I stood up, though doubting the strength of my legs, but apprehending that I must speak now, seizing the opportune moment, and disperse all lingering clouds of doubt and illusion. 'I would make a poor suitor in truth, for my heart is already given away. I love you, Cordelia! – and consequent upon your most welcome revelation, my Will and my Reason now join with my Heart, in preferring you above all others. If you will not have me, I must – I must –' 'I was meaning to say, I must depart, and glanced uncertainly towards the door, but at that instant, she seized me in her arms and kissed me!

Oh! – the joy that flooded my heart! – I had never imagined, never allowed myself to conceive such happiness! It seemed natural and easy to return her embraces – though having the advantage of me in height and strength, she pressed me to her so hard I could scarce breathe and was soon forced to entreat her for a moment's respite. As she released me, I saw that her eyes were shining and her cheeks flushed – all bitterness and cynicism vanished from her countenance – no longer the sad young man, but a woman of great beauty and noble demeanour. Our lips met again, this time with tender hesitancy.

'Oh Abby,' she breathed, 'stay with me, be mine – I will love you for ever!' Taking my hand, she covered it with kisses.

'Yes dearest, for a lifetime and more. We must never again be parted, I could not endure it. As to where we live,' I added, 'it hardly matters – this Castle is wholly delightful, but indeed I would welcome the opportunity of foreign travel.'

Our conversation continued a good while longer, mixed with a thousand caresses and sweet endearments, which having pity on my reader, I forbear to describe. At eleven o'clock, with exceeding reluctance, we descended to the ballroom, where Melissa welcomed us with composure and the merest flicker of a raised eyebrow. I was introduced to stately Amaryllis, Duchess of —, and a great number of other ladies, including several of the old nobility, others of scholarly renown or possessed of great artistic genius, and many fresh in the bloom and gaiety of youth. Having never before seen ladies dancing together, or paying such open tribute of sisterly kindness and affection, I revelled in the Spectacle; it recalled to me the poet's words:

> There all the happy souls that ever were,
> Shall meet with gladness in one theatre;
> And each shall know, there, one another's face,
> By beatific virtue of the place . . .

The central embellishment of the long refreshment table was an Ice Bowl, filled with chopped fruits; a device of marvellous conception and cunning execution; for though composed of frozen water it did not melt, only its frosty surface after several hours turned clear and glistened; and sweet pea flowers hung suspended therein, as if growing in air. This appeared to me an emblem of the heart: she who desires love must be content to wait in patience for her reward; break the bowl before it melts and you would tear and destroy the flowers – and so on.

I had almost forgot to say, Mr Hooker Waller came to a violent end – for having stayed late and drunk deep that night in the village tavern, and falling in with a pack of dastardly ruffians, and attempting in their company to rob a gentleman's carriage, he was first shot and then crushed by a rock. So all ends happily.

ALISON BECHDEL

SERIAL MONOGAMY

(1992)

Serial Monogamy

AFTER MY LAST BREAKUP, I DECIDED TO MAKE A SCRAPBOOK OF ALL MY EX-LOVERS.

old girlfriend memorabilia BOX #4

BEING ALMOST PATHOLOGICALLY ROMANTIC, I'D SALVAGED QUITE AN ARRAY OF FLOTSAM AND JETSAM FROM THE SHIPWRECKS OF MY VARIOUS RELATIONSHIPS OVER THE YEARS.

SCAB FROM #3'S FOREHEAD (HISTORIC BIKE WRECK)

GROCERY LIST COMPOSED BY #6

BRAID FROM WHEN #4 CUT HER HAIR OFF

#2'S MERIT LIGHT BUTT

#1'S SOCK LINT

I HOPED ORGANIZING IT ALL IN A BOOK LIKE THAT WOULD TAKE MY MIND OFF MY MISERY, AND MAYBE ALSO MAKE SOME **SENSE** OF THIS BAFFLING PROGRESSION OF FAILED VENTURES.

KLEENEX #5 CRIED IN

BUT WHEN I FINISHED, IT ALL LOOKED EVEN **MORE** MEANINGLESS. HAD I LOST MY YOUTHFUL ILLUSIONS?

FALL IN LOVE, PROCESS, BREAK UP; FALL IN LOVE, FIGHT, GET DUMPED; FALL IN LOVE, GET BORED, FALL OUT OF LOVE. WELL I'M THROUGH WITH IT.

COULDN'T CARE LESS

Even I Jane Knew

I DIDN'T HAVE MANY LEFT. I KNEW THAT MONOGAMY AND ROMANTIC LOVE WERE JUST MALE-SUPREMACIST CONSTRUCTS DESIGNED TO KEEP WOMEN IN THEIR PLACE...

THE WOMAN IN YOUR LIFE

WOH!

SELF-INFLICTED HAIRCUT

TOTALLY STONED

LAVENDER JANE LOVES WOMEN

GYN ECOLOGY

Age 21

I KNEW MY PARENTS' MARRIAGE WAS UNHAPPY, MY OWN LOVE LIFE WAS A SEEMINGLY UNENDING SERIES OF DISAPPOINTMENTS, AND NO ONE I EVER KNEW HAD BEEN IN A RELATIONSHIP FOR MORE THAN A YEAR, THAT I HAD ANY DESIRE TO EMULATE.

DON'T INTERRUPT ME!

IF YOU COULD TELL A STORY RIGHT, I WOULDN'T NEED TO!

10 YEARS & GOING STRONG!

BUT THERE WAS STILL A PART OF ME THAT BELIEVED, DESPITE ALL EVIDENCE TO THE CONTRARY, THAT ONE DAY I'D FIND THE LOVE OF MY LIFE, GET MARRIED, AND LIVE HAPPILY EVER AFTER WITH HER.

THIS JUST ISN'T WORKING OUT.

OKAY, FINE. LET'S BREAK UP.

PHEW! I WANNA BE AVAILABLE WHEN THE LOVE OF MY LIFE SHOWS UP!

I DUNNO WHY. MAYBE I WATCHED TOO MUCH TV AS A KID. I LOVED ALL THOSE DUMB, PATRIARCHAL SIT-COMS ABOUT BLISSFULLY WEDDED COUPLES AND HAPPY FAMILIES. LIKE, YOU KNEW NOTHING REALLY **BAD** WAS EVER GONNA HAPPEN IN THE BRADY'S SPLIT-LEVEL RANCH HOUSE.

SHAG HAIRCUT

... AND THEY KNEW IT WAS MUCH MORE THAN A HUNCH ...

SHAG CARPET

Age 11

BUT RECENTLY, EVEN THAT LITTLE BUBBLE WAS CRUELLY BURST FOR ME. THE BRADY BUNCH WAS EVEN MORE DYSFUNCTIONAL THAN **MY** FAMILY.

FLORENCE HENDERSON ADMITS TO TORRID ROMANCE WITH TV SON DURING PRODUCTION OF POPULAR SERIES

DANNY PARTRIDGE BOOKED ON ASSAULT CHARGE

EDDIE MUNSTER IN DRUG REHAB CLINIC

TIP O' TH' HED TO JORDES KATZ!

THAT REALLY PUSHED ME OVER THE EDGE. I KNOW IT WAS JUST A 70'S TV SHOW, BUT IT WAS ALL I HAD! NOW WHAT? IF TRUE LOVE IS JUST A MYTH, WHY DO I KEEP FALLING FOR IT? WHY AM I SO HELL-BENT ON PAIRING OFF?!

Age 31

NO TV

NO DRUGS

NO CARPET

Exxa

I KNOW THERE ARE ALTERNATIVES. CASUALLY GOING OUT WITH SEVERAL DIFFERENT WOMEN, FOR EXAMPLE. I THINK IT'S CALLED "DATING". BUT I'VE NEVER BEEN ABLE TO PULL IT OFF.

SO, UM, WOULDJA LIKE TO ... YOU KNOW, HAVE DINNER SOMETIME?

AND I CAN'T IMAGINE EVER HAVING THE ENERGY THAT COMMITTED NONMONOGAMY MUST REQUIRE.

OH, YES! THAT FEELS SO GOOD, UM....

DANG! IS THAT CARMEN? OR PHYLLIS?!

MAYBE **CELIBACY** IS THE ANSWER.

'TIS THE GIFT TO BE SIMPLE, 'TIS THE GIFT TO BE FREE . . .

• NO **INTIMACY** ISSUES!

• NO **CODEPENDENCE!**

• NO GETTING **DUMPED!**

. . . NO SEX. WELL . . . MAYBE WE COULD HAVE SEX, BUT JUST NOT GET ALL **EMOTIONAL** ABOUT IT. YEAH . . . THAT'S IT!

HEY, THANKS FOR THE ORGASMS!

SURE THING! YOU REALLY STIMU-LATED MY NERVOUS SYSTEM!

• NO JEALOUSY!
• NO PROCESSING!
• NO MESS!

. . . NO DRAMA. NAAH . . . THAT'S NOT IT EITHER. BUT SEX IS DEFIN-ITELY THE ROOT OF THE PROBLEM. THAT'S WHERE IT ALL BEGINS . . .

IF WE NEVER EXPERIENCED THAT INITIAL, OVER-POWERING ATTRACTION TO SOMEONE, DO YOU THINK IT WOULD EVER EVEN **OCCUR** TO US TO WANNA SHARE A **CHECKING ACCOUNT** WITH HER FOR THE REST OF OUR LIVES?!

I DON'T **THINK SO.**

IT'S A **TRICK.** YOU GO THROUGH THAT INITIAL PERIOD OF **TEMPORARY INSANITY,** YOU KNOW?

CRAZY WITH LOVE

WHERE ARE YOU GOING?

TO THE BATHROOM! I'LL BE RIGHT BACK!

WAIT! I'LL COME WITH YOU!

UNPAID BILLS

ESTRANGED FRIENDS

NEGLECTED WORK

THEN YOU WAKE UP 6 MONTHS LATER... AND FIND THAT THE TWO OF YOU ARE *JOINED* AT THE FRONTAL LOBE.

WAIT! IT GETS *BETTER!* AS WE CONTINUE THIS DOGGED QUEST FOR INTIMACY, WE LEARN TO QUESTION SOME OF OUR MOST *FUNDAMENTAL PRECONCEPTIONS* ABOUT LIFE!

STOP *NAGGING* ME! I DON'T CARE WHAT YOUR MOTHER SAID, THE WORLD WILL NOT END IF I LEAVE THE REFRIGERATOR OPEN LONGER THAN ONE SECOND!

NON-TOXIC WATER

SOON WE REALIZE THAT OUT OF ALL THE ELIGIBLE WOMEN IN THE WORLD, WE HAVE ONCE AGAIN MANAGED TO CHOOSE THE ONE GUARANTEED TO ~~DRIVE US THE CRAZIEST~~ TEACH US THE MOST.

I CAN'T *HELP* WHINING! IT WAS THE ONLY WAY I GOT MY MOTHER TO PAY ATTENTION TO ME! IRRITATING HER WAS BETTER THAN BEING IGNORED.

WELL MY MOTHER WHINED CONSTANTLY ABOUT EVERYTHING SO WE'D FEEL SORRY FOR HER. COULD YOU GIVE IT A REST? IT'S SO *IRRITATING!*

ANOTHER PERFECT MATCH!

NEXT, IF YOU'RE *LUCKY*, YOU'LL SETTLE INTO A *CALM* SORT OF *RUT* FOR A WHILE. YOU LEARN TO LIVE WITH THE GNAWING SENSE OF *DISILLUSIONMENT.*

NOT ONCE HAS SHE EVER WRITTEN ME A *SONNET!*

I WONDER WHAT IT WOULD BE LIKE TO HAVE A LOVER WHO WAS A *GOOD DANCER?*

FBI WARNING

THINGS CAN DRAG ON LIKE THAT FOR YEARS, BUT SOONER OR LATER, SOMETHING *SNAPS.* SO MAYBE YOU TRY THERAPY TOGETHER...

Kiss of Death
LESBIAN RELATIONSHIP COUNSELING INC.

MAYBE YOU DON'T. WHATEVER. THE POINT IS, IT'S *OVER.* NOW, (IF YOU HAVEN'T ALREADY DONE SO) YOU HOP INTO BED WITH THE NEXT PERSON WHO SEEMS REMOTELY INTERESTED IN YOU, AND THE WHOLE PROCESS STARTS ALL OVER AGAIN.

I JUST BROKE UP WITH SOMEONE YESTERDAY.

BUT I'M REALLY *RESOLVED* ABOUT IT.

WANT A *BACKRUB?*

THIS IS REALLY *BUMMING* YOU OUT, RIGHT?

WELL LISTEN TO THIS! NOT ONLY DO LESBIANS HAVE LESS SEX THAN HETS AND GAY MEN, WE BREAK UP MORE OFTEN! IT SAYS SO RIGHT HERE!

FUN STATISTICS ABOUT MIDDLE-CLASS WHITE PEOPLE

EVERYTHING YOU NEVER WANTED TO KNOW ABOUT AMERICAN COUPLES*

SCHWARTZ & BLUMSTEIN

* BUT WE'RE TOO BORED TO ASK.

I KNOW, IT'S REALLY NEGATIVE OF ME TO POINT THIS OUT. WE SHOULDN'T FORGET THAT DESPITE POWERFUL FORCES CONSPIR-ING TO KEEP US APART, THERE ARE PLENTY OF HAPPY, HEALTHY, LONG-TERM LESBIAN COUPLES OUT THERE!

I'VE JUST NEVER BEEN IN ONE, OKAY?

I DID THINK I'D BE WITH EACH OF THESE WOMEN FOREVER, THOUGH.

ALL THE GIRLS I'VE EVER LOVED

WELL, I GUESS I SORT OF STILL AM WITH EACH OF THEM. I MEAN, ONCE YOU'VE BEEN THAT CLOSE TO SOMEONE, THERE'S A CERTAIN CONNECTION YOU'LL ALWAYS HAVE BETWEEN YOU.

IT IS AN AREA WHICH WE CALL

The EX-LOVER ZONE

JUST WHEN YOU THINK YOU'RE FINALLY FEELING RESOLVED ABOUT THINGS . . .

A COMMITMENT CEREMONY? OF COURSE I'LL COME! I'M SO HAPPY FOR YOU!

YA DIDN'T KNOW WHAT THE @#*!/*#* THE WORD 'COMMITMENT' MEANT 5 YEARS AGO!!

YOU WILL OBSERVE BIZARRE BEHAVIORAL CHANGES IN ONCE-RATIONAL WOMEN! FOR EXAMPLE, I ONCE HAD A LOVER WHO I WAS ALWAYS NAGGING TO STAY HOME AND COOK MORE WITH ME . . .

YOU KNOW I HATE TO COOK! YOU'RE SUFFOCATING ME!

AFTER SHE GOT INVOLVED WITH SOMEONE ELSE, SHE WENT OUT AND BOUGHT A WHOLE SET OF BRAND NEW POTS AND PANS!

?

I DUNNO. I THOUGHT IT MIGHT BE NICE TO STAY HOME AND COOK MORE!

(JUST STOPPED BY FOR DOG VISITATION)

AND AS IF YOUR OWN ERSTWHILE PARTNERS DON'T MAKE LIFE STRANGE ENOUGH...

IS THIS HIP OR NUTS?

WOMAN MY EX LEFT ME FOR

EX

EX'S EX BEFORE ME

ME

BONA-FIDE ACTUAL OCCURRENCE!

COPING WITH THOSE OF YOUR CURRENT LOVER CAN BE POSITIVELY EERIE!

IT'S FUTILE TO TRY AND HIDE.

CAPACITY CROWD OF 5,000 KD LANG FANS

ME

MY LOVER

HER EX

HER EX'S NEW LOVER

ANOTHER BONA-FIDE TRUE ADVENTURE!

SO WHY BOTHER? IF YOU CAN'T BEAT 'EM, JOIN 'EM. I'M PROUD TO SAY THAT SOME OF MY **BEST FRIENDS** ARE EX-LOVERS! WEIRD AS IT CAN BE, THERE'S NOTHING QUITE LIKE THAT BOND. NO MATTER WHO YOU GET INVOLVED WITH SUBSEQUENTLY, YOUR EX WILL ALWAYS HAVE KNOWN YOU **LONGER**.

I'LL NEVER FORGET THE LOOK ON YOUR ROOMMATE'S FACE WHEN SHE WALKED IN ON US THAT MORNING!

HYUK!

IT'S KINDA NICE, ACTUALLY. TOUCHING, EVEN.

BUT I WANT MORE OUT OF LIFE THAN AN EXTENDED FAMILY OF EX-LOVERS!

I WANT THE PICKET COTTAGE! THE JOINT FENCE! THE ROSE-COVERED CHECKING ACCOUNT! I WANNA GO INTO SERIOUS, LONG-TERM DEBT WITH SOMEONE!

BUT I CAN NEVER SEEM TO GET OVER THE **HUMP** IN RELATIONSHIPS! WHEN I FIND OUT MY LOVER ISN'T *PERFECT*, LIKE *ME*, I *LOSE IT!*

GO AHEAD! ORDER THE MONGOLIAN BEEF! IF YOU WANNA EAT FLESH IT'S *YOUR* BUSINESS! JUST DON'T EXPECT TO KISS *ME* EVER AGAIN!

100% COWHIDE

I GET SO **THREATENED** WHEN WE HAVE DIFFERENT OPINIONS!

NO, THE *RIGHT* WAY IS WHEN IT ROLLS OVER THE TOP, LIKE *THIS!*

TAMPAX WHATTA DEAL!

32 FOR THE PRICE OF 40!

AND LIKE MOST LESBIANS, MY EXPECTATIONS ARE **ABSURDLY** HIGH.

I THINK WE WOULDN'T FIGHT SO MUCH IF YOU'D LEARN TO ADMIT YOU'RE *WRONG!* WHY DON'T YOU GO TO THERAPY? AND AL ANON? AND GET A HAIRCUT?!

I KNOW I'D BE BETTER AT RELATIONSHIPS IF I WERE ONLY MORE *ACCEPTING*, MORE *LAID-BACK*, MORE *IN-THE-MOMENT*, MORE AT *PEACE* WITH THE *UNIVERSE !!*

Say 100 X per day: "I AM LETTING GO OF TRYING TO CONTROL EVERYTHING IN THE WHOLE FUCKIN' WORLD."

I'M TRYING! I'M TRYING!

YOGA FOR INFLEXIBLE PEOPLE

MAYBE THE PROBLEM IS, I'M ASKING TOO MUCH. MAYBE YOU CAN'T *HAVE* BOTH LONG-TERM STABILITY AND SEARING PASSION.

NIRVANA THE EASY WAY.

OR FINELY-TUNED EMOTIONAL INTIMACY AND COMPATIBLE LIVING HABITS.

DON'T BE ALARMED! I CAN'T REALLY DO THIS!

OR HIGHLY-CHARGED INTELLECTUAL RAPPORT AND A SIMILAR TASTE IN MUSIC.

OR THIS EITHER.

BETH NUGENT
CITY OF BOYS

(1992)

'My little sweetheart,' she says, bringing her face close enough for me to see the fine net of lines that carves her face into a weathered stone. 'You love me, don't you little sweetheart, little lamb?'

Whether or not she listens anymore, I am not sure, but I always answer yes: yes, I always say, yes, I love you.

She is my mother, my father, my sister, brother, cousin, lover; she is everything I ever thought any one person needed in the world. She is everything but a boy.

'Boys,' she tells me. 'Boys will only break you.'

I know this. I watch them on the street corners, huddled under their puddles of blue smoke. They are as nervous as insects, always some part of their bodies in useless, agitated motion, a foot tapping, a jaw clenching, a finger drawing circles against a thigh, eyes in restless programmed movement as they watch women pass – they look from breasts to face to legs to breasts. They are never still and they twitch and jump when I walk by, but still I want them. I want them in the back seats of their cars; I want them under the bridge where the river meets the rocks in a slick slide of stone; I want them in the back rows of theaters and under the bushes and benches in the park.

'Boys,' she says. 'Don't even think about boys. Boys would only make you do things you don't know how to do and things you'd never want to do if you knew what they were. I know,' she says. 'I know plenty about boys.'

She is everything to me. She is not my mother, though I have allowed myself the luxury of sometimes believing myself her child. My mother is in Fairborn, Ohio, where she waits with my father for me to come home and marry a boy and become the woman into whom she still believes it is not too late for me to grow. Fairborn is a city full of boys and parking meters and the Air Force, but most of all it is a city full of my mother, and in my mind she looms over it like a cloud of radioactive dust. If I return, it will be to her. She is not why I left, she is not why I am here; she is just one thing I left, like all the things that trail behind us when we go from place to place, from birth to birth, from becoming to becoming. She is just another bread crumb, just another mother in the long series of mothers that let you go to become the woman you have to become. But you are always coming back to them.

Where I live now is also a city full of boys, and, coming here, I passed through hundreds of cities and they were all full of boys.

'Boys,' she tells me, 'are uninteresting, and when they grow up, they become men and become even more uninteresting.'

I know this too. I see how boys spend their days, either standing around or playing basketball or engaged in some irritating, persistent harangue, and I can draw my own conclusions as to what they talk about and as to the heights of which they are capable, and I see what they do all day, but still I want them.

The one time I pretended she was a boy, she knew it, because I closed my eyes; I never close my eyes, and when I came, she slapped me hard. 'I'm not a boy,' she said, 'just you remember that. You know who I am and just remember that I love you and no boy could ever love you like I do.'

Probably she is right. What boy could love with her slipping concentration? Probably no boy could ever achieve what she lets go with every day that comes between us, what she has lost in her long history of love.

What I do sometimes is slip out under her absent gaze.

'Where are you going, what are you going to do?' she says, and, wallowing in the luxury of thinking myself a child, I answer: 'Nowhere. Nothing.'

In their pure undirected, intoxicating meaninglessness, our conversations carry more significance than either of us is strong enough to bear, together or alone, and I drag it out into the streets today, a long weight trailing behind me, as I look for boys.

Today, I tell myself, is a perfect day for losing things, love and innocence, illusions and expectations; it is a day through which I will wander until I find the perfect boy.

Where we live, on the upper West Side, the streets are full of Puerto Rican men watching women. Carefully they examine each woman who passes; carefully they hold her with their eyes, as if they are somehow responsible for her continued existence on the street. Not a woman goes by untouched by the long leash of their looks.

'Oh, sssss,' they say. '*Mira, mira,*' and when a woman looks, they smile and hiss again through their shiny teeth. In their eyes are all the women they have watched walk by and cook and comb their black hair; all the women they have touched with their hands and all the women they have known live in their eyes and gleam out from within the dark. Their eyes are made only to see women on the streets.

Where we live, on West Eighty-third and Amsterdam, there are roaches and rats, but nothing matters as long as we're together, we say valiantly, longingly. Nothing matters, I say, stomping a roach, and nothing matters, she agrees, her eyes on a low-slung rat sidling by in the long hallway toward the little garbage room across from the door to our apartment. I told the super once that if he kept the garbage out on the street, perhaps the building would be less a home for vermin.

'What's vermin?' he wanted to know.

'Vermin,' I told him, 'is rats and roaches and huge black beetles scrabbling at the base of the toilet when you turn on the light at night. Vermin is all the noises at night, all the clicking and scratching and scurrying through the darkness.'

'No rats,' he said. 'Maybe a mouse or two, and maybe every now and then you'll see your roach eggs, but I keep this place clean.'

Together we watched as a big brown-shelled roach tried to creep past us on the wall. Neither of us moved to kill it, but when it stopped and waved its antennae, he brought his big fist down in a hard slam against the wall. He didn't look at the dead roach, but I could hardly take my eyes off it, perfectly flattened, as though it had been steamrolled against the side of his hand.

'Maybe a roach here and there,' he said, flicking the roach onto the floor without looking at it, 'but I keep this place clean. Maybe if you had a man around the house,' he said, trying to look past me into our apartment, 'you wouldn't have so much trouble with vermins.'

I pretended not to understand what he meant, and backed into the room. Rent control is not going to last forever in New York, and when it goes and all the Puerto Ricans have had to move to the Bronx, we will have to find jobs or hit the streets, but as long as we're together, as long as we have each other.

'We'll always have each other, won't we?' she says, lighting a cigarette and checking to see how many are left in her pack.

'Yes,' I always say, wondering if she's listening or just lost in a cigarette count. 'You'll always have me,' I say. Unless, I think, unless you leave me, or unless I grow up to become the woman my mother still thinks is possible.

*

Today is a day full of boys. They are everywhere, and I watch each of them, boys on motorcycles, boys in cars, on bicycles, leaning against walls, walking: I watch them all to see which of them in this city of boys is mine.

I am not so young and she is not so old, but rent control is not going to last forever, and someday I will be a woman. She wants, I tell myself, nothing more than me. Sometimes I think she must have been my mother, the way she loves me, but when I asked her if she were ever my mother, she touched my narrow breasts and said: 'Would your mother do that?' and ran her tongue over my skin and said: 'Or that? Would your mother know what you want, sweetheart? I'm not your mother,' she said. 'I stole you from a mattress downtown, just around the corner from where all the winos lie around in piss and wine and call for help and nobody listens. I saved you from that,' she said. But I remember too clearly the trip out here, in the middle of a car full of people full of drugs, most of them, and I remember how she found me standing just outside the porn theater on Ninety-eighth and Broadway, and she slipped me right from under the gaze of about a hundred curious Puerto Ricans.

'Does your mother know where you are?' she asked me.

I laughed and said my mother knew all she needed to know, and she said, 'Come home with me. I have somebody I want you to meet.' When she brought me home, she took me right over to a big man who lay on the couch watching television.

'Tito, this is Princess Grace,' she said, and Tito raised his heavy head from the pillow to look me over.

'She don't look like no princess to me,' was all he said.

I never thought much of Tito, and she never let him touch me, even though our apartment is only one room, and he was sick with wanting me. At night, after they'd finished with each other, she crept over to me in my corner and whispered in my ear, 'Sweetheart, you are my only one.'

As Tito snored through the nights, we'd do it at least one more time than they had, and she would sigh and say, 'Little sweetheart, you are the one I wanted all the time, even with all those other boys and girls who loved me, it was always you that I was looking for, you that I wanted.'

This is the kind of talk that kills me; this is the kind of talk that won me, in addition to the fact that she took me in from the hard streets full of boys and cops and taxicabs, and everywhere I looked, the hard eyes of innocence turned.

That first time with her, I felt as though my mother was curled up inside my own body giving birth to me; each time she let me go, I made my way back inside her.

The long car pulls up to the sidewalk and I bend to see if it has boys in it. It is full of them, so I say: 'Hey, can I have a ride?'

'Hey,' they say. 'Hey, the lady wants a ride. Where to?' they ask.

'Oh,' I say, 'wherever.' I look to see where they are heading. 'Uptown,' I say, and the door swings open, so I slide in. The oldest boy is probably sixteen and just got his driver's license, and he is driving his mother's car, a big Buick or Chevrolet or Monte Carlo – a mother's car. Each of the boys is different, but they are all exactly alike in the way that boys are, and right away I pick the one I want. He's the one who does not look at me, and he's the oldest, only a couple of years younger than I, and it is his mother's car we are in.

'How about a party?' the boys say. 'We know a good party uptown.'

'Let's just see,' I say. 'Let's just ride uptown and see.'

Sometimes I wake up to see her leaning on her thin knees against the wall that is stripped down to expose the rough brick beneath the plaster. I dream that she prays to keep me, but I am afraid that it is something else she prays for, a beginning, or an end, or something I don't know about. She came to bed once and laid her face against my breast, and I felt the imprint of the brick in the tender skin of her forehead.

She herself is not particularly religious, although the apartment is littered with the scraps of saints – holy relics of one sort or another: a strand of hair from the Christ child, a bit of fingernail from Saint Paul, a shred of the Virgin's robe. They are left over from Tito, who collected holy relics the way some people collect lucky pennies or matchbooks, as a kind of hedge against some inarticulated sense of disaster. They are just clutter here, though, in this small apartment where we live, and I suggested to her once that we throw them out. She picked up a piece of dried weed from Gethsemane and said, 'I don't think they're ours to throw out. Tito found them and if we got rid of them, who knows what might happen to Tito? Maybe they work is what I mean. And besides,' she went on, 'I don't think it's spiritually economical to be a skeptic about absolutely everything.'

When Tito left, his relics abandoned for some new hope, she was depressed for a day or two, but said finally that it really was the best for everybody, especially for the two of us, the single reality to which our lives have been refined. Tito said he was getting sick of watching two dykes moon over each other all the time, though I think he was just angry because she wouldn't let him touch me. I was all for it, I wanted him to touch me. That's what I came to this city for: to have someone like Tito touch me, someone to whom touching is all the reality of being, someone who doesn't do it in basements and think he has to marry you, someone who does it and doesn't think about the glory of love. But she wouldn't have it; she said if he ever touched me, she would send me back to the Ninety-eighth Street porn theater and let the Puerto Ricans make refried beans out of me, and as for Tito, he could go back to Rosa, his wife in Queens, and go back to work lugging papers for the *Daily News* and ride the subway every day and go home and listen to Rosa talk on the phone all night, instead of hanging out on street corners and playing cards with the men outside the schoolyard, like he did now. Because, she said, because she was paying the rent, and as long as rent control lasted in New York, she would continue to pay the rent, and she could live quite happily and satisfactorily by herself until she found the right sort of room-mate; one, she said, fingering the shiny satin of Tito's shirt, who paid the rent.

So Tito kept his distance and kept us both sick with his desire, and when she finally stopped sleeping with him and joined me on the mattress on the floor, even Tito could see that it wasn't going to be long before we'd be taking the bed and he would have to move to the floor. To save himself from that, he said one day that he guessed he was something of a fifth wheel around the joint, huh? and he'd found a nice Puerto Rican family that needed a man around the house and he supposed he'd just move in with them. I think he was only trying to save face, though, because one day when she was out buying cigarettes, he roused himself from the couch and away from the television, to say to me, 'You know, she was married before, you know.'

'I know that,' I said. 'I know all about that.'

How she pays the rent is with alimony that still comes in from her marriage and I know all about that and Tito wasn't telling me anything that I didn't know, so I looked back at the magazine I was reading and waited for him to go back to the television. He kept looking at me, so I got up to look out the window to see if I could see her coming back and if she had anything for me.

'What I'm trying to say,' he said, 'what I'm trying to tell you is that you're not the only one. You're not. I was the only one, too, the one she was always looking for. I was the one before you, and you're just the one before someone else.' I could see her rounding the corner from Ninety-sixth and Broadway, and could see that she had something in a bag for me, doughnuts or cookies. I said nothing, only looked out the window and counted the steps she took toward our building. She was leaning forward and listing slightly toward the wall, so I guessed that she must have had a few drinks in the bar where she always buys her cigarettes. When I could hear her key turning in the lock to the street door, I went to open our door for her and Tito reached out and grabbed me by the arm.

'Listen,' he said. 'You just listen. Nobody is ever the only one for nobody. Don't kid yourself.'

I pulled away and opened the door for her. When she came in, cold skin and wet, I put my face in her hair and breathed in the smell of gin and cigarettes, and all the meaning of my life.

The next day Tito left, but he didn't go far, because I still see him hanging out on street corners. Now all the women he has known are in his eyes, but mostly there is her, and when he looks at me, I cannot bear to see her lost in the dark there. Whenever I pass him, I always smile.

'Hey, Tiiiiiiito,' I say. '*Mira, mira*, huh?' And all his friends laugh, while Tito tries to look as though this is something he's planned himself, as though he has somehow elicited this remark from me.

I suppose one day Tito will use the key he forgot to leave behind to sneak in and cover me with his flagging desire, his fading regrets, and his disappointments, and she will move on then, away from me; but rent control will not last forever in New York, and I cannot think ahead to the beginnings and the ends for which she prays.

The boys in the car lean against one another and leer and twitch like tormented insects, exchanging glances that they think are far too subtle for me to understand, but I have come too far looking for too much to miss any of it. We drive too fast up Riverside, so that it's no time at all before the nice neighborhoods become slums full of women in windows, with colorful clothing slung over fire escapes, and, like a thick haze hanging over the city, the bright noise of salsa music. Like the sound of crickets threading through the Ohio summer nights, it sets the terms for everything.

'So,' one of them says, 'so where are you going, anyways?'

'Well,' I say. 'Well. I was thinking about going to the Bronx Botanical Gardens.'

The Bronx Botanical Gardens is no place I'd ever really want to go, but I feel it's important to maintain, at least in their eyes, some illusion of destination. If I was a bit more sure of myself, I'd suggest that we take the ferry over to Staten Island and do it in the park there. Then I could think of her.

When we went to Staten Island, it was cold and gray and windy; we got there and realized that there was nothing really that we wanted to see, that being in Staten Island was really not all that different from being in Manhattan.

'Or anywhere,' she said, looking down a street into a corridor of run-down clothing stores and insurance offices. It was Sunday, so everything was closed up tight and no one was on the street. Finally we found a coffee shop near the ferry station, where we drank Cokes and coffee, and she smoked cigarettes, while we waited for the boat to leave.

'Lezzes,' the counterman said to another man sitting at the counter eating a doughnut. 'What do you want to bet they're lezzes?'

The man eating the doughnut turned and looked us over.

'They're not so hot anyways,' he said. 'No big waste.'

She smiled and held her hand to my face for a second; the smoke from her cigarette drifted past my eyes into my hair.

'What a moment,' she said, 'to remember.'

On the way back, I watched the wind whip her face all out of any shape I knew, and when I caught the eyes of some boys on the ferry, she said, not looking at me, not taking her eyes from the concrete ripples of the robe at the feet of the Statue of Liberty just on our left, 'What you do is your own business, but don't expect me to love you forever if you do things like this. I'm not,' she said, turning to look me full in the face, 'your mother, you know. All I am is your lover, and nothing lasts forever.'

When we got off the ferry, I said: 'I don't expect you to love me forever,' and she said I was being promiscuous and quarrelsome, and she lit a cigarette as she walked down into the subway station. I watched her as she walked, and it seemed to me to be the first time I had ever seen her back, walking away from me, trailing a long blue string of smoke.

Something is going on with the boys, something has changed in the set of their faces, the way they hold their cigarettes, the way they nudge each other. Something changes when the light begins to fade, and one of them says to me: 'We have a clubhouse uptown, want to come there with us?'

'What kind of club,' I ask. 'What do you do there?'

'We drink whiskey,' they say, 'and take drugs and watch television.'

My boy, the one I have picked out of this whole city of boys, stares out the window, chewing at a toothpick he's got wedged somewhere in the depths of his jaw, and runs his finger over the slick plastic of the steering wheel. I can tell by his refusal to ask that he wants me to come. This, I suppose, is how to get to the center of boys, to go to their club. Boys are like pack creatures, and they always form clubs; it's as though they cannot help themselves. It's the single law of human nature that I have observed in my limited exposure to the world, that plays and plays and replays itself out with simple mindless consistency: where there are boys, there are clubs, and anywhere there is a club, it is bound to be full of boys, looking for the good times to be had just by being boys.

'Can I join?' I ask. This is what I will take back to her, cigarettes and a boy's club. This will keep her for me forever: that I have gone to the center of boys and have come back to her.

'Well,' they say, and smirk and grin and scratch at themselves. 'Well, there's an initiation.'

The oldest of the boys is younger than I, and yet, like boys everywhere, they all think that I don't know nearly so much as they do, as if being a woman somehow short-circuits my capacity for input. They have a language that they think only boys can understand, but understanding their language is the key to my success, so I smile and say: 'I will not fuck you all, separately or together.'

My boy looks over at me and permits himself a cool half-smile, and I am irritated that he now holds me in higher regard because I can speak a language that any idiot could learn.

Between us there are no small moments; we do not speak at all or we speak everything. Heat bills and toothpaste and dinner and all the dailiness of living are given no language in our time together. I realize that this kind of intensity cannot be sustained over a long period of time and that every small absence in our days signals an end between us. She tells me that I must never leave her, but what I know is that someday she will leave me with a fistful of marriage money to pay the rent as long as rent control lasts in New York, and I will see her wandering down the streets, see her in the arms of another, and I say to her sometimes late at night when she blows smoke rings at my breasts: 'Don't leave me. Don't ever ever leave me.'

'Life,' she always says to me, 'is one long leave-taking. Don't kid yourself,' she says. 'Kid,' and laughs. 'Anyways, you are my little sweetheart, and how could I ever leave you, and how could I leave this' – soft touch on my skin – 'and this, and this.'

She knows this kills me every time.

Their clubhouse is dirty and disorganized and everywhere there are mattresses and empty beer bottles and bags from McDonald's, and skittering through all of this mess are more roaches than I thought could exist in a single place, more roaches than there are boys in this city, more roaches than there are moments of love in this world.

The boys walk importantly in. This is their club; they are New York City boys and they take drugs and they have a club, and I watch as they scatter around and sit on mattresses and flip on the television. I hang back in the doorway and reach out to snag the corner of the jacket my boy is wearing. He turns to me without interest.

'How about some air?' I say.

'Let me just get high first,' he says, and he walks over to a chair and sits down and pulls out his works and cooks up his dope and ties up his arm and spends a good two minutes searching out a vein to pop. All over his hands and arms and probably his legs and feet and stomach are signs of collapse and ruin, as if his body has been created for a single purpose, and he has spent a busy and productive life systematically mining it for good places to fix.

I watch him do this while the other boys do their dope or roll their joints or pop their pills, and he offers me some. I say no, I'd rather keep a clear head, and how about some air?

I don't want him to hit a nod before any of it's even happened, but this is my experience with junkies, that they exit right out of every situation before it's even become a situation.

'Let's take the car,' he says.

'You are my sweetheart,' she says, 'and if you leave me, you will spend all your life coming back to me.' With her tongue and her words and the quiet movement of her hand over my skin, she has drawn for me all the limits of my life, and of my love. It is the one love that has created me and will contain me, and if she left me I'd be lonely, and I'd rather sleep in the streets with her hand between my legs forever than be lonely.

In the car, the boy slides his hand between my legs and then puts it on the steering wheel. A chill in the air, empty streets, and it's late. Every second takes me farther into the night away from her; every second sends me home. We drive to Inwood Park, and climb the fence so that we are only a few feet away from the Hudson.

'This is nothing like Ohio,' I say to him, and he lights a cigarette.

'Where's Ohio?'

'Don't you go to school?' I ask him. 'Don't you take geography?'

'I know what I need to know,' he says, and reaches over to unbutton my blouse. The thing about junkies is that they know they don't have much time, and the thing about boys is that they know how not to waste it.

'This is very romantic.' I say, as his fingers hit my nipples like a piece of ice. 'Do you come here often?'

What I like about this boy is that he just puts it right in. He just puts it in as though he does this all the time, as though he doesn't usually have to slide it through his fingers, or between his friends' rough lips; he just puts it in and comes like wet soap shooting out of a fist, and this is what I wanted. This is what I wanted, I say to myself as I watch the Hudson rolling brownly by over his shoulder. This is what I wanted, but all I think about is the way it is with us; this is what I wanted, but all I see is her face floating down the river, her eyes like pieces of moonlight caught in the water.

What I think is true doesn't matter anymore; what I think is false doesn't matter anymore. What I think at all doesn't matter anymore, because there is only her; like an image laid over my mind, she is superimposed on every thought I have. She sits by the window and looks out onto the street as though she is waiting for something, waiting for rent control to end, or waiting for something else to begin. She sits by the window waiting for something, and pulls a long string through her fingers. In the light from the window, I can see each of the bones in her hand; they make a delicate pattern that fades into the flesh and bone of her wrist.

'Don't ever change,' I say to her. 'Don't ever ever change.' She smiles and lets the string dangle from her hand.

'Nothing ever stays the same,' she says. 'You're old enough to know that, aren't you, sweetheart? Permanence,' she says, 'is nothing more than a desire for things to stay the same.'

I know this.

'Life is hard for me,' the boy says. 'What am I going to do with my life? I just hang around all day or drive my mother's car. Life is so hard. Everything will always be the same for me here in this city. It's going to eat me up, and spit me out, and I might as well never have been born.'

He looks poetically out over the river.

'I wanted a boy,' I say, 'not a poet.'

'I'm not a poet,' he says. 'I'm just a junkie, and you're nothing but a slut. You can get yourself home tonight.'

I say nothing and watch the Hudson roll by.

'I'm sorry,' he says. 'So what? So I'm a junkie and you're a slut, so what. Nothing ever changes. Besides,' he says, 'my teacher wants me to be a track star because I can run faster than anyone else in gym class. That's what he says.'

'Well, that sounds like a promising career,' I say, although I can imagine the teacher in his baggy sweatpants, his excitement rising as he stares at my boy and suggests afterschool workouts. 'Why don't you do that?'

'I'd have to give up smoking,' he says. 'And dope.'

Together we watch the river, and finally he says, 'Well. It's about time I was getting my mother's car home.'

'This is it?' I ask him.

'What were you expecting?' he says. 'I'm only a junkie. In two years I probably won't even be able to get it up anymore.'

'Look,' I say, coming in and walking over to where she sits by the window. 'Look. I am a marked woman. There is blood between my legs and it isn't yours.'

She looks at me, then looks back at what she was doing before I came in, blowing smoke rings that flatten against the dirty window. 'Did you bring me some cigarettes?' she asks, putting hers out in the ashtray that rests on the windowsill.

'A marked woman,' I say. 'Can't you see the blood?'

'I can't see anything,' she says, 'and I won't look until I have a cigarette.'

I give her the cigarettes I bought earlier. Even in the midst of becoming a woman, I have remembered the small things that please her. She lights one and inhales the smoke, then lets it slowly out through her nose and her mouth at the same time. She knows this kills me.

'Don't you see it?' I ask.

'I don't see anything,' she says. 'I don't see why you had to do this.'

She gets up and says, 'I'm going to bed now. I've been up all day and all night, and I'm tired and I want to go to sleep before the sun comes up.'

'I am a marked woman,' I say, lying beside her. 'Don't you feel it?'

'I don't feel anything,' she says, but she holds me, and together we wait patiently for the light. She is everything to me. In the stiff morning before the full gloom of city light falls on us, I turn to her face full of shadows.

'I am a marked woman,' I say. 'I am.'

'Quiet,' she says, and puts her dark hand gently over my mouth, then moves it over my throat onto the rise of my chest. Across town, no one notices when she does this. Nothing is changed anywhere when she does this.

'Quiet,' she says again. She presses her hand against my heart, and touches her face to mine and takes me with her into the motherless turning night. All moments stop here; this is the first and the last, and the only flesh is hers, the only touch her hand. Nothing else is, and together we turn under the stroke of the moon and the hiss of the stars; she is everything I will become, and together we become every memory that has ever been known.

MARGARET ATWOOD
COLD-BLOODED

(1992)

To my sisters, the Iridescent Ones, the Egg-Bearers, the Many-Faceted, greetings from the Planet of Moths.

At last we have succeeded in establishing contact with the creatures here who, in their ability to communicate, to live in colonies and to construct technologies, most resemble us, although in these particulars they have not advanced above a rudimentary level.

During our first observation of these 'blood-creatures', as we have termed them – after the colourful red liquid which is to be found inside their bodies, and which appears to be of great significance to them in their poems, wars and religious rituals – we supposed them incapable of speech, as those specimens we were able to examine entirely lacked the organs for it. They had no wing-casings with which to stribulate – indeed they had no wings; they had no mandibles to click; and the chemical method was unknown to them, since they were devoid of antennae. 'Smell', for them, is a perfunctory affair, confined to a flattened and numbed appendage on the front of the head. But after a time, we discovered that the incoherent squeakings and gruntings that emerged from them, especially when pinched, were in fact a form of language, and after that we made rapid progress.

We soon ascertained that their planet, named by us the Planet of Moths after its most prolific and noteworthy genus, is called by these creatures *Earth*. They have some notion that their ancestors were created from this substance; or so it is claimed in many of their charming but irrational folk-tales.

In an attempt to establish common ground, we asked them at what season they mated with and then devoured their males. Imagine our embarrassment when we discovered that those individuals with whom we were conversing *were* males! (It is very hard to tell the difference, as their males are not diminutive, as ours are, but if anything bigger. Also, lacking natural beauty – brilliantly patterned carapaces, diaphanous wings, luminescent eyes, and the like – they attempt to imitate our kind by placing upon their bodies various multicoloured draperies, which conceal their generative parts.)

We apologized for our *faux pas*, and inquired as to their own sexual practices. Picture our nausea and disgust when we discovered that it is the male, not the egg-bearer, which is the most prized among them! Abnormal as this will seem to you, my sisters, their leaders are for the most part male; which may account for their state of relative barbarism. Another peculiarity which must be noted is that, although they frequently kill them in many other ways, they rarely devour their females after procreation. This is a waste of protein; but then, they are a wasteful people.

We hastily abandoned this painful subject.

Next we asked them when they pupated. Here again, as in the case of 'clothing' – the draperies we have mentioned – we uncovered a fumbling attempt at imitation of our kind. At some indeterminate point in their life cycles, they cause themselves to be placed in artificial stone or wooden cocoons, or chrysalises. They have an idea that they will someday emerge from these in an altered state, which they symbolize with carvings of themselves with wings. However, we did not observe that any had actually done so.

It is as well to mention at this juncture that, in addition to the many species of moths for which it is justly famous among us, the Planet of Moths abounds in thousands of varieties of creatures which resemble our own distant ancestors. It seems that one of our previous attempts at colonization – an attempt so distant that our record of it is lost – must have borne fruit. However, these beings, although numerous and ingenious, are small in size and primitive in their social organization, and attempts to communicate with them were not – or have not been, so far – very successful. The blood-creatures are hostile towards them, and employ against them many poisonous sprays, traps and so forth, in addition to a sinister manual device termed a 'fly swatter'. It is agonizing indeed to watch one of these instruments of torture and death being wielded by the large and frenzied against the small and helpless; but the rules of diplomacy forbid our intervention. (Luckily the blood-creatures cannot understand what we say to one another about them in our own language.)

But despite all the machinery of destruction which is aimed at them, our distant relatives are more than holding their own. They feed on the crops and herd-animals and even on the flesh of the blood-creatures; they live in their homes, devour their clothes, hide and flourish in the very cracks of their floors. When the blood-creatures have succeeded at last in overbreeding themselves, as it seems their intention to do, or in exterminating one another, rest assured that our kind, already superior in both numbers and adaptability, will be poised to achieve the ascendency which is ours by natural right.

This will not happen tomorrow, but it will happen. As you know, my sisters, we have long been a patient race.

EMMA DONOGHUE
WORDS FOR THINGS

(1993)

The day before the governess came was even longer. Over a dish of cooling tea, Margaret watched her mother. Not the eyes, but the stiff powdery sweep of hair. She answered two questions – on the progress of her cross-stitch, and a French proverb – but missed the final one, on the origin of the word 'October'. Swallowing the tea noiselessly, Margaret allowed her eyes to unlatch the window, creep across the lawn. She thought she could smell another thatch singeing.

The next morning woke her breathless; one rib burned under the weight of whalebone. The dark was lifting reluctantly, an inch of wall at a time. Practised at distracting herself, Margaret reached down with one hand. She scrabbled under the mattress edge for the buckled volume. But it was gone, as if absorbed into the feathers. Confiscated on her mother's orders, no doubt. Clamping her eyes shut, Margaret focused on the rib, bending her anger into a manageable line. She lay flat until the room was full of faint light that snagged on the shapes of two small girls in the next bed.

Her belly rumbled. Margaret was hungry for words. None on the walls, except an edifying motto in cross-stitch hung over the ewer. Curling patterns on the curtains could sometimes be suggested into letters and then acrobatic words, but by now the light was too honest. She shut her eyes again, and called up a grey, wavering page with an ornate printer's mark at the top. 'The History of the Primdingle Family,' she spelled out, 'Part the Fifth.' Once she worked her way into the flow, she no longer needed to imagine the letters into existence one by one; the lines formed themselves, neat and crisp and believable. Her eyes flickered under their lids, scattering punctuation.

The black trunk sat in the hall, its brass worn at the edges. Dot caught her winter petticoat on it as she scuttled by. The governess was in the parlour, sipping cold tea. Mistress Mary, her employer called her; it was to be understood that the Irish preferred this traditional form of address, and besides, it avoided the outlandish surname. Her Ladyship showed no interest in wages, nor in the little school Mistress Mary ran in London, nor in her recent treatise on female education. Her Ladyship's questions sounded like statements. She outlined the children's day, hour by hour. They had been let run wild too long and now it was a race to make the eldest presentable for Dublin Castle in a bare two years. The girl was somewhat perverse, her Ladyship mentioned over the silver teapot, and seemed to be growing larger by the day.

Mistress Mary watched a minute grain of powder from her Ladyship's widow's peak drift down and alight on the surface of the tea. She had been here one hour and felt light with fatigue already. The three children were the kind of hoydens she liked least, the fourteen-year-old in particular having an unrestrained guffaw certain to set on edge the nerves of any potential suitors. The governess asked herself again why she had exiled herself among the wild Irish rather than scour pots for a living. 'But your mother was a native of this country, was she not, Mistress Mary? You are half one of us, then.' 'Oh, your Ladyship, I would not presume.' But that bony voice did remind the governess of her mother's limper tones. Bending her head over the tea, Mistress Mary heard in her gut the usual battle between gall and compassion.

Behind an oak, Margaret was shivering as she nipped her muslin skirts between her knees. If she stood narrow as a sapling she would not be seen. The outraged words of two languages carried across the field, equally indistinguishable. Dot would carry the news later: who said what, which of the usual threats and three-generation curses were made, which fists shaken in which faces. It had to be time for dinner, Margaret thought. She would go when the smoke rose white as feathers from the second thatch.

Stand up straight, her mother told her, 'You have been telling your sisters wicked make-believe once more. How can I persuade you of the difference between what is real and what is not?'

'I do not know, madam.'

'You will run mad before the age of sixteen and then I will be spared the trouble of finding a husband for you.'

'Yes, madam.'

'Have you forgotten who you are, girl?'

'Margaret King of the family of Lord and Lady Kingsborough of Kingsborough Estate.'

'Of which county?'

'Of the county of Cork in the kingdom of Ireland in the year of our Lord one thousand seven hundred and eighty-six.'

'Now go and wash your face so your new governess will not think you a peasant.'

In November the evictions were more plentiful, and Margaret wearied of them. The apple trees stooped under their cloaks of rain. Mistress Mary had been here three weeks. She and the girls were kept busy all day from half-past six to half-past five with a list of nonsensical duties. So-called accomplishments being in her view those things which were never fully accomplished. Mistress Mary kept biting her soft lips and thinking of Lisbon. Between them the children churned out acres of lace, lists of the tributaries of the Nile, piles of netted purses, and an assortment of complaints from violin, flute, and harpsichord. The two small girls could sing five songs in French without understanding any of the words, and frequently did. The harpsichord was often silent, on days when Margaret, blank-faced and docile, slipped away with a message for the cook and was not seen again.

Sometimes, losing herself along windy corridors, her air of calm efficiency beginning to slip, Mistress Mary caught sight of a long-booted ankle disappearing round a corner. Dot denied all knowledge. On the first occasion, the matter was mentioned to her Ladyship. Bruises slowed Margaret's walk for a week, though no one referred to them. After that, Mistress Mary kept silent about her pupil's comings and goings. I will conquer her with kindness, she promised herself. Tenderness will lead where birch cannot drive.

'Need the girl sleep in her stays, your Ladyship? She heaves so alarmingly at night when I look in on her. As your Ladyship wishes.'

Considering her governess's animated face bent over a letter, Margaret decided that here was one doll worth playing with. She knew how to do it. They always began stiff and proper but soon they went soft over you, and then every smile pulled their strings. Mostly they were lonely and despised themselves for not being mothers. The Mademoiselle in her last boarding-school was the easiest. Watch for the first signs – vague laughter, fingers against your cheek, a fuzziness about the hairline – and seize on her weakness. Ask her to help you tie the last bow of ribbon on your stomacher. Take her arm in yours while walking, beg to sit next to her at supper, even bring her apples if the case requires it. Mademoiselle, the poor toad, had reached the stage of hiding pears in Margaret's desk.

By December, Mistress Mary was astonished at her power over this sweet little girl. The dreadful laugh had muted to a wheeze of merriment between wide lips. Margaret sat on a footstool below her governess's needle, and chanted French songs of which she understood half the words. At night, she had

taken to pleading for Mistress Mary to come into her bedchamber; not Dot, nor any of the serving-maids, nor either of her
sisters, only Mistress Mary might lift off the muslin cap and
brush Margaret's long coarse hair. My little friend, the woman
called her, as a final favour, though when Margaret stood up she
had a good inch over her governess. They shared a smile, then.
Mistress Mary would have liked to be sure that they were
smiling at the same thing.

Another thing the governess could not understand is why
Margaret loved to read and hated to write.

Words were a treasure to be hoarded and never shared.

On Margaret's twelfth birthday, an event marked only by one
of her Ladyship's sudden visits to the schoolroom, she had been
discovered sitting under a desk with a very blunt quill, writing
'The History of the Quintumbly Family, The Third Chapter'.
Under interrogation in the parlour, Margaret could offer no
reason for such an outlay of precious time. She licked the corner
of her lips. Nor could she explain her knowledge of such an
unsuitable family, who, it seemed, kept tame weasels and sailed
down the Nile. Her Ladyship was disgusted at last to find that
the Quintumblys were merely fanciful, a pretend family. The rest
of the journal pleased her even less, being a daily account of
Margaret's less filial thoughts and sentiments. Having read a
sample of them aloud in a tone of wonder, her Ladyship picked
the limp book up by one corner and held it out to her daughter.
Margaret was halfway to the parlour fire before her mother's
voice tightened around her: did she mean to smoke them out
entirely? Dot was called for to carry the manuscript to the
gardener's bonfire, where it would do no harm.

From that day on the girl would write no words of her own,
only lists of French verbs and English wars. In the strongbox
behind her eyes, she stacked volumes of stories about her
pretend families. She sealed her lashes and reread the adventures
only in bed before it was light, in case anyone might catch her
lips moving. By day she stole other people's words: romances,
newspapers, treatises, anything left beside an armchair or in an

unlocked cabinet in the library. Margaret swallowed up the words and would give none back.

Laid low by one of her periodic fevers in January, the girl was starving for a story but could not concentrate enough to form the letters. What she did remember to do was to clamour for Mistress Mary to hold her hand. The governess flushed, and consented, after a little show of reluctance. Humouring the patient, she agreed to petty things, like brushing her own dark hair with Margaret's ivory brush. By suppertime, the girl was too worn out to think of anything endearing to say, but Mistress Mary leaned over and hushed her most tenderly.

In her sleep, the girl made hoarse cries, and threw the gentlest hand off her forehead. There was a girl in Dublin used to sleep in her stays, Dot remarked, that died from compunction of the organs. The governess heaved a breath and knocked on the parlour door. 'Most dangerous in her state of health, your Ladyship, eminent medical gentlemen agree.' The stays came off. Margaret tossed still, picking at invisible ribbons across her chest.

The girl woke one February twilight to find that her lie had come true. She could not bear to let the governess out of her sight. Her puzzled eyes followed every movement, and her voice was cracked and fractious. She insisted that she could not remember how to sew. There was nothing comfortable about this love.

Scrawny children plucked at Margaret's skirts as she walked between the burnt cottages, wheezing. She shared her pocketful of French grapes among them. Their ginger freckles stood out bold on transparent skin.

Hungry for the familiarity of words, the girl stole into the library. She knelt on the moving steps and pressed her face against the glass cases, following their bevelled edges with her lips. One of the cases would be left unlocked, if she had prayed hard enough the night before. Titles in winking gold leaf reached for her fingers. At first she looked for storybooks and engravings, but by March she had got a taste for books of words about words: dictionaries and lexicons and medical encyclope-dias. One strange fish of a word leapt into the mouth of another and that one into another, meanings hooked on each other, confusing and enticing her, until, after the hour or so she could steal from each day, Margaret was netted round with secret knowledge.

'There was a farmer went for the bailiff with a pitchfork last month,' Dot said. 'When they hanged him in Cork town his bit stuck up.' Margaret knew about bits and the getting of babies and the nine months; Mistress Mary, flushing slightly, said every girl should know the words for things.

'Why was I not born a boy,' Margaret asked her governess while walking in the orchard, 'or why was I born at all?' Mistress Mary was bewildered by the question. Margaret ex-plained: 'Girls are good for nothing in particular. In all the stories, boys can run and leap and save wounded animals. My mother says I am a mannish little trull. Already I am taller than ladies like you. So why may I not be a boy?'

'There is nothing wrong,' began Mistress Mary cautiously, 'with being manly, in the best sense. Manly virtues, you know, and masculine fortitude. You must not be afraid. No matter what anyone says. Even if they say things which, no doubt unintentionally, may seem unkind.'

Margaret kicked at a rotten apple.

'You must stand tall, like a tree,' explained the governess, gathering confidence. 'No matter how tall you grow you will be my little girl, and your head will always fit on my shoulder. Tall as a young tree,' she went on hurriedly, 'and you should move like one too. Why do you not romp and bound when I say you may; why do you cling to my side like a little doll?'

'My mother forbids it.'

'She cannot see through the garden wall. I give you permission.'

'She may ask why we spend so long in the orchard.'

'We are studying the names of the insects.'

And the governess tagged her on the shoulder and, picking up her skirts, hared off down a damp grassy path. Margaret was still considering the matter when she found her legs leaping away with her.

In the April evenings, Mistress Mary entertained the household with recitations and English country dances. Her Ladyship looked on, her hair whiter by the day. They argued over the number of buttons on the girls' boots.

When she grew up, Margaret had decided, she would make the bailiffs give all the rent back. The red-headed children would grow fat, and clap their hands when they saw her coming.

By May the air was white with blossom. Margaret could not swallow when she looked at her governess. Their hairs were mingled on the brush; Margaret teased them with her cold fingers. She could not seem to learn the rules of bodies. What Mistress Mary called innocent caresses were allowable, and these were: cheeks and foreheads, lips on the backs of hands, arms entwined in the orchard, heads briefly nested in grey satin skirts. But when Margaret slipped into the governess's chamber one morning and found her in shift and stockings, she earned a scathing glance. Gross familiarity, Mistress Mary called it, and immodest forwardness. When she had fastened her last button and called the girl back into the room, she explained more calmly that one must never forget the respect which one human creature owed another. Margaret could not see what respect had to do with dressing in separate rooms. She hung her head and thought of breakfast. 'Had any of the servants ever tried to teach her dirty indecent tricks?' 'No, mistress, Dot was always busy, and besides, she knew no tricks.'

It was June by the time she found that there were words for girls like her. Words tucked away in the library, locked only until you looked for them. Romp and hoyden she knew already. Tomboy was when she ran down the front staircase with her bootlaces undone. But there were sharper words as well, words that cut when she lifted them into her mouth to taste and whisper them. Tommie was when women kissed and pressed each other to their hearts, it said so in a dirty poem on the top shelf of the cabinet. Tribad was the same only worse. The word had to mean, she reasoned, along the lines of triangle and trimester, that she was three times as bad as other girls.

Margaret knelt up on the moving steps as the page fell open to that word again; her legs shook and her belly-rumbles echoed under the whalebone. Tribad meant if she let the badness take her, she would grow and grow. Already she was taller than anyone in the house except her mother. The book said she would grow down there until she became a hermaphrodite shown for pennies at the fair, or ran away in her brother's breeches (but she had no brother) and married a Dutch widow. The change was coming already. When the girl lay in bed on hot mornings the bit between her legs stirred and leapt like a minnow.

One noon she limped into the bedchamber, phantom blows from her mother's rod still landing on her calves. Dot was sweeping the cold floor, her broom trailing now as she gazed into the frontispiece of a book of travels.

'Give it,' said Margaret.

Dot regarded her, then stared at the book again, at its pages flattened by the grey morning light. She looked back at the girl as if trying to remember her name. Seizing the besom, Margaret threaded her fingers between the twigs, and set to bludgeoning the maid's thick body with the handle. The coarse petticoats dulled the impact; it sounded like a rug being beaten. She pursued Dot to the window with a constant hiss of phrases, from 'idle ignoramus' to 'tell my mother' to 'dirty goodfornothing inch of life'. Dot broke into a wail at last, expressive less of pain than of a willingness to get it over and done with. She stood in the corner, hunched over to protect her curves. Tears plummeted to the floorboards.

'Beg pardon,' Margaret instructed. Her ribs heaved and sank under the creaking corset.

'Beg pardon, miss,' Dot repeated, her tone neutral.

The broom was lowered but the eyes held.

Margaret had made it to the door before, with a lurch, she found herself sorry. She turned to see Dot industriously brushing her tears into the floor. She was so sorry it swamped her, left her feeble. Was there any comfort to give? A lump in one of the unmade beds reminded her, and she scrabbled under the coverlet. The doll she pulled out was missing one eye, but her pink damask skippers were good as new. The girl walked up behind Dot and tapped her on the shoulder with the doll's powdered head. 'Take her,' she said graciously, 'and leave off crying.'

Dot turns a face that was almost dry. 'What am I to do with that, miss?'

Margaret was disconcerted. Play with her, she could have said, but when? Dress her up, but in what? A shaky, benevolent smile. 'Perhaps you could beat her when you are angry.'

Weary, Dot considered the two faces. 'Get away out of that, miss,' she remarked at last, and walked from the room, trailing her broom behind her.

It was in the corner of the bedchamber that the governess found the girl a little later, her fingers dividing and dividing the doll's hair. She lifted Margaret's hands away gently. 'Girl, you harass my spirits. You are too old for your sisters' dolls, and what need has a healthy girl of wax toys when there is the wide world to play in?' If she noticed the stiffness in Margaret's legs, as they strolled in the orchard, she said nothing. They spoke of birds' nests, and poetry, and unrest among the French.

Mistress Mary had taken to writing a story in the bright July evenings. What was it about? 'Disappointment,' she murmured, and would tell no more. Feeling neglected, Margaret became clumsier, tripping over shoes and toppling an inkstand. The governess forgave her everything. One morning Margaret found a double cherry hung over the handle of her wardrobe. She knew she had the power now. It brought her no joy.

'I govern her completely,' Mistress Mary wrote to her sister. 'She is a fine girl, and it only takes a cherry to win a smile from her. Her violence of temper remains deplorable, but I myself never feel the effects of it. She is wax in my hands. The truth is, this girl is the only consolation of my life in this backwater. How I look forward to my brief escape!'

Nobody remembered to tell the children that their governess was spending two days with acquaintances in Tralee. Distracted by the details of mail coaches and hats, Mistress Mary was gone before breakfast. Dot, passing the girl on the back staircase, had only time to whisper that the governess was gone.

Margaret stood in the middle of the empty bedchamber. Sure enough, Mistress Mary's travelling cloak was missing for the first time since October. Margaret was oddly calm. Her mind was busy wondering what she had done wrong, what brief immodesty or careless phrase would make her governess punish her so, by leaving without a word. She noticed that the writing case had been left behind. No reason not to, now: she wrenched it open and took a handful of pages. 'Pity is one of my prevailing passions', she read, and 'this world is a desert to me' at the top of another leaf. For a few moments the girl stood, savouring the grandeur of the phrases. But then they were dust in her mouth. All these words, and not an inch of warm skin left. As if Mistress Mary, who had never seemed too fond of having a body, had escaped in the form of a bird or a cloud.

The words were building up behind her tongue, making her gag. Nine months she has been living behind my hair, thought Margaret; that is as long as a baby. She parted her lips to breathe and a howl split her open.

After that she remembered nothing until her mother was standing over her.

'Stop this fuss,' her Ladyship advised. 'You are making a grand calamity out of nothing at all. Recollect yourself. Who are you?'

'I don't know.'

'You are Margaret King, of . . .?'

'I don't remember.'

The girl stood, at the rod's pleasure. It beat and beat and could not touch her.

Due to the excessive regret the girl had shown at the briefest of partings with her governess, her Ladyship explained to the household, she had decided that Mistress Mary would not be coming back. The black trunk was sent off before breakfast.

By August, Margaret was bleeding inside. Feeling herself seep away, she was not surprised. But Dot saw the red path down the girl's stocking; she took her into a closet and explained the business of the rags. Margaret nodded but did not believe her. She knew it was the first sign of the change. Blood had to trickle as the growth sped and the new freakish flesh pushed through. When she was three inches long, she would run away to Galway fair and show herself for sixpences. The pretend families would come with her, riding in the ropes of her hair.

A republican in 1798, Margaret would spit at bailiffs. An adulteress in Italy, she would meet her governess's daughter, who never knew her mother, and would tell her, I knew your mother.

KATHY ACKER
THE LANGUAGE OF THE BODY

(1993)

I got married when I was very young. I did not know my husband . . .

The day after our wedding, *I had a dream about the world*:
  At the entrance to the world, I was about to have an abortion.
  I had had abortions before this.
  I had to decide whether or not I wanted an anesthetic. I guess that the doctor had asked me, but I don't remember that anyone was there. Thinking, I asked how much the abortion was going to hurt me. The doctor replied, 'Oh, there'll be pain . . .' in a voice that was trying to dismiss such pain. Since I knew that that type of voice meant that there would be a lot of pain, I chickened out. The blanket that was lying on top of me was yellow. I hate pain. I decided on anesthetic.
  All through the abortion, I was kind of conscious. While I was in this consciousness, a pillow, which was around my ass, inflated and I floated three feet up above the cot.
  After the abortion, my body was OK, so I left the hospital.

This was the scene of my marriage.

Then, I entered the real world (as opposed to that of the hospital). In a car. The car reached the end of the dirt road that lay beneath it: the main road began. At this spot, the man who was in the car with me informed me that I could drive.

But I had never driven a car. I began driving the black Bentley. To begin, I had to turn the car, but I had no idea how. Turning must have something to do with steering.

I was halfway into the turn and I couldn't see what was behind me.

'Don't worry about seeing,' my new husband said, 'I'll do the looking.'

I guess that he did because we, or I, successfully negotiated the huge Bentley onto a dirt road that led to our home.

Home was an army barracks.

There, in woods which, here and there, had been cleared, stood a number of cabin-like, but larger, buildings. My husband and I had to clear out of the one which had been relegated to us. Larry . . . is this my husband? . . . I don't think that I know my husband well . . . likes to keep his guinea pigs outside the cabin, in the forest's damp.

My guinea pigs are always safe and warm.

After we had abandoned that part of the army that had once been our home, I entered a cabin named *School*. An older man in a uniform, who was sitting behind a desk which was the only furniture in that large, wooden room, turned around toward me and spoke German. An unknown language.

My husband answered him in German that the files were Japanese.

From this exchange, I learned, primarily, that we had to evacuate because the Germans were coming.

I knew that there weren't any Jap files in the school, therefore, that my husband was trying to fool the German. I wondered whether he had succeeded.

After that dream, my husband drove by the hotel in which we would spend our honeymoon. We hadn't known it at that time. Everything just happened by chance.

For we had been planning to go to England by train, then by boat, but the train had derailed. We had had to spend the night in Ostend.

We had had to wait through the night.

In Ostend, wherever that was, or at the end of the world, we found a hotel. It was rising out of the decay. The name of the hotel was 'Etoile Rouge'.

'It's rather dead this time of year,' my husband said.

The insides were luxurious: in a lobby, a wide red-carpeted staircase, which resembled a slide, descended into Persian rug upon Persian rug. A fat clerk seemed to be the only person. He handed us the keys to the royal suite as if we mattered. Perhaps we did, for we were the only people here, in this area which the sun no longer visited.

The first time my husband had fucked me, I had grabbed for the beam which was above my head.

Afterwards I asked him whether he loved me.

He was falling into sleep. 'No.'

For the first time, he turned to me. 'Do you love me?'

I didn't know what to answer because of how he had answered. 'Of course I do.'

He replied that everything is good: 'I don't love you, you don't love me, therefore we were made for each other.'

That night I dreamed, as if this hotel was in a dream, that there was a magnificent family house open on every side to lawns which were rising upward.

I was given the room in which, from now on, I would be safe. For I was part of the family.

Nevertheless the evil people penetrated the house. In order to evade them, I climbed out a window.

Instead of reaching the outside where I would be safe, I found myself in a section of the grounds which had been closed-off into a parking lot.

I had to escape this parking lot so that the evil ones wouldn't get me.

The lot around which I was still wandering was either made

out of dirt or sand. Either case, off-white. Lying some distance from the house, it retained its oval shape.

No grass grew within this space.

While I neither slowly nor quickly was climbing over the lot's fence, the evil ones grabbed me.

Now, inside this enclosure, people, the ones who had been living in the house, and the evil ones played baseball. Played baseball because they had religion. I joined their game, though I couldn't play well, and while I was in the outfield, I looked for a way, a hole through which I could escape.

I couldn't find any whole.

Next, in the enclosure which was a hole, the original inhabitants of the mansion, none of whom were Christian, were being tortured in ways that reminded me visually of the last scene in *SALO*.

I have been captured as if I was a beast.

I wanted to run away from my husband.

The next morning turned blue, then red.

Afterwards, I descended into the hotel's lobby.

There was still no one there except for the clerk. Wrinkles had almost closed his eyes. I wandered over to one of the corners by the huge windows, away from the Persian carpets.

The emptiness of this lobby reminded me of animals. Though I adore them, I don't own any because I wouldn't remember to feed them.

Two women who seemed non-human walked into the hotel. The older was stunning, her hair absolutely white, dressed in black; after her, a boy who was actually a girl.

Whispering to the clerk who was shaking visibly, I asked who they were.

They are together.

Later that night, before I was able to meet them, I heard them talking to each other through the walls of their room.

'Let me go. Please. Let me go away.' I knew that this was the younger voice.

'I'll never let you go, Kata.'

The name was Kata.

'I'm going to leave you anyway.'

'Not again.' She was bored. The beautiful one.

'I'm going now.'

'Kata, you don't have the ability to leave me.'

'But you don't want me anymore. You want that American girl who's in this hotel.'

'And you need me.'

I hadn't yet heard this conversation. To me, the white-haired woman in her black seemed to be a jaguar, a jaguar inside a snake whose skin is three types of black.

It was as if she had once wrapped her scarf-belt around his monstrous head and in response, the cat, closing his eyes and placing the monstrous head in one of her hands, turned tame.

I felt as if the older woman was kissing me on the lips and I was very frightened.

I went upstairs, back to my husband, who had planned to visit Bruges where a number of murders had just taken place.

As usual he wore his sunglasses. We travelled through Bruges's labyrinths of canals until a dog started barking and sirens passed us by. We followed these sirens, away from the canal, to a mass of townspeople gathered around a white car.

A stretcher was leaving the vehicle.

A policeman muttered to my husband, 'Oh monsieur, it is horrible. . .terrible. . .the fourth this week . . . young girls, all of them. Beautiful, too. This one has been lying here four days. Mutilated, like the rest . . . not a drop of blood.'

My husband's blind eyes stared at no one.

For he was vulnerable. 'I don't understand.' To this policeman.

'None of us understands,' the policeman said.

The stretcher was returning, on it a body which was invisible, a red blanket over the body.

It must be a girl like me.

They took it away in the white car.

As we traveled away from that city, in a wide bus, I confided in my husband that I was scared.

I informed him that I was scared of him. 'Oh yes, Steven, you were pleased. You felt pleasure seeing the dead girl's body.'

'You're pleased saying this. We're getting to know each other.'

I let my head rest on his shoulder while one of my hands slowly undid his belt.

He didn't want me to touch him there.

On that bus, I fell into sleep and dreamed that I escaped Steven.

I had always known the city I was in, this city of murders, because it was my childhood. Narrow, filthy, dark streets, whose buildings are the same. Doors have decayed into walls.

It was the city in which I owned an apartment. Either I used to live here or I had never. The apartment, its insides, were decomposing like everything else. Three rooms, each the size of a piece of furniture. One-third of the bathroom was a shower stall, half rubble, without a bottom.

This tiny city part was bottomless.

I was now renting the apartment either to a punk or to a punk couple. If a punk and if I had lived in the apartment prior to my renting it, I lived with him. He had abandoned me. I feared that the filthy punk or punks were in the process of demolishing this architectural hole which was my cunt.

When I looked directly into my fear, I found it groundless. I fixed my apartment up and rented it to someone else for a hundred dollars a month above the mortgage payment.

I left the city in order to go into the country.

The first thing that I saw was a naked woman tossing a naked baby joyfully into the air. This, I thought, is how the people in Paradise live.

This country into which I had come, whose name was Marin, was like a countryclub. A mosquito stung me. The swelling quickly metamorphosed into a tremendous wart. Since I didn't belong in paradise, I ran to a group of students who right then were climbing over a mountain and into view.

Though I recognized one of them, Dale, I couldn't stay with him because his cock was soft.

I had nowhere to go and no one to be. Then, I remembered that I owned this apartment where everything's falling apart. That was safety.

After I had dreamed, I no longer wanted to leave my husband.

We returned to the hotel at the end of the world.

Before we had left, the woman who had white hair had invited my husband and I to have dinner with her and her young friend.

'Let us put unpleasant things out of our minds . . .'

A policeman had just left the room.

'. . . Let us resume the conversation we were having before we were interrupted,' she said. 'Steven; you don't mind me calling you Steven, do you?'

I noticed that my husband was staring at the girl who looked like a boy. I saw he wanted her.

'Steven, I was just explaining to your wife about the Báthorys. Three hundred years ago . . .

'Klara Báthory had married four husbands in succession. She had murdered the first two. Afterwards, she took a lover who was much younger than her . . .'

Steven returned.

'She smothered the boy in castles. Then, a pasha captured him; while the former was skewering and roasting him on a spit, the entire garrison raped Klara. They cut through the throat of the woman who was still living.

'It is a violent society.

'Klara's niece was Erzébeth Báthory, better known as "The Scarlet Witch".'

'She murdered almost 610 young women,' her secretary added.

'Yes, she kidnapped young girls in order to get their blood.'

'No.'

'She hung them up by their wrists, then whipped them until their tortured flesh was torn to shreds.' My husband spoke for the first time.

He, the Countess, and her friend were sitting together on a small sofa. I was perching on an armchair.

'Oh yes, and she clipped their fingers off with shears,' – the Countess.

'Pierced their nipples with needles, yes, then tore out the tips with silver pincers,' – my husband.

'Because human blood is an elixir,' – the Countess.

'. . . She bit them everywhere and pushed red hot pokers right into their faces . . .' – my husband.

'No!'

'And with the curses of witches . . .', said the young girl,

'And with the curses of witches, especially the sorceress Darvulia Anna, cut off pieces of their flesh, grilled them, then made them eat parts of their own bodies.'

'Go on go on go on.' – the girl.

'Kissed their veins with rusty nails,' – the woman whom I had desired.

'Go on go on go on,' – her lover.

'. . . and when the young girls parted their lips in order to screech, she plunged the flaming rod into the caverns of the throats . . .' my husband began taking over . . .

'No!'

'Your wife is very much in love with you, isn't she?' the Countess asked him.

'How does the story end?' my husband replied.

Ran into one of the room's corners. I shivered because I didn't want to hear anymore, but I couldn't stop.

'The cops walled her up in her room. Day after day and night after night, her beautiful, pale hands were held against each other as if in a prayer . . .

'It was her as a child: As was the custom of the country in those days, her husband-to-be's mother had taken her away, at age eleven, from her wealthy fashionable world, when she was still gay, still full of hope, and placed her in the room of Protestantism where she was locked up, locked in, forbidden to see to hear to touch anything or anybody. From now on, her mother-in-law announced, your life is only to be Christianity and your husband. As soon as she could, this once-wealthy child reacted violently.

'One day, a mysterious woman disguised as a boy visited Erzébeth. Together they began torturing women whom Erzébeth loved . . .'

'. . . the lost dream . . .' – the girl.

'How does the story end?' – Steven.

'I don't want sexuality!' I yelled before this end had come, 'I don't want to become diseased.' . . .

I have run away from everyone.

But I can't bear no sex, no human communication.

I've begun a journey to make sex live, to find the relation between language and the body rather than this sexuality that's presented by society as diseased.

My body seems to reject ordinary language.

If I can find the language of the body, I can find where sex is lying.

While I masturbate, I'll try to hear the language that's there.

Masturbation Journal

DAY 1

(This might not make any sense.)
the movement in my clit is like going, a ⎫ this is still
movement, in a wave → my expectation ⎭ description

*

I haven't gone anywhere, to the realm, yet.

'strap' → it begins

There is nothing: it is here that language enters:

1. To calm the irritation. Just calm the irritation. Where is the opening, the door that opens?

Irritation is happy to be touched, but if it turns too expectant or excited without relaxing, it will become rigid.

The arising is a single, growing clit;

2. lose myself (beginning to lose myself)

3. becoming music. The more I become it, the more I trust it, hold on, just hold on, follow, don't have to do anything else.

4. purely holding on. Now, the more, the better. I'm there, I'm there, (have made the transfer to another person which is music)

going over.

DAY 2

It starts with bodily irritation, but then one has to forget the body, leave the body, leave the body until the body quivers un-controllably.

messages will reach me from the lost sailor.

Entering the room. the dust.
Room after room like levels of the body. Here is no dialectic.
In this room, everything hangs out: nipples scrape against air;

buttocks thrust out so that the asshole is open, and all that was inside is now outside

now it starts. it: actual touching. This is the beginning of feeling.

DAY 3

It happened very fast and I couldn't stop it (in order) to write. First, relaxing so that the ground, the body had become ground, was able to feel sensation. To do nothing else. Then, my clit was alive.

(Here's the problem with coming: One enters the territory whose threshold is coming and wants to stay there forever. While *crossing the threshold*, language is forbidden; having crossed, it's possible to have language.)

As soon as my body relaxed into only being receiver, I entered into music or began a journey that was rhythmic, wave-like, in time. For waves in time = music. Each time a wave falls, I'm able to feel more sensation. Why? Something to do with breathing. When a wave falls, I exhale. Then, at the bottom of exhalation, the physical sensation has to be (already allowable allowed) strong enough and wanting or desiring enough for the whole to turn into physical sensation; at this point, still desiring where there's no body left to become desire, at this point *failure*, the whole turns over into something else.

I have described the entrance into the other world where all is a kind of ease. This other world is also the world within dream.

Now I am going to go to the ball.

Here's a speech or dream about going to the ball:
    In the beginning, I was sleeping with two women.
    At first I didn't understand fucking with women. But the second time I fucked with one of them, I began to like the sex a lot.

One day, Rodney, a friend who's a drag-queen, invited me to a drag-queen ball. We were in a one-story beach house which was divided in three parts. I decided (though now I don't know why) to go to this ball as Patti Page. I said Patti Page, but I bet that I meant Doris Day. (When I had been growing up, Doris Day in *Pillow Talk* was the most repulsive female there was.)

'Oh,' said Rodney, 'everyone's going to the ball.'

To be Patti Page, I had to have the right wig.

My girlfriend returned to my bedroom which overlooked the ocean. When we made love, I sat on her and ground my cunt into hers. Afterwards, I traveled into the city because I had to go to the bank and to re-register. But I was too late in that location where the stars sit in darkness to accomplish any of these tasks on account of which I had decided to come . . . here . . .

And so I returned home . . .

Within the section of the tri-part building that was simultaneously walled and wall-less, the part next to the beach, my motorcycle was sinking into sands now more water than substance. The whole room was flooding as if from a cunt.

There the girl whom I despise most in this world, a skinny blonde, was putting clothes on. She told me she was going to the ball. But I still wanted to go. This ex-junky whose name was Kathy was attending the ball with her roommate.

Who was I going to go to the ball with? I remembered that I hated my loneliness.

If I'm going really to be Patti Page, I have to have a handbag just like my grandmother used to carry. Where am I going to find this kind of bag?

As I was looking for a bag, Rodney walked into the room. It was the large room that bordered both on the flooded room and on the beach. This room, unlike the other, possessed walls.

I hadn't known that Rodney was still in this house.

'Why don't you come with me?'

Suddenly, I had my period. This blood was brown and smelly. Actually it looked like shit. I was holding a Tampax that was full of the stuff. Some had smeared itself over my left upper leg. I solved all these problems by plugging the hole up with a clean Tampax.

Rodney told an old cleaning-lady who was now standing in the room that I was smelly. I was. Yuck. I wandered back, while I was beginning to wonder what dress I would wear, into the walled room and found deodorant Kotexes in a plastic garbage pail. They don't hurt the way that Tampaxes do.

Now that I no longer smell, I can decide what I am going to wear. I have learned from Rodney to do what I want: I will dress in full formal.

And Rodney will be waiting for me, in the office located in the night at the end of the street, beyond a door marked by a black O.

JEANETTE WINTERSON
THE POETICS OF SEX

(1993)

Why Do You Sleep with Girls?

My lover Picasso is going through her Blue Period. In the past
her periods have always been red. Radish red, bull red, red like
rose hips bursting seed. Lava red when she was called Pompeii
and in her Destructive Period. The stench of her, the brack of
her, the rolling splitting cunt of her. Squat like a Sumo, ham
thighs, loins of pork, beefy upper cuts and breasts of lamb. I can
steal her heart like a bird's egg.

She rushes for me bull-subtle, butching at the gate as if she's
come to stud. She bellows at the window, bloods the pavement
with desire. She says, 'You don't need to be Rapunzel to let
down your hair.' I know the game. I know enough to flick my
hind-quarters and skip away. I'm not a flirt. She can smell the
dirt on me and that makes her swell. That's what makes my lithe
lover bull-rush-thin fat me. How she fats me. She plumps me,
pats me, squeezes and feeds me. Feeds me up with lust till I'm as
fat as she is. We're fat for each other we sapling girls. We neat
clean branching girls get thick with sex. You are wide enough
for my hips like roses, I will cover you with my petals, cover

you with the scent of me. Cover girl wide for the weight of my cargo. My bull-lover makes a matador out of me. She circles me and in her rough-made ring I am complete. I like the dressing up, the little jackets, the silk tights, I like her shiny hide, the deep tanned leather of her. It is she who has given me the power of the sword. I used it once but when I cut at her it was my close fit flesh that frilled into a hem of blood. She lay beside me slender as a horn. Her little jacket and silk tights impeccable. In my broken ring I sweated muck and couldn't speak. We are quick-change artists we girls.

Which One of You is the Man?

Picasso's veins are kingfisher blue and kingfisher shy. The first time I slept with her I couldn't see through the marble columns of her legs or beyond the opaque density of each arm. A sculptor by trade Picasso is her own model.

The blue that runs through her is sanguine. One stroke of the knife and she changes colour. Every month and she changes colour. Deep pools of blue silk drop from her. I know her by the lakes she leaves on the way to the bedroom. Her braces cascade over the stair-rail, she wears earrings of lapis lazuli which I have caught cup-handed, chasing her *déshabillée*.

When she sheds she sheds it all. Her skin comes away with her clothes. On those days I have been able to see the blood-depot of her heart. On those days it was possible to record the patience of her digestive juices and the relentlessness of her lungs. Her breath is blue in the cold air. She breathes into the blue winter like a Madonna of the Frost. I think it right to kneel and the view is good.

She does perform miracles but they are of the physical kind and ordered by her Rule of Thumb to the lower regions. She goes among the poor with every kind of salve unmindful of reward. She dresses in blue she tells me so that they will know she is a saint and it is saintly to taste the waters of so many untried wells.

I have been jealous of course. I have punished her good deeds with some alms-giving of my own. It's not the answer, I can't catch her by copying her, I can't draw her with a borrowed stencil. She is all the things a lover should be and quite a few a lover should not. Pin her down? She's not a butterfly. I'm not a wrestler. She's not a target. I'm not a gun. Tell you what she is? She's not Lot no. 27 and I'm not one to brag.

We were by the sea yesterday and the sea was heavy with salt so that our hair was braided with it. There was salt on our hands and in our wounds where we'd been fighting. 'Don't hurt me,' I said and I unbuttoned my shirt so that she could look at my breasts if she wanted to. 'I'm no saint,' she said and that was true, true too that our feet are the same size. The rocks were reptile blue and the sky that balanced on the top of the cliffs was sheer blue. Picasso made me put on her jersey and drink dark tea from a fifties-flask.

'It's winter,' she said. 'Let's go.'

We did go, leaving the summer behind, leaving a trail of footprints two by two in identical four. I don't know that anyone following could have told you which was which and if they had there would have been no trace by morning.

What Do Lesbians Do in Bed?

Under cover of the sheets the tabloid world of lust and vice is useful only in so much as Picasso can wipe her brushes on it. Beneath the sheets we practise Montparnasse, that is Picasso offers to paint me but we have sex instead.

We met at Art School on a shiny corridor. She came towards me so swiftly that the linoleum dissolved under her feet. I thought, 'A woman who can do that to an oil cloth can certainly do something for me.' I made the first move. I took her by her pony-tail the way a hero grabs a runaway horse. She was taken aback. When she turned round I kissed her ruby mouth and took a sample of her sea blue eyes. She was salty, well preserved, well made and curved like a wave. I thought, 'This is the place to go surfing.' We went back to her studio, where naturally enough, there was a small easel and a big bed. 'My work comes first,' she said, 'Would you mind?', and not waiting for an answer she mixed an ochre wash before taking me like a dog my breasts hanging over the pillow.

Not so fast Picasso, I too can rumple you like a farm hand, roll you like good tobacco leaf against my thighs. I can take that arrogant throat and cut it with desire. I can make you dumb with longing, tease you like a doxy on a date.

Slowly now Picasso, where the falling light hits the floor. Lie with me in the bruised light that leaves dark patches on your chest. You look tubercular, so thin and mottled, quiescent now. I picked you up and carried you to the bed dusty with ill-use. I found a newspaper under the sheets advertising rationing.

The girl on the canvas was sulky. She hadn't come to be painted. I'd heard all about you my tear-away tiger, so fierce, so unruly. But the truth is other as truth always is. What holds the small space between my legs is not your artistic tongue not any of the other parts you play at will but the universe we make together beneath the sheets.

We were in our igloo and it couldn't have been snugger. White on white on white on white. Sheet Picasso me sheet. Who was on top depends on where you're standing but as we were lying down it didn't matter.

What an Eskimo I am, breaking her seductive ice and putting in my hand for fish. How she wriggles, slithers, twists to resist me but I can bait her and I do. A fine catch, one in each hand and one in my mouth. Impressive for a winter afternoon and the stove gone out and the rent to pay. We were warm and rich and white. I had so much enjoyed my visit.

'Come again?' she asked. Yes tomorrow, under the sodium street lights, under the tick of the clock. Under my obligations, my history, my fears, this now. This fizzy, giddy all consuming now. I will not let time lie to me. I will not listen to dead voices or unborn pain. 'What if?' has no power against 'What if not?'

The not of you is unbearable. I must have you. Let them laugh those scorn-eyed anti-romantics. Love is not the oil and I am not the machine. Love is you and here I am. Now.

Were You Born a Lesbian?

Picasso was an unlikely mother but I owe myself to her. We are honour-bound, love-bound, bound by cords too robust for those healthy hospital scissors. She baptized me from her own font and said, 'I name thee Sappho.' People often ask if we are mother and child.

I could say yes, I could say no, both statements would be true, the way that lesbians are true, at least to one another if not to the world. I am no stranger to the truth but very uncomfortable about the lies that have dogged me since my birth. It is no surprise that we do not always remember our name.

I am proud to be Picasso's lover in spite of the queer looks we get when holding hands on busy streets. 'Mummy, why is that man staring at us?' I said when only one month old. 'Don't worry dear, he can't help it, he's got something wrong with his eyes.'

We need more Labradors. The world is full of blind people. They don't see Picasso and me dignified in our love. They see perverts, inverts, tribades, homosexuals. They see circus freaks and Satan worshippers, girl-catchers and porno turn-ons. Picasso says they don't know how to look at pictures either.

Were You Born a Lesbian?

A fairy in a pink tutu came to Picasso and said, 'I bring you tidings of great joy. All by yourself with no one to help you, you will give birth to a sex toy who has a way with words. You will call her Sappho and she will be a pain in the ass to all men.'

'Can't you see I've got a picture to finish?' said Picasso.

'Take a break,' said the fairy. 'There's more to life than Art.'

'Where?' said Picasso whose first name wasn't Mary.

'Between your legs,' said Gabriel.

'Forget it. Don't you know I paint with my clit?'

'Here, try a brush,' said the fairy offering her a fat one.

'I've had all the brushes I need,' said Picasso.

'Too late,' said the fairy. 'Here she comes.'

Picasso slammed the door on her studio and ran across to the Art College where she had to give a class. She was angry so that her breath burnt the air. She was angry so that her feet dissolved the thin lino tiles already scuffed to ruin by generations of brogues. There was no one in the corridor or if there was she was no one. Picasso didn't recognize her, she had her eyes on the door and the door looked away. Picasso, running down the clean corridor, was suddenly trip-wired, badly thrown, her hair came away from her glorious head. She was being scalped. She was being mugged. She was detonated on a long fuse of sex. Her body was halfway out of the third-floor window and there was a demon against her mouth. A poker-red pushing babe crying, 'Feed me, Feed me now.'

Picasso took her home, what else could she do? She took her home to straighten her out and had her kinky side up. She mated with this creature she had borne and began to feel that maybe the Greek gods knew a thing or two. Flesh of her flesh she fucked her.

They were quiet then because Sappho hadn't learned a language. She was still two greedy hands and an open mouth. She throbbed like an outboard motor, she was as sophisticated as a ham sandwich. She had nothing to offer but herself, and Picasso, who thought she had seen it all before, smiled like a child, and fell in love.

Why Do You Hate Men?

Here comes Sappho, scorching the history books with tongues of flame. Never mind the poetry feel the erection. Oh yes, women get erect, today my body is stiff with sex. When I see a word held hostage to manhood I have to rescue it. Sweet trembling word, locked in a tower, tired of your Prince coming and coming. I will scale you and discover that size is no object especially when we're talking inches.

I like to be a hero, like to come back to my island full of girls carrying a net of words forbidden them. Poor girls, they are locked outside their words just as the words are locked into meaning. Such a lot of locking up goes on on the Mainland but here on Lesbos our doors are always open.

Stay inside, don't walk the streets, bar the windows, keep your mouth shut, keep your legs together, strap your purse around your neck, don't wear valuables, don't look up, don't talk to strangers, don't risk it, don't try it. He means she but not when He means Men. Mainland is a Private Club.

That's all right boys, so is this. This delicious unacknowledged island where we are naked with each other. The boat that brings us here will crack beneath your weight. This is territory you cannot invade.

We lay on the bed, Picasso and I, listening to the terrible bawling of Salami. Salami is a male artist who wants to be a Lesbian.

'I'll pay you twice the rent,' he cries, fingering his greasy wallet. 'I'll paint you for posterity. I love women, don't you know? Oh God I wish I was a woman, wafer-thin like you, I could circle you with one hand.' He belches.

Picasso is unimpressed. She says, 'The world is full of heterosexuals, go and find one, half a dozen, swallow them like oysters, but get out.'

'Oh whip me,' says Salami getting moist.

We know the pattern. In half an hour he'll be violent and when he's threatened us enough, he'll go to the sleaze pit and watch two girls for the price of a steak.

As soon as he left we forgot about him. Making love we made a dictionary of forbidden words. We are words, sentences, stories, books. You are my New Testament. We are a gospel to each other, I am your annunciation, revelation. You are my St Mark, winged lion at your feet. I'll have you, and the lion too, buck under you till you learn how to saddle me. Don't dig those spurs too deep. It's not so simple this lexographic love. When you have sunk me to the pit I'll mine you in return and we shall be husbands to each other as well as wives.

I'll tell you something Salami, a woman can get hard and keep it there all night and when she's not required to stand she knows how to roll. She can do it any way up and her lover always comes. There are no frigid lesbians, think of that.

On this island where we live, keeping what we do not tell, we have found the infinite variety of Woman. On the Mainland, Woman is largely extinct in all but a couple of obvious forms. She is still cultivated as a cash crop but is nowhere to be found growing wild.

Salami hates to hear us fuck. He bangs on the wall like a zealot at an orgy. 'Go home,' we say, but he doesn't. He'd rather lie against the skirting-board complaining that we stop him painting. The real trouble is that we have rescued a word not allowed to our kind. He hears it pounding through the wall day and night. He smells it on our clothes and sees it smeared on our faces. We are happy Picasso and I. Happy.

Don't You Find There's Something Missing?

I thought I had lost Picasso. I thought the bright form that shapes my days had left me. I was loose at the edges, liquid with uncertainty. The taut lines of love slackened. I felt myself unravelling backwards, away from her. Would the thinning thread snap?

For seven years she and I had been in love. Love between lovers, love between mother and child. Love between man and wife. Love between friends. I had been all of those things to her and she had been all of those things to me. What we were we were in equal parts and twin souls to one another. We like to play roles but we know who we are. You are beauty to me Picasso. Not only sensuous beauty that pleases the eye but artistic beauty that challenges it. Sometimes you are ugly in your beauty, magnificently ugly and you frighten me for all the right reasons.

I did not tell you this yesterday or the day before. Habit had silenced me the way habit does. So used to a thing no need to speak it, so well known the action no need to describe it. But I know that speech is freedom which is not the same as freedom of speech. I have no right to say what I please when I please but I have the gift of words with which to bless you. Bless you Picasso. Bless you for your straight body like a spire. You are the landmark that leads me through the streets of the everyday. You take me past the little houses towards the church where we worship. I do worship you because you are worthy of praise. Bless you Picasso for your able hands that carry the paint to the unbirthed canvas. Your fingers were red when you fucked me and my body striped with joy. I miss the weals of our passion just as I miss the daily tenderness of choosing you. Choosing you above all others, my pearl of great price.

My feelings for you are Biblical; that is they are intense, reckless arrogant, risky and unconcerned with the way of the world. I flaunt my bleeding wounds, madden with my certainty. The Kingdom of Heaven is within you Picasso. Bless you.

There is something missing and that is you. Your clothes were gone yesterday, your easel was packed flat and silent against the wall. When I got up and left our unmade bed there was the smell of coffee in the house but not the smell of you. I looked in the mirror and I knew who was to blame. Why take the perfect thing and smash it? Some goods are smashed that cannot be replaced.

It has been difficult this last year. Love is difficult. Love gets harder, which is not the same as to say that it gets harder to love. You are not hard to love. You are hard to love well. Your standards are high, you won't settle for the quick way out which is why you made for the door. If I am honest I will admit that I have always wanted to avoid love. Yes give me romance, give me sex, give me fights, give me all the parts of love but not the simple single word which is so complex and demands the best of me this hour this minute this forever.

Picasso won't paint the same picture twice. She says develop or die. She won't let yesterday's love suffice for today. She makes it new, she remixes her colours and stretches her canvas until it sighs. My mother was glad when she heard we'd split up. She said, 'Now you can come back to the Mainland. I'll send Phaeon to pick you up.' Phaeon runs a little business called Lesbian Tours. He drives his motor-boat round and round the island, just outside the one mile exclusion zone. He points out famous lesbians to sight-seers who always say, 'But she's so attractive!' or 'She's so ugly!'

'Yeah,' says Phaeon, 'and you know what? They're all in love with me.' One sight-seer shakes his head like a collecting box for a good cause. 'Can't you just ask one of 'em?' he says. 'I can ask them anything,' says Phaeon, who never waits to hear the answer.

Why Do You Sleep with Girls?

Picasso has loved me for fifty years and she loves me still. We got through the charcoal tunnel where the sun stopped rising. We no longer dress in grey.

On that day I told you about I took my coat and followed her footprints across the ice. As she walked the world froze up behind her. There was nothing for me to return to, if I failed, I failed alone. Despair made it too dark to see, I had to travel by radar, tracking her warmth in front of me. It's fashionable now to say that any mistake is made by both of you. That's not always true. One person can easily kill another.

Hang on me my darling like rubies round my neck. Slip onto

my finger like a ring. Give me your rose for my buttonhole. Let me leaf through you before I read you out loud.

Picasso warms my freezing heart on the furnace of her belly. Her belly is stoked to blazing with love of me. I have learned to feed her every day, to feed her full of fuel that I gladly find. I have unlocked the storehouses of love. On the Mainland they teach you to save for a rainy day. The truth is that love needs no saving. It is fresh or not at all. We are fresh and plentiful. She is my harvest and I am hers. She seeds me and reaps me, we fall into one another's laps. Her seas are thick with fish for my rod. I have rodded her through and through.

She is painting today. The room is orange with effort. She is painting today and I have written this.

NOTES ON THE AUTHORS

KATHY ACKER (1948–   ). In the 1960s Acker hung out in New York with the Fluxus group and underground film-makers. She was later involved in the early punk rock scene, and her intelligent and experimental writing owes much of its vivacity and punch to these influences. Her books include *Blood and Guts in High School* (1978), *Great Expectations* (1982), *Empire of the Senseless* (1988) and *In Memoriam to Identity* (1990). Her work is intimately involved with notions of desire and expression, but not necessarily with conventional concepts of meaning: 'I realized that this relation, the area between language and the body, is connected to the imagination, desire, those realms that escape meaning, at least what we want to mean, rational meaning . . .' Exploring this terrain continues in her next book *My Mother: Demonology*, as well as in 'The Language of the Body'.

DOROTHY ALLISON, lives in San Francisco. She is the author of a book of poetry, *The Women Who Hate Me*, a collection of short stories, called *Trash*, and a novel, *Bastard out of Carolina*.

She uses repetition and reinvention to make her acid stories.

MARGARET ATWOOD (1938–   ). A leading writer whose impressive range of fiction, poetry and criticism displays both her consummate skill with words and her precise and analytic philosophy. Accessible and intellectual, knife-sharp and melting, her works include *The Circle Game* (1967), *The Edible Woman* (1969), *Lady Oracle* (1976), *The Handmaid's Tale* (1985), *Cat's Eye* (1988), *Interlunar* (1988), and *Wilderness Tips* (1990). 'Cold-blooded' is taken from her most recent collection of short pieces, *Good Bones* (1992).

ANN BANNON. Bannon's five lesbian pulp novels *Odd Girl Out* (1957), *Women in the Shadows* (1959), *I am a Woman* (1959), *Journey to a Woman* (1960) and *Beebo Brinker* (1962) rapidly became cult sanity-saving classics for many women in America. With their hugely successful re-publication by the Naiad Press, Bannon reassessed her work; 'The books as they stand have fifties flaws. They are, in effect, the offspring of their special era, with its biases. But they speak truly of that time and place as I knew it.'

DJUNA BARNES (1892–1982) was the author of *The Book of Repulsive Women* (1915), *A Night among the Horses*, (1929), *Ryder* (1928), *Nightwood* (1936), and *The Antiphon* (1958). Her juvenilia has been recently collected in *Smoke and Other Early Stories* (1982) and *I Could Never be Lonely without a Husband* (1985). Her work has suffered for many years from critical misreading and, like that of other women in the Modernist period, it has been overshadowed. But her dense and allusive prose, as well as her witty style in pastiche, is now being newly appreciated.

ALISON BECHDEL (1960–   ) describes herself as an astrology-dependent, lentil-lapping leftist. She lives in Vermont and has four collections of *Dykes to Watch Out For* cartoons in print.

NICOLE BROSSARD (1943–   ) was co-founder of the cultural

journal *La Barre du jour*, published in Canada from 1965. An inspiring, original and impassioned writer, she is recognized as the leader of the avant-garde in Quebec and her reputation has spread with the translation of her work. Her books include *Daydream Mechanics* (1980) and *The Aerial Letter* (1988).

REBECCA BROWN (1956–   ). A bold writer whose tender treatment of violence, cruelty and obsession has never received the attention it deserves. Brown has published two novels, *The Haunted House* and *The Children's Crusade*, and a collection of painful stories, *The Terrible Girls*. Her forthcoming book, *Annie Oakley's Girl*, will be published in 1993.

PAT CALIFIA (1954–   ) is a defiant celebrant of lesbian sado-masochism, a champion in the eyes of some readers, a weirdo according to others. Her books include *Macho Sluts* (1989) and *Sapphistry* – a sex-education text whose title has generated many variants in academic feminist criticism.

COLETTE (1873–1954) is a versatile writer whose work started with the *Claudine* novels at the beginning of the century, went on to the self-conscious and writerly autobiography of *My Apprentice-ships* (1936) and then to the lyrical experiment of genre- and gender-crossing in works such as *The Pure and the Impure* (1941).

H.D. (Hilda Doolittle) (1886–1961). Travelling to Europe with her lover Frances Gregg, she fell in with Ezra Pound, who named her 'H.D. Imagiste'. As a contributor to that experimental movement her fugitive poems still stand out among the mediocre writings of the First World War. An acute and demanding writer, H.D.'s poems are still extraordinary. More extraordinary is the fact that she is only just finding her rightful place in the literary history of the twentieth century.

ISAK DINESEN (Karen Blixen) (1885–1962). Her taken pseudonym means 'laughter' (Isak) and, like Homer's gods, her accomplished short stories adopt an ironic perspective on the little affairs of women and men. Detached in tone, and highly organized in design, her *Seven Gothic Tales* (1934), *Last Tales* (1957) and *Anecdotes of Destiny* (1958) are mistresspieces of the form. She is, however, best known today for the more sensational aspects of her life and the revelations of her quasi-autobiographical experience recorded in *Out of Africa* (1937).

EMMA DONOGHUE (1969–   ). The youngest of eight children, and the youngest in this collection, Emma Donoghue was born in Ireland and is presently working for a postgraduate degree. She has written two novels and is ready for more.

FRANCES GAPPER (1957–   ) is the author of *Saints and Adventurers* (1988).

JEWELLE GOMEZ is a black activist who lives in New York and works as an arts administrator. She has published *Flamingoes and Bears* and *The Lipstick Papers*. Her most recent work is *The Gilda Stories*, which tells of a girl born into slavery in the nineteenth century who lives as a vampire into the twenty-first.

RADCLYFFE HALL (1880–1943). Publicist, saint, martyr and burden for all lesbians. Hall led a brave crusade in the face of society's – and her own – misconceptions of what it meant to be lesbian. She wrote (some quite good) poetry as well as *The Unlit Lamp* (1924), *The Forge* (1924), *Adam's Breed* (1926) and *The Master of the House* (1924). Her most famous novel is *The Well of Loneliness* (1928). Its explicit study of the condition of the 'invert' makes it essential reading. But its miserable conclusion of isolation and oddity makes it a curse and a challenge. Father to daughter, as she tries to come out: 'You don't need to tell me. I know about lesbians; I've read *How Deep is My Well . . .*'

SARAH ORNE JEWETT (1849–1909). Born in Maine, Jewett was

distantly descended from Anne Bradstreet and wore her literary credentials with pride. Her life was marked by serious friendships with women, culminating in a lifelong 'Boston marriage' with Annie Fields after the latter was widowed. Writing 'imaginative realism' (her term) Jewett produced *Deephaven* (1877), where two young women attempt to emulate the Ladies of Llangollen, *A Country Doctor* (1884), about a woman's aspiration to practise medicine, and *The Country of the Pointed Firs* (1896), where matriarchy rules.

ANNA LIVIA (1955–   ) is the author of *Relatively Norma*, *Accommodation Offered* and a collection of love stories entitled *Incidents Involving Warmth*. Her most recent title is *Minimax* (1991), which is a comic fiction whose characters include Natalie Barney and Renée Vivien.

SARA MAITLAND (1950–   ) is a forceful and intelligent thinker and, as a writer, at her best when she measures stereotypes and archetypes to stretch their resonance beyond their immediate context. *Daughters of Jerusalem* (1978) and her numerous critical writings are good examples. Her ironic but celebratory account of the enthusiasms of the 1960s and of early feminism is to be found in 'Lullaby for my Dyke and Her Cat' and in *Very Heaven: Looking Back at the 1960s* (1988).

KATHERINE MANSFIELD (1888–1923). In Virginia Woolf's book, Mansfield's work was 'the only writing I have ever been jealous of'. It's easy to see why. Taut and economical, Mansfield's prose is lean, without fat. Critics have trouble with her stories. They can see that they are very often about relationships, but rarely do they perceive their subtle feminist and political contexts. For typical Mansfield double-talk see 'Bliss' or 'A Modern Soul'.

MERRIL MUSHROOM (1942–   ) is an American writer who has provided much insightful documentation of the gay scenes of the 1950s and 1960s. She has written *The Daughters of Khaton* (1987), a science-fiction novel where a group of space explorers land upon a planet entirely inhabited by girls and women.

JOAN NESTLE (1940–   ). American, Jew, socialist, feminist, teacher, herstory archivist, femme and sexpot. Nestle is brave because she exposes herself, as a 1950s femme, as a 1980s feminist, as a consumer of anonymous sex, as a lover of her lover's cock, as a woman desiring women. As she is, so are her writings; brave, absurd and true.

ANAÏS NIN (1903–77). A theorist on fiction before she was a practitioner, Nin was an early defender of experiment in general and D. H. Lawrence in particular. *House of Incest* (1936) is a prose poem which was followed by *Winter of Artifice* (1939), and her 'roman fleuve' *Cities of the Interior*, which is made up of *This Hunger* (1945), *Ladders to Fire* (1946) and four other related but discrete parts. In all of this not just the style, but the characters, their psychology and sexuality is all 'fluid'. Nin's *Diary* (1966, and continued to 1984) and her erotica, *The Delta of Venus* (1977), reveal her to be a sophisticated student of human behaviour and a discerning roué in matters of the flesh.

BETH NUGENT (1955–   ) lives in Evanston, Illinois.

JAYNE ANNE PHILLIPS (1952–   ). Her first book *Sweethearts* (1976) deals, in brief haphazard scenes, with the violence and obsession of adolescent sexuality, intermittently and piercingly felt, obscurely and accidentally focused. Phillips herself calls her girls 'ambisexual; that is sexual in relation to everything alive'. They remain a persuasive subject for her, as the wiping out of difference in desire reappears in *Counting* (1978), *Black Tickets* (1979), *Fast Lanes* (1984) and her forthcoming novel *In Summer Camps*.

JANE RULE (1931–   ) was an early and important spokeswoman for lesbians in literature and academia. Her critical book *Lesbian Images* (1975) and her books of essays, *The Outlander* (1981) and *A Hot-Eyed Moderate* (1985) are essential reading. Of her novels, *Desert of the Heart* (1964) was made into a cult film by Donna Deitch. Other fiction includes *Against the Season* (1971) and *Contract with the World* (1980).

GERTRUDE STEIN (1874–1946). An avant-garde writer whose best work remains avant old and new guards. Rigorous in the intelligent application of theory – see especially *Composition as Explanation* (1926) and *Narration* (1935) – she was undaunted by misunderstanding and ridicule and produced important creative expositions which still startle: *Tender Buttons* (1914) and *The Autobiography of Alice B. Toklas* (1933). Her special method of repetition with variation is present in 'Miss Furr and Miss Skeene', as is her delight in the duplicity of words. Gertrude and Alice are rivalled only by Radclyffe 'John' Hall and Una Troubridge as herstory's most celebrated lesbian lovers.

DOROTHY STRACHEY (1866–1960). She translated Gide but wrote only the one novel, *Olivia*, which seems to have been based upon her experiences at a well-known girls' school in Switzerland.

RENÉE VIVIEN (1877–1909) was the pseudonym of Pauline Mary Tarn, who, fleeing from the expectations of her family, saw and loved Natalie Barney, for whom she wrote *Une Femme m'apparut* (1904). Her first volume of poetry was *Études et Préludes* (1901), and she continued to write, live, drink and not eat with uniform intensity until her early death.

JEANETTE WINTERSON (1959–). An admirer and master of the English language, Winterson's position as the leader of her literary generation delights her passionate adherents and infuriates her passionate detractors. There is no middle ground. She is the author of *Oranges are not the Only Fruit* (1985), *The Passion*

(1987), *Sexing the Cherry* (1989) and *Written on the Body* (1992).

MONIQUE WITTIG (1935–   ). With the publication of *L'Opoponax* (1957) Wittig was named as a promising writer of the *nouveau roman*, but she did not come into her individual voice until politics met artistic discourse in the lesbian war with patriarchy enacted in *Les Guérillères* (1969). *Le Corps Lesbien* (1973) is another theory-fiction, while the essays 'The Straight Mind' and 'The Mark of Gender' are theory about fiction.

VIRGINIA WOOLF (1882–1941). She may be the darling of feminist criticism as postgraduate students queue up to register their dissertation on 'this and that and Virginia', but this big bad Woolf has, as yet, quite failed to blow down the straw houses of conventional Modernist criticism. But then, there are a lot of little pigs helping to keep the hovels of reputation intact . . . Her own mansion is large and spacious. Her novels include *The Voyage Out* (1915), *Night and Day* (1919), *Mrs Dalloway* (1925), *To the Lighthouse* (1927) *The Waves* (1931), *The Years* (1937) and *Between the Acts* (1941). She also wrote *A Room of One's Own* (*1929*), on how you have to have money and privacy to be a writer, *Flush* (1933), on the difficulty of reconciling one's dog to the arrival of one's lover, and *Orlando* (1928), a love-letter to another woman which also happens to expatiate upon the necessity of independence and a well-developed sense of self-esteem in the lives of girls and women.